MAMIGON

MAMIGON

A Novel by
Jack Hashian

Coward, McCann & Geoghegan
New York

Copyright © 1982 by James T. Hashian
All rights reserved. This book, or parts thereof, may not be
reproduced in any form without permission in writing from the
publisher. Published on the same day in Canada by General
Publishing Co. Limited, Toronto.

Library of Congress Cataloging in Publication Data

Hashian, Jack.
Mamigon: a novel.

I. Title.
PS3558.A7234M3   1982   813'.54   82-5081
ISBN 0-698-11186-9   AACR2

PRINTED IN THE UNITED STATES OF AMERICA

Dedicated to my friend
George Cabot Lodge
who told me to write this twenty years ago

FOREWORD

This is the story of Mamigon . . . soldier, sailor, blacksmith, truck-driver.

It is also a story about Armenians—not the gentle and sensitive Armenians of William Saroyan and Elia Kazan—but the Armenians descended from those who first cast iron and rode their horses roughshod and bloodily through the Bronze Age; of Armenians descended from those who beat back the Persian hordes of Darius and Cyrus, the Greek phalanxes, the Roman legions, holding out for centuries at the crossroads of civilization, the Golden Crescent, only to embrace Christianity and finally fall to the sword of Islam 900 years ago as they repeatedly and meekly turned the other cheek.

This is the story of Mamigon, a modern-day Armenian at the start of World War I who did not know how to turn the other cheek. It is a story of vengeance and death as he tracks the killer of his family across the suddenly hostile homeland of his fathers to the bewildering shores of the New World.

It is a story of bloodshed and tears not meant for the meek or squeamish. It is the story of the Turkish massacre of Armenians, told not as a history but as a developing tale based on fact with characters whose experiences have long since been buried with their bones in the hard clay of the Anatolian Plain or in the rocky ground of New England.

The details, descriptions, and atrocities encompassed in this tale are based on British Foreign Office Miscellaneous Document No. 31 (1916), called "The Treatment of Armenians in the Ottoman Empire, 1915–1916." The document was presented by Viscount Bryce to Viscount Grey of Fallodon, secretary of state for foreign affairs. It was written by Viscount Bryce after an examination and collation of evidence from American, Danish, Swiss, German, and Italian witnesses, by "a young historian of high academic distinction, Mr. Arnold J. Toynbee, late Fellow of Balliol College, Oxford."

Viscount Bryce, who gave that credit to Toynbee, also wrote in the preface to Miscellaneous Document No. 31 "that nothing has been admitted the substantial truth of which seems open to reasonable doubt. Facts only have been dealt with; questions of future policy [for the government] have been carefully avoided. . . ."

Any resemblance to persons living or dead is purely coincidental, except for obvious references to historical personages, places, and events included for the sake of verisimilitude.

J.H.

BOOK I

Turkey

1 &ORDERS

"Do you think we will have much trouble with them, chief?"

"Not one flea bite, *yarbay*. They are Armenians, are they not?"

"I do not grasp your meaning." The young lieutenant wasn't used to unstated metaphors.

"I have not met many of those infidels who have not been docile in the presence of their masters. They will do exactly what we tell them to do." Tallal Kosmanli, the police chief, had such conviction in his voice the lieutenant was impressed.

"How will we treat them . . . you know . . . as guests, as wards, as . . .?"

Tallal burst into loud laughter. "Guests? . . . Wards? We will treat them as prisoners of war!"

"Prisoners of war . . .?

"Yes. If we treat them as such we should have no trouble."

"Perhaps, agha, but if I may note, women, children, and old men are not used to taking military orders."

"I have little doubt that a naked sword will give them instant training, *yarbay*."

"They will be innocent of military ways."

"My father used to say, innocence is like still waters; it will only react when it is touched . . . and my sword is for touching . . ."

"I would rather touch those young women with the sword between my legs."

"Perhaps you have left your senses, *yarbay*. One moment you are concerned about how carefully we should treat them . . . will they be able to take orders . . ." he mimicked the lieutenant, "and the next you are talking about sticking the women. They will be my charges, not playthings for the men."

"Enough, enough, chief, do not get your balls in an uproar." The lieutenant was an officer in the militia while his superior was a civilian police chief, the *emniyet muduru* from Yosghat. "All I know is that the journey will be boring, the nights will be long, and you and your men will yearn for the warm thighs women hide so well."

"Your ears are filled with sand. I said we cannot touch them, not a hair."

"Yes, I heard you, my chief. That is what the orders say, but you heard what happened in the eastern provinces." The *yarbay* sounded as if he were being cheated.

"Oh, enough of this baying at the moon. Each of us has his assignment and I, for one, will do my duty."

"And, I will do mine, verily. It is just that my militia unit has orders to round up the men and take them to a camp and your police troop is to take care of the women and children. You cannot sit there on your horse and tell me you and your men will not have some fun with them."

"Camel dung, *yarbay*. Camel dung and spit!"

"All right, wait and see. I read some of the secret reports from the east covering the past six months. Once those women are without their menfolk, our troops seem to find ways of enjoying them."

"Well, it will not happen, lieutenant, it will just not happen. With the help of Allah, I will do what has to be done, nothing more, nothing less."

"Mark my words, *bey*, remember them well. It might not happen right away but I do not think you and your men are any different from the others who had similar assignments. But, I wish you well."

Tallal didn't respond. He shifted his lean buttocks in the saddle and squinted in the glare of the hot August sun down the road he had just traveled. A column of horsemen, three abreast, followed in tight formation, with the rear lost in a haze of dust. He nodded, grateful that the hours and hours of formation drill were showing results. The last thing he wanted right now was to see his *polis* unit straggling and lagging on the road in the presence of the militia company that rode with them.

Tallal's unit, consisting mostly of illiterate recruits from the dregs of the Turkish populace, had been trained mercilessly by a German cadre after getting off to a bad start. The problem was that the youthful Turks could not distinguish literally, between left and right. Tallal could never figure out why they had this difficulty, since every Moslem knew the admonition that the left hand—*never the right hand*—was to be used to perform one's private sanitary duties. Why then, he wondered, did they become so confused in marching or drill formations when commanded to march or face to the right or left? Finally, some now-forgotten genius had supplied onions and garlic cloves to his company and proceeded to confound the regiment with his unit's precise marching. With a small onion bound in the right hand and a garlic clove in the left, the recruits turned and moved in either direction in response to the orders: "Turn to the onion" or "Eyes to the garlic." The method proved effective, if a bit alliaceous downwind as the herbs warmed up in sweaty palms.

The olive-drab column wound its way slowly along the rock-strewn roadway, which was just wide enough for three horses. Behind Tallal and the *yarbay*, the militia lieutenant, were 180 men, all with rifles slung across their sweat-stained backs, swords dangling from their belts, and *tozlooks* binding their legs from ankle to knee. What differentiated the two groups in the column was the headgear. The first half wore flat-topped *kalpaks*, indicating they were militia or regulars; the remainder wore black felt fezzes, showing them to be *polis*, the gendarmerie.

The two officers were armed with handguns rather than rifles, their guns and swords supported by Sam Brownes. On their legs they wore black leather puttees, their shine dulled by a heavy coating of dust. Tallal, defying his superiors, wore a spiked German officer's helmet and carried a riding crop with a red fingerloop. He loved every bit of the show he put on with his white Arab stallion under him, complete with a Hungarian cavalry saddle.

Tallal stole a glance at the *yarbay*, sitting astride a spindle-legged roan and wearing his *kalpak* with a red band and thought the lieutenant looked positively pedestrian by comparison. Because officers purchased their own equipment in the Turkish army, differences in family wealth showed up in such outward trappings. Tallal was the son of a *vali*, in fact, the son of the governor of the Yosghat vilayet, while the *yarbay* had entered the *mektebi* for military cadets in Constantinople directly from a big farm in the hinterlands. The lieutenant couldn't be more than twenty-two or twenty-three, Tallel estimated, and he was making a valiant try at growing a mustache. Tallal wondered if the young man had guessed what their mission was all about. As the *emniyet muduru*, Tallal found himself with an assignment he didn't care for, one he would rather shirk. All anyone knew, except for Tallal, was that the force would eventually end up in Aleppo, far to the south, on the edge of the great desert that made up more than half of the Ottoman Empire they were sworn to defend. There were no complaints. Riding horseback within the boundaries of one's own country was easy and safe duty in wartime. It was better than manning the trenches in the Dardanelles or being sent to the eastern frontier to face the wild Cossacks. Most Turkish subjects, Moslem and Christian alike, had taken pride in the way their soldiers, under the command of Mustapha Kemal, had been repulsing the invasion of the French and English at Gallipoli. For five months now, the enemy had been effectively contained and the German staff had made certain its Turkish ally had the arms and instructions to be even more effective as the enemy continued to force the battle.

Tallal's verbal orders had been simple and direct: Remove everyone from the Armenian village of Yosghat Dagh. Send the men of military age to a work camp under escort of the militia. All the rest—women, children, the old—were to be herded to Aleppo, nearly a thousand kilometers away, picking up more exiles from villages along the way. And, kill any and all who resisted. He was given a packet to be opened only when he arrived at Yosghat Dagh.

What puzzled Tallal was that there really didn't seem to be any need for the undertaking. Even his father, who was responsible for the safety and welfare of the province, was not convinced that this action was necessary. But orders were orders, and who was the *vali*, or his son, the *polis* chief, to question the decision and, by implication, the wisdom of the Young Turks who now ruled Turkey? This type of maneuver, if you could call it such, certainly hadn't been taught to young Tallal at *Harbiye*, the Turkish military academy or *mektebi* he had attended in Constantinople.

But, praise be to Allah, the orders were simple and direct. The difficulty was the human factor. For Tallal there was more involved than merely dealing with strangers, but only he knew that. During his years at the academy, Tallal had been friends with another cadet from his district, a tall Armenian named Mamigon from the mountain hamlet of Yosghat Dagh, the very place the troop was headed for now. He didn't relish the thought of facing his friend under the circumstances. They had studied together, served together at Gallipoli, where Mamigon had been decorated for valor, and had hunted together in these very hills. Oh, pig shit. He would face up to the situation when it presented itself.

Pig shit, again! Tallal had looked back once more and had seen that the supply carts or *arabas* were falling too far behind. The oxen were too slow and could not keep up with the horses. He raised his right arm and brought the column to a halt.

"Get the men and horses in the shade of those rocks, lieutenant. I want to talk to the troops while we wait for those damned *arabas* to catch up."

With the men dismounted and in the shade and time to kill, Tallal figured it was a good opportunity to read the contents of the sealed packet given him when he received his verbal orders from the provincial governor, his father.

"What's the matter?" blurted the militia lieutenant, who was watching Tallal's face as he broke the seal and read the single sheet of paper.

"Here, read it yourself."

It was a copy of a wire from Tallat Pasha, the Minister of the Interior in Constantinople, addressed to the governors of the provinces, dated March 9, 1915. It read:

> Although the extermination of the Armenian element had been decided upon earlier than this, circumstances did not permit us to carry out this sacred intention. Now that all obstacles have been eliminated, the time has come for redeeming our fatherland from this dangerous element.
>
> All rights of the Armenians to live and work on Turkish soil have been completely canceled, and with regard to this the Government takes all responsibility on itself and has commanded that no Armenians, even babies in the cradle are to be spared. The results of the compliance of this order have been seen in some provinces; it is urgently recommended that you should not be moved to feelings of pity; by putting an end to them all, try with all your might to obliterate the very name Armenian from Turkey. See to it that those to whom you entrust the carrying out of this purpose are patriotic and reliable men.

The lieutenant looked up from the paper, a smile growing across his mouth: "Does this mean what I think it means?"

"No doubt about it, lieutenant. By the Beard of the Prophet, we have some interesting work ahead of us!"

"Then, all those oral orders to separate the able bodied men and march them to Ankara for work was a sham."

"It was."

"What do we do with the menfolk?" The smile on the lieutenant's face showed he didn't think the question to be more than rhetorical.

"You kill them."

"When?"

"Not in the village, certainly! We will separate them from their families, first. You will march them off out of sight from the village and send them to their nonbelievers' hell."

"Is there any special way they should be dispatched? I have never been instructed in mass killing."

"We do not have machine guns, so I will leave the manner of killing entirely up to you and your men."

"Shall we tell the troops now?"

"No. I do not want anything to happen until I give the word. If some of our men become impatient at the fun in store for them, they may get out of hand before we are ready."

Tallal had had misgivings about the men assigned to his command, but now he understood. Most of the recruits had been inmates of military stockades and the lice-ridden jails of the cities. This assignment was going to be mean work, and the government was making certain the men given the task were mostly the empire's psychopaths, misfits, and killers. The squeamish would be out of place in this adventure. It was going to take more than military discipline to keep his *polis* in line . . . and the message affirmed that he wouldn't have to; he only had to let the base nature of these men take its course.

Tallal had the column brought to attention and told them they were going to go into the Armenian village of Yosghat Dagh. They were going to separate the men from the women, children, and the old folks. The militia would escort the men to a work camp near Angora. The rest would be allowed to carry whatever they could on their backs or on their mules or horses, if they had any, to exile, to exile in the area of Aleppo. Yes, carts were to be allowed. This command was carrying out the orders of the government's Committee of Union and Progress. Turkey was not to be for Armenians anymore. Resistance by the populace was to be dealt with firmly. If arms of any kind were found, they were to be confiscated and the man or men in the family placed under arrest. We are doing this because the government considers Armenians to be a danger to the security of this country. We cannot fight our enemies at our borders and worry about our rear. The troop was to pick up additional exiles in two other villages on the way to Aleppo. Those were the orders.

The *arabas* creaked up to position, and Tallal gave the word for the column to mount up and proceed. As he rode closer and closer to Yosghat Dagh, the confrontation with his Armenian friend Mamigon tugged at his thoughts. The big man was still a reserve officer in the Turkish Army. Mamigon had been released from active duty at the same time as Tallal, shortly after Mamigon had been wounded four months ago. How would he face his friend? How was he going to tell Mamigon that he was now considered a potential threat to the country's safety? He realized that much of what would happen when they met would depend on Mamigon's reaction. He would wait and see.

His heart did a quick flip as his thoughts automatically shifted from

Mamigon to Mamigon's wife, the vivacious, comely Ahgavni. Unlike the Moslems, the infidel Armenians, who were Christians, didn't veil their women. Ahgavni had served Tallal coffee and *pahklava* and *tahn* on at least a dozen occasions when he had visited their house after hunting trips with Mamigon. It was unfair to test a man the way these Christians went about it, he thought. Moslem women were covered completely, from head to foot, with only the eyes visible. Most non-Moslem women walked around in public with their faces uncovered, a "nudity" that was provocative, to say the least.

Ahgavni's shy smile and furtive sidelong glances contrasted with what he had experienced in other infidel households, where the women's attitude seemed dominated by a subtle aura of fear. Of course, the presence of his great friend, Ahgavni's husband, would have a lot to do with the lack of fear in this case, he supposed.

Tallal didn't have much use for Armenians in general. It's too bad they're so damned uppity and act so superior to the rest of us, he thought. It's our country and those infidels treat us like second class citizens . . . when they get the chance. Double damn them. They're the storekeepers, the bankers, the teachers, the builders, the scientists, and yes, even the farmers—all know-it-alls. When the Christians observe one of their holy days—and they seem to have a million of them—the marketplace almost completely shuts down because they own the stalls, the banks, the stores, and even the baking ovens. When the Moslems mark one of their holy days, the bazaars are wide open and going full blast as if the Moslem majority was a distinct minority. The only time the Turks really get back at these people—Greeks included—is tax time, when the collectors, backed by *polis*, exact punitive levies.

Of course, Mamigon and his family were not like most Armenians he knew. They were friendly and open. Mamigon's mother doted on Tallal every time he visited.

The smile on Tallal's face vanished as his horse rounded a huge rock on the road and Yosghat Dagh's mud-brick houses came into view.

2 ⚭ MASSACRE

Mamigon didn't know it as he loped easily along in the bright sunshine, but he was running to his destiny as an outlaw—wanted dead or alive by the Turkish police. The big man was feeling good about the sound of his heavy boots crunching the gravel and padding the dust of the trail, feeling good about the light breeze caressing his brow, feeling good about the heft of the pheasants he was carrying in both hands, and feeling good about the way his balls bumped easily against his thighs, first on one side, then the other as he ran. He would be home in the morning early enough to catch most of the

Mass and would be able to spend some time on the Sabbath with his family before going to work the next morning. He knew his lateness for Sunday services tomorrow would be forgiven by the *der-hire*, Father Vasken, once he gave the benignly shrewd little priest with the pointed chin whiskers a brace of pheasants for his table, part of the sixteen he had bagged on his Saturday hunt.

"Keep up, man . . . keep up."

"I am . . . *puff* . . . keeping up . . . *puff.*"

"You must do better, my brother."

"Is that smoke I see . . . *puff* . . . through those rocks ahead?"

"I see nothing . . . watch the trail . . . it's bad along here."

Mamigon had turned his head to check Aram to make certain the younger man was keeping up with him. Mamigon had developed a system of covering distances efficiently. It involved trotting for about 5 kilometers, walking 2, and so on, alternating the pace until it was time to eat or rest. Aram, not quite nineteen, constantly complained about the run-walk-run routine imposed on him arbitrarily because that was the hunting routine of his older brother. The younger man was nearly 6 feet 2 already, and would probably be taller than his older brother eventually. Aram carried four of the pheasants, changing hands constantly and puffing loudly, more to impress Mamigon with the fact that he didn't like the routine than being actually in distress.

"Enough, brother . . . *puff* . . . I can take care of myself."

"We certainly bagged a fine collection of birds."

"Yes . . . *puff* . . . our mother is going to like these . . . they are plump."

"You speak the truth, Aram, Mother is going to like them."

"I believe Ahgavni . . . *puff* . . . is not going to be as impressed."

He grinned at the mention of his wife. She would grumble at all the feather plucking she and the rest of the women in the household would have to do, as if they weren't always plucking and cleaning hens to make broth for pilaf. The household was constantly aflutter with skirts, what with six brothers and their wives all living together in his father's bulging mud-brick home with the series of ells the old man had added to accommodate his offspring. When in hell would some of them move out, he thought without rancor. It was the biggest family unit in Yosghat Dagh, and just feeding everyone at the same time was as hectic as preparing a meal for the hungry at the annual church picnic. Well, it wasn't his problem, really, as long as they all preferred it that way and were happy. Armenian families were large, not due entirely to innate fecundity. When a girl was married, she usually went to live with the bridegroom's family, where she was dominated by her mother-in-law and any older daughters and sisters-in-law in that family. Mamigon was the sixth son to marry, and his wife automatically moved in with the rest and was called *harse* or bride. Even though she had now been married six years, she was still called *harse* and would continue to be until the youngest and last brother, Aram, brought home a bride. Mamigon grinned at the thought of the not-so-subtle pecking order that this custom imposed. His wife had the least status in the household because she was the newest and youngest, only twenty-two. He chuckled as another thought occurred to him. Aram's future wife would be called *harse* forever since there would be no brides to follow.

The trail he was on in the rugged, rocky foothills was one he could claim as his own creation. Since he was a boy old enough to use the ancient hornbow given him by his father, he had been trotting off to the rugged vastness of the mountains near his hamlet to hunt game. Now that he was a man of twenty-eight with a wife, three young children, and another on the way, the hunt was his one release from his dawn-to-dusk work as the blacksmith and ironmonger for his hamlet and surrounding countryside. He had replaced his father as the village smith, after returning from his three-year stint in the army. He had spent two of those three years as a cadet in the *Harbiye*. Then, as a second lieutenant, he had been a platoon leader in the opening battles at Cannakale Bogazi, the straits the enemy called the Dardanelles where the spit of land, Gallipoli, was being contested. The wounds in his arms, legs, and left side were enough to get him sent home. He wondered what good his knowledge of German, learned at the military academy, would do him now that he spent his life as a blacksmith, forging shoes for riding and work horses, shears for the sheepmen and rug makers, plowshares for the farmers, and sundry pans of simple but serviceable design.

It was the easiness of the work that made life boring for Mamigon, who stood over 6 feet, 5 inches high and could lift 100 pounds with either hand. His strength had persuaded his father to choose Mamigon, rather than any of his six other sons, as his apprentice. Mamigon looked forward to the day he would bring his brother Aram, now running behind him on the trail, into the shop. That could mean perhaps an extra day in the hills doing what he liked best, hunting and fishing, accompanied by his huge retriever, Aslan. He had bought Aslan from a traveling storyteller four years ago when the dog was a pup, and the two had become inseparable. He had named the dog Aslan, Turkish for lion, when the puppy attacked a big snake without hesitation—and killed it—the day after he joined the household.

"Mamigon . . . *puff* . . . I am sure I saw heavy smoke again . . . *puff*."

"I do not see anything . . ."

"It is only when we top a rise . . . *puff* . . . and I can see ahead."

"Very well, brother, I will keep my eyes open. Do not lose the birds. Too many would be disappointed." Mamigon realized immediately he shouldn't have added that about losing the birds. It had been difficult to adjust to Aram when he had returned from the army. Aram was just thirteen when he left and was a man now and Mamigon knew he was forgetting too often to treat him as one.

Over the years, Mamigon had provided half the village with game he brought down with his bow. It was half the village because most inhabitants of an Armenian village on the Anatolian Plain of Asia Minor were related in some fashion. Residents of a village or hamlet of Christians in a country ruled by Moslems tended to stay put. Armenian communities were everywhere. They resided in totally Armenian communities such as Yosghat Dagh; they resided in sections of cities and large towns, comprising as much as half the population, sharing their lives with Turkish neighbors and households or whole neighborhoods of Kurds, Kizibashis, Persians, Lazes, Circassians, Yezidis, Greeks, Nestorians, Jacobites, and even Gypsies. Assyrians, Sunni Arabs, Lebons, and Hebrews completed the major groups, all remnants of the civilizations that had flourished and waned in what had been for hundreds of centuries the crossroads of civilization with Mount Ararat in ancient Armenia as the hub of the universe.

While Armenians were not considered first class citizens, because they were infidels, they were generally left alone by their Moslem masters to practice their religion, conduct their own schools and perpetuate their own languages and culture. As long as they paid their taxes and their young men served in the army (or paid substitutes to serve for them), the government did not interfere beyond a constantly ominous, niggling harassment. Mamigon had been treated like any other Turkish soldier when he led his company against the French invasion on the mainland of Turkey at Kum Kale when the Allies opened their drive to capture Constantinople by landing their main force on the Gallipoli peninsula in April. The Turkish commander, Mustapha Kemal Pasha himself, had decorated and promoted the young Armenian after Mamigon had crawled two-hundred meters under heavy enemy fire with a machine gun on his back to where a Turkish unit was being shot to pieces. He rallied the only sergeant still alive and ordered him to lead his surviving men back while he covered them with the gun. He managed the machine gun until nightfall and dragged the gun back, counting seventeen bullet nicks on his body, three serious enough to send him home from the war. The sergeant he had rescued had kissed him on both cheeks and had stayed by Mamigon's side during the treatment of his wounds at the aid station.

In the meantime, his newfound friend in the army, Tallal Kosmanli, had been ordered home for official paramilitary duty in the vilayet of Yosghat, governed by his father. The Turk and Armenian had continued their friendship, going on many hunting trips together.

Mamigon frowned as he realized that Tallal had not visited in the past few weeks, although he had been an almost weekly hunting companion after they returned from service.

While the Turk's presence had annoyed some of the villagers, Mamigon and his family treated Tallal with the same hospitality they would have offered a visiting Armenian. Tallal was a smart, shrewd man with a heavy eye for the women, a proclivity that only made Mamigon smile indulgently. Tallal never made overtures to the women in Mamigon's village, though he talked a lot about them.

"That big one we just passed at the sheepfold, have you been sticking her? You know, the one with those magnificent blooming melons."

"Such questions . . . you must mean Mariam."

"I guess that is the one. The only way I could improve Allah's design for that one is if she had three of them."

"Three? Three what?"

"Three full, blooming casabahs in a row. That way, I could suckle at the middle one while I caress the other two . . . and I would be sticking her at the same time." Tallal's eyes had a faraway look and his tongue was running across his thin lips.

"Enough, you dog in heat. I see the picture all too plainly for me." Mamigon had a small smile on his face. He was always uncomfortable when Tallal articulated his sexual desires and fantasies. "Mariam is fetching, for certain, even without a third one. Tallal, what you have to learn yet is that a beautiful woman is hell, purgatory and paradise."

"All three? Very well, tell me."

"I was unhappy when my father told me that arrangements had been made for me to marry this certain girl. I told Father she was homely. Be satisfied and happy, my son, he said. A beautiful woman is the hell of the soul, the purgatory of the purse, and a paradise for the eyes only."

"Was he right?"

"No, my father was wrong. Ahgavni is my paradise. There is no hell or purgatory."

"A thousand pardons, my infidel friend, but I would still like to see Mariam with three of them."

"Oofah, Tallal, your mind is in a single channel."

"By the beard of my father, why not? What else is there other than good food and a good probe?" Seeing the semblance of a grin on Mamigon's face, Tallal shifted his thoughts slightly. "You know, all the years I have known you in the army you never once talked about your women . . . or any woman."

"Truly, there was nothing I could have said that you did not know, old pistol."

"Not even that Circassian blonde I saw you with after graduation?"

"Ah, Tallal, there is so little to tell. We were lonely, we liked each other, and spent the evening together playing backgammon."

"See how I talk in truth? You did not tell me a thing! Tell me now, did you stick her?"

"Very well. I will indulge you this once . . . since you do not know who she is and will probably never cross her path. She offered herself. I am ashamed to say I offended her sensibilities by refusing. No, we did nothing that would interest you at all."

"Nothing?"

"Nothing, you Turkish stilleto . . . stop prying."

"Would you stick her if you met her now?"

"I am married. I was then. I am now."

"Eh? Is that an ordination for celibacy?"

"Tallal, I have offspring I want to be able to look in the eye."

"I notice you did not mention your wife."

"She is not to be mentioned in such barracks talk." The Armenian's face had darkened as he snapped out the words.

"You do not think much of me, eh?"

"Like a brother, Tallal, I love you."

"Then, what was that tone of reproval?"

"I am an old bear, Tallal . . . I am a one-woman man."

"So am I, Big One, so am I . . . one woman at a time. Har . . . har."

Mamigon had joined the Turk in laughter, clapping him on the back. Tallal had been good company. He would certainly appear soon with a string of ribald tales. Mamigon secretly wished he could be more free in his thoughts and actions, like Tallal. In such conversations, he always felt less an adult and more a boy.

Mamigon was feeling good. With seven brothers, their six wives, sixteen offspring, his father and mother, and all the in-laws and cousins and aunts in the hamlet, the fourteen pheasants he had to distribute would not go very far. Oh well, it wasn't a matter of need that motivated his hunting trips. Pheasant, grouse, rabbit, mountain goat, and venison helped change the fare at the table.

Mamigon's skill with the hornbow, made of laminated rams' horns, was of such deadly accuracy that he never missed when he loosed an arrow. If the prey was in range, it was dead. He hammered out his own iron tips for the arrows he fashioned from willow and kept a supply of several hundred. Making them gave him something to do when he ran out of work in the barnlike shop next to his father's house.

As the sun set, Mamigon came upon the last campsite he would make before leaving in the morning for home. Aram gathered some firewood while Mamigon dressed one of the pheasants for the meal. After they ate, the brothers took their ease, watching the fire burn down to a smoldering mound, both peaceful with their own thoughts until sleep knitted up their eyelids.

The brothers were up at dawn. The clear mountain air had a heavy tinge of white smoke that wafted by in intermittent, barely discernible clouds. Mamigon began sweeping the lower lands with squinted eyes in the half-light of early morning.

"Aram . . . Am I seeing things or is the smoke coming from the direction of our village?"

The younger man looked hard for a few seconds. "It might be the brushes near the. . . ."

"It *is* the village . . . my God . . . let's go!"

They scooped up their things and began a steady trot for home, about ten kilometers away. The closer they got, the more worried they became. Flames licked up here and there but the main emanation was smoke. Even with the smoke, at half a kilometer, Mamigon could not see anything amiss except for an annoying difference in the standard view of the village his eye had come to expect.

He suddenly realized what it was: The round church tower that dominated the village cluster was minus its Byzantine conical dome with the cross at its peak. And as he got closer he could see that the roofs of most of the structures had been burned out.

Mamigon increased his running pace, leaving Aram far behind by the time he entered the outskirts of the village.

It was Sunday morning and everyone should have been in church. Everyone seemed to be outside on the main street, dead. Bodies of women and children everywhere. The older thinnest women were mostly clothed, the younger women and the plump ones of all ages were mostly naked . . . even the little girls and little boys, some with their heads bashed in, some with deep, fatal cuts across their fronts or backs, but all dead in the grotesque positions the body assumes when life strains to remain during the final agonies.

The twisted, bent, huddled, sprawling bodies were not all due to the inflicted pain of death. The killers had made obscene jokes out of some. Even in death the faces of two young women were hideously contorted. They were sharing in their sex the deeply imbedded ends of a police club with their bodies slammed against each other at the crotch, their legs scissoring each other.

Mamigon tried to avert his gaze as he ran along, becoming shorter and shorter of breath in reaction to what he was discovering in what was once his peaceful village. Some of the women had the flesh around their pinned wrists rubbed off to the bone as they must have twisted and pulled in total pain and terror: they had died with oil-soaked remnants of clothing stuffed in their sex and burned. Some had simply bled to death, their hands still trying to cover the raw wounds where their breasts had been lopped off.

Cristos! Cristos! Holy Father, what is this . . .

The naked corpses of eight pregnant women were carrying something else in death. The taut cloth stretched on large wooden hoops used to separate grain from chaff had been ripped out, the hoops broken in two, and the semicircles of wood shoved through each victim's sex and out through a slit sliced across the belly. One of the hoop ends had speared a fetus and its tiny head was peeking out, its deep purple color in sharp contrast to the ghastly white and crimson of its mother's belly.

Mamigon kept on trotting, his heart in his mouth, his eyes straining down the street toward his own house. He had to dodge not only bodies but broken furniture and bedding and all the rest of the things that make up a home . . . dragged out of the houses to see better what to loot. The houses, with their broken and smashed windows, seemed to stare at him with hollow eyes as he ran by.

He passed the village well in the center of the town and averted his eyes again once he realized what made the well look so much bigger. Five naked women draped the lip of the well on their bellies, their heads dangling inside. Their hips and white bottoms were starkly exposed with the haft of bayonets driven through their sex to pin them to the wooden sill of the well. From the heavy pools of blood at their lifeless toes, the women had obviously been killed by the bayonets thrust into them after they had been bent over the well.

Mamigon's total horror and bewilderment was not at all abated at the sight of Father Vasken. The delightful old priest had no twinkle in his staring eyes. There was not a stitch on him, hanging by his neck from a tripod gibbet, the stump of his severed penis sporting the tail of a goat. *Cristos!* Mamigon had forced himself to look once more at the priest's face to see why it was so disfigured. A sliced-off vaginal opening had been planted on his face, his nose sticking out through the orifice.

Where were the men? Except for Father Vasken, Mamigon had yet to see a single male adult other than ninety-year-old Baron Sourapian, his head almost severed from his shoulders. What in the name of God was going on! What hound of hell had visited his village? Who could have done this? He ran grimly on, breathlessly on through the smoking ruins and corpses to his house. It was a burned wreck. The first thing he saw was his wife, by herself, in the middle of the street.

Mamigon stood stock still for a second, then raised his arms, his face to the heavens, and gave out with one long roar of rage, a roar that reverberated in the haunting stillness of the scene. Then he ran to her side.

She was completely naked, her body tied spreadeagled to stakes, her belly ripped open and an embryo among the entrails spilling to the dust beside her bloody torso.

He let a whimper escape as his wildly searching eyes caught sight of his three little children, their heads smashed in, tossed like torn-up stuffed dolls in a heap near the house.

He roared again, his hands touching his face, his teeth bared, his huge frame drawn and tense, unable to believe, unable to understand, unable to accept anything he was seeing.

He brought his hands down as he spotted his mother, lying on her side, in total repose with a bullet hole between her eyes.

Mamigon had not moved from the spot near his murdered wife. He seemed rooted there, shaking like a leaf one moment and drawing up tense the next. His eyes caught sight of his nephews and nieces, all thirteen of them, cast about like driftwood, either brained or deeply cut by what must have been a heavy saber.

Off by the corner of the house near the forge were four of his five sisters-in-law, hardly recognizable by Mamigon. He had never seen them naked . . . naked and dead with iron pokers from his forge sticking out between their purposely drawn-up thighs, their bottoms resting in coagulated pools of their own blood, now dark brown and part of the mud.

Then he heard it, a low moan, and looked around frantically. There almost hidden by the corner of the house, his oldest brother Ardavast.

He was still alive but with life ebbing as blood oozed from around the bayonets driven into his shoulders and legs to pin him to the ground, a viciously slow way to die.

"Ardavast! Ardavast! It is Mamigon."

"Mamigon . . . Your . . . friend . . . Ta . . . Tallal . . . Tallal . . . kill . . . killed us . . . laughed as he . . ."

"Ardavast! Don't die, my brother . . . Don't . . . Where are the men-folk?"

But he was dead, his last words whispered in a final struggle over the massive lethargy of death.

Those last words were hard for Mamigon to grasp. What was that he said? Tallal? Tallal Bey? Tallal, who had fought beside him against the French? Tallal, who had gone hunting with him? Tallal, whose life Mamigon had saved from the tusks of a charging boar? Tallal, who had broken bread with him, served by his mother and his wife when they returned from the hunt? NO!

But Ardavast had said so with his dying breath. Mamigon stumbled back to the scene he hoped had been an illusion, a nightmare.

He gently gathered and held each of his little children to his chest, calling their names, crying and moaning softly for a moment before he laid them next to their mother's body. He cut the fetters holding his wife, closed her eyes, and held her head close to his, weeping quietly in a last farewell. "My poor baby girl," he kept saying over and over again in choking moans. He had thought of her that way since he wed her when she was sixteen. Aslan crept up carefully and slowly on his haunches and nudged Mamigon, big solemn eyes showing bewilderment at the strange noises his master was making.

Mamigon was still holding Ahgavni, rocking the lifeless, bloody form when Aram arrived. He howled long and loud as if in pain, seated on the ground next to his mother, his hands flat on the ground, beseeching her to open her eyes and speak to him.

Time stood still for the brothers as they sat with their slaughtered family amidst the carnage that reeked of blood and white wreaths of smoke.

The grief-stricken pair finally dug a big hole in the sheepfold behind the ruins of their house and carefully placed into it what was once their family, the twenty-three members they could find. The father, four brothers, and a sister-in-law were missing. The flies and vultures were beginning to arrive to feast as the sun rose higher.

Mamigon's anguish and bewilderment began to turn slowly into deep-seated rage.

"Where were you, God? Where *were* you, today?" he roared at the sky. "Are you really there, oh God? Do you care? Is this what happens to the innocents who believe in you? Give me a sign . . . tell me you made a mistake today . . . show me you exist." He was out of breath, his chest heaving, his facial muscles drawn taut. The long silence after his outburst seemed to be the answer he expected. He deliberately spat hard at the earth and looked up again. Nothing.

Mamigon nodded. All right, he would find Tallal, and if Tallal was responsible for the mayhem here, he would pay for it, magnificently. Yes, Tallal and everyone else who had a bloody hand.

He looked at Aram, who had remained at a respectful distance, never having heard his brother sound so wild. "They are going to die, Aram, all of the ruthless sons of hell . . . every single dog-mother's son who had a hand in this."

"Do you know who, brother?"

"I am certain. I just do not know why."

"Who?"

"Tallal."

"Tallal? You don't mean . . ."

"Yes. My friend Tallal. My good friend . . ." He spat with a snap of his head.

"But why? Why?"

"I am going after them. I am going to find out before I kill them as painfully as they killed our family."

"I am going with you."

Mamigon sized up his nineteen-year-old sibling. "Aram, we are done with tears and breast beating. Let us move on. Help me get things together that we shall need. Go find the pheasants I dropped back there somewhere and let us see if we can find anything in this hellhole we can use."

Between them they found some *piddeh*, some jerked beef, *fetah*, and a couple of woolen blankets in which to roll them. Aram found an old Turkish scimitar in the blackened schoolhouse ruins. Mamigon rummaged among the smashed works at his forge and found the two bags of iron arrowheads he had fashioned to augment his supply for the hornbow.

They were ready to go. Mamigon walked slowly back to the sheepfold and knelt at the fresh mound of earth that now covered his loved ones. Aram followed.

"I swear to you, my children, my wife, my mother, my brothers and sisters, I will not rest until your killers have died at my hand. Rest, now, in peace."

Mamigon did not cross himself. He did not invoke his God. He turned away quickly and, with Aram a step behind, left the wrecked, corpse-strewn village, sticking to his alternating run-walk-run system.

They did not look back.

3 PURSUIT

The trail was easy to follow. They were on horseback and there were nearly two hundred of them, Mamigon judged from the hoofprints and droppings, all heading southeast. The Turks had at least a twelve-hour start from all the signs. Ox-drawn *arabas* were bringing up the rear . . . the rear because their wheel tracks were untrampled. That meant that the Turks would not be able to travel faster than a good walking pace—the pace of the oxen. The big man figured he would catch up in about six hours with his run-walk system.

Aram slowed him down. The younger man couldn't keep up with his brother, and Mamigon didn't want to run ahead and take the chance of Aram catching up at an inopportune or dangerous moment, so they walked more than they ran. Nightfall was on them and the exhausted pair still had not caught up. The following morning, about an hour after they started, the brothers came upon three naked bodies, those of a young boy and two young women, all three with deep cuts where the neck meets the shoulder. The faces looked familiar, but the brothers could not identify them. They buried the bodies and added rock covers because the graves were not deep.

The sun was at its peak when the pursuers saw the dust raised by their quarry, about 8 kilometers ahead. Mamigon took his time, lagging now to keep out of sight until he chose to be seen. He caught up with them at nightfall.

There were a hundred men making camp in an open space among the rocks and stunted shrubs of the dry mountain fastness. Huddled together on one side and watched over by four rifle-bearing guards was about a score of women from the village. The light was nearly gone, but Mamigon could see their uniforms; the men were a unit of *polis*, young men recruited for emergency service by the vilayets to perform police duties. Each gendarme would be armed with a rifle and a sword.

Suddenly they heard wild screams and outbursts of laughter. Mamigon took Aram and the dog out of earshot of the camp. Aram was shaking and Mamigon was glad his brother was with him; otherwise he would have yielded to his violent urge to charge into the camp and stop what was going on. But he would have died, he knew, leaving Aram totally alone. Instead he waited.When the camp fires were dull glows and the bivouac was quiet, he crawled up to the camp carrying only the scimitar. There was only one sentry in sight, sitting on a boulder, totally at ease, picking his teeth, his rifle at his side. The Turks had nothing to fear. Who would dare attack an armed camp?

Mamigon was puzzled. He couldn't have been that wrong about the signs on the trail. There had to have been about two hundred horses in the group. Yet, there were certainly fewer than a hundred men in the camp. He crawled in a wide circle around the camp to where the horses were tethered. He could make out about ninety. He sat for nearly an hour thinking what to do next. Getting to Tallal was going to be difficult on a one-on-one basis. Doing something about the women captives was a new consideration, something he had not thought of when he set out after the Turks. All right, he would bide his time and, he hoped, make things happen. He decided to rejoin Aram and crawled to a safe distance from the camp before he walked.

"Some of our women from the village are back there, Aram."

"I thought so. Who are they, Turks?"

"Yes. Looks like a *polis* troop."

"Did you see Siranoush with the women?"

"No . . . I could not tell in the dark."

"Was Tallal there?"

"I did not see him, but he must be. Those women are . . ."

"What was all the screaming and yelling about?"

"Nothing important, brother."

"You looked as if you found worms in your pilaf, Mamigon. What is happening?"

"I said it is nothing. Let us leave it at that."

"There you go, worms in your pilaf again . . ."

"Get some sleep." Mamigon patted Aram on the shoulder and sat down with Aslan to feed him bits of dried beef. The big dog had had little chance to fend for himself during the pursuit, and Mamigon cupped some of the precious water they were carrying in a goatskin bag for Aslan to lap up. Have to find some fresh water soon, he thought.

The cold of the night dissipated quickly with the first rays of the sun. The rocky, barren foothills provided excellent cover for Mamigon and his company of boy and dog. They watched as the troop rode slowly down the winding, narrow road. The big Armenian's eyes were on the leader, a slight but well-proportioned figure astride a white Arabian, wearing a German helmet with a spike on the crown, his right arm akimbo. Tallal! Tallal, you godforsaken, lecherous son of a dog whelped on a dung heap. You won't live out the day . . .

Mamagon knew the country perfectly. He trotted along a ravine, leading his brother, until they reached a rocky promontory that overlooked the roadway. He was ahead of the column, which was slowed by the entourage of women and the four *arabas*. He sent his brother, with Aslan on a leash, to high cover, checked his quiver, selected two arrows, and waited until the column came into view. They were in bow range in five minutes. Mamigon was accurate, deadly accurate, up to 400 meters. The Turks, with their excellent Mauser 98s, had a range up to 700 meters, though Mamigon guessed most of them would be lucky to hit anything even at 400. Mamigon knew how bad the Turks were with their rifles. "They can slice off an ear without touching a hair but they can't hit the side of a mountain with their rifles," had been his lament at Gallipoli.

At the instant Mamigon unleashed his arrow at Tallal, his horse reared in fright at a hissing snake, tossing the rider sprawling to the dust. The arrow thumped into the Arabian's neck, bringing an almost human scream from the animal and sending it in a frenzied gallop down the road. Mamigon's next arrow was for Tallal's lieutenant, who died instantly with the shaft in his eye socket, still trying to draw his pistol. The troop reacted but made the mistake of firing hastily from horseback, a poor platform.

"Tallal . . . Tallal . . . . you bloodless whelp of a wolf," was the roar heard from the rocks as the Turks dismounted to clamber up the rock-stitched slope after the assailant they had seen briefly. Mamigon circled back, darting from rocks to shrubs to rocks, killing two more men silently with his hornbow. He worked his way to the rear of where the column had stopped and saw that the women were still standing, cowering on the roadway in front of the four ox carts, guarded by the four drivers. He crawled down to bow range and killed three of the men before the last driver ran out of range, up the opposite slope and into the dwarf shrubs. Mamigon stood up quickly and waved to the women to come to him. They broke into a run in his direction, holding up what remained of their tattered skirts, screaming, shouting. The Turks were doing the same—howling, shouting—as they stood up and began converging on Mamigon and the approaching women. Mamigon braced himself for a last stand, looking carefully at the charging men for some sign of Tallal. The bastard must be well back of his men, he thought. The women were about 200 meters from the slope where some cover was available. Mamigon counted his arrows—twelve.

The nearest man that he could see was coming into range, leading a cohort of about fifty or so darting, dodging riflemen who were showing great respect for the hidden bowman. A dozen rifles spat lead as Mamigon suddenly stood up to lose an arrow into the chest of the closest target. He counted to three, stood up again and killed another, crawling man, counted to four, did it again, counted to two, again, changing his timing constantly to put the enemy off pace. He was down to eight arrows; the women were almost there, but so were the Turks, who began firing at the women now. One of the women seemed to trip in midstride and crumpled to the dust, lying motionless.

Mamigon spat in disgust. They were going to kill him just like they killed her, impersonally. What a way to die! He wasn't going to save the women, he wasn't even going to get Tallal, and those approaching riflemen were such poor shots he would probably be hit a dozen times before they could finish him off. He hoped Aram would get away at least.

He never missed when he strung and loosed one of his missiles. He had only six arrows now, the closest Turk was about 80 meters away, and the women, close enough to recognize their own village blacksmith, began shouting his name.

He stood up for the last time, dropping another man who had his rifle at the ready. There was a sudden stillness as everyone in the savage arena anticipated the end.

Then a voice boomed out from above, on the flank of the advancing Turks, "All right, my bravos, leave no shit-whelped Turk alive!" It was Aram's voice.

Mamigon took the cue and motioned toward the Turks:

"Wait . . . wait until I kill five more cowards before you attack!"

That was enough. The Turks broke their advance, scampered for their horses on the road and galloped down the valley. Mamigon could see Tallal's spiked helmet leading the way.

The sudden quiet was finally broken by cries of relief from the women, all in their teens and early twenties and all of them familiar to Mamigon. He looked eagerly among the bruised, cut, tattered, and disheveled group, eighteen in all, patting heads and embracing some as he looked for his missing young sister-in-law, Siranoush. When he finally asked for her by name, a brief silence resulted.

"Tallal took her the first night," someone said in a hushed voice. "She spat in his face as he forced her in front of everyone . . . so he cut her throat after he was through." The women began to cry and babble about what had happened to them and their families. Aram and the dog joined the group at this point, and Mamigon raised his arms for silence.

"Not now, please. We must get out of here first. Aram, you saved our lives, boy. You go quickly and gather up as many rifles, pistols, and bandoliers as you can carry. Take some of the stronger women with you. Collect canteens, too. I need two women for each of those *arabas* to get them off the road and see what we need from them. All right, let's go, Y'Allah."

The collection from among the dead proved to be needless. The four carts had extra rifles and pistols and ammunition as well as tins of cheese soaking in salt, sugar, cloves of garlic, onions . . . and four boxes filled with gold and silver jewelry and expensive baubles stripped from the homes and bodies of the victims.

The newly freed captives stuffed knapsacks with food and canteens to be filled at the nearest water source, and each was given two bandoliers with cartridge clips for the Mausers. Everyone, including the men, put on a pair of ill-fitting but useful new boots. Mamigon and Aram equipped themselves with an extra bag with four Navy Colt revolvers they found in the carts. Then the band sat down for a quick council.

"Does anyone know where Tallal was heading?"

"Gemerek," was the reply from a dozen voices.

"Gemerek? That is about 90 kilometers from here. It is another Armenian village. I have cousins living there. About five hundred families in all," Mamigon said out loud, more as a reflection than an effort to be informative.

"I am sure I heard one of the Turks say they would be heading east from Gemerek and end up in a place called Gurin where they were going to meet up with more soldiers."

"That's a good two hundred kilometers from here. I don't know how we can get to Gemerek before Tallal and his men to warn the village, and reaching Gurin seems hopeless. Those jackals have horses."

Mamigon sat silent for a long time, pondering the situation. The group sat silent also, somberly contemplating the probable fate of the people of Gemerek and Gurin and who knew where else. Mamigon knew he had to do something about the women. Aram was a useful and easy companion, but the women were going to be a terrible hindrance and responsibility. He had to think of their safety before he could think of anything else. He shook his head. Tallal would have to wait, but he had to check on a thought that was nagging him.

"Listen, I counted two hundred horses when I was following you and when I came on your camp the first time I am certain there were less than a hundred. Does anyone have an explanation for me?"

Araxy answered immediately, "You're right about the count. Half the mounted men were soldiers under an army lieutenant. They didn't want to ride at the pace set by the oxen so they continued on ahead, as we overheard, to Gemerek."

"So, the soldiers are ahead of Tallal Bey and his men? All right, that settles it. We will move quietly, carefully, mostly during the night to the seacoast near Adana. That's about 350 kilometers to the south, I estimate. I'll try to get you on a boat to Cyprus where the Greeks will take care of you. Divide up the gold and silver equally among you, and there should be plenty to keep you alive for a while. What say you?"

The women stared at him with big eyes. One, a twelve-year-old called Rachell, whose face was swollen and bruised from repeated slaps, began to whimper, "I . . . I don't think I can walk much farther . . ."

"Everyone has to walk. There is no other way."

Rachell leaned over to Araxy beside her and whispered at length.

"Rachell has something wrong with her. She's been bleeding badly and can't stop the blood," Araxy said.

"Well, let's take a look and bandage it up."

"You can't, Mamigon Agha. It's . . . it's not a place you can bandage." Araxy seemed embarrassed. She looked at the ground and said quietly, "They took turns with her because she was a virgin. They tore her insides."

Mamigon raised her hands to stop her explanation, but she looked steadily downward and finished. "There were sixteen virgins in the group they took along. Rachell is the only one left. We'll never forget their screams."

As if on signal, all of them began wailing with the exception of Rachell, who seemed to be in a stupor.

"Enough, enough. We'll carry Rachell, then. Oh, yes, I want all of you to pick out an army cap for yourself from that cart and make sure it fits you with your hair tucked up into it. And, pick out a pair of trousers and wear them with your skirts inside. All right, get ready to leave."

He pulled Aram aside, talked to him in a low voice, and, with the women shielding his movements, he slipped behind a rocky outcrop with a loaded rifle and sat down, his knees pulled up.

"Don't look back at me as you walk away," Mamigon said. "I'll catch up soon."

There was about an hour of daylight left as the tatterdemalion group struggled up the hillside, away from the roadway and the carts.

Mamigon didn't move or look around. As the last of the refugees moved out of view, he heard dislodged rock rolling down with a clatter from the opposite slope to the roadway. Then, some curses as someone slipped and fell. Mamigon waited. He had not forgotten the *araba* driver who had run away up the other side of the road.

Very carefully, Mamigon turned and peered around the rock he was behind. The driver was almost to the roadside. He was looking across the way down to Mamigon's right, where a *polis* with an arrow in his chest was making feeble attempts to stand up.

Mamigon stood up, his Mauser aimed at the driver. The target immediately threw up his hands: "*Aman, aman,* don't kill me, in the name of Allah!"

"You excrement of a dog, why not? Haven't you killed anyone lately?"

"Y–Yes."

"Helpless girls, boys, women, men?"

"I only killed one man who tried to take my *araba*, honestly."

He was not more than a boy, Mamigon saw; a boy with a big wart under his left cheekbone who was wetting his pants as he spoke.

"Why should I let you live, boy?"

"I . . . I don't know . . . please, you're a Christian . . ."

"Christian, am I, you bastard Moslem. Am I supposed to turn the other cheek? Don't believe it. Before I kill you, bury that woman over there."

The boy ran to one of the carts, pulled out a shovel, and dug a grave where Mamigon showed him. He rolled the body onto one of the cart covers and the woman, no more than a girl, whose name Mamigon couldn't recall, was covered over.

"All right, now unhitch those oxen so they can forage, and take off another of those cart covers and leave it on the road."

The boy took off the halters and released the wagon trees from each brace of oxen to free the dumb brutes. After he finished the task, he raised his hands again, facing the big Armenian.

Mamigon said nothing, turned to the mortally wounded man who had sat down against a boulder, holding his chest around the imbedded arrow, blood flowing in spurts fom his mouth. The rifle in Mamigon's hands barked once and, with a bullet through his ear, the man's slow death became instant. Mamigon turned back to the driver.

"Your name, boy?"

"Enver, Enver Dash. I am only sixteen."

"All right, run for your life and never let me gaze on you again."

The boy was off in a flash, back up the road the troop had traveled. Mamigon located all the bodies of the men he had killed—thirteen of them—and wondered how he could make his mark. He would decapitate them . . . that would scare the living . . . if they thought they could lose their heads. The evil grin on Mamigon's face vanished as he thought of something else . . . emasculation. The Turks had a penchant for Armenian women. Mamigon had never seen an unveiled Turkish woman. They must be real dogs if the Turks were so crazy about Armenian girls. Armenian women were just not safe in the presence of Turks or Kurds. No question about it. Mamigon had known this most of his life, but attributed the whole thing to male gusto . . . until now. He changed his mind. He suddenly knew what his mark was going to be.

Finished, he found some sulphur matches and set fire to the *arabas* before he left, rolling up and taking the cart cover with him.

He felt he had made a mistake in letting the boy go, but he didn't dwell on it. He had more important things on his mind. Like, what was he going to do with all those women?

Mamigon had climbed to the ridge and had begun his descent on the other side so he was unaware of the figure of a man tracing his steps from one fallen Turk to another at the scene of the battle.

Mamigon caught up with the group in less than an hour. They were sitting in a grove of trees without a fire, shivering in the night cold. The arid Anatolian Plain was hot during the day and usually in the 40s and 50s at night during the summer months. It would have been hopelessly cold if it had been winter.

"How's Rachell?"

The woman Araxy was holding the girl in her arms, trying to keep her warm. She shook her head. Mamigon didn't need more than that for an answer. He caught sight of Aram who appeared out of the gloom.

"Aram, let's cut a couple of branches about 2-meters long and see if we can make a litter to carry her."

"What happend back there? I thought I heard a shot."

"I did some cleaning up." From the tone of his voice, Aram knew enough not to question his brother further. They found a tree that had fairly straight branches, chopped off two, removed the offshoots, and bridged the limbs with the canvas from the cart to support Rachell's body.

"We'll rest for an hour and start off. Araxy, see that everyone takes one-hour turns carrying Rachell. She shouldn't be too heavy."

Mamigon looked over his charges. The Turks had gathered up the prettiest women and girls in the village to carry off to use as they pleased. The eighteen survivors seemed to be the youngest ones. Araxy couldn't be twenty yet. He knew Mariam, the baker's daughter, was not quite seventeen. Hripseme, the best dancer in the village, was eighteen. Takuhe, the young wife of the schoolteacher, was maybe twenty. Eksah, wife of the wool merchant, was nineteen. All of them had three things in common: They were all married women less than a week ago, they were all probably young widows now, and each had been mass raped and used sexually in a variety of ways.

As he thought about the young women who had become his responsibility, another thought that he had tried repeatedly to suppress forced its way into his consciousness. His dead wife. He had married her when she was sixteen, about the average age for young women to marry, in his village, and she was dead at twenty-two. What haunted Mamigon was the sight of her lifeless, mutilated, naked body. He had never seen her naked. Never once in their six years as husband and wife. He had touched her, made love to her, felt the warmth of her body, the touch of her hands, but it had always been in the secret of night, without sound or light of any kind. It would have been a breach of good manners to have anyone else in the family know that a couple was having sex, especially *enjoying* sex.

Talking about their intimacies was another taboo. Except once, a year or so after marriage and a month after she had borne him a daughter. They had been alone at the well drawing water for the wash, Mamigon turning the crank.

"I caught you watching me when I was feeding the baby." Ahgavni stared down the well as she said it.

"I'm sorry. Didn't mean to embarrass you." He didn't look at her either.

"I was not embarrassed, man of mine."

"You looked absolutely wonderful. Your . . . your . . ."

"Yes, they're heavy with milk. I wish you would . . . you would touch me tonight."

"Is it all right? I mean, are you able to . . ."

"Oh, yes, of course. I was wondering when you would show interest again."

"I have always been interested, Ahgavni. I was waiting for you to . . ."

Her voice was low and soft as she looked at him for the first time during the exchange of words and said, "I cannot wait."

"I cannot either. Wish we could go off somewhere and be alone."

"Man of mine, do you want to cause a scandal?" She had never once called him by his given name. It was always *martuz*, "man of mine." Mothers and sisters only addressed the men in the familiar.

"We are living in a hypocritical world, Ahgavni. The whole world makes love but no one wants to admit it. No one wants to admit that copulation is what produces babies. We have to sneak it as if we were not married and were doing it behind the barn." His voice had risen.

"Shhhh. Do you want everyone to hear? Be patient. I just hope the baby does not cry tonight and wake up everybody. We will have to be extra careful and quiet."

Mamigon could not get the sight of her naked body out of his mind. Her legs, her thighs, and arms, even in death, had been beautiful. He shuddered in disgust at himself for thinking about her that way and that emotion turned into greater rage at those who had, ironically, revealed her nakedness to him.

He looked at the fitfully napping forms of his charges, their female shapes indistinguishable in the baggy trousers, heavy boots, and shawled torsos. Would they ever be the same again, after what they had been through? Would they be able to relate naturally to men? He thought they were lucky to be alive, but for how long? Mamigon had doubts about his ability to protect so many of them on such a long trip through wild, rough country inhabited by wolves and bears and boars, not to mention the major threat of the Turkish soldiers and civilians. He couldn't figure out what was going on in the country. What had happened in his village? Why? That was the question. As if in answer, Takuhe and Hester, oldest daughter of the village priest, sat up where they had bundled together for warmth, and seeing Mamigon seated against a tree with a rifle across his lap and Aslan stretched out beside him, joined him.

"Is it all right for us to sit with you?" Village women did not sit with men who were not members of the family.

"Of course, of course. There cannot be custom between us in this time and place."

"How did you get away when the Turks came?" Takuhe asked.

"I was not at home. I was out hunting with my brother, Aram."

"Oh . . . Do you know what happened?"

"Only what I saw when I came back. What happened? Why was everyone killed?"

"It was early in the morning," Hester said, "and my brother had just brought in a pail of goat's milk when we heard three shots. He ran out to see what it was and came back to tell us that the Turkish police were in the square and that all men had to report to the square right away."

"What was the reason? Conscription?"

"That is what some of us thought," Takuhe said, taking up the story. "When all the men were there, some of us came out to see what was happening. We recognized Tallal Bey, your friend, Mamigon Agha, in full army dress, in charge of about two hundred gendarmes and soldiers. They were all riding horses. He looked around and asked for you by name."

"He asked for me?" Mamigon nodded to himself. By this time, the rest of the women, except for three still sleeping, had gathered around.

"Yes, he did. Tallal then said boys thirteen years old and up must join the men in the square. The boys came out and joined the men. There must have been about four hundred or more, it was so crowded." Takuhe began to cry. Araxy broke in at this point, almost in a frenzy as she talked.

"Tallal Bey announced that everyone would have to leave the village. He said the men were going to work for the army and that the women and children and old folks were going to be taken into exile to the south.

"Father Vasken pushed his way to the front of the men to ask Tallal what madman had ordered such an inhuman thing—breaking up families and driving people from their homes and livelihoods."

"Tallal said no one was to question the orders. They had to be complied with immediately. He said that he had his orders and would carry them out to the letter. He asked for you, again, but no one knew where you were," Araxy said, almost accusingly.

"Father Vasken might have caused the bloodshed, Mamigon Agha. Our priest raised his fists in the air and told the men in the village not to obey the orders."

"Tallal warned him to keep quiet or face the consequences. Father Vasken replied that only God had consequences for him. Tallal ordered his men to seize the priest. Two *polis* grabbed Father Vasken. Then, Baron Hovsep's two wrestler sons jumped forward and pulled the Father back. The Turks began to fight their way into the crowd and then a shot came from somewhere and one of the Turkish soldiers still on horseback fell dead.

"Everybody stopped in their tracks. Tallal formed a square of soldiers with rifles at their shoulders, ready to fire. They grabbed Father Vasken again, this time without a fight. That dead soldier shocked all of us.

"Tallal shouted he was going to make an example of Father Vasken. He yelled something to his men, and three heavy poles were brought from one of the carts. They set them up in a triangle, dragged our priest to it, and we suddenly realized they were going to hang him.

"We saw it, this time, when the shot came again. It was from the loft of your forge, Mamigon Agha.

"Another soldier, next to Tallal, fell off his horse, dead. Tallal ordered everyone not to move. He spurred up to your house and forge with his pistol out and called for you to come out. Your mother came running out with her hands up toward Tallal, pleading to wait. She wasn't able to say what she wanted Tallal to wait for. He shot her dead in her tracks, Mamigon Agha."

Mamigon nodded absently and waved to Araxy to continue.

"Tallal ordered a squad to go into the forge. They found your brother Ardavast with your army rifle. Tallal had him held down and they drove stakes through his shoulders and knees, leaving him to die . . . His screams were horrible . . ."

"Who killed my wife and children?"

"Tallal did. But it happened later. Tallal rode back to the square where we all were and had his men tear off Father Vasken's clothes and jerk him to the top of the tripod, off his feet. He . . . he . . . strangled slowly. It was . . ."

"All right, so they hanged Father Vasken. Why was everybody killed?"

"Believe it or not, it was Father Vasken again. In one of his convulsions he kicked the rifle butt of one of the Turks standing too close; the rifle fired and the bullet killed another soldier, this one on the ground.

"That shooting was all that Tallal Bey was able to accept, I guess. He was wild with rage. He ordered his men to take all the men from the village to the cow pasture—you know, Baron Hovsep's.

"They marched the men and boys, my father, my husband, my brothers—everyone—to the pasture and then began shooting them. Shooting them! Some of the men tried to run away and they were cut down with swords. Some tried to attack the horsemen, but they were just as helpless. Everybody was dead or dying in twenty minutes."

There was a hush as the women relived the scene. Hester broke the silence.

"We were going crazy at what was happening. Tallal Bey rode back from the pasture and went straight to your house, Mamigon Agha. He called out to your wife. She came out with a big knife and Tallal kicked her in the jaw, knocking her unconscious to the ground. Then he got off his horse and . . ."

"That's enough, enough," Mamigon said softly without emotion on his face. "Did anyone find out why this all happened?"

"I heard one policeman say something about 'let your Christ save you now.' "

"I heard an officer say 'that's what people get who want their homeland back from their conquerors.' "

"They spent the whole day as if they were on a picnic, robbing our homes, killing the old women and young children, doing . . . doing awful things to the rest of us. They would make our mothers watch before they killed them. Then they set fire to all the buildings and left, taking a few of us along."

"Wake up the rest and let us be off," Mamigon said by way of ending the conversation. "Make Rachell comfortable on the litter and treat her gently."

The girl didn't weigh more than 70 pounds, but the rough terrain, the climbing and descending, was a trial for everyone. It didn't last long. Rachell died the second night, quietly, so quietly the bearers did not know they were carrying a corpse until the little band stopped for food and rest. Mamigon buried her with the cart cover as her shroud. Everyone was crying again. A little service was held, with the recitation of the Lord's Prayer and a quiet rendition of the requiem from the Armenian Mass. Rachell turned out to be the first person from Mamigon's village since the massacre, outside of his own family, to receive a decent burial. The grave was left unmarked.

Mamigon summed up the situation. "I figure we have traveled about 50, maybe 60 kilometers in two days. That little stream we crossed back there was nothing. We must cross a big river, I think tomorrow, and then we will hit the real mountains. We shall face our greatest danger in the mountains because there are only a few narrow paths and we may meet people we don't want to meet. So, I will teach all of you how to use the rifles. We will start right here and now."

He had everyone, including Aram, sit in a half-circle around him, each with a Mauser, as he demonstrated how to load the weapon. He slipped a clip of five cartridges from his bandolier, pulled back the bolt at the breech to open the firing chamber, and pushed the clip down into the magazine as the strip holding the clip fell off. Then he pushed the bolt forward all the way and down, noting that the rifle was now loaded and ready to fire. He had everyone follow the routine. "Every time you pull the trigger," he said, "you have to pull the bolt up and back to release the spent cartridge, then forward and down to fire again." He noted that the Mauser 98 weighed about 9 pounds and would be difficult for some of them to handle. He had each woman lie on her stomach and simulate firing with the elbows on the ground to steady the rifle. He cautioned that the rifle butt must always be snug against the shoulder when the trigger is squeezed, to minimize the punch of the strong recoil. He ended the lecture by showing them how to sight and aim the pieces.

Mamigon couldn't help remembering that he had to instruct all these strangers, females, that when they moved their bowels or passed water, to dig a hole at least a foot deep and cover the offal firmly. Trackers, he had told them. If anyone took up their trail, he wasn't going to make it any easier for them, that's all. He couldn't look them in the eye as he told them about the procedure. The chore became so onerous that the women made a pact to try to go together in small groups and use one big hole instead of digging private ones. And they solved the problem of wiping themselves by using leaves, an unsatisfactory expedient but better than nothing. Mamigon had not instructed them about that bit of personal hygiene. He knew that in a very short time the limited intake of food and water would eventually produce small balls of dry excreta, leaving no residue around the anus. Oofah, what a state of affairs, having to think about such things!

The small band ate what they carried off from the *arabas* and each mouthful on this, the third day, became more precious and more boring.

"I am off with Aslan to see about some game. Maybe we should have something good to eat for once. Aram, follow that star and you will not lose your direction. I will be back after sunup."

Two hours after sunrise Mamigon was calculating he should be back with his troop when he heard the scream. It came from the tree-filled hillock ahead, but he couldn't see a thing. He put down his rifle and knapsack containing the six grouse he had shot with his bow and told Aslan to stay where he was. Grabbing his bow and scimitar, he crept up the hill.

His stealth for a man his size was astonishing. He moved noiselessly, something he had learned in hunting easily startled game. When he reached the edge of the clearing, he froze. Aram, blood trickling from a gash on his skull, was tied to a tree. Mamigon could see eight soldiers, one holding a rifle on the women, huddled together near the tree. Seven of the Turks were chortling and giving advice to the eighth, who had one of the women on her back with her boots and trousers off, her bottom completely exposed, and her big skirt pulled up over her arms and face. He was on top of her, his right hand bunching the skirt to render her arms immobile, and he was trying to force entry, seeking to control her gyrations with his other hand. The men thought it was very funny. Aram was looking, the women were not. The Turks had stacked their Mausers, but their swords were hanging from their belts.

The soldier guarding the women died instantly with an arrow in his heart. Two seconds later the would-be public rapist had a shaft through his rib cage, and he was coughing blood all over his intended victim as he fell over from the impact. It happened so fast that it took another second or two for the others to leap to their feet, diving for the rifle stack about 6 meters away.

Mamigon beat them to it, blocking the way, the heavy scimitar in his right hand. He had discarded his bow and quiver, and he was not smiling even though his teeth were bare.

"My name is Mamigon, son of Magaros of Yosghat Dagh, you Turkish pigs!"

The six, not believing the size of this lunatic and his audacity at bracing six soldiers of the sultan all by himself, drew their swords and approached him slowly. Without taking his eyes off of them, Mamigon swung his left leg and kicked the rifles backward to the base of the big cypress. He backed up until he was standing against the tree, the tip of his sword weaving in small arcs. The soldiers formed a wide semicircle; then shouting "Y'Allah" as a signal, they lunged at him in unison.

Instantly, Mamigon leaned to the right, not moving his feet, his powerful blacksmith's right arm tight across his chest, his sword cocked, pointing to the left. In one motion, the scimitar came whistling in front of him in a vicious upward arc, taking off the extended sword arm of the second man from the right and chopping through the neck of the farthest man on the right. Simultaneously, Mamigon grabbed the trunk of the tree with his left hand just as his prolonged leaning position was about to unbalance him. The momentum of the scimitar, coupled with the hand on the tree as the axis, swung Mamigon around the trunk, coming up now to the first man on the left. The scimitar took up its deadly work again, taking off the elbow of the next man, stopping with a thud in the side of his chest. Mamigon scrambled erect and faced the last two. They were wide-eyed in terror and began backing away. The one on the ground with the bleeding arm, the bone sticking through, was crying for mercy and help.

"Come on . . . come on, fight an armed man for once."

They turned and ran. Mamigon just stood there, watching them. Aram and the women were petrified at the bloody scene, which had taken less than thirty seconds. Mamigon sat down suddenly among the dead and dying, his right hand covering his face, not moving for such a long time that Aram finally called out for someone to untie him.

Aram's cry jogged the intended rape victim. She slowly uncovered her face to see what had happened. It was Mariam. She scrambled up when she realized that Baron Mamigon was sitting nearby and began to cry in relief as she ran over to the other women, tripping over a body as she went.

Mamigon shook himself, stood up, and checked Aram's head wound. It was a cut from a rifle butt and was not serious. It would heal. He told Aram to go get the stuff down the hillside, where he would find Aslan. Then he turned to the women.

"Was anyone else molested other than . . . ?" He noticed Araxy then as several heads turned to look at her when he asked the question. She had her arms folded across her chest, holding on to herself. "Are you hurt?"

She nodded slowly. Mamigon saw she wasn't wearing her soldiers pants. That told him all he wanted to know. "Where are you hurt?"

She shook her head. Her eyes were big, and Mamigon noticed that her mouth—an elegant, delicate mouth, he thought—became hard every so often, as if she were stifling sound . . . or pain.

"I will not ask you again. What is the matter?" Everyone stayed still, taking turns looking at Mamigon and Araxy. Then she spoke.

"The one there that was holding the rifle on us . . . he attacked me first before they picked on Mariam. I am hurt."

"Is . . . is there anything I can do?"

Araxy looked around at the company, bewildered. "We know not what to do and I am ashamed to . . . But, it is hurting very much and bleeding badly." With that, she beckoned Mamigon to her and took her arms away as she opened her bodice. The right side of her blouse was soaked with blood. "The man almost bit it off," she said, exposing a handsome breast that had blood welling from the base of the nipple, the nipple itself dangling.

Mamigon covered his eyes with his hands for a moment, then issued quick orders to the women to gather twigs for a small fire, put some salt and water in the rice pan, and find a bandolier, a clove of garlic, and the cleanest piece of petticoat around. He himself dug up a small handful of dark earth, chopped the garlic into it and wet the mixture.

Mamigon had Araxy lie down while he checked her condition. The left breast was bright red, and Mamigon thought it would become black and blue in a few hours. The right nipple was in one piece, hanging by a thread of skin. He could only see this for a second, when he cleared the blood.

The fire was started, and the water was suspended over it to boil. When Aram returned, he was put in charge of the water detail. The women were all too conscious that Aram was a boy and were determined not to abet his already accelerated education in the female anatomy if they could help it.

A piece of petticoat was produced, and Mamigon had it boiled first. The water was changed and brought to a boil and the salt added.

"We must remove all the clothes from your upper body, I am sorry."

"I care not, Mamigon Agha. It hurts too much. I care not . . ."

One of the women helped Araxy undress, removing the bloodstained garments one by one. The salt water was ready.

"This is going to hurt even more, but it is the only thing that might save you from the poisons of that man's mouth."

Mamigon washed away as much of the blood as possible, pinching the base of the damaged nipple to stop the bleeding. Araxy groaned in pain. After he finished cleaning her, with the help of Takuhe, he carefully placed the nipple in its natural position and pressed the boiled cloth in several folds over the area. Then he applied the garlicky mud over the cloth, and pressed the bandolier, from which the cartridges had been removed, across the wound area while Takuhe pulled the ends around Araxy's chest. The bleeding stopped.

Araxy stared at Mamigon, then began to cry, shaking her head. "Until last week, only one man had ever seen my body. Then a few days later at least a dozen—I lost count—have used me, touched me in every imaginable way. And now, one of my late husband's friends knows of my body. You know? I have stopped caring . . . I have stopped caring, do you understand, Mamigon Agha?"

Mamigon simply patted her head, nodding in understanding.

"This, too, shall pass . . . but not right away, woman. I must change that bandage every other day." He turned to his little company. "You were fortunate today. I know not what happened, but we must be very careful from now on. They know we are here now. I do not know how long it will take for them to begin following us, so we must move in daylight as well. Go on ahead with Aram. I will be right along."

Mamigon gathered up the eight rifles, stuck them individually into the ground up to the trigger guard, with each weapon cocked, and fired each one. Each gun burst at the breech, making it useless as a weapon. Then he went to each of the six soldiers—they were all dead now—and made his mark on each.

* * *

In the middle of the afternoon, the Turks caught up with them. Mamigon had been watching the rear carefully, with Aram and the dog in front as point. He saw the soldiers, twenty-four of them, stream down a hillside about a kilometer back, in single file. The terrain was hilly and rocky but there weren't enough trees to provide much shelter for an ambush. The Turks, of course, would know their prey's exact strength. But, would they?

After Aram and the women had trudged through a long, shallow defile, he trotted up to them and told them to stop.

"There are twenty-four Turks behind us and they are going to overtake us." Mamigon had to raise his arms and shake his head at the cries of fear that went up.

"We will stop them. Put on your soldier hats with your hair up into them. Break up into two groups of five and thirteen. Five of you will go back with me down the ravine along one side and find places for each of you to hide. Then I will take the rest of you on the opposite side and do the same thing. Aram and I will be in the center, Aram with you thirteen. Now, you all know how to fire those rifles. Fire them with the barrels resting on something in front. I do not expect you to hit anything. It is only important that you fire. And, only when I tell you to. My five will fire when I raise one hand. You on the opposite side will fire when I raise both hands. If I swing my arm in a circle, both sides fire. But, please, only fire when I signal and only one shot. Watch me. Do not worry about the Turks. If I am killed, do what you think best. Remember, if you do as I say, you will have a chance to live."

He took his five along the top of the ridge and placed them about 5 meters apart behind rocks and boulders. He did the same with the second group. Then he took Aslan down the trail, being careful not to walk near the path he and the band had walked on originally, and had the big dog sit in a depression, out of sight from the path. Mamigon told Aslan to stay, and received a lick of understanding on his hand. Mamigon then trotted up the side of the ravine and took his place midway in the line of his five women. Aram took a similar position directly opposite with his thirteen, all spread on each side for about 50 meters.

Mamigon marveled at the women's silent acceptance of his decisions. It was a drastically different world for them, this one, and they had no previous precept or concept to follow. So they did what they were told, dumbly, though fearfully.

The Turks appeared in about five minutes, walking purposefully, the point man scanning the ground for the footprints that told him they were on the right track. They were strung out for about 40 meters. Mamigon waited until the entire pursuit group was sandwiched between his guns, strung two arrows in quick succession, felling the officer behind the point man and then the last man in the column, before raising both his arms. Instantly, fourteen rifles spat in ragged fire from Aram's side. Two men went down and the rest retreated and scurried up the slope toward Mamigon's group. The first fusillade had convinced them that everybody must be on Aram's slope. Another arrow found its mark quietly before Mamigon raised one arm. His side erupted in fire from six rifles, and four men dropped. The soldiers broke for the path, except for two who continued upward. Mamigon dropped them with two quick shots. As the Turks scrambled back to the path, Mamigon stuck his hand up in a whirling motion. Both sides fired at once. Only two men went down. Mamigon snarled and fired once more, dropping another before he slammed a new clip into the magazine and began firing rapidly. The Turks hesitated and started up Aram's slope. Mamigon waited for them to move at least 10 meters, then stuck up both arms. Aram's side fired, and he signaled again with both arms. They fired again, and four men tumbled down. There were six soldiers still standing. Mamigon whistled. A brown whirlwind of fur and teeth hurtled down the path toward the Turks. Mamigon slammed two more shots into them, leaped up and scrambled down the slope, his hunting knife out, hollering imprecations loudly in Turkish. His shots and Aslan's fangs now had accounted for three. The three remaining soldiers began running in the direction they had come from. Mamigon raised his arm in a whirl once more, and again, and the ravine resounded with thundering rifles, Mamigon's whoops, and Aslan's growls and barks. Mamigon caught up with a limping man and dispatched him with his knife. One man got away. When he ran back to the arena, the women were subdued, shocked by the death they had personally perpetrated. Aslan went around among the dead, coming to a point when one of the bodies still showed signs of life. Mamigon delivered coups de grâce to six of them. He couldn't help them, and he couldn't leave them for the wolves to chew on while they were still alive.

Not a soul in his little band had suffered even a scratch.

"All right, gather your things, and be off. You did well as amateur rifles. I will be right with you."

There were twenty-three of them this time. It was going to take a while, but he was determined. He stopped beside each dead man, turning some face up to use his knife. He noticed that there was no welling of blood when he cut into the skin. Dead men don't bleed.

He walked up the draw, took one last look at his late foes, and trotted off after his charges.

Mamigon didn't see the figure slip out from among the rocks on the hillside and trace his steps again among the dead.

5 ❧ BRANDED

Tallal had new orders, but this time they were not directed toward an entire village. They concerned the apprehension of one man, a man who had once been his friend and who he could now consider a mortal enemy. In his heart he did not blame Mamigon, but circumstances had dictated a course of action he had not contemplated, not wished, not dreamed could have occurred. But, the die was cast—*kismet*—and the Armenian would have to pay with his life for what he had done and, no doubt, would continue to do.

Tallal left out one or two bits of information, and added others, that tinted black and gray the picture he painted to the military provost marshal at Sivas, the closest military district headquarters, where he reported what was happening in the province. In reporting his loss of sixteen men, he did not think it necessary to mention that he had known Mamigon as a comrade in arms or that he had raped and killed the Armenian's wife, his children, and family. What for? It did not have any bearing on the fact that the village of Yosghat Dagh had revolted, incited by Mamigon to resist, and three of his men had died during his efforts to suppress the revolt. Of course, the village population had been almost annihilated. That *had* been a bit difficult for the provost to swallow. All of them, he asked? Yes, it had been necessary because once a few reacted, the rest followed with table knives, shovels, and sickles and whatnot. The old men and women and little children, too? Well, you know how those things happen. My men lost control of themselves when they saw their comrades cut down. It wasn't total annihilation, though. Many of the women and children and the old escaped. We just couldn't take the time to make a wide search and round them all up. That's why we burned the village, so they wouldn't be able to go back. But, there is no doubt that Mamigon, the ringleader, escaped with some armed men. These we must hunt down before he gathers more strength. That is why I am here. I need help in obtaining more men and equipment. The provost was quizzical.

"It is too late for you to rendezvous at Gemerek . . ."

"Cancel my mission is what you are suggesting, sir?"

"I am not sure. Your casualties were eighteen percent." The provost stared at his desk top.

"We were attacked by a superior. . . ."

"Superior? Superior, my grandfather! How effective could untrained mountain peasants be against our men?"

"Surprise, sir. We did not expect to . . ."

"Close your mouth, sir. You get yourself deeper and deeper in unmilitary bull dung. It is written that he who is prepared is superior. Would you have me believe that you were surprised by a superior military force?"

Tallal licked his thin lips in total frustration. He had not expected this kind of treatment from a half-assed colonel. The dapper little prick must have missed some good ass last night. "I only ask you to believe that the possibility of enemy action was not indicated in advance and not expected."

"How many were in the enemy force?"

"We estimated about a hundred."

"What was your kill?"

"About twenty, twenty-five . . ."

"You do not know? You left the field of combat to the enemy?" The provost now knew that Tallal had been routed. It was fruitless to continue the session. "I will recommend the transfer of fifteen militia to your command and replenish the equipment you lost. And one last thing for your helmet spike: Try not to let your men kill *every* Armenian. Save a few for the sake of appearances. Now go."

Tallal gave the briefest of salutes and grinned once his back was turned. That balls-licking provost still didn't know the real story.

His orders now, after a five-hour wait for the telegraph wires to respond, were to join up with the army unit at Gurin and help escort Armenian exiles to Aleppo. Once that was done, his troop was to hunt down Mamigon and his army. In the meantime, another cavalry unit would be detached from the division heading for Van and deployed to the foothills to see what luck it would have in tracking down the Armenian band.

"This Armenian has become a dangerous outlaw. He has violated the rules of law and decency and he must pay for it," the provost said. A reward of 5,000 *lira* was posted for Mamigon's capture, dead or alive, and handbills were struck off for distribution throughout the eastern provinces. Other than his extraordinary size, the description of the wanted man—black hair, brown eyes, heavy mustache, and probably a beard because he wouldn't be able to shave under the circumstances—wasn't much of a description. It would fit many, many men living on the Anatolian Plain—Turks, Kurds, and Armenians alike.

Tallal was well on his way the next morning to Gurin before he realized that he had left out an important fact in providing Mamigon's description. Mamigon spoke only Turkish and German, the German he had learned at the military academy. It was a nicety, but Tallal should have indicated that the hunted man could not speak Armenian, an ability the Turkish hunters would assume. Well, he would set that straight the first chance he got.

Things seemed brighter for Tallal. The ambush on the road and rescue of the captive women could have darkened his career for certain. But the men in his company had kept quiet about the incident—it would have reflected on them, too—and he was no worse off this morning than he was on the morning he left his father's house to begin his new duties. In fact, he was at peace with the world. He had spent the night in the company of two whores, one Armenian, the other Egyptian. Their combined ministrations left him totally limp and he had slept through the night as if drugged. No, Mamigon was not going to be a problem at all.

6 &⁂ TOIL AND TROUBLE

The end of the fourth day of walking brought the little band to the bank of Kizil Irmak, a deep river that had its sources in the far northeast headlands, looped southward past Kaisaria, and turned again and flowed back north to empty into the Black Sea. Mamigon figured they were about 50 to

60 kilometers west of the Ottoman Ganjak capital of Kaisaria, where many Armenians lived. Once they crossed the river he knew they had about 200 kilometers to go, as the eagle flies, to reach the seacoast near Mersina. It meant crossing the Taurus Daglari, a range of mountains sweeping along the southern portion of Turkey with crags up to 8,000 feet. It was going to be difficult. But first there was the river. They couldn't wade across it as they did the smaller stream they had crossed only yesterday. This one had crested at least two months ago and at the end of August was down a bit, but it still presented a formidable barrier.

"You stay with the women this time, and I'll go see what there is," Aram announced as they stood watching the flow.

"All right, Aram. I don't have to tell you to be careful."

Aram grinned at him and trotted upstream to see if anything was available for crossing the river. He came back in two hours, exhausted, with nothing to report.

Mamigon took up the search, heading downstream. He hadn't gone 30 meters when he came upon a rowboat, in perfect condition, tied with a new painter to a tree close to the bank, well hidden from view from the river. Mamigon crouched low and looked around from the vantage of the bushes he found close to the bank. There was nothing. No sign of life, no path to the bank, no apparent reason for that boat to be tied up there. His band was so close he could have called them, but he didn't dare. He settled down to wait. He wasn't there long, no more than ten minutes, when the bushes behind him began to rustle, and the sound and movement came rapidly closer to him. A man and a woman appeared about 4 meters from Mamigon, looking warily in all directions. They were naked. The woman's black hair hung in long matted and filthy strands, reaching her hips. Her breasts were young and huge. Mamigon was so close he could see the stretch marks on her breasts and abdomen and a slight telltale sag to her almost flat belly, indicating recent motherhood. The man was equally filthy and had only one eye. His right eye socket was empty and its upper lid had been cut recently. They saw Mamigon. The woman smiled at him vacuously, making no attempt to hide her nudity, as the Armenian stood up. The man looked wildly desperate as he scrambled about for something to defend himself.

"Be not afraid, be not afraid." Mamigon raised both hands. He spoke in Turkish.

"Did you find my baby boy?" The woman said it in Turkish also, with a smile, holding out her hands to the big man. Mamigon looked at the man who now pulled the woman gently to him and stepped slightly in front of her.

"Please, *effendi*, we are helpless, as you can see . . ."

"I can see that. What is happening? Who are you? Where are your clothes?"

"Are . . . are you a . . . Turk?"

"Kill such a thought. I am Armenian, a *High*."

"Thank God, thank God! Maybe you can help us. We are *Highs* too."

"Good, but what are you doing here? Are you alone?"

"Did you find my baby boy . . . ?"

"Ssssh, Mariam. Be quiet. We lost our three-week-old baby boy in the river and my wife has gone out her mind. We . . ."

"Wait. Is that why you are undressed in the middle of the wilderness? You lost your baby in the river? Is that your boat over there?" Mamigon was getting confused.

"Yes . . . no. Let me tell you. We are from Kaisaria. The Turkish gendarmerie came to our city last week, ordered us out of our homes with whatever belongings we could carry, saying the area was not safe for Armenians anymore, and marched us 40 kilometers to the river. They had some big cattle barges there and loaded us onto them. When we got to the middle of the river, the armed police made us take off all our clothes and then pushed us into the water. Any who tried to stay because they could not swim were shot. My wife was carrying the baby in her arms. There were many women with little children and babies. Some were pregnant.

"We jumped off the barge and Mariam would not let me hold the baby. We cannot swim and tried to stay afloat, keeping the baby's head out of the water. There were others all around us, splashing around, screaming for help, trying to get to the shore. We kept passing the baby back and forth between us. He was bawling from the cold water and the repeated dunking, choking on the river water." The man began crying. Mariam kept smiling. He stifled his sobs and continued when he saw Mamigon's stoic face.

"The current separated us and we each thought the other had the baby . . . Vartanig is gone, poor little baby, poor little baby . . ." He was crying again. Mamigon only stared.

"I was about to give up. I could not stay up anymore, I was so tired, when something hit me on the head. It was that rowboat, floating free down the river, and Mariam was hanging on to the other end. We were in the river at least an hour before we came ashore here. We never got into the boat. She went crazy when she discovered that I did not have Vartanig. Oh, my name is Sarkis Vartabedian. Who are you?"

"My name is Mamigon, son of Magaros of Yosghat Dagh. But come, we are wasting time. I have some people with me. Here, wear my jacket for now, and bring her along. We will get her covered in no time. No, no, do not give her the jacket. There are seventeen women a few meters from here."

Before they got to camp, Sarkis told Mamigon that very few had escaped drowning because the Turks had mounted men on both shores who killed anyone who managed to swim to the river banks.

"How did you lose your eye? It looks like a new loss."

"I begged the Turks not to push my wife and baby into the water. Before I could finish one of them pushed me over the side by sticking his knife in my eye. The Turks have gone mad. I know not why they suddenly hate us so much . . ."

Takuhe was the first to see the three approaching and raced up to them, taking off her shawl and tossing it toward Sarkis. Mariam kept asking for her baby, and all the women who had lost their own started a fresh round of wailing that Mamigon had to quell. Mariam's breasts had to be bound tightly to relieve the pain from the milk she had been producing, with no taker now.

Mamigon introduced Sarkis and announced the discovery of the boat; the massacre was detailed by Sarkis as he was outfitted in a loose-fitting uniform and a patch devised for his aching eye cavity.

"We must wait until dark to go over, five at a time," Mamigon said. "That means nine trips on the open water, five over and four back. And, we must do it before the moon comes up."

"Now, how many of you think you hit anyone when you fired your rifles back at the ravine?"

"I know I hit three of them." It was Araxy.

"I am certain I got two, if not more," said Soorpuhie, a sixteen-year-old who had been married only seven months ago.

"All right, I want you two, and two more of you, to stand watch with your rifles when I begin rowing the rest of you over. Aram will go with the first group so that he can stand guard across the river. Sarkis, you take your wife in the first group. It will be about a thirty-minute turnaround for each trip. Let us rest now."

On the second trip over, the boat bumped into something in the river, then bumped into something else. Mamigon stopped rowing and allowed the boat to drift as he scanned the dark surface. They were logs . . . no . . . bodies, naked bodies. There seemed to be hundreds of them. Too many to count. He gestured for quiet, just in case the women reacted, pulled a corpse toward the boat with one of the paddles, and asked Takuhe, who was in the sternsheets, if she would grab the hair of the dead man's head nearest her so that it could be dragged to the bank. A shuddering Takuhe did what she was asked. When they reached the shore, Mamigon looked over the bloated body. There were no marks of violence on it. It was the body of a drowning victim that had spent some time at the bottom and then had risen to the surface to float with the current. One look at his genitals and Mamigon knew he was a Christian. He called Sarkis who identified him as a cobbler from Kaisaria.

The remaining trips back for the rest of the company turned into a horror as a head or arm or leg or chest of a corpse had to be pushed down with almost every bite of the oar before it could enter the water.

Mamigon breathed easier when the last river crossing was completed without incident. What in the name of Christ was going on? Was everybody being killed? Why?

The stories told by both the women of Yosghat Dagh and Vartabedian described what had happened. There was no real explanation, though— nothing concrete to explain why all of this was happening. Nevertheless, Mamigon knew what he had to do now. The people he was guiding to safety needed more than an escort. They would have to have some basic ability to defend themselves. The country was going crazy, and he was not going to count on any standard prescriptions a more normal situation might have suggested.

"I think we will spend a day or two right here," he announced. "It's as good a spot as any. I want to teach all of you as much as I can in some basic self-defense and fighting techniques. If anything happens to me, I do not want you to be completely helpless."

The first lesson was devoted to unarmed self-defense. "Now, a man's most vulnerable points, those that can render him helpless, are his eyes, his nose, his throat, his stomach, and his crotch. Does anyone know what's your best weapon? Your feet. Aram, cut down a branch over there with a fork in it."

Mamigon fashioned the branch and then held it so its Y was inverted about three feet off the ground. He told each of the women to practice kicking hard upward to catch the fork of the branch, not with their toes but with their ankles, pointing out that they couldn't miss the target if the man's thighs guided the foot in its upward arc. The knee was to be used in closer combat. He repeated the warning that such a move had to succeed the first time because there would be no second chance.

"A man will be helpless for a good minute, at least, if you make good, hard contact. But your move will have to be fast, very fast, and you cannot telegraph that you are going to do it.

"The stomach is the next target for your feet. Forget about the crotch if you are on the ground on your back. Pull both knees back to your chest with your legs flat against your thighs, looking as if you are inviting him to mount you—do not look so shocked, this is shocking business. When you think he is close enough, brace your shoulders as best you can and throw both your heels at his stomach. That should knock his air out and if you are lucky, give his heart a good jolt.

"Forget putting your feet above the stomach for obvious reasons. Use your hands for his throat and face. Wait until the last minute, if his hands become occupied with you, and jam your fingers into his eyes. No scratching, just pushing with your fingers stiff out like fork tines. If you can swing your arm back, and his throat is clear, don't try to choke him—you don't have the strength or the time. Hit him as hard as you can in the Adam's apple. Hard. That blow can smash his larynx and he will not be able to breathe. Smashing his nose upward with the heel of your palm is another way to kill all of his interest.

"If you do not succeed in doing any of these things, and the man is about to grab you, let him. But quickly hold on to his neck or upper body and push backward, rolling with his forward push. As you do it, pull up your feet and he will most likely land on you, but your knees should be between you so that you can heave him off.

"All right, these are basics. We will now drill in these techniques, first slowly, to see what it all will mean to you in required strength and balance. Only Mrs. Vartabedian and Araxy are excused at this time."

It was difficult and almost laughable at first. Mamigon was chagrined at their lack of understanding of what was meant by vicious force. Not until he actually slammed some of the women with the back of his hand on their arms and shoulders were they able to understand what he meant by "hitting hard."

By sunset, the women were a grinning but exhausted lot. They felt more confident about the quickness of their feet. Practice would be the byword from now on, Mamigon said as he announced that the next day would be devoted to armed combat.

A much more sober group listened, all eyes riveted on the gleaming dagger Mamigon held, as he demonstrated defenses against a plunging knife.

"If the knife is coming at you, grab for the wrist or forearm and use the weight and force of the man's arm to push yourself, your neck or chest, sideways from the knife point. Do not worry about the knife cutting your arm. It is a cheap wound compared to penetration of your neck or chest. If the knife is being held against your neck, forget everything. Move not a hair. You can die instantly and therefore, must do exactly as you are told . . . unless he intends to dispatch you then and there."

Mamigon held the knife in a position of attack and had each of the women first grab his wrist with both hands and use their right hand to push away in a sideways motion. He pointed out that not much movement to the side was needed to escape the knife blade. Never try to stop the downward thrust of the knife. You don't have the strength, he warned.

Again, at sunset, the women were exhausted, but this time it was a somber group. Not a one was sure she would be able to escape a knife attack.

He spent the third day drilling the women in the use of the Mausers in concerted and staggered fire. The first thing he taught them was the proper place to fit the butt of the rifles against their shoulders. Most had suffered sore shoulders after their brief stint as riflemen at the ambush in the ravine. Mamigon issued pistols to four of the women: they were too small and their arms were not long enough to handle the rifles properly. So as not to draw unwanted attention, they did not use live ammunition, but the women learned and seemed to learn well. Mamigon had trained many a raw recruit in his time in the army and he came to the conclusion that women, in general, seemed to have better hand-to-eye coordination than men. At least it seemed so in his brief experience now with this group. He was constantly surprised when he touched one of them to feel the softness and lightness, the complete lack of sinew and brawn.

There was no question in his mind; the women could have absorbed weeks and weeks of training and could have been ready to make a fine showing, but there was not time, no time for anything except a hard, fast run to the southern coastline and a heavy reliance on good luck and a benign God in heaven.

Mamigon's band began traversing the foothills of the Taurus range the fourth day after crossing, covering only 80 kilometers in two days. They began meeting more and more people as they got into the mountains, where the few travelers were concentrated on a small number of available paths.

Mamigon made short work of a small band of Kurdish brigands who swooped down on him, thinking he was alone. He killed five with rapid fire from his Mauser, and when Aram and the rest of the band arrived—looking like a squad of soldiers—that was all the Kurds needed to give up the try.

There was a hand-to-hand fight with three Turks who probably thought one man would be no match for their three. Mamigon fought with two of them, one, who was almost as big as the Armenian, expertly wielded a knife at his throat. Aslan finished ripping out the larynx of a pistoleer and turned to the two on top of his master. His leap ended on the tip of the long knife, but not before his extended paws had gouged out the eyes of his killer.

Mamigon cried when he buried Aslan—only the second time Aram had seen his brother cry, he announced in awed tones to the band. He had cried when he had buried his wife and family, but who wouldn't.

Mamigon's battle cries and shouts were always in Turkish. He couldn't speak Armenian at all, a common circumstance in some Armenian villages in central Turkey. The simple dominance of the Turkish culture prevailed when the Armenian community was tiny, surrounded by Turkish towns and villages. He did know some classic Armenian, the Armenian of the apostolic church rites, by rote. It is a language with just a few similarities to the Armenian vernacular, much like Italian is to Latin.

The women in the band of fugitives he led spoke Turkish exclusively too, though all were Armenian and Christian, the latter being synonymous in the old country. Over the centuries, those Armenians residing in areas predominantly Turkish gradually lost their own language and took up that of their ancient conquerors. The Turkish they spoke, however, was something resembling the queer admixture of French and English the French Canadians speak in Quebec Province. Mamigon's village, or *kiugh*, was so deeply penetrated by the Turkish culture that the inhabitants there spoke the language as perfectly as the neighboring Turks.

As they were running low on food staples such as salt, bread, and rice, Mamigon decided to replenish the supply at the next village they came upon. He collected the plainest gold rings from the collection the women carried and bided his time. About noon the next day, far below in a green valley surrounded by meadows dotted with sheep, he saw a cluster of about sixty homes. It was time to go. He told Aram to keep moving south among the scrub trees and mount shrubs. He would see what he could buy down there and catch up. He completely disarmed himself except for a short knife that most men carried in that part of the world. Then he asked if any of the women could spare enough underskirt to make a turban for him. Now, with his turban, his lambskin vest, black woolen shirt with long sleeves, black woolen breeches with the ends stuffed into his black boots, he looked about as Turkish or Kurdish as any man in Asia Minor.

In half an hour he was within shouting distance of the village, having waved and yelled greetings to a shepherd on the way. He could hear window shutters creak slightly as the inhabitants peeked out at the tall stranger. Some small children ran up to him, laughing and tugging at his pants. Mamigon inquired about a store and the village oven where the women baked their daily supply of bread. A small boy with a toothless grin pointed up the only street, a dusty, rutted avenue without sidewalks or shade. Two men seated in front of a one-story house got up and approached Mamigon.

"*Gewn oodin, bey.*"

"Good day to you, too. Can you tell me where I can buy some bread and salt and, perhaps, some rice?"

The two nodded and the older one, a man about fifty, spoke. "I think the trader over there will be able to help you," he said, pointing to a larger structure just beyond the square. "Can we be of any help?" The question was more of a gambit to learn about the tall one rather than a real offer.

"No, thank you much. I just need a few things and I'll be on my way."

Mamigon went to the building, stepped through the open door, and found the typical trading store so familiar to him. Bags and bags of different types of grains and dried beans and split peas, boxes and tins of preserved staples, sheets of sun-dried mush from apples and pear, apricots, dates, and raisins. The smell of onions and garlic, tinged with cumin. The trader and his family would be living in the rear of the building. Flies were everywhere, scrambling among the edibles. The heat in the place so was stifling, it was cool outside by comparison.

Mamigon selected as much as he could carry, with the help of the bald-headed rotund storekeeper who, he suspected, leaned on the weights a bit when the cloth bags were placed on the scales. Mamigon was about to produce his little string bag with the trinkets to pay when someone walked into the store behind him.

"Pay attention, you. Turn around so I can see who you are."

Mamigon turned quickly at the commanding sound of the voice and broke into a broad smile at the sight of a Turkish army *bash chowoosh,* a master sergeant.

"Hmmm. You have his height, all right. Come on out here."

Mamigon was ushered out into the bright sunlight, looking at a squadron of Turkish cavalry, regulars. They were a handsome lot, he thought, sitting straight and tall in their saddles, their heads covered with *kalpaks*—flat-topped, visorless caps—the tips of their lances aflutter with short yellow ribbons. They had rifles slung on their backs and swords at their belts. The *suvari,* in twos, was strung out beyond the outskirts of the village.

"Who are you?" The question came from the officer with a red mohair-lined cap seated on a gray horse beside the storefront. His youthful, carefully groomed appearance was marred only by scars of the smallpox he had survived.

Mamigon bowed slightly before he answered, his right hand on his heart. "Oh powerful one, I am the son of Mustapha, the *terzi* of a small village near Yosghat. May you be graced with the spirit of our Lord, Mohammed." He had seen many a peasant being interrogated respond with equal if not more servility when he was in the army.

"What is your name and what are you doing in these parts?" The question was a good one since Mamigon was easily 100 kilometers from where he said he came from. Inhabitants of small Anatolian villages weren't apt to be travelers, especially the son of a tailor.

"I am called Ishmael, your magnificence. I was on my way to the great city of Adana, where I am to purchase swelling glasses for our village physician to use on my mother. His supply was accidentally broken, and we were told we could get them only in Constantinople or Adana." Swelling glasses! Mamigon had thought quickly to come forth with that one. Physicians or healers used them when patients complained of back or chest miseries. Lengths of string tallow candles were coiled up to resemble a cobra ready to strike; the wick, standing about two inches, would be lit and as many as six to eight of them placed on flat surfaces of the back or chest or abdomen. The glasses would be inverted over them, the flame would burn up the oxygen, and the flesh would bulge up about a half inch or so, trying to fill the vacuum. This was supposed to draw out, through the bulge, the toxins or whatever was causing the patient his distress.

The officer pondered Mamigon's reply. "What are you doing here?"

"I was accosted by brigands, *albay*. They took all the supplies I had except for my little knife. They thought the two coins I had were all the valuables because they missed this little purse that was going to pay for the glasses. I wish I had met you yesterday when I was being robbed . . ."

"What did the brigands look like? How many were there?"

"There were nine of them, *albay*, and they were speaking a language I couldn't understand." Mamigon thought it best not to recognize the captain's rank from his insignia.

"I am not a colonel, I'm a *yuz bash*. Could it have been Armenian?"

"No, your lordship . . . I mean captain. I have met those *giavours* occasionally in Yosghat and I would have recognized that stupid tongue."

The officer looked at his *yarbay* next to him, exchanging glances.

"Was their leader as big as you?"

"No sir. He was about the size of your *chowoosh*, the one that brought me out of the store."

"We are seeking a man about your height or taller. He has a younger man and a big dog with him, and he is traveling around the country with a harem of slatterns. Have you heard or seen anything of such a band?"

"A . . . a harem? Slatterns?"

The office glared at him, then rattled off a long sentence or two, ending up in a barking command.

Mamigon stared blankly, obviously puzzled.

"I just spoke to you in Armenian, dolt. I said your mother was a diseased streetwalker, that your father had copulated with an overgrown jackass to whelp you, and that I had ordered you to kiss my saddle-sore backside."

Mamigon feigned anger, then smiled weakly as the troop erupted in loud laughter.

The officer, still grinning at the delight of his men, slowly dismounted and walked toward Mamigon. Silence settled heavily on the scene; the long line of cavalry, the elegant officer approaching the tall, slightly bent figure of the mountain peasant, the sergeant close by, watching the big man, and the few bravely curious village men looking on from a respectful distance. They knew that soldiers, when in doubt, were quicker to hurt or kill than to bother with niceties or facts.

"I am not convinced, big one. I have a feeling about you." The captain's eyes were speculative.

Mamigon forgot to be servile. He straightened up and stared down at the captain, dropping the forced smile from his face. "It is truly written, one must trust his feelings if the mind does not understand the words."

"It is also written in the Law of Retaliation that death removes all doubt."

"That would be an easy solution for you, my lord . . ." Mamigon was now beginning to wonder if he was going to get away with his life . . . "but it would be difficult for me to complete my errand to Adana."

"I have trouble, big one, believing you to be who you say you are. You could easily be the Armenian we are looking for. Armenians are devious and sly by nature. You could be the hawk fluttering like the crow."

Mamigon was pondering an answer when the sergeant asked the captain if he could speak. The *chowoosh* stepped up to the captain when the latter had nodded his assent and whispered in his ear. After several nods back and forth the captain turned back to Mamigon.

"You say you are Turkish, and therefore, a Moslem. You can prove that, of course?"

"Prove? I have told you who I am and you do not believe. How can I prove when there is nothing more than my word?"

"Verily, you can, big one. We are all circumcised at five years when we come of age. Christian infidels are not. Are you circumcised?"

"Yes, thank Allah, if that is all the proof you need. I am."

"Show me."

"A believer's word should be sufficient among believers, my lord. The sacrificial barber in Yosghat, Ben Achmed, the Arab, performed the ceremony. Is that enough?"

"Show me."

Mamigon decided to play out the game now that he felt he was safe. Ben Achmed certainly had performed the circumcision on him, but at the age of three. His mother had noticed that the boy urinated a spray and she had difficulty peeling back the foreskin to clean him. When he became irritable (he never cried) she also discovered that his nascent erections were causing him great pain. It was decided he would have to be taken to a Turkish community where circumcision was a routine practice. His father, Mesrop, took him to Yosghat where Ben Achmed had relieved him of the sliver of skin at great but temporary pain. The Arab barber would take no money because the little boy did not cry, a sign, he said, that the boy would become a great warrior. His brothers had constantly joshed Mamigon in his young years about Ben Achmed. Only the sharp reaction from Mamigon's father had prevented the brothers from calling him "Turk" thereafter. Mamigon did not move to comply with the captain's order.

The sergeant called out and a trooper ran to Mamigon's side and both men pinned the Armenian's arms. The captain took the sergeant's short sword and for a moment Mamigon thought it was all over as the officer shoved the point at his stomach. He cut the belt with a deft flick of the blade and Mamigon's britches dropped around his ankles. Underclothes were an affectation of city dwellers and his privates were immediately exposed.

The captain hardly looked. "I am glad you are one of us, Ishmael," he said, using for the first time the name Mamigon had provided. "Why were you so mulish in this small matter?" The *yuz bash* was grinning, as were the troops.

"Exposing oneself for sport among women is a necessary pleasure, my lord. But, showing myself to a whole company of men?"

"Your bashfulness almost sent you to paradise before your time. Fix your britches and be on your way. May Allah go with you."

"*Allah ismarladik,*" Mamigon replied in kind, holding his britches as he bowed, backing away, mumbling, "I'll see all of you in hell." He had feared the captain would have his purchases checked. The quantities would have given him away. He went back into the store, got a piece of rope for his pants, paid for the provisions, and ordered a demitasse of coffee to while away some time.

The storekeeper was happy to comply. It wasn't often that he made such a single large sale, and he welcomed the chance to exchange news from other regions. He had no way of knowing that Mamigon was prolonging the conversation to avoid letting the Turkish squadron see the direction he took from the village.

He reached his band just before nightfall and was greeted by Aram.

"What happened back there, my brother?"

"Nothing important, Aram."

"Why have you changed the belt on your trousers?"

"You have the eyes of the eagle. That's good." He told Aram without detail how the Turks had tried to trick him into speaking Armenian and then checked him to see if he were really a Moslem.

"Saint Gregory was watching over you, my brother," was all Aram could say, even though he had a thousand questions he wanted to ask his taciturn sibling.

Aram in fact was beginning to feel some resentment. His brother paid no more attention to him than he did to the women. He treated him with the same distant deference and preoccupation, almost as if none of them was present. Their relationship had changed subtly from that of naturally easygoing brothers to that of father and son. Aram was getting the same reactions from Mamigon that he had experienced from his father. His feelings of respect and awe had transferred. It was so strong that he could not bring himself to joke with Mamigon or confide in him.

The nineteen-year-old had seen things that even in his wildest young fantasies he had not envisioned. He had seen animals in the barnyard do it but never humans, including himself. He had never seen a woman's breast—at the most an ankle and calf on accidental occasions when women were cleaning around the house. But now he had witnessed two rapes—

well, nearly two—and couldn't get over the horrible fascination of the events. He was deeply ashamed that he had been unable to stop watching what had gone on. He had watched the rest of the women, too, as the soldier had taken Araxy. Yes, more than a few were stealing looks. They had all experienced the deep, degrading sense of being treated as a dehumanized piece of meat. They had been exposed to things they had never dreamed of in their innocence and had participated in actions that had driven some of them starkly insane. But they couldn't help stealing glances—there, but for the temporary grace of God, go I. He had heard some of the women talking at night when they thought he was asleep. What had caused Rachell's death was that the soldiers couldn't enter her, she had been so small and tight, so they had reamed her open with the handle of a sword. They were still shuddering, remembering Rachell's wild screams of pain. After five or six men had spent themselves in her, they had folded her up and held her for another group to spend themselves in her anus. The soldiers had not conducted mass raping sessions with the women they had taken with them. They had used one or two at a time for the entertainment of any and all.

Aram heard more about the sexual practices of men and women than he had guessed were possible. The Turks had broken the neck of one little boy, no more than nine or ten, because he constantly cried—before, during, and after submission. Aram couldn't believe what he was hearing surreptitiously, and he wouldn't dare question them for fear of being cut off from future eavesdropping.

What had baffled him most were some references they made to taking it in their mouths and being forced to swallow something. The women seemed to react with the greatest repugnance to these things, mentioning horrible smells, scabs, sores, and just plain filth in the conversations, all in bated whispers as if they had to compare reactions to make certain they were not alone in their feelings of despair, disgust, and humiliation.

Aram was smitten by a girl who seemed to be a generation older then he. Anoush was no more than fifteen and had been a bride for five months before the end came. He noticed her eyes first. They were big and round and brown and they occasionally danced with a rare light. Once, when he found her sniffing back some sobs as they trudged along, he had unthinkingly placed an arm around her shoulders. Her sudden and horrified revulsion at his touch shocked him deeply. It must have shocked her, too, although she didn't say a word to him then. At the next rest stop, she went over to where he sat watching the trail and nodded and touched his shoulder briefly before turning away. Aram realized then that every eye in the camp was upon him—and her—and he resolved to keep his distance from then on.

He wasn't able to keep his resolve, however. The next morning he awoke to find Anoush curled up beside him, one of her arms thrown across his chest. He slipped out from under the arm without awakening her. But the rest of the group had seen them. He shrugged his shoulders and joined his brother, who didn't say a word. Later that day, as they met changing positions on the trail, Mamigon stopped his brother.

"I know you did not seek her out but none of these women are for us."

"I am not looking for a woman, any woman, my brother."

"I am not saying you are. These are things that can happen at any time. Now is not the time for anything except for temperance and survival."

"Brother, I will not turn her away if she wants to be near me. I . . . I want to be near her, I know that."

"That is exactly what I am talking about. You must resist getting close to her. She is . . . all of them are . . . wounded animals. They are looking for a safe place to lick their wounds. You and I could easily become havens for them. It would be wrong, my brother."

"Do not tell me of right and wrong, my brother." Aram was startled to hear himself talk to his older brother like that. Mamigon smiled, nodding.

"It is happening. You could end up fighting me over the love of a woman who, right now, does not know what she is doing. I must protect you as well as her from the evil consequences of such a liaison."

"Protect me? What the hell are you talking about?"

"Aram, you have seen much . . . too much for a young man who has yet to have any of the normal responsibilities of life. There is no doubt, though, that you are now in the world of men.

"This world is different from your world of a month ago. You were not taught anything about the world of women because it was not necessary. Unfortunately, you are learning in a terrible way. All I have to say on this subject is this one admonition: Excitement in your nether region at the sight of a female must be controlled."

Aram stared angrily at his brother for a moment, then stalked off. Christ, big brother was going to be worse than his father!

As it turned out, the confrontation was unnecessary. The women had developed a tremendous amount of camaraderie from their wild, common experiences and did not let each other out of their sight. Aram was never able to be alone with Anoush long enough to exchange more than a good morning or a good night.

Mamigon's days spent as a young hunter of wild game helped him in his new role as the hunted. At one point, as he climbed a narrow mountain path with a steep shoulder of rocks on one side and a deep, sloping ravine on the other, he thought he heard something ahead. He had Aram take the women into the rocks and wait for him to give the word. He went up the sloping path another 100 meters or so and then quietly slipped behind some boulders for cover. And he waited. Nothing, nothing for about five minutes. Mamigon stepped out onto the trail, almost colliding with two turbaned figures, slightly bent over, seeking the tracks of whatever had made the sounds the pair had apparently heard a few minutes ago.

The three squared off, Mamigon drawing the scimitar and the duo producing long, wicked-looking knives. They stared at each other, silently, eyes locked on eyes. The one with an ugly cicatrix along his right cheekbone broke the silence: "You are quick to seek battle, big one." The other began moving sideways.

"In wild country one does not expect warm embraces."

"We are not wild. We are peaceful travelers."

"Aye, you two look about as peaceful as wild dogs. If you are as you say, then be on your way and I shall go mine."

"Of course, we will, but first, what have you in your packs?"

"Ah . . . the usual question of peaceful travelers." Mamigon was grinning slightly as the scimitar in his hand began a purposeful twitching, pointing to his left side. "I have what only bloodied steel will discover."

The invitation was accepted. Cicatrix lunged at Mamigon as an Italian fencing master might do, lurching forward and down, resting on the palm of his left hand as his outstretched right arm thrust his sword tip at Mamigon's chest. Simultaneously, his comrade, who had moved almost to Mamigon's left side, brought his sword in a flat, whistling slash aimed at Mamigon's head.

Mamigon danced backward to avoid the sword's thrust from below, swinging the scimitar up and backward across his left ear to parry the vicious slash at his neck. The blades clanged loudly, followed by a high-pitched scream of pain as the slasher felt the bite of the scimitar, which had been in a perfect position following the parry to sweep down into his right shoulder near the neck. From the rocky side, Cicatrix lunged again, his sword pointing at the seemingly distracted giant now freeing his scimitar from his victim's shoulder blade. Mamigon caught the glint of the heavy saber coming at him. He pirouetted like a bullfighter, grasped the sword in the middle of the blade as it gleamed by, inches from his belly, and gave it a mighty yank in the direction it was going. The momentum of the sword thrust, coupled with the heavy yank on the blade in the same direction, propelled the man's body over the edge of the path and down the rocky slope. His wild, long scream of terror ended abruptly as he landed on his neck on the rocks far below.

One less predator in the world, Mamigon thought, shaking his head. He turned his gaze back to the man he had cut badly. The eyes were sick and he was bleeding heavily from the gash at the base of his neck. Should he shoot him? He was going to die anyway . . .

The wounded man must have had the heart of a bear, Mamigon thought later, because the next thing he knew a small one-shot derringer was being leveled at his face. It never went off. A rifle barked and the man's face disappeared in a slur of blood and bone.

Mamigon waved at Aram down the slope where his brother was lowering his Mauser. He came bounding up, leading the women.

"It is the second time you have saved my life, my brother." He slapped the beaming Aram on a shoulder.

They pushed the body over the side and went on.

Three days later, the band of refugees was picking its way up a steep defile when Turkish cavalry caught up with them. Mamigon had watched the approaching horsemen, about fifty of them, for more than an hour from a succession of vantages.

The terrain favored the pursued. Cavalry tactics would be impossible.

The horsemen, already riding in single file, would have to dismount soon and lead their gingerly stepping mounts up the steeper, rock-strewn slash on the mountainside. It was not much more than a deep water sluice for rains and freshets. A mountain goat would have trouble crossing it.

"We have no chance in the open, once we pass through," Mamigon whispered to his brother so the women wouldn't hear. "You keep them on the move. I shall stop them, if I can, right here. Leave me two full bandoliers for my rifle. Now, get going, my brother."

Aram's protests—he wanted to stay—were fruitless. "You must stay with those girls. What will they do if both of us are killed? Now, be off. I will be all right," he said, patting his rifle. They shook hands, the younger man's eyes brimming, the older one's mouth in a wide grin, the whiteness of his teeth accentuated by his huge handle-bar mustache.

Mamigon found the likeliest spot to make his stand, a slight turn in the passage where it narrowed so much that no more than one horse could get through at a time. He had learned his military lessons well at the *Harbiye*. The situation would be classic: one man holding off an army because the army—in this case about fifty horsemen—could not present more than one man at a time at the front.

He leaned his Mauser against the rock wall, piled six cartridge clips beside the rifle, checked his pistol to make sure all chambers were filled, counted his homemade iron-tipped arrows—twenty-two—unslung his hornbow, and sat down to wait. It was good to rest. He wondered if his luck would hold out.

In ten minutes, the clattering of rocks down the draw alerted Mamigon. The point man came within 200 meters, holding the bridle of his horse as he stumbled and slipped up the path. His rifle was slung on his back, his lance jerked around in its upright saddle scabbard, his sword at his belt.

He died without a sound, falling forward as Mamigon's arrow chunked into his heart. The horse stopped in its tracks, the dead man's hand still hooked to the reins.

"Hey, get up, you lazy . . ." was all the second trooper could say as he peered around the dead man's horse before the arrow reached his brain.

Mamigon growled in frustration. The horses were blocking his view. They were blocking the Turks, too, and it wasn't long before they acted. A white kerchief on a lance emerged from among the horses and Mamigon recognized the pockmarked young *yuz bash*, the captain, who had flicked off his belt back in the Turkish village.

"Whoever you are, I want to talk." He had taken three steps forward before he called out.

Mamigon stuck his head out farther. He wasn't wearing the turban he had contrived for his trip into the village, but the captain recognized him.

"It is . . . you, Ishmael, the tailor's son!"

"No, *effendi*, it is Magaros of Yosghat Dagh, the blacksmith."

"Ah . . . the outlaw."

"What do you want?"

"Can we talk?"

"Talk."

"Give yourself up. You have no chance. You will be treated fairly."

"Perhaps, before you hang me."

"Suit yourself then. My men will kill you all."

Mamigon didn't reply. He was watching some activity down toward the middle of the column of horses and men. It was bunching up near the center to leave an open area. The area was about 600 meters from him and he could see the men handing along heavy objects from the pack mules in the rear.

"Did you hear me?"

The Armenian was too engrossed in the bustle well behind the captain to pay attention to him. Well, I'll be damned, he thought. It's one of those . . . it's a *Ballongeschutz*, a Krupp balloon gun. The Germans had used it first in the siege of Paris to shoot down French observation balloons in 1871. He had seen the weapon demonstrated as a modified grenade launcher at the academy. The barrel, slightly less than 2 meters long, was now being brought up to position, followed by the mounting which had been cut down to about 2 meters so that the gun didn't point to the sky. It had a steel stock, trigger, and trigger guard. The muzzle could be swung around rapidly and the gunner could aim it like a rifle, from a crouch, with a set of rear sights.

Mamigon's fascination almost made him forget that all of it was meant for his early and quick demise. He was still remembering the instructions offered by the German officer at the academy. The gun used a 3-kilogram grenade with a charge that propelled it more than 600 meters before it exploded.

He figured the gun would be aimed a bit over his head for a good trajectory, and knowing that cavalrymen made poor artillerymen, he decided to wait and see how badly they worked the piece.

The gunner slipped a shell into the breech, turned the crank to cock it, braced the stock against his shoulder as he crouched, took aim, and fired.

The crash of the gun and following boom of the exploding shell was far to the right. The gunner went through the motions again with his weapon, which looked like a stationary telescope, and fired. It was to the left this time but closer to the defile. Shattered shale showered on Mamigon.

Hhmm. The gunner might get lucky. Oh, well, I'd better stop this . . . here goes: 600 meters range, no windage, flip up the rear sight for elevation, aim, squeeze . . . bang.

The slug from the Mauser slammed into the gunner who just managed to pull the balloon gun's trigger as he slumped sideways, swinging the gun muzzle erratically.

The explosive burrowed into the wall 2 meters from the gun mount with a roaring blast, causing a chain reaction:

—The direct hit churned huge sections off the granite face of the defile.

—A huge cloud of gray rock dust shrouded the scene.

—Five horses and seven men were buried under tons of rock.

—A new wall of rock debris stoppered the defile upwards of 15 meters.

—The horses surviving in front bolted ahead, trampling some of the men and scrambling past Mamigon, twenty of them.

The sudden silence was pierced by an occasional scream or cry from a downed horse or an injured trooper at the base of the talus.

Mamigon peered down on the carnage once the horses got by. The captain was rallying about a dozen of his battered, split company, all dusted in light gray, flesh and clothing alike.

It was going to be sheer murder as far as Mamigon could see. They would have to move up toward his position with no cover. They couldn't retreat. The Turks flattened out on the ground and began snaking toward him on their bellies. There were thirteen altogether.

It was no good. Mamigon was well above them. He closed his eyes for a moment, gritted his teeth, and began picking them off, one by one, from the rear man forward. Five died before the captain stood up, drawing his sword, his legs spread, looking up the draw in challenge. Mamigon smiled. He liked that kind of courage—if I am to die I will die like a man.

Mamigon stepped out from his cover, rifle still in hand. Neither said a word for a good minute. Then, the Turk spoke.

"You shoot well."

"My countrymen, the Turks, taught me."

"Why have you turned against us?"

Mamigon spat first. "My country has turned on me, on mine, because we are not Moslems."

"I know not of such things. My orders are to bring you in."

"I know all about orders . . . the *Harbiye*, Class of 1912. Climb back over the rocks and see to the rest of your men. They need you now."

"Not without you, mister."

"You have no choice. Get back there or die."

The Turk remained, motionless.

"All right, captain. Disarm your men and start climbing back there or you are all dead men. I mean it." Mamigon flourished the Mauser as if the 9-pound weapon weren't much more than a twig in his huge fist.

It was all over for words, deeds remained. The captain sheathed his sword, had the casualties checked to see if anyone was still alive, picked his way back among the bodies, and stared back once more when he reached the base of the rock pile. The seven other survivors had climbed up ahead of him

"I will see you in hell," the Armenian yelled by way of farewell. The *yuz bash* saluted and clambered up to disappear over the top.

Mamigon waited a while, then looked over the latest crop of candidates for his special hell. He didn't have the heart to mark them. They had died badly but bravely. He gathered his arms and trotted up the defile after his band.

* * *

Night came in two hours and a quarter moon eventually shed some small light on the trail. Mamigon caught up with the horses. The dumb brutes had simply stopped after their wild, stumbling run up the defile had sapped their fear and energy.

Mamigon grabbed the tail of the last animal and whooped it up to get them moving again. The horses would be surefooted in the dark and he trotted behind the herd without loosing his hold.

Dawn found the horses and the man in a broadening downward trail with a gradually deepening cliff on one side. There was no sign of Aram or the women. He halted each horse as he caught up with it, stripped each of saddle and hackamore, and tossed the gear down the cliff. He wasn't about to let the Turks catch up and find fully saddled mounts ready for pursuit.

He joined his band an hour after daybreak without seeing or hearing his pursuers again. Mamigon was certain the *yuz bash* would follow. He certainly couldn't return to headquarters with two-thirds of his command wiped out and report that one man had been responsible for the casualties. And had escaped? No, the captain plainly couldn't give up now.

On the eighth day the ragtag band of refugees came across the railroad line that connected, in a roundabout way, Constantinople and Adana near the Mediterranean. Walking the tracks would have been an easy way to get to the coast, but the dangers were too great.

The band crossed the tracks and were heading for a line of trees when a long line of horsemen in *serpoosh*, the olive drab of the army uniform, galvanized the women into flight, their faces etched with fear, except for Mariam who was still seeking her drowned baby. They reached the trees in two minutes or so.

If the women had not panicked, they might not have attracted attention because from a distance they looked like a group of foot soldiers. But the pell-mell run must have certainly aroused the curiosity of the cavalry commander. He was going to investigate, no doubt about it, and Mamigon's band could not stand investigation.

Mamigon split them into two firing groups again. "I don't want everyone firing at once. These men are trained soldiers. They will wait for your volley, take their losses, and advance on you as the smoke from your rifles blinds your aim. All right, now. Aram, you take your eight rifles over there and aim in the direction of that big boulder. I'll have my group down this way and we'll aim in the direction of that boulder, too. It's called enfilading fire. Now, listen. You must hold your fire until my group fires. Count to three and then fire. Then we'll fire after we count to three. In that way, we won't waste bullets hitting the same target more than once. Remember, lie flat on the ground, using a tree to cover most of you. Prop your rifle on a rock or a branch. Whatever you do, do not stand up. If you get too frightened to fire, try taking deep breaths and think of what they did to your families. OK? Any questions?

"What about us with the pistols?" It was little Anoush.

"Good. I want the four of you to stay behind Aram's group. Do not shoot until you see the enemy at this point," Mamigon said, pointing to a low prickly green bush no more than 30 meters from the tree line. "Remember, hold the pistol with both hands, always bring the barrel down toward the target and squeeze the trigger when you see him. Do not wait to get better aim. It will not help your aim. It will get worse. Bring the pistol down from over your head and squeeze when you see the target and KEEP BOTH YOUR EYES OPEN."

He didn't have the heart to tell them that if the cavalrymen got as far as that bush he pointed out, the defenders were as good as killed or captured.

"Now remember, men . . . I mean girls . . . women . . . oh, what the hell . . . remember. You have plenty of bullets. Pile all the clips behind your tree and pretend you are in a drill for me. Now, get into position."

Mamigon placed everyone in a line of defense that was actually a roughly straight line except that the rifles in the two groups were pointing ever so slightly toward the center of the line, about 400 meters in the distance where the big boulder was. Anything that came between the boulder and the tree-line would be greeted with lead from the left and the right. The center, close to the tree line, would be the safest place to be—if you could get that close.

The horsemen were less than a kilometer away now. The column had broken into a canter and would be in front of them in less than 2 minutes, Mamigon figured. The trick was to get them to attack frontally.

"Remember everything I told you," he said in one last warning. "Varta-bedian Agha, you stay with Araxy in my group if I do not return. Araxy, take charge and give the order to fire when you see me raise my hand, right?"

She nodded in puzzlement as Mamigon stepped out from among the trees and sauntered toward the boulder, waving at the approaching cavalry, his rifle cradled in his arms. He walked all the way out to the huge rock, leaned against the side facing the direction of the riders, and waited until the lead riders were in range of his Mauser. Then the rifle was at his shoulder in a flash, spitting out the five rounds in the clip. Four men toppled from their saddles. Mamigon turned and ran directly away from the now shouting horsemen, who spurred up in pursuit. About fifty or sixty of them, closing in rapidly, followed the Armenian's dash into the range of the hidden rifles. With a quick look, Mamigon calculated that the main body was now abreast of his rifles and he raised his left arm. A ragged volley erupted from the trees, and Mamigon headed directly to the flank to get to his people. He counted to himself, and good old Aram responded on the count of three with his fire. The horsemen immediately began veering away from the trees to get out of range, clambering up the embankment to the rail line. Three horses and seven riders were left behind, two men still alive.

Mamigon could only guess what would happen now. Behind the cover of the embankment, the cavalry would probably split into two units, ride about a half a kilometer apart, burst over the rail line, and ride into the trees to flank the enemy on both sides in a pincer movement.

"Everybody up and run like rabbits to the back. I want a new line of fire, exactly like this one, but this time they will be in among the trees looking for us up front."

They understood and ran deep into the trees until Mamigon called halt and strung the line out again.

"I am going back to the front line we just left. Fire at no one on foot until I yell 'Yosghat' when I get back so you do not shoot me by mistake. Good luck."

Mamigon ran back to the treeline and waited. He didn't have to wait long. The horsemen were foolishly ducking and dodging branches as they rode their mounts in the underbrush of the woods. Mamigon snapped off three shots to his right and two to his left, fell to his knees and began to crawl back to the hidden rifles. The Turks began shooting indiscriminately, mostly at imaginary targets in the spotted light of the woods with the sun creating its own natural camouflage.

The military man in Mamigon groaned even as he grinned at the sound of a mounting crescendo of rifle fire behind him. The Turks were shooting at each other, mistaking those who had dismounted as the enemy and apparently, as more dismounted, the firefight began in earnest. Mamigon thought he must have killed the commander and the lieutenant of the unit as they were approaching, otherwise the fiasco he was hearing would have been halted quickly, if begun at all. Cavalrymen never like to leave their mounts when they are about to fight, and this occasion was obviously no exception. They had ridden directly into the woods in a flanking attack from both sides and had been duped into firing at each other.

Mamigon got back to the band, waved to the first one he saw, Baron Vartabedian, to tell everyone to fall back quietly, and the group retreated as fast as they could, with the sound of heavy firing growing dimmer with every meter they ran.

Suddenly, a Turkish sergeant on a strawberry roan appeared with two troopers in front of the running group. They scrambled off their horses and fired rapidly at the women, almost into their faces. The three riders had apparently made a wide loop and intercepted their quarry. Four of the ragtag band fell before Mamigon's group dropped to their knees and killed the three with a heavy volley. Mamigon, who had been bringing up the rear, shouted orders to keep on running. There was no time for stopping—the four remained where they fell.

The brief fusillade must have been heard by the main force of Turks back at the point of initial contact.

Some of Mamigon's band nudged or tugged at one another; they could hear horses approaching. There wasn't much place to hide. Groundcover had gradually disappeared in the sparsely wooded glade. Darkness would be their only salvation, but that was at least a half hour away.

Mamigon did some quick thinking. If the Turks had learned anything from their encounter, they would be dismounted now and leading their horses. They were probably without commissioned officers—being led by a sergeant. There were probably fifty of them, give or take twenty, depending on how many casualties they had inflicted upon themselves in the initial confusion.

The Turks would be operating under one major handicap: They had not seen the size of the force that had ambushed them. They would be wary, jumpy, overly cautious for certain. That gave Mamigon an idea.

"Gather, quickly! Each of you pick a tree and stand behind it, sideways if necessary, away from where they will be coming. Do not move!"

"I am going back to see if I can find that sergeant we killed. I need his clothes and his horse."

"If all goes well, I will be back. If not, Aram and Araxy will try to get you to the coast. Good luck . . ."

He found the dead sergeant just as gun shots echoed from the direction of his little band.

"Cristos! What the hell is going on!"

He took time enough to grab the dead man's *kalpak*, which he put on his head. He tore off the blood-soaked uniform jacket and slipped awkwardly into it as he ran, passing his Mauser back and forth in each hand to get his arms through the sleeves.

He couldn't waste time looking for the roan, not while the shots were increasing in number and tempo.

He almost ran into a Turk crouching behind a boulder, snapping off shots toward . . . Mamigon groaned at the sight.

There was a line of about a dozen soldiers on the right, behind trees and boulders, firing at Mamigon's band.

There was Mariam, the loony one, wandering around with that vacant smile amidst the gunfire, yelling her baby's name.

There was Araxy, on her belly, crawling toward Mariam, a pistol in one hand, a knife in the other.

And there was Aram, running from tree to tree, yelling support to the women, firing his rifle from each position.

The Turkish line was gathering strength with each passing moment as the rest of the unit came up. Someone had smartly got the Turks out of the woods and brought them to flank the fleeing band.

Mamigon had run to his right toward the Turkish line. The crouching Turk saw him, waved at him, and snapped off another shot.

"It is another trap," Mamigon hollered above the firing. "Get word to the *bash chowoosh* to fall back."

The private stared at Mamigon's bent figure and noticed the three bloody holes in the big man's uniform. "I am hit bad, boy. The rebel Armenians are using these women as decoys . . . three hundred of them coming up on your right flank . . . Get the *chowoosh* to pull the men out before it is useless . . ." Mamigon feigned death as he fell over on his face.

The private didn't have to be urged. He even forgot to crawl, standing up and running to the center of the line.

The Turks suddenly stopped firing as orders were barked up and down the line and within minutes the drumbeat of galloping horses could be heard receding in the distance.

Mariam was untouched. The Turks must have ignored an obvious crazy.

Araxy had screamed when she saw Mamigon in his bloody jacket and kissed him soundly when her fears were allayed.

Aram had the look of a tough veteran, grinning his appreciation at the outcome of events.

Mamigon left three more of the women for the wolves and vultures. He took the time to run among the bodies of the cavalrymen in the grove to make his mark, once the women had regrouped and headed out.

7 &ESCAPE

Mamigon figured that in one more night they would be close to the coast and, he hoped, escape for the women. He sat in a clump of evergreens on a ledge overlooking the campsite when he realized that one of the women was climbing up the slope to reach him. It was Araxy, the woman with the forthright manner and the mending breast that would never suckle a child. She had the looks that could have driven a single man crazy, Mamigon thought.

"What are you doing up here? You ought to be resting. How does your chest feel?"

"It is feeling better every day, thanks to you. I could not rest, so I came to keep you company."

"I am not good company, woman. I must keep my eyes on our surroundings."

"You can do that, Mamigon Agha. I will just talk, if you mind not."

"I mind not."

"Aram tells us you will not be going with us if we find a boat."

"Aram talks too much."

"It is true?"

"Yes."

"Why? Your whole family is dead. You have nowhere to go. What would be the sense of staying in this land?"

"I have my reasons, woman."

"Could you . . . would you tell me?"

Mamigon turned to look at her. "Why are you bothering me with such questions?"

"Because I . . . I care for you, that is why." There was defiance in her tone.

"Care for me? What do you mean, woman? Have you lost your mind?"

"I have not lost my mind . . . I have lost my heart to you."

"What? Are you crazy? Leave me! Now!"

"I will not go away. I am not mindless. There is no one like you. I would be truly crazy if I did not speak my mind to you. Do not you understand? There is no one to speak for me now."

He knew all too well what she was talking about, her desperation. Not one of the women—the girls—in his unhappy troop would or could be married if their past were ever known.

An unmarried woman a few years over twenty was considered unmarriageable in any case, and, of course, she would be a virgin. No question at all about that. Chastity was a woman's crown.

When a woman was still not spoken for in her late teens, she became an object of great concern to her mother and the matchmakers would knock themselves out trying to find her a husband, it didn't matter who it was— just as long as she was married. It was considered a disgrace, a blotch on the family name, if the young woman was not married. It was also a simple matter of economics as to who would care for her in her old age once her parents died. It was not uncommon, therefore, to see a rich old widower taking a twenty-year-old woman to wife; it was more important that she be married than that she be happy.

Thus, girls were usually married shortly after they reached puberty. There was little chance for a girl to lose virginity before marriage under such circumstances, but if it did happen, marriage became out of the question. If she were not banned from her father's household to God knows where, the girl would become, literally, the scullery maid, doing the bidding of every female in the household. And she could not eat with the family.

But a widow who had been raped? Absolutely untouchable! That was what these women faced, but Mamigon couldn't think about such things anymore. It was a different world. This woman Araxy was being impossible!

"Oofah, woman, have you forgotten your dead husband and my dead wife so quickly, so easily?"

"Please, Mamigon, it has been little more than two weeks since that dreadful first day, and I no longer know who I am, where I am, and how I will survive. The only thing that makes any sense to me in this world now is you. And I want to be with you as long as God allows me to. Is that too strange, too crazy, too much to ask?"

Mamigon stared at her for a long time. Then, without a word, he reached for her, pulled her to his chest, and embraced her, chin over shoulder. Tears rolled down his face. He held her for a long time with neither of them speaking.

"I have watched you as you tend to my wound. I am not stupid, Mamigon Agha. I see things in your eyes you will not admit to me."

"Watch your brazen tongue. I warn you, woman," Mamigon said, but he did not release her.

"Stop making sounds like a soldier and sound human for once."

"All right, I will tell you. I will tell you with great shame that I want you.

I want you to be with me, at my side, at all times. Is that what you want me to say?"

"Ah, yes, but you are saying it as if it will not happen."

"It cannot happen. I would be embarrassed before my young brother. Such a situation would tear this group apart, do you not see?"

Araxy sighed. Mamigon continued:

"I, too, know not who I am. My soul is dead. I feel as lost as you do, my girl. But, I have vowed on the grave of my family that I will not rest until those who killed them will pay for it in their own blood."

"Have you not done enough, then, to have kept your vow?"

"Not until Tallal Bey is dead."

"How are you, one man, going to do this? He has soldiers all around him and you have traveled far away from where he said he would be."

"I almost had him once. I will try again and again until one of us is dead. I had to struggle with myself not to abandon all of you when I had to make the choice of protecting you or pursuing Tallal."

Araxy pushed away and looked into Mamigon's eyes.

"I have been wondering why you seemed so angry, so short with us. So, that is the reason. We interfered with your vow of revenge . . ."

"No, I have not been angry, and you have not really interfered, just delayed me."

"Do you think God has chosen you as His avenging angel?"

"No, Araxy, there is no God. I am just as an instrument perhaps to save you and your sisters. I do not believe for one moment that He would approve of my vow of revenge if there were a God."

"Well, I guess there is no convincing you that you should try to get away with us."

"No, there is not."

"Then I shall pray to the God you deny for your salvation."

"Salvation of my soul, only, woman . . ."

"Only . . . only your soul? Why not your life?"

"You cannot ask your God to take sides."

"Take sides?"

"Yes. My enemies . . . our enemies are the children of this God as much as you are . . . If you pray for me, you are asking God to take sides."

"You are really something, Mamigon Agha."

He stared at her, shaking his head.

Without another word Araxy pulled away from Mamigon and picked her way back down the slope to the camp.

Mamigon felt a wave of bitterness. He felt she was right, but there was no turning back now. For that matter, where would he take her? How would they live? How could he think of her while his wife and children were barely cold in the ground? The sight of Araxy's breasts was constantly on his mind, however, and he realized that his mouth went dry every time she was ready to have her bandage changed. The emergency repair, for what it was, seemed to have worked. The third examination in six days showed redness around the wound but no signs of infection. The nipple seemed to have the same color as its mate, a good sign, Mamigon thought.

Mamigon thought it ironic that he had been able to help Araxy because of what he had learned from Tallal that day when he had saved his friend from the boar. Mamigon's arrow had killed the boar but not before one of its razor sharp tusks gouged into the back of Tallal's right hand, tearing up the skin and laying the bones open. Mamigon used the saltwater treatment and mudpack then and wrapped the hand tightly with his scarf to stop the bleeding. Tallal escaped with full use of the hand, but the back portion was deeply scarred with livid ridges. The skin and flesh mended without benefit of sutures because the men did not return to the village until three days after the damage was done.

As darkness began to fill the deep valleys and gorges of the mountains, the band again began its march toward the sea. Mamigon felt they would reach the coast by morning, exactly where he did not know. He was certain of one thing: The population in this area was heavily Turkish. Then suddenly they came across another rail line and Mamigon knew where they were. It was the line between Adana and Mersina. Mersina would be to the west, Tarsus and Adana to the east. They would have to circle northwest to get clear of Mersina and then south of the shoreline. Other areas between Mersina and Adana were too populated to be safe. He remembered the trips he had taken with his father, three times in the past—which now seemed centuries ago— to buy cloth goods and spices from the merchants of the big city near the coast, and he had not forgotten the surrounding country.

During the night they walked past Mersina to its north, giving it a wide berth, and began angling toward the coastline. Mamigon wasn't sure what they would do once they got there, but at least it was their immediate destination. The going was much easier although the chance of meeting strangers was a constant danger. When they heard the surf pounding in the distance, Mamigon began looking for a safe place for the group to camp. Their food had held out fairly well. Because they had camped during the daylight hours, they had been able to build quick small fires to boil rice. They had eaten game Mamigon shot, half-cooked because they couldn't afford to let the fire smoke once the fat began to ooze out.

Mamigon went directly to the ocean and walked the beach. His enthusiasm was mostly gone. He didn't know why he cared so much a few days ago—cared whether he was successful or not. He felt a deep sense of loss, almost as deep as when he found his murdered family. It was the seashore. This is where he had promised to bring those poor lost souls, and he had left seven of them dead a few short kilometers from here. The tragic Baron Vartabedian was dead. Pretty little Anoush was lying back there, probably unburied, with the top of her head blown off. And, Mariam, the baker's daughter, whom he had rescued from rape, and yes, Takuhe. Vartabedian's poor, deranged wife was now without anyone to take care of her. Bull dung and camel dung! Enough of this, he thought. Pay better attention to the seashore. The shoreline began to rise the farther he walked until the beach was bordered by steep cliffs. Then he found it: a deep overhang with crumbled rocks in front, an excellent place to bivouac. By dawn, the fourteen in the cavelike opening watched the sea roll toward the beach, something only Mamigon had ever seen before.

The ocean rolled in as the tide rose, and just when Mamigon feared he had made a mistake and the ocean would pour into the cavern, the tide stopped rising and began its ebb. All their footprints in the sand were washed out: a good omen in Mamigon's eyes.

Daylight was on the wane, and there hadn't been a soul on land or sea visible from their vantage. They spent a nervous night, wondering about tomorrow. The second day was also barren of a single sign of life other than foraging albatross. Mamigon told the group that if nothing happened on the third day they would have to move out and look for a boat. They were running out of the little food they had left.

Mamigon went on a tour near daybreak, timing it so that high tide would erase his footsteps by the time he got back to the cavern. Then he saw it: a big sail, all white, approaching the beach in front of the cavern. Mamigon began to run, feeling he had to get there before something happened that might be beyond his control. His only weapon was a pistol stuck in his cummerbund. He had intentionally left his other arms behind, in order not to attract too much attention if he were seen.

When he got near enough, he saw Aram waving a white cloth and the sailboat heading for it. Mamigon reached the cavern, told everyone to stay put, and waded out into the surf with his hands high, waving. The boat came tossing heavily across the surf and lurched to a stop in the sand with about a foot of freeboard exposed. A cross was nailed to the mast, visible as the sail came down. Three men and a woman were on board. One of the men, a small, wiry fellow with a clipped mustache, close-cropped hair and steady brown eyes spoke up.

Mamigon was stumped. He couldn't understand the language.

"*Oorum?*" It was the word for Greek in Turkish.

"Ah! You are a Turk?" The man on the boat spoke in Turkish.

"*Hayir. Ben Ermeni.*"

"Then why do you speak in Turkish if you are Armenian?"

"I speak no Armenian."

"An Armenian who cannot speak Armenian? Ha, ha, ha. You must be a damned Turk or a poor liar."

"Please, mister, I am an Armenian from a village where we only speak Turkish."

"Sure, sure, and I am the King of Greece who dives for sponges to make a living." He turned to give some orders to the people on the boat. The other men leaped into the surf to push the boat free of sand.

Before Mamigon could speak again, the man on deck raised his forefinger and asked: "What do you want anyway, Turk or no Turk? And who are those people over there under the cliff?"

"May Allah be with you," Mamigon said. "We have escaped some terrible massacres in my village and I have twelve young women and my brother here. We have traveled nearly 350 kilometers. I am hoping someone like you will take them to safety. You will be well paid."

The man on the boat held his chin for a moment. "Yes, I heard some rumors about the Armenians when I was in Tarsus yesterday. But, how do I know this is not a trick?"

"I do not know, mister, but here is my pistol to show you I do not mean you any harm," and Mamigon tossed his revolver onto the boat's deck.

The boatman glanced at the revolver, and then suddenly yelled "Soldiers!" and began screaming to the men to push away the boat.

Mamigon looked back at the beach, fearing the worst. It was the women, with their hair tucked up under their forage caps, their rifles slung on their backs, their trousers and their boots.

"Take your damned hats off," Mamigon roared, waving.

The women, as if on puppet strings, pulled off their hats. Their hair came tumbling down around their shoulders.

"Your trousers, take them off, too."

The women sat on the sand and pulled off their army pants. When they stood up again in their crumpled skirts they had some semblance of femininity.

The boatman's fear-filled eyes turned soft at the sight.

"My God, they scared me," he said in Greek, then repeated it in Turkish. "All right, I will listen to what you have to say."

Mamigon recounted briefly what had happened and why they were there. He mentioned that the boatman could have a whole bag of silver, gold, and jewels if he would take the women and Aram to Cyprus. As he finished speaking, Mamigon's charges arrived at the water's edge. The boatman looked at them carefully. Their gaunt, haunted expression, their filthy clothes, their wide, beseeching eyes, were enough for him.

"My name is Dimitri Panagos of Crete. This is my wife, Theodora, the best cook in all the islands, and these are my brother and brother-in-law. I am a Christian. I will certainly help you."

"Thank you, Panagos Agha. We have a pasha's ransom in gold and silver that should more than pay you for your help."

"Do not insult me, Turkish-speaking Armenian. Your Turkish tongue, like the Turks, is uncivilized. I would not dream of accepting anything for a Christian act of mercy."

Mamigon muttered something inaudible. Then he said, pointing to the Mausers, "There are fourteen of those, as you can see. I'll keep one for myself with as much ammunition as I can carry. You can have the rest. They should bring a good price in the market."

"Can you damned Armenians ever do anything without talking trade? All right, I will take the rifles. Now, why do you wish to take these poor souls to Cyprus? It is under the rule of the British, and they will have all kinds of rules about such people. I will take them to my country and hope for the best. Is that all right with you?"

"Anything you say, Panagos Agha."

"And, why are not you coming along. Is my boat not good enough for you?"

"I have unfinished business here."

From the look that came across Mamigon's face, Dimitri understood.

"All right, all right. Get your people on board. I care not to hang on this beach too long."

Mamigon turned to Aram, embraced him tenderly for a moment, whispered in his ear, and turned away, tears glistening his eyes. Araxy came up, embraced him solidly, and turned to the boat. Each of the women did the same.

Dimitri had everyone move to the stern of his boat and the bow lifted free of the sand. The sail was hoisted, the boat stopped wallowing and gathered headway as it responded to the rudder hard alee, and began swooping and bucking surf to the ocean sea.

The little sponge diver, standing at the stern manning the tiller, suddenly raised his left arm straight up and yelled at the lone figure on the beach:

"*Bahbahm*, what are you called?"

"Mamigon."

"What kind of a name is that . . . Macedonian?"

"Armenian . . . Armenian kings, you dumb Greek."

"All you damned Armenians think you are royalty."

Mamigon raised both arms with clenched fists and grinned broadly. The boat was almost out of earshot. He stood watching the boat move away; the wind tugged at his hair and clothes as he waved again.

They're going nuts, he thought, as he saw them jumping up and down on the deck, waving frantically as the sails disappeared behind a spit of land a kilometer away. A wail of grief wafted back before the wind shredded it and folded it into the crashing surf.

He stood motionless, raised his right hand in one last small gesture of farewell, and headed for the overhang to collect his gear.

The *yuz bash* and the remnants of his command from the balloon gun incident, eighteen in all, were strung out, flat on their bellies, along the top of the cliff, their rifles trained on him.

Mamigon didn't break his stride when he saw them. No wonder his people on the boat had been agitated . . . and he didn't even have his pistol. Did the Turks know his weapons were cached under the cliff? No, not likely. They must have arrived as the boat was well out to sea, otherwise he would have been warned in time from the boat. No, the Turks had no idea there was a cavern below them. All they knew was that their nemesis was less than 80 meters from them, apparently unarmed, and nowhere to run or to hide. He was as good as dead.

Mamigon raised his arms as he continued walking toward them. The captain stood up in the center of the line and watched, his arms akimbo, slightly puzzled by the seeming unconcern of his quarry. All the captain had to do was give the word and seventeen bullets would converge on the approaching target.

Mamigon was still 30 meters from the cliff, which rose about 12 meters from the beach, when he shouted suddenly, pointing down the beach to the left. In the split second of distraction he created, the big man sprinted for the overhang.

The clifftop came alive with the rattle and flash of rifle fire, the round uneven and badly aimed. Mamigon gained 3 meters.

The second round was fired again too hastily but enough rifles were aimed true to have hit the runner if Mamigon had not stumbled to the ground. His driving feet had reached loose sand. But he gained another 6 meters.

He maintained his forward tumbling momentum, using the wrestling skills he learned at the academy to propel himself safely under an umbrella of lead as the third volley was delivered—but high. Mamigon gained another 5 meters.

The cavalrymen were now scrambling to their feet and edging to the rim of the cliff as the runner gained his legs to make a final dash to safety, 10 meters away.

The captain's dismay was growing with every round fired and every meter gained. Enough of this horse shit! He had been drawing his Luger as he watched. He stepped to the edge of the cliff and very carefully, with great deliberation, punched out six slugs at the runner below, now only 5 meters from the cliff base.

Three slugs hit into the sand behind. A fourth tore Mamigon's left pectoral, skimming downward across his ribs. A fifth chewed through the outer flesh of the right thigh. The sixth sighed through his groin, nicking his penis and tearing open the scrotum.

Mamigon yelled as if a mule had kicked him, did a somersault as he bent to embrace the locus of the excruciating pain, and ended up in a sprawl on his back under the overhang.

"We got the sonovabitch . . . We nailed the bastard . . . Good shooting, sir . . . Where did he go?"

When they got down to the beach they found him astride the rock debris in front of the overhang, breathing laboriously, blood soaking the clothes of his chest, his crotch, and his thigh.

"Is he alive?"

"Looks like it, captain, barely."

Mamigon's eyes were open and glazed from the trauma. Rifles were cocked for the coup de grace.

"Hold it, men. Let him suffer. We have made a eunuch out of him. He will die slowly, knowing that Allah's ways are avenging and just."

"I will see you in hell." Mamigon croaked out the words.

The captain laughed. "Fall in, men. We have a long way to go and on foot."

Mamigon closed his eyes, a grayness pervading his senses, listening to the muffled footsteps in the sand fading away.

He moaned, opened his eyes, and was bemused to see them again—four or five—surrounding him. They must've come back . . . no . . . they weren't soldiers . . . women . . . yes, women . . . hell, he must be dead . . . one minute soldiers leaving . . . the next . . . all those women. He closed his eyes.

"He has passed out again."

"Huh?"

"Mamigon . . ?"

"Huh."

"Mamigon? It is Araxy. How do you feel?"

"Arax . . . Araxy? Where did you come from?" He opened his eyes wider and realized his head was propped up on something, his body on a blanket covering the sandy floor under the overhang. His entire band of women—and Aram—were now crowding in, shaking hands, and hugging one another.

"You are all right, now, Mamigon Agha. You will be all right, thank God."

"What . . . How . . . ?" His voice was weak, almost womanish.

"We found you . . . we came back when we saw the Turks. We . . ."

Mamigon groaned in anguish. "Get away from here! They might see you!"

"Rest easy, brother. They are far gone by now. You have been out of it for two days. You lost a lot of blood," Aram said. "We will get some broth into you. Do not move, please, you are all stitched up."

"What happened? You say I have been unconscious?"

"Yes. This is the morning of the third day since you were shot." Aram continued. "When we saw the Turks all lined up behind you, nobody wanted to leave until we knew what happened to you. We beached the boat on the other side of the spit and ran back. It was almost a kilometer and we ended up on the cliff. We could not see a soul. We were about to give up, thinking they had taken you away when we saw all those footprints going to our overhang.

"We thought you were dead, big brother. Dimitri's wife here, Theodora, examined you and said if the bleeding could be stopped you could be saved." Aram grinned as Mamigon began looking and became aware that he was naked under a blanket, except for the bandages.

"She sewed up deep cuts for many a sponge diver when they tangled with sharp things in the water, so Theodora took over. She had Araxy help her and you will be as good as new, big brother."

"Hey, the Turks did not see your rifle and stuff in the back, is not that fortunate!" Aram knew his brother was painfully bashful and tried to shift topics.

Dimitri pushed through the crowd to shake Mamigon's hand. "You take it easy today, Mamigon Agha. We will put you on the boat tomorrow and get you out of here."

Mamigon nodded, taking some broth spooned out to him by the dark-eyed slim Greek woman who had doctored him. She saw the look in his eyes, motioned to her husband, and whispered to him.

Dimitri waved everyone out of earshot, except for his wife who, with downcast eyes, kept on feeding the Armenian and blushing at the same time. "Your wounds on the chest and thigh were not much more than deep cuts, Agha. Theodora closed them up easily. You . . . no, Theodora does not understand Turkish . . . you are a lucky man. Your balls were nicked but not smashed, my wife says. The bullet made everything look like noodle soup, though. She sewed up the . . . bag, and also the cut on your *papaz*. You will be fine. I know not if you will ever be able to father children, but *kismet*."

"I should be able to get up, then?"

"Not until tomorrow, I think. The wounds can break open if you move too much, and we are still worried about infection. You ran a high fever yesterday and last night. By the way, who is Ahgavni? You kept calling her."

"My murdered wife."

"I am sorry, Mamigon Agha."

"I feel bad about you, Panagos Agha. On account of me, you have been delayed now for days and I . . ."

"Quiet, Turkish-speaking Armenian. I told you you had an uncivilized tongue. If I want to help you, I will help without you getting excited."

Mamigon closed his eyes, smiling wanly, groped for and found Theodora's reluctant hand, and dropped off to sleep.

8   TATIOS

Mamigon worked his way up the steep path toward the notch in the spine of the mountain ridge. He was getting tired of the constant struggle upward and then the inevitable slipping and sliding and near plunges to eternity on the downward trails. He had abandoned the safer and better mountain paths on his trek north from the seacoast. A lone man armed with a rifle, a bow and quiver, a scimitar, a heavy dagger, a pistol in his belt, a backpack, and a bag slung over his shoulders would attract too much attention. It was attention he could not afford. His goal was to get back to the midlands. Perhaps Tallal had been detained in the area around Gurin, where the girls had said his unit was heading. Encounters with travelers on the regularly used ways would delay him and might even be fatal. It would take a little longer over the vertible goat paths he was treading, but at least he felt he had a better chance of reaching the Gurin area.

He felt truly lonely for the first time in his life. It had taken all his powers of persuasion to convince Dimitri and Aram that he should remain. The Greek, finally convinced, had insisted on staying two more days to make sure Mamigon could tend his own wounds. Now, his loneliness was assuaged only by the easing of his concern for the safety of the young people he had shepherded to the coast. He was hungry, his canteen was almost empty, his bootsoles were in shreds and his feet were bleeding as he climbed to the notch in the towering granite of the mountain slopes.

He never walked over the crest of a ridge; he approached each apex on his hands and knees, peered over and down, and then made a descent if all was clear. It took him three days to travel what he estimated was about 100 kilometers before he descended into the valley embracing the flow of the Sihoun River. The river flowed down from the northeast, the direction he wanted to go. The going along the river bank was a Sunday stroll compared to what he had experienced up to then, but it was extremely hazardous in terms of being seen. After four close calls, Mamigon gave up and settled in a heavy outgrowth, waiting until nightfall to continue. The first night he had to cross a deep tributary to the Sihoun and soon realized he was approaching a village or town. There were fenced pastures and paths, and he could smell occasional outhouses upwind of him. When he thought he was getting too close, Mamigon stopped near a big tree he thought he would be able to recognize again because of the giant Y branch formation. He removed his scimitar, bow and quiver, rifle and bag of pistols, and buried them in some bushes at the base of the tree. Armed only with a pistol, he walked into what turned out to be a good-sized village. He could tell from the church that it was an Armenian village.

It was late, about two hours after supper time, and he wondered who would be up and around. The village had a well in the center of it, and a boy was filling a bucket there.

"Hello. What place is this?" The boy didn't understand Turkish. He shook his head. "Mamigon," he said, pointing to himself, and then pointed expectantly at the boy.

"Krikor," the boy said, and smiled. He had recognized Mamigon's Armenian name. He beckoned Mamigon to follow him. The boy led the big man to a mud house five houses away. He ran in while Mamigon waited and two men appeared at the door.

"*Ben Ermeni, turka-khos Ermeni,*" Mamigon said.

"I speak Turkish," the older of the two said. "Who are you and what do you want?"

"I am on my way to Gurin and I am wondering where I am."

"You are in Yerebakan and you look tired. Please come in and rest."

"Thank you, I am tired a bit. I am from a *kiugh* near Yosghat."

"Ah, that is why you speak no Armenian. But, come in, come in. Then we will talk. My name is Dikrahnian."

The family seemed to consist at least of a father, mother, and four sons. The wife appeared when Dikrahnian called out her name, Ahrussyag. There would probably be other women in the house, but they would not appear when a strange male was present.

"My name is Mamigon, son of Magaros. I am an ironmonger and blacksmith. I am on my way to Gurin. Have you heard any news from up that way?"

"Please sit down first and have something to eat. You are hungry, are you not?"

"Thank you, I will not stand on ceremony. A piece of cheese and some bread would do." Mamigon had never been able to understand the games Armenians played about accepting food in another's house when it was offered. The host had to ask three times. The visitor would refuse twice and accept only if it were offered the third time and then only if really expected to say yes.

The men sat in a circle on rugs piled around the edge of the room facing the visitor. The father seemed to be about forty; the sons ranged from about twelve to maybe twenty years. The boy who had been at the well was not there.

"No, we have heard nothing from Gurin or thereabouts. Why do you ask?"

"You have heard nothing at all about what is happening in the country?"

"We have heard some rumors about Armenians being molested by government troops, but nothing definite."

At this point, the food was brought in and Mamigon smiled politely at the woman who offered a tray with some cold baked lamb, spring onions, cheese, *pideh*, yogurt, and a jug of water. She seemed a bit frightened, barely smiled back, and withdrew hurriedly.

Mamigon excused himself and quickly devoured everything on the tray without another word. He had crossed himself before he ate and again when he finished, saying his grace silently. There was an immediate change in the demeanor of his hosts.

Baron Dikrahnian called out to his wife to serve coffee and told his oldest son to tell Krikor "nevermind."

Dikrahnian smiled uneasily at Mamigon. "We really knew not who you were. We were not too sure you were Armenian as you claimed and I . . . I sent my boy to alert the village for possible trouble."

"Trouble? From me? What made you change your mind?"

"A true Moslem would have died rather than cross himself."

"Tell me, Dikrahnian Agha, what is going on that you expected trouble from someone like me, even if I had been a Turk?"

"This village is in the jurisdiction of the *vali* of Sis. Only yesterday a notice was posted in the square from the *vali* that all Armenians had two weeks notice either to renounce Christianity and embrace Islam or be prepared to pack up and leave the country. I thought you might have been sent from Sis to feel us out."

Mamigon thought that one over before he asked softly: "And have you made a decision?"

"The village council met and we sent an emissary to Sis to find out exactly what was meant by leaving the country."

"Is not the posted notice plain enough? May I see it?"

They took Mamigon to the church where a large piece of heavy paper had been nailed to the wooden door. Mamigon read every word of it. It was a proclamation, issued by the Ottoman government in Constantinople. It read:

* * *

Our fellow countrymen, the Armenians, who form one of the racial elements of the Ottoman Empire, having taken up, as a result of foreign instigation for many years past, with a lot of false ideas of a nature to disturb the public order; and because of the fact that they brought about bloody happenings and have attempted to destroy the peace and security of the Ottoman state and the safety and interests of their fellow countrymen, as well as of themselves; and, moreover, as they have now dared to join themselves to the enemy of their existence and to the enemies now at war with our state—

Our Government is compelled to adopt extraordinary measures and sacrifices, both for the preservation of the order and security of the country and for the welfare and the continuation of the existence of the Armenian community.

Therefore, as a measure to be applied until the conclusion of the war, the Armenians have to be sent away to places which have been prepared in the interior vilayets; and a literal obedience to the following orders, in a categorical manner, is accordingly enjoined on all Ottomans:

First, All Armenians, with the exception of the sick, are obliged to leave within five days from the date of this proclamation, by villages or quarters, and under the escort of the gendarmerie.

Second, Though they are free to carry with them on their journey the articles of their movable property which they desire, they are forbidden to sell their lands and their extra effects, or to leave the latter here and there with other people, because their exile is only temporary and their landed property, and the effects they will be unable to take with them, will be taken care of under the supervision of the Government, and stored in closed and protected buildings. Anyone who sells or attempts to take care of his movable effects or landed poperty in a manner contrary to this order, shall be sent before the court martial. They are free to sell to the Government only the articles which may answer the needs of the Army.

Third, All Armenians who are sent away will be under the protection of the Government and will be assured safe conduct of their persons as well as their effects.

Fourth, Anyone in the land, in any status or position, who attempts to harm or molest the Armenians on their way will be sent before the court martial.

Fifth, Since the Armenians are obliged to submit to this decision of the Government, if some of them attempt to use arms against the soldiers or gendarmes, arms shall be employed against them and they shall be taken, dead or alive. In like manner those who, in opposition to the Government's decision, refrain from leaving or seek to hide themselves—if they are sheltered or given food and assistance, the persons who thus shelter or aid them shall be sent before the court martial for execution.

"What does that mean—here—where it says 'they have now dared to join themselves to the enemy of their existence?' Who do they mean?"

"I believe they mean the Russians, Mamigon Agha."

"Well, it sounds reasonable enough for a government action, and I do not think your emissary is going to find anything helpful at all."

"We are hopeful that there might be some options."

"I am afraid your options are those of a chicken on the chopping block, my newfound friend. Please call the menfolk to some place we can talk. I must talk to all of you."

Dikrahnian agreed. Krikor had already alerted many of the men, in any case, and everyone gathered at the church. Mamigon excused himself for speaking in Turkish and then told them what had happened in his village and the experiences he had had in the meantime. Many in the audience were disbelieving. Some said the people in Mamigon's village may have committed a terrible wrong, causing unpremeditated overreaction by the Turkish police. Others said his story about what happened—or was supposed to have happened—in Kaisaria was secondhand information at best. The bodies in the river could have been the result of a big boat accident on the Kizil Irmak. Still others thought the Turkish *vali* may have overstepped his bounds as head of the *sandjaki* and the men felt that the *bey* of the Adana province would overturn the *vali's* ridiculous orders, proclamation or no.

"We know who you are now. You are that mad Armenian the Government has posted a reward for." It was the tall man who had advanced the thought that Mamigon's villagers had done something rash to cause the massacre there.

"I will not mince words with you, *baron*. You are saying I am sick in the mind, and therefore nothing I have said is true. Is that right?"

The tall one squirmed a bit before answering. "Well, perhaps not sick but it obviously is Armenians like you who are bringing the wrath of the government down on our heads."

"Oh? You believe that because I have been shoeing horses for fifteen years in a little village, the government became irritated, eh? You believe that because I served in the army, the government doesn't like me? You believe that because I went on many hunting trips with the son of the *vali* of Yosghat, who broke bread at my table, caused bad feelings, eh? Or, maybe you believe that like a good Christian I should have turned the other cheek when the government's police raped and killed my wife, killed my children, my father and mother and five of my brothers, eh? I do not think I can understand your kind of thinking, *baron*."

"We are in your debt, Mamigon Agha, for talking to us. Many thanks." Dikrahnian rushed in to close the conference before it got out of hand.

"No thanks necessary, Dikrahnian Agha. I will leave you with this thought: You cannot trust the Turk, my brothers. I have nothing more to say. I have warned you."

Mamigon went back to where he had cached his arms, hung his possessions on himself and walked back through Yerebakan on his way north, passing the eyes of the entire population of the hamlet. Not another word was said to him. When he saw the children looking saucer-eyed at his regalia, he wanted to cry. He knew the little ones wouldn't be spared, and their attraction to such unfamiliar sights would bring terror and death in the days ahead; he was sure of it. If the people here were anything like the people in his own village, they regarded themselves as Turkish citizens and could not, would not, believe that the government, their government, would ever do anything really bad to them. Mamigon knew that a month ago he would have thought the same thing, even though everyone knew about the massacres perpetrated by Sultan Hamid. But, the sultan was a stupid conniver who was kicked out by his own army officers.

Mamigon put plenty of room between himself and the Turkish village of Fekke on the river and crossed the river below it. He estimated he was about 150 kilometers from Gurin, but he wasn't too sure exactly where he was. The country was unfamiliar to him and he made it a practice not to meet or be seen by anyone, if he could help it.

Yerebakan was now one full day behind him, and he had about an hour of daylight left when he reached the top of a ridge on his hands and knees, as usual, and stopped dead, slipping to a prone position among the trees and bushes. Far below, in a broad valley dotted with daisies and cowslips, was a strange sight. It looked like a bedraggled army of men, women and children—mostly women and children—all trudging slowly toward the southeast. There were about three thousand of them, strung out for nearly 2 kilometers, some with oxcarts, some riding asses, most everyone carrying belongings of some kind, some carrying children, others helping the elderly among them.

Mamigon's eyes glittered. Flanking the horde were what looked like three hundred or so men on horseback, two-thirds of them policemen armed with rifles and swords, and the rest mounted horse soldiers or cavalry, he wasn't sure. As they convoyed the army of civilians, their speculating eyes never left the younger females in the crowd. The horsemen laughed, talked loudly and shouted cries of approval occasionally at a particularly handsome woman, but kept their distance along the flanks at about 15 to 20 meters.

The convoy was halfway past Mamigon when a guttural wail of fear swirled up from the crowd below. A small figure of a girl had tottered away from the main body and was heading for the horsemen. A rider spurred his horse toward the girl and ran directly into her, slamming her to the ground. An older woman, screaming like a banshee, ran to the motionless form with her arms thrust forward and was also run down by the rider's horse. The horseman then carefully leaned downward and deftly slit her throat with the tip of his sword. The wailing from a thousand throats finally subsided to a moan, much like a dying wind among the pines.

Mamigon didn't move a muscle. What in the name of *Soorp* Mariam was
going on? Where's Saint Mary? Why are they being killed like animals?

"On your life, do not move!"

Mamigon stared straight ahead but he could see the outline of someone on
his left, holding something over his head. The command was in Turkish.

"I am still. What do you want?"

"Where is your horse, Turkish dog?"

Mamigon slowly turned his head to look into the bony, intense face of a
man with a huge head of hair, a long, scraggly mustache under his flaring
nose. He was on his knees, holding a knotty club high in the air, ready to
brain Mamigon. Mamigon fell to his side and snapped into a roll toward the
fellow, reaching him as the club bit into the dirt where he had been. Mamigon was on top of him in an instant, an elbow pressing down on his assailant's throat. The man's thrashing steadily lost its sharpness, and he was
almost motionless when Mamigon let up and stood back, an arrow now
strung to his bow, pointing at the reviving form.

The man groaned and sat up, his hands about his almost crushed neck.

"Go on, kill me," he croaked, looking without expression at the
ground.

"Who are you?"

The man hesitated. This big, wild-looking man armed to the teeth could
be a Kurd, from the looks of him.

"You speak, now, or die," Mamigon said.

"I am Armenian."

"Truly, you say? What are you up to?"

"My sisters may be down there."

Mamigon thought this over before answering.

"What do you think you are doing?"

"I was going to save them from you jackals."

"What is all that down there?"

"You know not?"

"What is this, lesson time in the schoolhouse? Tell me, man."

"Those are most of the women from a town called Gurin, up north. The
Turkish army is walking them into exile to the Syrian desert."

"Where are the menfolk? I do not see too many, only a few old ones."

"They gathered up all the able-bodied men outside of town and told them
they had to go to Moush to help the army build something or another. The
men were loaded into oxcarts and taken away. Do you know what the Turks
did? They made the men undress, pile their clothes back on the carts and
then the soldiers drew their firewood hatchets and hacked them to death.
Chopped them down, with blood spurting everywhere. The screams! It was
the bloodiest, most godforsaken thing I have ever seen. It took two bloody
hours to finish the massacre. My God, my God."

Mamigon listened.

"How do you know all this? Were you one of the men from Gurin?"

"No . . . Yes . . . No. I was living in Constantinople until two weeks
ago. I heard rumors from some of my Turkish friends about what was going

to happen to Armenians in the eastern provinces. I wrote two letters to my family in Gurin and never got a reply. So, I traveled out here to find out what was going on."

Mamigon shifted his eyes to the valley below. "We will talk later. They are moving away and I think we should keep as close as we can. What did you have in mind about a rescue?"

The bony Armenian looked closely at Mamigon before he answered. "If you are not a Turk or a Kurd and you are not going to kill me, then who are you and what are you doing up here?"

Mamigon shook his head. "It matters not who I am. I am nobody now. Let it be enough for you to know that you now have an ally."

"Are you Armenian?"

"Yes, but stop this talk. Let us see what we can do. First, take these two revolvers. I see you do not have arms," Mamigon said, handing over two mismatched handguns from his canvas bag. "These are bandoliers that go with them . . . here. I hope you know how to use them."

"I know how. But, now that I am armed, I know not what to do about anything. There are too many Turks . . ."

"Our first task is to keep close to them . . . until it gets dark. Then we can do something. Can you ride?"

"I am the best horseman in Turkey," he replied matter-of-factly as if everyone in the realm knew that.

"Good. I like a man with confidence. What is your name, *kimikli*, bony one?"

"Tatios is good enough, mister. I really know not who you are and the less you know about me, the better."

"Tatios it is. Let us go. Do you have anything with you?"

Tatios produced a dufflebag containing some dried beef, cheese, unleavened bread, a comb, razor, some socks, and a small book.

"What is that book, the Bible?"

"No it is a book of poems written in Greek by the Englishman Byron. Second to Shakespeare's translations in the German, I think this man has a touch of literary genius."

They followed the convoy below them until dark; when cook fires began to dot the little plain, they stopped and set up camp. Tatios took up his narrative as they ate some cheese and chewed on dried beef. He said he took the train to Ankara, the end of the line east, bought a horse and saddle and set off for Gurin, a good 400 kilometers eastward.

"I ran into some trouble near Yosghat. Some troops were not going to honor my pass until their commander told them to let me go. I went by a little village that was just a smoking ruin, and I really began to worry. When I approached Gemerek, I decided to go around it instead of through the town. I could see smoke and I was not sure what was going on. You know, by this time, I was really getting worried about my family. My father's place is about 4 kilometers to the southeast of Gurin. So, instead of heading directly for Gurin, I angled to the south of it. I was about 20 kilometers away when I heard the wildest shouts and screams. I took no more chances at this point. I tied my horse to a tree and crept up to the next rise. God! May I never see that sight again! Axing people to death! Unarmed, naked men holding up their arms to ward off the blades from their chests and necks and faces! I recognized many of the men being killed. The Turks loved their job. I know not what revolted me more, the blood-curdling screams and sobs or the laughter of the Turks. Most of the men died in a special way. The Turks would make a feint for the head, and when his victim instinctively threw up his hands, the axe would come around and up into the groin. Of course, the victim would immediately bring his hands down and bend, just in time to catch the axe in his skull or back. *Sacre bleu!* After the last man was down, the Turks carefully cleaned themselves, wiping off each other of blood spatters, and left those piles of naked bodies, many dismembered, ready for the wolves.

"It was like an ancient battlefield except that all the dead were from one army and none had even a broken sword in his hand to indicate that his death may have been valiant. Talk about Dante's Inferno . . .

"I went down to see if anyone was left alive after waiting until I was sure those brave bastards were not coming back. I found two. They were past help but were able to tell me what had gone on in the village. I stayed with them until they died, went back for my horse and rode hard for my father's place. You can imagine how I was feeling about what I dared not hope to find.

"My worst fears came true. I found my father's body in front of the house, his head barely attached. I found seven of my sisters killed and left in hellish positions as if they had been denizens of Sodom and Gomorrah. The smell made me vomit. I found my youngest sister, Lucine, hiding in a hay cart, practically out of her mind. She had witnessed the whole thing and had stayed in the cart for two days until I came along. She told me she had been playing in the cart when the Turk *suvari* squadron rode up. They never saw Lucine. They went right into the house, came out dragging my father, made him kneel—with his daughters, my sisters, forced to look on—and struck off his head. Then they went to work on the women. Lucine said she covered her ears and tried not to hear the rest of the terrible screams and sounds until the cavalry squadron left." Tatios paused at this point to catch up with his emotions.

"Please, please, go on with your report."

"Oh, yes, anyway, while I was looking around for my other sisters and my younger brother, Lucine screamed a warning that someone was coming. It turned out to be an old Turkish friend of my father's, Mustapha. They had played backgammon together for as long as I can remember. I had my horse in the barn so he did not know anyone was around as we watched from the house. Mustapha ran over to my father's body, cursed mightily at the sight, and just sat down and sobbed without control, holding my father's cold hand in his.

"We came out at this point and Mustapha immediately put his arms around both of us, kissing and hugging as if we were his own family. To make a long story short, he insisted that Lucine's place was in the safety of his home, where he would pass her off as one of his nieces. He knew what was going on and begged me to ride to the coast and seek sanctuary anywhere but in the empire of the Ottomans.

"I left Lucine with him. I had misgivings but he seemed to speak common sense. I had not gone 5 kilometers away when I came across bodies of women and children dotting the trail of what must have been an army of them. I caught up to them yesterday and I am fairly certain they are most of the survivors of Gurin.

"Bad luck caught up with me, though. I had hobbled my horse to let it graze, but in the morning—this morning—it was gone. You know the rest. I met you and here we are."

Mamigon marveled at the narration. "Tell me, do you know anything about the Turks—who they are, where they came from?"

"From the looks of their uniforms, they are policemen and horse soldiers. They seem to have very little discipline and poor leadership. Their officers seem lax."

"That is good. The toughest and best fighters are those with discipline. Perhaps we can do some damage and save a few lives in the bargain."

"I wish I knew whether my sisters and brother were down there."

"We will find out, worry not."

"How are we going to do that?"

"Not 'we,' you."

"Me?"

"Of course. I know not what they look like. How many sisters do you have?"

"There were ten . . . and three boys in the family. Right now I know not how many of us are left, but I cannot account for two sisters and my younger brother who were at home. My oldest brother and I have been living in Constantinople."

"You had ten sisters and two brothers?"

"Yes. There is a funny story we tell about how there got to be so many of us, too. Would you care to hear it?"

Mamigon shrugged, so Tatios continued: "We had a big place. My father raised cattle, horses and sheep, oats and barley. He was a *Haji*, my father. He had made the trip to Jerusalem twelve times and everyone called him *Haji* Hagop as a sign of honor. My father, may his soul rest in light, had a problem. He had, like most fathers, wanted sons. My mother Mariam had presented him with three daughters in the first six years of marriage.

"So he took her with him on one of his hegiras to Jerusalem and exhorted the Almighty for a change in natal venue.

"Lo, my brother Harootune was born. Thank God, my father must have cried in gratitude, for he had a new church built in the village in honor of his first male child. God apparently was not impressed because Mama presented *Haji* Hagop with three more girls, two years between each. It is said he was terribly ill-tempered about this and took her, like a culprit of some kind, back to Jerusalem, ostensibly to give spiritual guidance to her deliveries.

"I was the result and Papa had a new schoolhouse built to commemorate the event. Trips to the Holy Land notwithstanding, once back on the Anatolian Plain, Mama produced three more girls like clockwork in six years time, again.

"My father, or *Haji Bey* as the Turks called him out of respect for his great wealth and spiritual devotion, gave up taking her to Jerusalem at this point. I think God rewarded him for his forbearance with a third son, my brother, Ishiak.

"He tried again for a son, of course, and only God knows if the arrival of his tenth daughter—and thirteenth child—was to have meant two more girls to come. My mother, may she rest in light, died in childbirth.

"I suppose she was fortunate. If she had lived she would have witnessed and felt the barbarity the Turk is capable of perpetrating." Tatios had tears in his eyes and stopped talking.

Mamigon waited several minutes before he spoke. "You seem to be an educated man. Tell me something. Ever since I can remember, the Turks have been giving us *Highs* a bad time. I even heard they killed a lot of us back thirty-five or forty years ago in the towns near the Russian border. What's going on? What is the trouble between us *Highs* and the Turks?"

"I suppose you feel great hate for the Turk, now that he has killed your loved ones?"

Mamigon didn't answer. He looked at him steadily for a moment as if to ask if Tatios did not feel the same way.

The thin man hunkered down on his haunches, smiling. "You know, it would be downright ignorant to say the Armenians are being killed or exiled, now, simply because the Turks are savage, brutal, inhuman—doing this just because we are not one of them.

"Well, they certainly are savage, brutal, and inhuman, but not because they are simply bad people. They follow the main precepts of the Koran which are charity, hospitality, fidelity to one's word, and protection of widows and orphans. But, there is some history you should know about. This land we call our homeland was overrun and conquered by the Turks almost 900 years ago. We lost our kingdom and our kings, our land and our political rights—everything except our language and our religion, which our conquerors let us keep. We lost our country fair and square, if you want to call invasion and war the way to lose one's birthright. But we did. We lost.

"Anyway, about fifty or sixty years ago, we began making political trouble for the sultans of Turkey by demanding representation in their civil service and more equality. After all, our boys were serving in the Turkish army and died by the thousands in the Crimea."

"How do you know so much?"

"My father sent me to follow my older brother to school in Paris. When I finished last year, I joined my brother in publishing a French-Armenian newspaper in Constantinople. We are not liked there by the Turks, but we are tolerated . . . shall I go on?" Mamigon nodded.

"Let's see, it is 1915 now . . . back about thirty-five years, around

1880, the Turkish government realized it had a real Armenian question: What to do with a minority population of a different race and religion that suddenly wants equality and a larger political role in the country you have ruled for almost a thousand years?

"And the Turks had another problem. The Czar's army at its eastern borders was getting to be a real headache. There were all kinds of rumors of Armenians aiding and abetting the Russians and even plotting to seize Turkish soil.

"As far as the Turk was concerned, there was only one way to deal with rebels: kill them, wipe out all nests of activity. So it started on the orders of Sultan Hamid in 1894. The Turks began killing, first the men, then everyone in a village.

"You know, if it were not for Danish and German and American missionaries out in the eastern provinces, I do not think the world would ever have known about what was going on. The government tried to keep all news out of the provinces under the carpet.

"The organized massacres have been going, off and on, for nearly forty years now, but you can see what has happened. The Turkish government has given up."

"What do you mean, given up? They are still butchering us."

"No, no. Do not you see, they have decided to kick the lot of us out of the country. I think trying to kill two million people is just too much. So, obviously they are sending us into exile . . . those they have not killed already or kill along the way. I do not think the plan of the government is to kill any more of us. I think the killing that is going on is ad hoc, excuse me, I mean unplanned. The soldiers and police escorts are having their grisly fun . . . mostly they are undisciplined recruits hired to get the job done."

"Where are the *Highs* being exiled?"

"Ah! That is where the brutality is evident. Are the Turks putting us on boats and saying go away? Are they putting us on trains and sending us off? No. They are marching us by the thousands to their deserts to the south to die eventually of thirst and starvation. That is the heartless brutality of it. Do not kill us outright, as you have done up to now. Kill us indirectly and say you had nothing to do with the deaths!"

Mamigon sighed as he absorbed the picture of what it was all about. This bony fellow was a book of information. He wished he had known him in better times. He thought he would have enjoyed passing the time with him, talking over coffee. But it was time to get back to the situation at hand.

"I think you should get in among the captives tonight. You will have to shave that mustache of yours and walk with them at least a day until you locate your family, if they are there. A big blanket over your head and a stoop should do it. What think you?"

Tatios thought of it for a while, then silently rummaged in his duffle for his shaving equipment, wet his face with water from Mamigon's canteen, and scraped away without benefit of mirror. At about an hour before sunup, the two approached the huge sprawl of the night bivouac. The men checked the two pistols that Tatios shoved firmly into his belt underneath his shirt, they shook hands, and Tatios crawled into the darkness.

With dawn, the groups of women came alive with activity. From his vantage back on the ridge, Mamigon wondered what there was to do. They didn't have any fires—they didn't have much to eat. Nevertheless, everyone was moving around. The guards had their own fires, and the army cooks were busy feeding the soldiers and police. In a half hour the long serpentine column was on the move, the riders taking up their positions along both flanks. Mamigon looked hard for a shape that he could distinguish as Tatios. He was glad he could not pick him out of the crowd. If he had been able to spot his friend at this distance, the Turks would certainly have been able to pick him out from under their noses. The plan was for Tatios to get to the head of the convoy and walk slowly, allowing the exiles to move past him as he worked his way to the rear. If his family were among them, he would alert them where to position themselves in the night camp to make rescue easier.

In the late afternoon, Mamigon became uneasy. He still couldn't spot Tatios. The sun was blazing warm, just right for the vultures that wheeled with infinite patience overhead. Where was the skinny idiot? Mamigon realized immediately that he had called Tatios an idiot because the man's erudition had disturbed him. He'd never met anyone like him.

The march was approaching what looked like several square miles of forest at the base of some foothills rising from the valley floor. Mamigon broke into a trot, deciding to reach the woods ahead of the column. The trees would give him cover and he would be better able to see Tatios. He hadn't taken five steps when he heard the sound of a commotion erupting near the end of the column. Mamigon watched as an old lady, stooped and limping, wandered into the open space near the horsemen. The marchers screamed, knowing she faced certain death. The rider closest to the stooped old lady raised his sword as he rode up to her. Then a shot rang out and the horseman flipped backward from the impact of the slug, sliding off his horse's rump. Instantly, the old woman's black shawl fell off and she became a bushy-haired man leaping onto the vacated saddle, grabbing the reins, bringing up the horse on its hind legs as its forelegs pawed the air. The rider wheeled the animal sharply around and raced down the flank, he now dropped the reins and had a pistol in both fists as he guided his mount with his knees and heels. The whole episode occurred so quickly the soldiers remained in line at intervals, shepherding the line of march. As the rider—it was Tatios—approached each soldier, one of his pistols snapped and the soldier went down. After he had dispatched three in this fashion, a roar of anger swelled from the Turkish horsemen who spurred their mounts in a concerted effort to get the lethal horseman whose proximity meant death.

Tatios began angling his ride toward the ridge where he thought Mamigon might be. Mamigon saw what he was up to. Tatios would be a bit off target, but that was fine. Mamigon would be able to flank the pursuers. He sat down beside a tree, fascinated at the fantastic antics of his companion, making sure his weapons were ready. Tatios leaned forward on his horse's neck, looking back to see how he was doing.

Mamigon watched intently, then slowly raised his Mauser as the lead pursuer came into range, waited a few seconds, and fired. The Turk's horse went down. At least a hundred if not more of the Turkish unit were after Tatios. They must have missed the source of the bullet that knocked down the horse. But they understood instantly when the next man swayed suddenly and fell, because they could see that Tatios had not turned and fired at them. Then, when another rider was hit, they saw the smoke and flash from the ridge to their left.

The pursuers slowed down. Meanwhile, some of the women took the opportunity to break away and head toward the woods and the ridge, ignoring the danger they faced as they ran past their captors. Seeing this, Mamigon put down his rifle, grabbed his bow and, taking aim at the sky, loosed an arrow toward the troopers who had not given up the chase. The arrow came down and plunged through a soldier's chest and lodged in the back of his horse. Bowmen, too? The Turks reined up almost to a man at the sight of the arrow. The lead rider, who hadn't seen what happened, provided further cause for astonishment as he died grabbing at an arrow that slammed into his guts.

Tatios had seen the last muzzle flash and angled his ride slightly toward Mamigon. The Turks were suddenly surrounded by a flood of would-be escapers who ran by them toward the woods. The first man who raised his sword died from Mamigon's next rifle shot. More rapid fire from the trees convinced the Turks that there must be a pretty good-sized force there. They wheeled their mounts to get out of range, forgetting the women temporarily.

Tatios reached the tree line, hauled up his horse short, whirled around and rode hard back toward the plain. Mamigon almost forgot to stay hidden as he watched with fascination as the rider galloped steadily toward three riderless horses, swoop down upon one, grab the hanging reins, and start back for the woods, leading the frightened animal. The Turks fired rapidly but the horses and rider escaped unscathed. Mamigon stood shaking his head at the scene. The thin one might have been bragging when he said he was the best rider in Turkey, but Mamigon, at the moment, was certain it was true.

Tatios rode up, grinning broadly with a fine set of white teeth, slipped easily out of the saddle, tied up both horses and ran to Mamigon, almost breathless.

"Thanks. How are we doing?"

"Oofah, you madman, what was that all about?"

"I could not find my family and I was not going to walk with all those pathetic, godforsaken creatures another meter, that is all."

"You could have been killed."

"I was not, thanks, but I do not think the Turks are going to give us time to gloat over this. That is why I rode back to get that other horse."

Mamigon looked back at the plain. Many of the women and children, maybe thirty, had gained the woods but for what good? They had nowhere to go, no food, and he was desperate at the thought that his actions had given them hope.

"What are we going to do about them?" Mamigon waved his arm in the direction of the fugitives who had reached the sanctuary of the woods.

"What are we going to do about *them*?" Tatios waved his arm in the direction of the main body of women and children still under the watch of the Turks.

Mamigon followed the wave of the arm and his casual look slowly turned into an intense stare. His eyes hardened, the alae of his nostrils turned white.

He was watching the Turkish horsemen who had returned to the main body where the commander had just reached them from the head of the long column. The officer wore a spiked German helmet. Mamigon could not miss the familiar figure. "Tallal!" he blurted out through a hard, drawn mouth. "It is that craven dog, Tallal Bey," he said, turning to a startled Tatios . . . startled at the sudden intensity and rage he could see and hear in the voice of his companion.

"Tallal Bey? Who are you talking about? Do you know one of the Turks down there?"

"Yes, the one with the German helmet, the leader . . . He is the one I am after . . . The butcher who slaughtered everyone in my village . . . He . . . "

"Are you certain?"

"One of my brothers told me as he died." Mamigon said the words in a low tone, shaking his head, stopping further words from Tatios. He was recalling the devastation he had been suppressing as much as he could . . . the devastation of the spirit that had dominated him in the little corner of hell that had been, until that fateful day, his happy home. He remembered now, not so much the sights that had smashed into his psyche with the force of a cannonball, but the little things he had had to do once the all-pervasive shock had diminished enough to allow him to think, to make him do things he would never forget, never.

Sitting there next to his dead wife, he had first called out to Aram to go to the sheepfold behind their house and begin digging a grave for the family. He would join him as soon as he could. What he had to do he did not want his brother to have to see.

He would never forget what he had to do. He had cut the thin ropes holding his wife's arms up over her head and those at her ankles that were holding her legs apart, and almost in tears at the violence he was using on what had once been his softly animate, loving wife, pulled her arms down and closed her legs, overcoming the powerful muscular freeze of rigor mortis.

He would never forget what he had done next, unable to recall later a rational motive. He had carefully picked up the tiny embryo that would have been his fourth child, still attached to the umbilical cord, brushed off the street dirt mingled with caked blood and dried mucus, kissed the pathetic, wrinkled shape whose oversized head had the classic weeping visage of a fetus, and carefully slipped it back into the gory cavity that had been its brief home. He took off his waist sash and bound his wife's middle to cover the gaping would. He then had removed his waistcoat and covered as much of her nakedness as he could. He had kissed her cold forehead once again before he moved on.

He would never forget, never, tenderly gathering up his two-year-old son, Hovsep; his four-year-old son, Dikran; and his six-year-old daughter, Mariam, unable to do anything about them—their eyes . . . their eyes. He had cried uncontrollably, moaning and rocking, calling out each one's name, choking as his breath caught in his throat. The killer had apparently held the little children by their ankles and had dashed their heads against the stone base of the house, crushing the back of their skulls. The eyes had popped out . . . and . . . and . . . he couldn't fix them for fear of hurting them . . . even in death . . . oooh, God!

He would never forget kneeling beside his brother's body and working out the bayonets imbedded in the dirt through his body, the jostling suddenly causing a chattering moan from the corpse as some trapped air escaped through the larynx. He had grabbed the still-warm body, thinking Ardavast was alive, and held him close, calling his name. It had been utterly cruel for him.

He would never forget having to go to each of his sisters-in-law, all in their early twenties. He couldn't bury anyone in his family in the gross positions assumed in their death throes, either naturally or induced. He had pulled out and tossed as far as his strength could manage the deeply imbedded pokers from between their legs. Then, he had had to use the full weight of his body on two of them to overcome the rigor mortis and flatten out and bring together the suggestively positioned legs and thighs. The third one had no rigor mortis. He did not have anything handy to cover their nakedness at that point. He had hoped his brothers, wherever they were, would forgive him for having gained such intimate carnal knowledge of their wives . . .

He would never forget the new horror he had felt when he discovered that his little nieces, none of whom was more than eleven, had been used sexually before they had been brained. Caked blood blotched the whiteness between their childish thighs.

He would never forget the ultimate cruelty of all—spading dirt on the mangled, butchered, smashed, violated bodies of his family in the ragged hole he and his brother had dug.

And, he would never forget trotting back to the church to take the priest down from the unsightly dominance he had involuntarily assumed over the scene of his slaughtered flock. The uncontrollable defecation at the instant of strangulation, in dried rivulets on the backs of his legs, must have been the final indignity sought for the priest by his executioners. Mamigon had ripped off the gross adornment on Father Vasken's face and elsewhere before lowering the body to the ground and covering it with the priest's own robe, tossed nearby. He had found the donor of the ghastly nasal adornment, the priest's own wife, inside the church, stripped naked and propped up sitting on the altar facing the nave. Her blood had splattered everywhere. Her tormentors had spread her dangling legs where she sat, as if to welcome parishioners with her ugly, gaping mutilation.

He would never forget, never, those and a hundred other things he did and saw before he could get away from the village.

Tatios finally spoke: "What are you going to do?"

"He is going to die before the sun sets, my friend." His voice had certainty.

"Do you have a plan? May I be of help?"

"I am not certain of the outcome of this, Tatios. If you ride with me, it may well be to your death."

"I am prepared to die if I can take at least one Turk with me. I shall never forget their enjoyment as they axed to death those men and boys from my village."

They looked at one another. "We are going to die, but let us not die too easily, my skinny friend. We will ride to the head of the column. When we get there, you take the flank down your right and I will take the other flank. They are bad shots but watch out for their sword play, they are good at that."

They rode silently among the trees, going over the ridge to cover their movements, ignoring the shouts and pleas of some of the refugees who had gotten close enough to call them. Now was no time to be protective. Now was the time to die, taking as many of the enemy as possible with you.

Mamigon felt uncomfortable in the saddle. He had rarely ridden—only to see if the horse he had shod at his shop took well to the shoes he had fashioned and nailed on—and the damned saddle was not much more than a leather sheet with a small upsweep for his ass. He noticed that Tatios was at home on his horse, a big gray gelding. Tatios raised his hand and they stopped.

"I want to fix the stirrups on your horse, my large friend. They are too high and you are riding on your behind. If you keep that up you will not be able to walk or ride tomorrow . . . if there is a tomorrow."

Tatios had Mamigon dangle his legs and reset the buckles on the stirrups. "Stand in them more than sitting on the horse, eh?"

Mamigon checked out the new arrangement, nodded in satisfaction, and dismounted.

"Now is as good a time as any to get rid of some of this gear we have," he said. "If we die, we will not need it. If we live, we can come back for it."

They left everything they had stashed away under a large clump of bushes and piled some heavy rocks on top of the food supply to discourage animals. Both were now armed only with pistols and a scimitar—Tatios with two pistols, Mamigon with one and the big, curving sword.

They remounted and in another five minutes were ahead of the column of refugees, protected from view by the trees. Mamigon got off his horse and told Tatios to watch the horses while he moved up to see what the situation was. He left a reluctant Tatios and crept forward about 100 meters until he could see their target. The Turks had fallen back into line on both sides. A burial detail could be seen far back to the left, taking care of the men who had been killed. The diggers were being guarded from attack by about fifty men, all at the ready, scanning the tree line where Mamigon's fire had come from.

He crawled back to where Tatios was waiting. "Tallal is there, up front. Make sure you leave him to me when we ride out. You will know who he is, the one with the spike on his helmet." Mamigon was hefting his scimitar.

Tatios nodded, looking askance at Mamigon. "You do not look too calm. Do not do anything fancy . . . just kill him. I think a bullet would do nicely."

"A bullet is too clean, too quick for that misbegotten dog. He must know who kills him. Mount up, let us go, and may Allah be with you."

The two rode side by side to the tree line, then kicked their horses into a gallop, heading for the point of the column about 700 meters ahead. Mamigon rode with the scimitar pointing to the ground; Tatios rode with a pistol in each hand, guiding his horse with his knees and heels. As they galloped closer and into rifle range, the pair split gradually, Tatios angling to the right, Mamigon riding straight for the leader. Tallal saw them and drew his saber, pointing to the pair, shouting. Rifles began to pop, a sound that meant the targets were upwind. Tatios's big toothy grin was spread across his face now. Mamigon raised his scimitar over his head. The closer they rode the heavier the firing became as the Turks spurred up to reach the head of the column. Tallal was yelling "*Cha-book! Cha-book!*" waving his sword for his men to come quickly. The women were screaming.

Mamigon now began to yell: "Tallal, Tallal, you treacherous dog . . . Mamigon . . . Mamigon . . ." He was less than 10 meters now, his scimitar was almost back behind his right ear, set for the lethal swing.

As the two got close enough for contact, a bullet spanged into the scimitar, snapping it in two, 6 inches from the tip. Simultaneously, Tallal, who had not expected anything so fortuitous, rolled backward off his horse. He wasn't having any of the scimitar. As he rolled off, the Luger he had in his hand fired blindly. Mamigon's slash, with half a shortened blade went for naught, and he was immediately surrounded by three *polis* with drawn sabers. He hacked off the hand of one who had waited too long to bring his sword down, killed the next man with his revolver, and grunted in pain as the third man's saber caught him on his right hip. He tumbled from his horse.

Meanwhile, Tatios's blazing handguns were taking their toll, and the horsemen on his side of the column began to rein up their mounts to veer off from engagement with him. Tatios reined up also, wheeled his horse and rode directly through the intervening horde of women toward Mamigon, screaming "*pahtz, pahtz*" to make way for him.

He could see Mamigon now. The giant was standing with his back to his horse, a shortened scimitar in one hand, a pistol in the other, flailing away and firing. Tatios kicked his horse, which was trying to avoid stepping on bodies in the way, trying to get to Mamigon's side. He began firing as the way finally opened up, but it seemed as if every Turk in the march was now shooting at him. His horse went down. He grabbed a riderless horse, losing one of his pistols in the effort, threw one leg across the saddle and galloped straight for the timber line. He couldn't help Mamigon.

Mamigon snarled out baiting epithets at the Turks as he fought. He saw Tatios try to get to him, saw Tatios extricate himself from his hopeless spot, and . . . regained consciousness wondering where he was.

9 ✦ JOUSTING

Tatios rode hard for the trees as bullets zinged by. He heeled his horse up the slope, gained the cover of the woods, and stole a quick look back to see how many were in pursuit. None. All he could see was a clutch of uniforms in a tight circle where the big fellow was, and he couldn't see anything to indicate that the fight was still going on. So—his name was Mamigon. He shuddered when he recalled the roaring, bloodlust vengeance in Mamigon's voice letting Tallal know that the Turk's nemesis was riding down on him. Well, I told him, nothing fancy, use a gun, Tatios thought sadly. Now he had gone to his Maker. He wondered if Mamigon had taken Tallal with him. If the Turk wasn't dead, it would have to be the Turk's lucky day.

He pulled up his animal to a walk and finally stopped and dismounted to get a better look. The crowd around Mamigon's last stand was dispersing. Then his eyes grew wide and a grin lit up his face. It couldn't be, but it was—the big fellow was alive: you don't bother to tie the legs and hands of a dead man—which the Turks were doing.

Tatios was elated at first but only for a few moments. Alive, but for how long in the hands of his mortal enemies? He wondered why they hadn't killed him on the spot. What could they be saving him for? Tatios gave up all thought of riding off. He had to find out what was going on. One of the supply carts was brought up and Mamigon was dumped into it, head first, and the forced march of the women resumed.

Tatios didn't bother to mount, not at the pace the march was going. He walked along for a while until he noticed he had company. The women and children who had escaped from the march, and who had hidden among the trees and bushes when they heard him galloping into the woods on the ridge, were converging on him from everywhere. Tatios stopped.

"All right, everybody, keep your voices down and let us talk."

"Please, help us." An older woman, beshawled as all the women were, spoke.

"Help you? How can I help you? What can I do for you, *bahbahm*?"

"I know not, but you are the only armed Armenian man around, and we know not where we are or where we can go."

"Where were the Turks taking you?"

"From what we heard they were taking us to somewhere near Aleppo."

"How do you know that?"

"They did not try to hide their intentions. You can see they did not care whether we died on the way or not."

Tatios nodded. "But what can I do, where can I take you so that you will be safe? I know not where to go myself. Do you have any food?" As the import of his words sank in, many in the group, which had swelled to about three hundred, began to cry. Tatios cursed.

"All right, all right, let us stay together then, and perhaps God will smile on us. But place not too much faith in that. He seems to have forgotten us, for all our past devotions."

"That is blasphemy, young man, and I, for one, will not hear of it." The admonisher was a young woman.

"Blasphemy, eh? Where has He been these past few days? Tell me."

"He sent you and that other man, did He not?"

"Certainly He did, but for what good? You may all still die of thirst and starvation, only I will be with you, that is all He has done so far."

"May your mouth dry up." She was indignant. Tatios chuckled. Armenians were prissy clean when it came to swearwords. The men swore in Turkish, the most expressive and wondrous language when it came to profanities concerning one's progenitors and whatnot. But Armenians resorted to imprecations, curses, with simple directness, certainly not giving a thought to the consequences: May your mouth dry up. May your eyes see no light. May your ears crawl with ants. May your fingers stiffen into sticks. Tatios had always thought the Armenian curses were far more terrible than the Turkish profanities.

"No predictions, please. We may all have dry mouths before this is over. Our only hope is to get to the coast somewhere and leave our homeland. Does anyone have any better thought?"

"What about refuge in Russia?"

"Russia? I figure we are about 200 kilometers from Harpout and Harpout is about 350 kilometers from the Russian border. We are talking about wild, mountainous country heavily populated by Turks as well as Kurds. No, I do not think we would have much luck heading east for Russia. I think our best outlook is to head south through the mountains and find the sea west of Aleppo."

"Are you not Tatios, son of *Haji* Hagop?" It was the same woman who had talked back to him. "I think you left home six years ago to study at the university . . ."

"Why yes, who are you? Does anyone else remember me?" Tatios was smiling. It was good to be among friends. Several voices chimed recognition.

"I am Miss Eksah, sister of Bedros Drevanian. He went to . . ."

"My God! You are the sister of Bedros, who went to the university the same time I . . ."

"The same. He mentioned you many times in his letters from Paris. I remember when you left Gurin for school with Bedros. You had a mustache, then."

"Where is Bedros now?"

Her eyes suddenly welled with tears. "They took him away with all the other men and boys and . . ."

Tatios walked quickly over to her side and embraced her. "Say not any more. We cannot dwell on what has happened." Her tears had been a signal for remembrance, however, and the entire company was in tears.

"The Turks have my friend down there. Before we do anything about ourselves, I have to see about freeing him. He is in that *araba* with the light canvas cover. Until I come back, please stay together, and none of you go over the ridge top where you could be seen."

He hobbled his horse so it could graze among the sparse ground cover and went down the slope to the tree line. The convoy was almost past, with the eleven *arabas* in the rear. There wasn't much daylight left and Tatios went back for his horse to follow the column until it stopped for the night. He checked his pistol. He still had a full bandolier. If he could rescue Mamigon, he knew he would feel a lot better. Well, he would see about that. He spent nearly two hours looking for the arms cache and retrieved two more pistols. Then he waited half the night for the campfires to die down. The gendarmerie maintained their watch halfheartedly. At best, they had one antagonist, the horseman with two guns, and what could one man do against an army of 400? The big man rumored to have killed so many Turks was tied up like a sheep, so they had nothing to fear.

Tatios crawled around until he came as close as he could to the *araba* that contained Mamigon. The oxen drawing the carts had been loosed to graze. The carts were drawn up alongside each other in a line, behind the women but within the circle of sentries. Tatios counted only four guards along the entire rear of the column. But a fifth guard was sitting on the tailboard of the cart containing Mamigon, the third vehicle from the nearest end. The guard had propped himself against a corner of the cart, his legs drawn up, his rifle across his lap, and he seemed to be dozing, if not asleep.

There was no moon, for which Tatios was thankful. Now, all he had to do was creep through the sentries, eliminate the guard on the cart, free Mamigon, and crawl out to freedom. Hah!

He crawled back until he thought it safe to stand up and ran back to the trees, up the slope. He found the women, all wide-awake, knowing that Tatios was going to try something.

"Where is Eksah?"

"Here."

"I need your help, but it will be dangerous for you."

"I will help." He couldn't see her face, other than an outline, in the dark, but her voice was reassuringly calm, he thought.

"Come with me then, and I will tell you what to do. For the rest of you, pass the word. Whatever sounds or alarms you hear, do not move away or try to find out what is happening. If I succeed, I shall be back before dawn.

If I fail, you will know by sunup and do your best to get to the seacoast to the south."

Tatios and Eksah crossed back over the ridge and went down into the valley, Tatios giving her instructions as they went along. They stopped at the tree line and she gave Tatios's arm a squeeze as he left her, heading for the camp.

When he got close enough, he crouched down and moved carefully on all fours. He counted continuously as he went. Now! Just as he counted to fifty, a shot rang out from the direction he had come. Good girl, he thought.

Instantly, the sentries crouched low, scanning the direction of the muzzle flash. Another shot, and everybody, soldiers and civilians, began watching and waiting for something to happen. It was too dark to see anything, and Tatios crawled between two sentries standing about 40 meters apart and made the cover of the nearest cart. Mamigon's cart was easy to get to. Tatios realized that the guard was now on his feet, standing about an arm's length from the back of the cart, staring into the darkness, like all the rest. He belted his pistol, drew his knife, clenched it with his teeth, and crawled into the *araba* from the front end. He groped about until he felt Mamigon's head and whispered his own name. A grunt was his reply. Tatios moved closer, found the bound hands and cut the ropes. He did the same with the fetters at the feet and quietly rubbed Mamigon's wrists to bring back the circulation. Mamigon said he had been hit on the head and was in a lot of pain. His hands must be black by now, he guessed. Tatios continued the rubbing for several minutes until Mamigon signaled that it was enough.

"Those motherless whelps have not given me water. I am desperate for water."

"We will get you some once we are out of here."

Tatios handed him a pistol, and Mamigon whispered that he wanted the knife. Tatios handed it over and Mamigon patted him on the shoulders, saying: "All right, you go now. I will stay here."

"What?" The exclamation was almost shouted.

"Quiet. You go now, Tatios. You have done well."

"Do not be a fool, Mamigon." It was the first time Tatios had used the big fellow's name. "There will be some more shots soon and it will give us a chance to get away from here."

"You are wasting time, and even your life."

"I am not going without you."

"Look, Tatios, when they look in here and see two of us, we will both be shish kebab. You will be robbing me of my only chance to get close to Tallal. Leave my bow and rifle where I left them on the ridge and go, in the name of your father!"

Tatios pondered the man's words, gave the blacksmith a strong handclasp and slipped out the front of the cart, just as new shots echoed from the ridge.

Mamigon, armed now with a knife and pistol, sighed and reflected on his situation. He heard hoofbeats racing up from the van and knew that Tallal would certainly be coming to investigate the state of his captivity. He heard

Tallal shout and assumed his former position just in time. The guard stuck his head into the dark *araba*, felt the prisoner's legs, and shouted out that the prisoner was still there. A ragged volley of rifle fire punctuated the night; then a long cheer arose from the soldiers. They must have shot Tatios. Tallal ordered the guard tripled, and quiet descended on the scene. Mamigon knew that Tallal's decision not to kill him right away meant that something special in the way of death was being planned for him. He felt he would have a chance to kill Tallal if the Turks were caught by surprise. He took his pistol and shoved it into the band at the small of his back. With a piece of cloth from his torn shirt he tied the knife to the inside of his bare thigh, with the handle stuck up under his testicles. He would have to wait and see if the Turks were as devout Sunni Moslems, the orthodox group, as he was counting on them to be. Oofah, his left hip was throbbing. The man who hit him with his saber in the fight had knocked him off his horse with the blow. It was accidental. The swordsman had slashed downward and missed Mamigon, but had swung the heavy weapon back to parry the expected riposte from Mamigon—which never came—and hit Mamigon's hip with the back of the saber. Mamigon thought his hip was broken, but he couldn't tell because the pain and feeling was not something he had experienced before. But, he really needed water, water . . .

He must have fallen asleep because the next thing he knew rude hands were pushing and shoving him, and light filled the little cart. Two men dragged him out and stood him up between them, in front of Tallal, who was sitting on his horse. The black Arabian stallion pawed at the sod which, in early September, was dry under the hot sun. Mamigon stared steadily into Tallal's face, the latter averting any eye contact.

"They untied him but could not rescue him, sir," one of them said.

"I did not want to be rescued." Mamigon said it deliberately in a loud voice, which cracked from lack of water. It brought a roar of laughter from the troops; at least 200 of them had formed a wide circle ready for the fun Tallal must have promised.

"I did not want to leave you gallant, brave soldiers because your leader was the man who killed my parents, my brothers, my children, and molested my wife before he killed her." More laughing approval greeted Mamigon's words. Moslem warriors were perfectly free to kill infidels or *giavours*, as non-Moslems are called, in any way they chose. It was the Law of Retaliation, the addendum to the Koran.

"That begger you call your pasha broke bread at my table and ate my salt. He is my brother!" An instant hush settled over the jostling, jesting troops.

"And the mother of my children, who had fed him many times and who had called him 'brother,' became the object, first of his lust and then of his knife." The silence was heavy. A true Moslem would not, could not, visit harm on a person at whose table he had broken bread and eaten salt. And he could never violate a woman once she had called him her brother. It was so written in the Koran. What was this *giavour* saying?

Tallal suddenly spurred his horse and slammed the heel of his boot into

Mamigon's face. Mamigon rolled back, grabbing the proffered boot with both hands and dragged Tallal off his passing horse. Tallal, Mamigon, and the two men who thought they were holding their prisoner, all fell in a tangled heap.

The soldiers closest to the melee quickly sorted out the pile and pulled Mamigon back under restraint. Any army lieutenant, the *yarbay* in command of the smaller unit of horse soldiers, spoke up.

"Your words are meant to delay your death, *giavour Ermeni*."

"My words are not empty. I saved the life of that cowardly son of a dog whelped on a dung heap. He is not fit to lead you."

"You infidel eater of pig testicles, I will hang you slowly, tear out your lying tongue and use your filthy carcass for target practice as you die from a thousand wounds." Tallal had spoken for the first time. He was feeling the tension around him and did not like the way things were getting out of hand. He felt uncomfortable, too, not being on his horse where he felt much stronger.

"You have no choice but to kill me right now. You know I can prove what I say."

"Proof? What proof could you possibly have, infidel?" The *yarbay* was not to be denied. He liked the fancy uniform Tallal was wearing. If Tallal could be discredited . . .

Mamigon looked directly into the eyes of the lieutenant. "I saved that miserable excuse of a man from the tusks of a boar. The back of his right hand was badly torn. I saved his hand, but it is deeply scarred. If he removes his riding gauntlet you will see three badly mended folds of skin and flesh. At the right corner, near his little finger, you will see this." Mamigon shook himself loose from the men holding his arms and drew a letter in a patch of brown earth.

Only a slight breeze rustling the cart covers disturbed the silence as everyone looked at Tallal. The men in the back strained to see and hear. The *yarbay* was getting nervous. What had started out as a good way of baiting the hated infidel had turned into something he did not feel he could handle without risk to his future in the army. How was he going to get the glove off Tallal's hand? He looked at the huge Armenian who seemed to be favoring his left leg, or was it his hip? The man was obviously hurt. It gave him an idea.

"Tell us, infidel dog, what is it that you scratched in the dirt?"

"It is the initial to my name." The tension broke again as everyone within earshot broke out in laughter again.

"Ha, hah. You branded your brother before you bound his wounds? Har, ha . . ."

"My dead wife's hand branded him." Deep silence again. Listening to this *giavour* was better than sitting around a fire listening to a traveling storyteller.

"I used my neck scarf to bind him. There were seven of us brothers before you killed five of them. Our wives embroidered our initials on the scarves to tell them apart in the wash. When I bound his hand, the embroidered part pressed into the raw flesh, and his hand healed with the letter cleanly marked forever on his hand. Show the hand, if you dare, you pigdog. It will match the figure in the dirt."

"Wait, wait," the *yarbay* said, waving his arms. "I have a way to settle this, if Tallal Bey will agree."

Tallal squared his shoulders and looked around him. The peasant faces of the young *polis* and soldiers looked eager, anticipatory. Pestering women on the trail was getting to be routine. This situation was something they could talk about later.

"Let me hear what you have in mind, lieutenant." Tallal was sure he was going to kill this upstart *yarbay* "accidentally" at the next opportunity.

"Why do you not challenge this big infidel oaf to take the glove off your hand, if he can?"

Tallal thought it over a second or two. "We cannot arm him."

Mamigon acted reluctant. "I do not see that I should provide more entertainment for you. Kill me and get it over with. I have told you what kind of a man you are following. I have nothing more to say or do."

"Shut your mouth, infidel. This concerns the business of our Lord Mohammed and what He has written. You have become a tool for the strengthening of our will to serve Him. If what you say is true, we will let you go . . . . after we make sure you will never be able to fight against us."

Mamigon smiled. He would be as good as dead under those unstated circumstances, but he wasn't dead yet. "I cannot play this game without rules. Would you have that dung heap completely armed? Kill me now, I will not filthy my hands on that maggot. I am dying of thirst, anyway."

Tallal lit one of his flat cigarettes. He too had noticed that the Armenian limped. Guns were out of the question. He was too good a shot. Swords and knives were doubtful; the man was good with them. He was too big to consider wrestling . . . "Give him some water." He would show the men he was a man of compassion.

"What about a fire tug?" The *yarbay* had provided the answer. It was a popular one as the men roared their approval.

Tallal nodded his consent. Mamigon nodded in understanding. The lieutenant had noticed his hip, too. So, it was going to be two legs against one, eh?

"Light up the fire right here," the lieutenant shouted, pointing to the middle of what had become the arena of confrontation. A sergeant snapped out orders and several squads left to collect kindling and tree limbs.

Mamigon had heard tell of a fire tug but he had never put much faith in the tales. It was a simple trial of strength. The gladiators were placed equidistant from the fire and, on signal, one tried to pull the other into the fire. They had to stay within a 4-meter alley drawn in the dirt, leading to the fire. There were no other rules.

"We need a rope about 20 meters long, *cha-book!*" The lieutenant acted like a young boy in his enthusiasm. Everyone seemed happy. Everyone except Tallal Bey, Mamigon thought. He wondered if the pistol stuck in his band under his loose overshirt would be discovered. His estimation of the

Sunni Moslem regard for the precepts and teachings of the Prophet Mohammed had proved correct. But he had not known where it would lead, and now that he had a glimmer, he wasn't too sure he shouldn't have escaped in the darkness with Tatios. He noticed that the captive women had not decamped. With most of the escort around the carts preparing for the fire tug, the hundred or so militia left to guard the women would have been hard put to prevent wholesale escapes. So, everything was at a standstill, awaiting the outcome of the fire tug.

A roaring bonfire was started and everyone stood around waiting for the flames to die down. Mamigon's two guards began chatting with each other. Tallal stood slightly off from his men, on the opposite side of the fire from Mamigon. The Armenian took a half step toward the fire, seemingly wrapped in deep thought. He tried to hunker down in front of the burning wood but his hip screamed in pain. He stepped closer to the fire. His guards were not a step beyond.

Tallal was half turned away from the fire, his arms folded, his eyes almost slits, barely visible in the sunlight.

All of a sudden, a family of field mice, unable to stand the growing heat that had radiated down to their subterranean cave, began streaming out of a hole almost at the base of the fire. Mamigon scrambled rapidly forward, drawing an instant round of laughter from those who saw him, as he pawed madly at the ground among the scattering mice.

The laughter stopped short as Mamigon suddenly hurtled himself beyond the fire at Tallal's rooted figure. Tallal did not move fast enough. Mamigon first grabbed the hem of the Turk's tunic, then yanked him closer to seize Tallal by the throat.

Both men toppled to the ground, the Turk's throat in a vicious grip that would break his windpipe and strangle him. Tallal flailed about wildly. Mamigon was snarling like a lion, his pent-up fury unleashed at last.

It was over in a second. A rifle butt slammed a glancing blow off the attacker's head, knocking him senseless.

When Mamigon came to with a buzzing head, the fire had reached the ember stage and he had been dragged back to his side of the fire. Not a word was said to him as a long rope was produced and each man was tied to an end by his left wrist. Tallal still had his gauntlets on, apparently not the worse from the attack.

The rope was wet down to prevent it from igniting over the fire and the two were positioned for the contest. Then, the lieutenant fired his pistol to start the contest.

Both men pulled back simultaneously. The three-strand rope became so taut water squirted from it.

The two men eyed each other, taking tentative tugs on the rope. Mamigon, standing slightly sideways toward his right, used only his tied hand. Tallal stood squarely, using his right hand to bolster his tied hand. It was easy to see that Mamigon was standing that way to favor his left leg. He couldn't afford to put any weight on it. He knew it. Tallal knew it. Everyone could see it.

Tallal gave a mighty heave on the rope, rocking back on his heels as he did.

Mamigon counted by slipping half way down on his right side and digging in with the side of his right foot. Only his extra weight saved him from being toppled immediately.

Tallal leaped erect, using the rope to pull him up, and gave Mamigon sudden slack.

Mamigon crashed to the ground. Knowing the rope would tighten immediately, he flexed his arm for the jolt from Tallal and used the Turk's hard pull to get back up on his feet. He almost screamed in pain when he put part of his weight on his left leg and something moved in his hip.

Tallal quickly turned his back on Mamigon, and, with the rope over his left shoulder, leaned forward and hauled as if he were pulling a wagon.

Mamigon ran toward the fire, hopping mostly on one leg.

Tallal sprawled on his face with the sudden slack.

Mamigon reeled in the slack swiftly, running back as he did, and gave a heavy jerk on the line.

Tallal, scrambling to his feet, trying to regain his balance, fell face forward toward the fire, his tied arm strung out as if pointing the way.

Mamigon kept the rope taut, slowly pulling Tallal toward the fire, now only a couple of meters away. The rope was so close to the embers it began to steam.

Tallal made one desperate move to bring his feet under him. It was his undoing. His drawn-up legs brought him closer and he fell on his chest directly on the fire. Immediately, his tunic began to smolder and his cry of fear echoed from the hills.

Mamigon limped to the smoking figure, which had rolled off the embers, grabbed the right hand and pulled off the glove. As if the body attached to the hand was so much trash, Mamigon dragged up the arm at the wrist and held Tallal's hand outward at his eye level as he slowly turned to show off the back of the hand. Tallal offered no resistance. The terms of the fire tug could not be ignored.

The troops had gathered close when Tallal landed in the fire, but gave up any thought of interfering when the fallen man rolled off the coals and Mamigon had grabbed the right hand.

There was no question about it. The back of Tallal's hand was exactly as Mamigon had described it.

A hush blanketed the onlookers as the need to see and listen rippled to the rear ranks. Mamigon had planted his bad foot on Tallal's back and simply stood where he was, waiting for the reaction.

"He spoke the truth." The lieutenant made his words loud and accusatory.

"Let the *giavour* go!" someone in the ranks shouted.

"He has paid enough!" another voice yelled. That seemed to be the consensus as the words were repeated in ragged chorus.

It seemed to be a period of indecision for the *yarbay* who was, at the moment, the psychological leader of the police and militia.

Mamigon stepped back from Tallal's prone figure, gritting his teeth as he realized that he had had Tallal in his grasp and had found it impossible to harm the Turk. All eyes had been on him, and he knew that at least one man among the several hundred watching would have been quick enough to dispatch him before he could find his pistol or knife to finish Tallal. It was still a good day for Mamigon—he was still alive, a condition he did not think he would be experiencing for too long into the day. He had been right. You couldn't trust a Turk's mental processes except in matters concerning what he feared or understood through his religion. They were awesomely courageous; they were expert riders; they were devastating with swords and knives; they were extremely protective of their families; and they had a rigid sense of right and wrong as dictated by the Koran. Mamigon knew of a Turkish family that had, in mutual agreement with another family, killed a daughter while the other had killed a son because the two young people had secretly fallen in love and had had intercourse. The sin of sins. Their pleas that they wanted to marry had had no bearing on their fate. The Holy Book had written the penalty for such an act. Mamigon knew he was going to touch a sensitive chord among the troops because the Koran was clear about the obligation of a man to protect a woman who called him brother.

Mamigon had studied the Koran, sura by sura, when he was at the academy. The Holy Book had helped bring order out of a land beset by chaos over the centuries. The Koran was also the main reason there was such a schism between Moslems and those they called nonbelievers. Nonbelievers were infidels, of course, because the teachings of the Prophet Mohammed were absolute gospel and could not be denied. Moslems did not place the teachings of Noah, Abraham, Moses and Christ at the level of Mohammed; the first four were all great prophets, as far as the Moslems were concerned, but certainly not to follow when one had the Prophet Mohammed. Christians and Hebrews were simply misguided and should be converted to Islam, by the sword if necessary, for their own good.

Mamigon's train of thought was interrupted by the insistent voice of the lieutenant, pressing Tallal. "What are we going to do with the prisoner? We agreed to let him go if what he said turned out to be true."

"True or not, we cannot let him go, lieutenant."

"I realize that the promise was made to an infidel, but as true men of Islam we have no choice but to keep our word."

"Lieutenant," Tallal said with emphasis on the title to remind his listener who he was, "lieutenant, we have no choice in the matter. Our prisoner is someone special. The government wants him."

"Someone special? What do you mean?"

Tallal looked uncomfortable. "The man has a price on his head and I am going to deliver him to the first military district we reach, I think Marash."

"A . . . a price? How much?"

"A thousand *lira*."

"When did you know about this?"

"I learned about it in Sivas."

"We have eaten the dung! Why did not you say anything about it?"

"Lieutenant, I do not like the way you are talking to me. The fact is, this *giavour* was not a part of our existence until he attacked us. Now, you know. What difference does it make?"

For answer, the lieutenant turned quickly to his top sergeant, the *bash chowoosh*. "Have the men fall in for parade." A chain of shouted orders brought both units into two groups, facing each other, 20 meters apart, with the *polis* unit in triple depth. Tallal and the lieutenant were in the center. Mamigon was two steps away, guarded by two *polis*.

Tallal was shaking his head, looking at the lieutenant. "I do not know why I am allowing all of this to happen, but go ahead, tell the men what you have in mind. But, remember, I am still your commanding officer."

"Temporarily, for the duration of this trek, you are, sir. Those are my orders, but I expect to take other action once we complete this mission. Now, I am going to address the men." He squared his stance and barked out his words. "The prisoner, who brought disgrace to our commanding officer, is a wanted man, an outlaw. The government has a thousand *lira* reward for him—dead or alive?" He looked to Tallal for confirmation of this aspect and Tallal nodded. "We told the prisoner that if he defeated the *emniyet muduru* and proved his charges, we would let him go. Our word as followers of Islam seems to be tested by the demands of the government. Since we were not told by the police chief until now that the government wanted this man, we do not seem to be bound by what we promised the prisoner. The police chief and I want you to know the reason we are not letting the prisoner go as we had promised. Sergeant, are there any questions?"

The *bash chowoosh* stepped off two steps, turned around and faced the army unit, listened to one of the men, and then addressed the lieutenant. "The men feel the infidel accounted for himself with courage. They want to know what it is that he has done that has placed him outside the law."

The lieutenant looked to Tallal.

"Men, the captive attacked my *polis* troop while it was in peaceful performance of its duties. He has been leading a band of rebels and more than a dozen of my men have fallen to his bullets and arrows."

He answered the troops' next question with less enthusiasm. "I had not given any thought to the reward money. I believe all of you should share in it. That means that if we split up the thousand *liras* by 400, that would mean about 250 *piasters* apiece. That is nearly three months pay, men."

The troops broke out with a roar of approval. Tallal wondered what the reaction would have been if they had known he was holding back four thousand *liras*. Mamigon was trussed up again and pushed into the *araba*. The mood of the entire company changed as the men were dismissed to take up the march again to the south.

The cart began to move and Mamigon tried to get some sleep. For some reason, his hip was not throbbing much and he felt some ease in his lower frame. He wondered if he had done something to help the hip in that last straining moment when he had applied his full weight to his left side by error.

His drowsy thoughts turned to Tatios. From everything he had heard, there was no doubt about it, Tatios was dead. He wondered who had fired those shots from the trees. He had hoped Tatios would get away—he was a great man . . . The whole world was going mad, and he was in the middle of the madness, a madness he could not have envisioned a few weeks ago in the peace of his little village . . . Someone was coming, riding up to the cart and talking to the driver. The driver was told to pull the cart over to the side when they stopped at noon, and to stay and guard the prisoner.

Mamigon's hands were swollen again from the tightness of the cords, and he knew that trying to hold his pistol would be useless. He wouldn't be able to slip his index finger, which was big to begin with, into the trigger guard. He would have to wait his chance, but he knew that time was against him now. His knife was still where he had secreted it. It was chafing him badly and he didn't think he could get to it, the way he was trussed up, but it was worth a try.

Mamigon's wrists were tied behind his back but that was all. His arms had not been tied to his body. He rolled over on his stomach and pulled at his shirt flap to move it up above his belt. He found the butt of the pistol and managed, after several awkward tugs with his still fingers, to pull it out and let it drop to his side. He barely had feeling in his fingers. He sucked in his stomach to make room for his hands under the belt. Once he worked his hands under the belt, he forced them down over his buttocks and rolled over on his side, the belt now straining tightly across his abdomen and his sides. His hands, one totally useless from being tied across the other at the wrists, reached below his crotch now, and he searched feebly for the twisted cloth rope he had fashioned to hold the knife. He found it, pressed his middle fingers into his thigh, hooked them to the cloth and gave it a strong jerk. The cloth rope parted but not until the pressure had dug the tip of the knife into his flesh, causing it to bleed.

Mamigon pulled his arms out and took a few breaths to regain his strength. Balancing himself in the swaying cart, he got up on his knees to allow the knife to fall inside his breeches. Then he watched the driver, whose back covered most of the opening in front. The driver would have to move aside on his seat and bend his head to look into the cart, something he had not done more than once as far as Mamigon could tell. Mamigon knew that if he tried to stand up enough to let the knife fall through his pants leg, he risked being detected by the driver. He decided to take the chance even though a sudden lurch of the cart might throw him against the sides and make enough noise to give him away.

He stood up, bent over at the hips because of the limited head room, and the knife slipped down and clattered on the cart bed.

Mamigon dropped instantly to the floor as the driver moved aside to look in. He was the boy with the wart on his face.

"Cannot you miss some of those holes, you misbegotten son of a scabrous trollop?" Mamigon snarled. The driver laughed enthusiastically.

"You do not remember me, do you? I am the one you let go after I buried the girl. Oh, my mother's soup, you are going to get yours, you oversized pile of dogshit."

"I remember you, now. Your name is Enver, the man who pisses in his pants. Well, I suppose Tallal is going to kill me in some fancy way?"

"Not for you, you poor infidel bastard . . ."

"Oh, I know, you are going to cut off my nose and my ears . . ."

"Hah, hah, you only wish."

"Oh? My genitals, then? That is nothing unusual."

The driver, who had been turning his head as he talked but had not tried to look back, now bent around and looked in.

"At noon today, when we stop, we are going to do just one thing to you." He grinned broadly, anticipating the impact of what he was about to say. "We are going to snip the tendons of the heel on both your feet!"

Mamigon groaned loudly for the benefit of the driver. Enver loved the reaction, and he broke out into a lively Turkish tune as he drove the oxen.

If the Turks managed to do that to him, Mamigon knew he would be dead in short order. A human can't walk with his feet dangling from the calfbone. He had seen a man once who had one foot like that. He had a string from his big toe to his ankle to keep the foot from dragging while he used a cane to get around. With both feet in that predicament, mobility would be practically nil.

He searched around behind him, found the knife, and managed to work his hands around it, the palm of one hand pressing the flat of the blade against the back of his other hand. He tried to work it so that the blade would slip upright into one of the seams in the cart bed. After many trials, he succeeded and the blade disappeared up to the handle. With great difficulty, he brought his body up over the knife handle, felt the handle with his hands, and settled down on it, positioning his hands so that the cords around his wrists would be over the blade when he pushed the handle flat. He had to make sure the blade didn't come all the way out of the crack. It didn't. Calling up all his strength as he kept his body bridged up by his drawn up legs, he sawed on the blade until one cord parted. No blood came from his wrist. His hands were free. He settled to his side and carefully worked the cords loose. Then he brought his arms around in front, sighing in relief at the movement, though they began to throb and hurt as the blood began to circulate. In another five minutes he could move his fingers; in ten minutes he had some feeling back; in twenty minutes he was able to pick up the pistol and put it back in his belt, in front. He retrieved the knife from the crack and held the weapon, a good six inches of blade, sharpened on both edges.

He looked out the back. He had at least an hour. He looked at the back of the driver, who was still singing, and cautiously peeked around the edge of the cart cover in back. There were no riders bringing up the rear. Army wagons or carts were usually the last units in the column. There were no camp followers in this type of activity—the troops were having all the fun they needed with their charges. The situation proved to be exactly what Mamigon needed. Looking back down the trail, he could see three bodies dotting the passage of the column.

Mamigon didn't wait another second. He slipped off the tailboard of the *araba* and lay still on the ground, his knife under him. He held his breath. Not a sound, no alarm, yet. He waited . . . and waited. Enver's tune didn't miss a note as it faded into the distance. The stridulous sound of the cart wheels receded. He didn't move a hair. Nothing. He knew he had to wait. If any of the hundreds of eyes up ahead glanced back as he stood up and tried to get away, it would be all over. As the sun beat down on his prone body, flies began buzzing around, and a big beetle that had escaped being crushed by all those feet up ahead, crawled up his arm and disappeared in a rent in his sleeve. He didn't move despite a terrible urge to get up and run. He wondered when they would stop for the noon meal. That's when the search would start. No question about it.

After ten minutes that seemed to be hours, he raised his head enough to look. The carts were almost out of sight. He would wait another five minutes and begin crawling to the trees up the slope to his right, about 100 meters away. He waited until the tops of the carts disappeared and began his crawl. It took him a good ten minutes to do it, but he reached the first tree. He stood up and realized for the first time that he had not been bothered by his hip as he crawled. Now there was only a twinge of pain and he could walk with a slight limp. What had been the matter? he wondered. Could it have been that his hipbone had slipped out of its socket and then had popped back? But he wasn't going to question his good fortune. He began his trek back to the place where he hoped to retrieve his equipment. It seemed like a generation since he had shed the stuff to ride with Tatios into the head of the column to challenge Tallal. Now Tallal was gone again and he was certain the man would be heading back eventually to Yosghat, where he came from. And where Mamigon came from.

Would it be a good plan simply to go back to his home country and wait for him? It would be dangerous, and the outcome would certainly be doubtful. But what else could he do? Why was he, Mamigon, alive while everyone in his family except Aram was dead? He surely had made a fool out of Tallal in front of all those men. That wasn't enough, though, not for a wife and three little children, not for a father and a mother, not for five brothers and sisters-in-law, not enough for thirteen nephews and nieces, and not enough for the whole village. He would have to pay with his life.

Without realizing it, Mamigon's pace had quickened as he thought about Tallal, and he gained new inspiration. Yes, he would wait for the bastard in Yosghat, or anywhere else necessary, to exact payment, small that it would be.

Mamigon had been traveling for at least twenty minutes, staying high in the tree line, when he heard them. Horsemen, apparently on both sides of the valley, weaving their way through the trees. They had their swords out and were literally beating the bushes for him. Not wasting a moment, he found a big spruce with a heavy outgrowth of needles and climbed up into it as far as he could. The climb was not what his left hip needed at this time, and it protested with added pain. Mamigon settled himself and waited with drawn pistol.

The riders came, looking around almost casually, beat a few outgrowths with the flat of their swords, and moved on. Mamigon stayed where he was until he saw them return to the column an hour later, about a hundred of them. They had probably come to the conclusion that he wouldn't get very far—unarmed, without food, and with a bad leg. He decided to stay in the tree until dusk before he moved again. No sense taking any more chances at this time. Later, he would find his cached belongings, if they were still there, and head north again. He did not know that every army post, every police station, every public building had a poster seeking his apprehension, dead or alive, for 5,000 *liras* or pounds Turkish.

10 &SAFETY

When Tatios slipped out of the cart, he headed away from the spot where Eksah was firing the pistol. The soldiers would be looking in that direction. He crawled diagonally until he was sure he had cleared the line where the sentries had stood and then began the long, careful traverse on his hands and knees to get back to the trees. In the distance he could see a dark area where the men gathered, their numbers swelling with new arrivals who had been disturbed from their sleep. Tatios's knees began to feel the stones and roughness of the earth as his trousers, meant for sedate city wear, became threadbare. He had only about ten more meters to go when . . . BANG . . . his pistol fired. The gun had eased slowly out of his belt as he crawled along the ground. When it hit the ground, the safety must have been off and, somehow, the hammer hit the cartridge.

Tatios wasn't hit, but the flash gave at least 25 riflemen a target in the blackness, and the volley was deafening. They ran for the target, now carrying a torch, and found him, his face covered with blood, blood spilling from his mouth.

"We got him! We killed the other one!" A couple of the militia gave the body a few hard kicks, and the men walked quietly back to the camp.

"He sure could ride," someone said. The body was left to rot or be eaten.

Higher up, at the tree line, Eksah stood with an arm around a tree trunk to steady herself. She couldn't imagine what had happened. The darkness that had concealed Tatios's and presumably Mamigon's movements as they crawled to safety from the Turks had hidden the two from her eyes as well. Then, after the fusillade of shots aimed at the source of the gunshot less than ten meters from her, Tatios's form became dimly discernible in the torch light, and she saw the soldiers kick his body and then leave.

She gasped at the sight. So, Tatios Effendi was dead and who knows what happened to the big fellow? She couldn't see another body. Strangely enough, she wasn't overcome with any great sense of grief, just a touch of sadness. She had witnessed too much to allow a simple death of a person she hardly knew to disturb her composure. He was a fine man, though . . .

She stuck the pistol she had been firing, as the diversion planned by Tatios, into her waistband and made her way back to the rest of her companions.

"They both died." It was simple and direct. There was only a slight murmur from the gathering. "There is no use staying here for them to find us. Let us let Tatios Effendi's horse lead the way for us in the darkness. It is best we get as far away as possible from here. I will keep the pistol, even though it only has one pellet in it. Let us go."

The sun was well past its meridian when a careful look at Tatios's crumpled form would have revealed that it wasn't exactly still. The arms made feeble attempts at movement. Then a groan came, weak, but a groan. The body moved again two hours later with a louder groan. Tatios got his hands to his head. It was splitting with pain. He felt a leathery stiffness on his face. It was dried blood, thick and hard. He raised himself by his arms and collapsed immediately, unconscious again. About an hour later he stirred again. Without trying to get up, he felt his face and head. One of his touches made him wince. There seemed to be a long, deep gash across his skull as if his hair had been parted perfectly almost on the center line. There was another one just over his right ear. He took stock of himself. There didn't seem to be any other wounds. His mouth felt rancid and full of curds. Dried blood. The skull wounds had bled instantly and freely when he had been hit. He had fallen with his face in a perfect position for his open mouth to accept some of the massive flow. And he didn't know it, but that accidental blood flow had saved his life. The blood had flowed into his open mouth, pooled in his inner cheek, and poured out. The torch-bearing Turks had seen massive head wounds and a sure sign of a mortal wound—blood seeping heavily from the mouth. He couldn't understand why his ribs were killing him on one side. But he was alive and the valley was strangely silent. He could see the remains of a big fire near the spot where the carts had been. He wasn't even sure of the time span . . . but he was alive . . . and alone. The combination of pain in his head and his ribs was not bad enough to cause him to vomit, but he almost did when he discovered that he was spitting out flies that had crawled into his mouth as he lay unconscious. The flies had also saved him from closer scrutiny. The Turks had come back looking for Mamigon just after the noon hour and had seen the flies covering his face and crawling in and out of his mouth, feeding on the best protein on earth, blood.

He stayed the rest of the daylight hours flat on his back, to compensate for the pain in his head. What in the name of the Four Horsemen was he going to do? He felt too weak to sit up, much less stand up. He had no food, no weapons, nothing. The women must have given him up for dead. They might have at least checked . . . Camel dung! They probably didn't have a chance. Despite growing hunger and thirst, he fell off into a fitful sleep and didn't open his eyes again until the night wore into day. He was now ravenous as well as thirsty, but he felt a lot stronger. He turned over on his belly, drew up his knees and slowly gained his feet, swaying, as he headed for the trees for support, about ten meters away. He reached a tree, hung to it as the world tilted and yawed about him, and sat down again. He realized he must have a concussion and nothing would help that except total physical quiet and rest. He had a small grin working as he thought over his predicament. He knew he should stay sedentary for at least two or three days but that he would probably die of thirst if he stuck to that plan. As it was, he had little choice, unless he wanted to stumble around and fall and hurt himself. The body repairs itself to some extent, and he fell into a daze, sitting against the tree at whose base he had slipped.

Tatios had been the cock-o'-the-walk in Constantinople before the Turks destroyed his world. He was a newspaper editor and was renowned for his voice as the leading deacon and choir director at the Armenian cathedral, chanting the ancient liturgical music in a powerful tenor, weakening the knees of many a lass. He sported a broad, flowing mustache, wore vested suits and spats on his shoes, and carried a silver-knobbed cane. He was a fine solo dancer. Along with his older brother Harootune, he had graduated from the Sorbonne in Paris, spoke seven languages fluently, and was able to write and read in fourteen, including Sanskrit. Now a scarecrow covered with blood, his mind wandered. He argued in French with his brother about the wording of a story. He pleaded with his mother in Armenian for more cold *tahn*. He sang a naughty off-key ditty in Turkish about a belly dancer. He pleaded again for more *tahn*, cool and wet. He exhorted the gods in Greek to let his horse win the race. He shouted in Arabic the QED to a geometric formula. He sobbed for plain ice water if the *tahn* was not ready yet. He whimpered at the loss of his *bella* Katarina in Italian. He smiled with his eyes closed and called out for Sophia . . . and jerked awake.

"Hey. What are you doing here all alone?"

"Eh?" Tatios made out a blurred shape, a shape that had shaken his shoulder.

"I say, what are you doing here? Who are you?"

"Eh? *Como* . . .?"

"Speak up, man—what's the matter with you? You're covered with blood."

"I cannot dance, my darling Sophia. I do not feel well . . ."

"For God's sake, my good fellow, snap to it. Are you Italian?" Tatios had muttered his response in that language.

"Ah, the Italians . . . the greatest people on earth . . ." His chin dropped to his chest and he slid to his left side, unconscious again.

The man trying to get an intelligible response from Tatios looked entirely out of place. Well over six feet tall, with a sandy, cropped mustache and matching hair, he was dressed in western clothes consisting of knee-high polished boots, a tweed jacket, a white shirt and black four-in-hand, topped by a tweed cap. Harry Sears was beginning to regret his impulse to see who was singing in the minor key with such abandon up there in the trees. The song that had caught his attention was sung in Turkish but now the man spoke Italian. Well, he could at least make the poor devil comfortable before he left, he thought.

He examined Tatios's head carefully and decided the best he could do for him was to clean the wounds. He went to his mule, which he had tied to a tree, rummaged through his saddle packs and produced a large medical bag. He doused a piece of gauze with water from his canteen and began cleaning up the caked blood to see what the damage was. There were two creases, one on the top exposing a bit of skull, another on the side, just a deep scratch. The fellow was lucky, he thought. Just a fraction more and he would certainly have been dead. He must be suffering from a concussion. While the man was unconscious, he stitched the deep scalp wound together to cover the area where the skull was exposed.

Harry Sears wasn't the cursing kind, but he was irritated. What could he do about this man, leave him? He had to be on his way, he was late, and now this . . . He covered his patient with the big slicker he carried on the mule and settled down next to him. Building a small fire, he boiled some rice to eat with his jerked beef. He shouldn't have stopped, he kept telling himself, but every time he looked at the sleeping man, he knew he had no choice. He had seen too much death lately and should have been inured to such things, he told himself, but the hell of it was that it would have been hell for him not to do what was right. Both men slept through the night.

"Hello? Who are you? Water, water." This time, it was Harry Sears who was awakened with several nudges. My God, the man was a Turk. He was speaking in Turkish.

"Well, hello. I see you are better. I don't speak Turkish. I am an American."

"*Parlez-vous Français? Donnez moi d'eau potable . . .*"

"*En peu, monsieur. Je parle l'Anglais et Ermenli . . .*"

"You speak Armenian! I am Armenian. Please, a drink of water."

"Good, good. At least we can understand each other. Tell me, who are you and what are you doing in the wilderness in this condition?" He talked as Tatios gulped water from his canteen.

"It is a long story but I am curious about you. You first spoke to me in English and I think you mentioned American. Are you?" In Armenian the question came out "You American are?"

"Yes, I'm an American. My name is Harry Sears. I've been in Turkey for the last four years as a medical aide at the American Mission in Van." Sears ended his words with expectant nods. He wasn't disappointed.

"The Americans in Van! You have been operating a hospital and a school there for years. I wrote about the mission for the French newspapers only last year! Why Miss Knapp and Mrs. Raynolds are veritable angels . . ." He began to gasp, his face paled, and he fell back exhausted from his excitement.

Sears wondered who he could be. He wrote about the mission for the French press? "Take your ease, man, take your ease. We shall talk when you are feeling better."

When Tatios came to—after falling into another stupor which lasted five hours—Sears had some soft rice for him and a broth from some beef he had boiled. The ingestion of food made him drowsy and Tatios fell asleep again, not awakening until the next morning. After another bowl of broth, they talked.

Harry Sears left the mission in Van, which had been defended by a thousand Armenian men, after the Turks had laid siege to it with 5,000 troops and artillery. The siege was lifted at the approach of a Russian brigade. Sears, who had been told to report to the American station in Aleppo, had decided to follow orders, even though everyone in Van left for the Russian border, including the Americans.

"Were Miss Knapp and Mrs. Raynolds safe?"

"Yes, the last I know. Mrs. Raynolds came down with a severe case of dysentery, but she was able to leave in one of the carts."

"Is Aleppo still in Turkish hands?"

"As far as I know. There's a German hospital and mission there like the one we operated in Van. I'm supposed to see what help I can give any of the missions there. It's been reported that a tremendous number of Armenian exiles are being funneled through Aleppo."

Tatios shook his head. "I cannot believe what is going on. I do not want to hear any more. We are being eliminated as a people."

"I can't say you are wrong about that, but what I can't seem to understand is why. Do you have any ideas?"

"Mr. Sears—All right, I will call you Harry—Harry, when the Ottomans took us over, we were classed as *rayah* or cattle. For centuries the Moslems encouraged the Armenians to form communities of their own. We became *Millets*, which first meant unshackled herds but has now come to mean religious sects.

"It is really interesting what happens to a conquered people when the conqueror says, in our instance, look, I am giving you religious, cultural, and social autonomy . . . but stay away from politics and political expression. You will have no say in how this country is run."

"That doesn't sound too bad a situation for a conquered people and I hope you don't take offense, Tatios."

"Of course not, Harry. Sultan Mohammed II chartered the Armenian *Millet* in 1462; the Armenian Catholic *Millet* was chartered in 1830, and the *Millet* of Armenian Protestants was chartered in 1840, when your American group came over to Van . . ."

"Excuse me, Tatios. Where did you go to school?"

"I studied at that French nuthouse they call the Sorbonne. I can handle seven languages pretty well and I can read fourteen altogether, but, as you can see, I cannot speak English. I know not what made me think I would not need it."

"What religion are you?"

"I am an Armenian, a member of the Armenian Apostolic Church of St. Gregory the Illuminator. Incidentally, I would like to ask you a question. What makes you Protestants think that the Armenians needed to be converted? Here we are, a truly original group, conducting services so steeped in the original that our liturgical music sounds like the Hebraic fabric from which Christianity sprung. Then, lo and behold, a new religious sect that broke off in the protest from the Roman Church comes over to this ancient land to convert us. Convert us to what, may I ask?"

Sears had begun to laugh halfway through the declamation, shaking his head. "Every time I talk to an Armenian who knows anything at all, he asks me the same question, although you have posed it the best. Frankly, I don't know why, except that when one believes strongly that his own religion is the true road to salvation and ultimate grace, then one may be excused if he wants to spread the good word to all mankind so that mankind may be saved. Does that sound too pompous?"

"I wager you have not found the Armenians eager to change."

"You're right, Tatios. You have always had a certain tenacity about your religion. I think it has been your salvation as a people, living in an area where for centuries crisscrossing armies have devastated and obliterated entire civilizations in a matter of days. But we've digressed . . ."

"Where was I . . . Oh, yes, the most important question is whether the Armenians ever sought sovereignty or independence or other forms of political separatism. The key is that no portion of the Ottoman Empire was exclusively inhabited by the Armenians. They were, literally, everywhere, in every province; and nowhere were they even in an absolute majority."

Sears felt as if he were back at Harvard in Professor Lowell's course in European History II. "What happened?"

"What happened was that Abdul Hamid came to the throne when General Grant was your president. Sultan Hamid singled out the Armenians after Turkey sued for peace with the Russians in 1878. Once all the foreigners were gone and interest in Turkish affairs from the outside diminished, Hamid resurrected and encouraged a fierce Moslem minority, the Kurds, to do what they wished with their Armenian neighbors.

"We were butchered in 1894 as a starter. Turkish regulars, joined by Hamidie Kurds, massacred the men, women, and children in Sassoun and Moush, then Trebizond and then in all the principal towns of the empire, including Constantinople.

"To show you how wrong Sultan Hamid was about the attitude of the Armenians toward their homeland and the government, consider what happened when Hamid was thrown out in 1908 by the Young Turk Revolution.

"They threw themselves into the service of the new regime, convinced that the new government would institute reforms and make the country a stable place.

"It was all camel dung. Even after the terrible massacres at Adana less than a year after the new constitution was proclaimed, the Armenians— we're really trusting people, Harry—showed their continued loyalty to the government by serving in the army with such valor on the Balkan Front that they were publicly commended.

"But, all of a sudden, after the Gallipoli victory, the Turkish government contended that the Armenians had suddenly reversed and shifted their loyalties and were now treacherously plotting for the destruction of the Ottoman Empire. That's about the whole story as I know it . . ."

Sears nodded. He wished he could have such a talk with a Turkish scholar to see if there was another side to this story. "What about you? What are we going to do about you now?"

"You have taken care of me, Harry. I think I can manage now. I must find my way to the coast and see if I can leave this godforsaken land."

"You can travel with me for as long as you want. I don't have too much food or water but we can share it."

"That's very kind of you, Harry, but I would only delay you even more."

"Don't be proud. I am going to Aleppo to help people just such as you. You are coming with me. Old Tom can carry us both."

It was still morning when the two set off. Sears estimated they were about 60 miles from Aleppo; Tatios said it was about 100 kilometers. They made some rapid calculations and agreed they were both right, give or take a few miles or a few kilometers. They knew they were somewhere near Aintab, the big Armenian city Sears was heading for when he discovered Tatios.

"With you along, I think we can't go near the city," Sears said. "If the country is being ravaged the way it seems to be, Aintab is probably no place for anyone to be right now. What do you think?"

"I think you are right. But these mountains make it tough to travel. It would be easier for you to go there and take the high road to Aleppo. The road joins the railroad track east of Killis. You ought to let me off somewhere soon and make your own way. If you give me a knife, I think I can fend for myself, once I get rid of this sickening headache . . ."

"No, no, I'm taking you with me. If I had some extra clothes I could have passed you off as one of us, but I don't and you look like exactly what you are, a fugitive from the Turks." They both laughed. But their laughter was cut short. Up ahead, on the narrow path in the defile they were riding appeared the head of a column of soldiers, horse soldiers.

"Quick! They cannot see me behind you," Tatios said. "Sidle the mule to those big rocks and I will get off and hide."

Sears angled the mule to the rocks, and Tatios slipped off and disappeared. The American continued riding without a break and raised his right hand in response to a similar gesture from the Turkish lead. Sears produced a big leather folder from his jacket and showed a safe conduct pass which all Americans had been issued by the vilayet when hostilities had broken out between Turkey and the Entente.

The officer looked over the papers carefully, looked up and down at Sears.

"*Amerikanlu?*"

"*Avet, Amerikanlu. Ben Turkjeh hayir khonooshmam, bey.*" Sears used the only Turkish he knew to say he couldn't speak the language.

The Turk grinned at his accent, shook his head, and gestured to Sears to fall in with the company.

Sears, smiling, shook his head. "Aleppo, *bey,* Aleppo," and he indicated he would be going on in that direction.

The officer shook his head emphatically and, grabbing the mule's reins, dragged Sears behind him beside the next horseman, to whom he handed the reins. He was giving Sears no choice. They rode past the spot where Tatios was hiding and disappeared around a bend.

Tatios settled down in a cranny and promptly fell asleep—his damaged head insisted on it. It was dark when he arose and set off without ado down the path. There was nothing to delay him—no food, no water, no tools or weapons to help him get food or defend himself. He almost felt like running, but his head wasn't on right yet. He walked for six hours until the first glimmer of light from the east appeared, then found a likely spot in the rocks to sit out the daylight again. The going was getting a little easier as the terrain began to give way to the foothills and the desert beyond. He didn't know how long he could last without food and water. He was suffering from lack of both. He took one last look at the brown, barren countryside and closed his eyes. At least he could sleep.

He slept. The wind from the south soughed up and swept the heat of the day across the land.

He slept. A long, black snake slithered up to his sleeping form, decided it was too big to eat, and retreated.

He slept. The sun turned bright orange, its color filtering through the humidity of a distant sky, and sank into the brown umber of the land.

He awoke to total darkness and had to rub his eyes to make certain they were open. His need for water became immediately apparent as his leathery tongue stuck to his palate. He stood up, shakily, and began his walk. The stars appeared.

"I'm not going to give up. Not this old boy," he muttered. He had to get out of this predicament and tell the world what was going on here. He'd write articles for all of the world's leading newspapers, in their own languages. But he had to have water.

Tatios stumbled along in the dark, keeping on the roadway by finding the wheel ruts to guide him. A pair of gray wolves trailed him but kept their distance. They were older and had learned that these two-legged creatures could be lethal. The wolves gave up toward dawn and ambled off.

Tatios found another spot in the growing light among the rocks where he would spend the day. There wouldn't be much shade but, at least, he wouldn't be exerting himself in the heat. He slept, fitfully. When the sun's rays crept over his inert form, he finally awoke and crawled to another shaded spot. The noonday sun deprived him of all shade, finally. He staggered to his feet and continued his trek.

Sunset found him on his hands and knees, crawling, crawling, slumping down on his face, up his hands and knees again, crawling.

"I'm going to get out of this alive . . . alive. This is no way to die. Got to find water." He crawled on. It was the second day since Sears left him. He was still on the road to Aleppo and that was all he was certain of.

As the light began to fade—it faded quickly in desert lands—he noticed a stand of trees, no more than four of them. Trees! Trees meant a water source . . . there must be water.

Tatios lifted himself to his feet and almost ran toward the outgrowth. All he could find was a depression centered roughly among the cypresses that indicated that water might have collected there during the spring.

· He found a large stone and threw it with what little strength he had against a boulder. He had to throw it four times before the stone shattered. One piece was broken with a flat face and a sharp edge.

He got on his knees in the middle of the 3-meter wide depression and dug into the claylike ground. He dug a deeper and deeper hole with a widening parameter for nearly an exhausting hour before the earth became damp.

Tatios stretched out for half the night and dozed off before he could continue. The stars provided him enough light to see what he was doing. Another 15 centimeters and the earth became slushy. He dug frantically now, the excitement of finding water giving him new strength.

He tore off the lower part of his shirt and scooped some of the mud into it. He bundled up the goo, held it over his upturned mouth and squeezed it. Water, muddy brown and gritty, trickled into his mouth. He repeated the trick over and over again, careless of the grit, aware only of the wetness that slaked his tongue, his palate, and his throat. He fell asleep, totally exhausted by his digging efforts.

It was a couple of hours past daybreak when he was awakened by the chattering of two chipmunks reveling at the brink of the water hole he had created.

During the night the hole had filled up halfway with water, the scent attracting the chipmunks.

Tatios rolled over onto his belly and stuck his face into the half-meter wide pool he had created and drank his fill of the slightly brackish liquid. His wasted innards gave it up almost immediately. The pain of heaving was almost unbearable. He felt as if he was heaving up his very guts. He fell asleep again.

When he awoke, it was a family of field mice running around and over his arm near the pool that brought him to. This time, he drank less copiously, a few sips at intervals. The water stayed down.

When darkness came, he had to make a serious decision: stay near his precious water or go on. He was feeling much better even though the lack of food was sapping him by the hour.

"One more night and day here, old boy. One more night and day. That ought to take care of my water level for a few more days." He had nothing with which to carry water.

His body was so desiccated, it wasn't until the following evening, toward nightfall when he was ready to continue his walk, that his body passed a trickle of urine—deep orange, almost brown.

He took one last, long drink, forcing himself to fill up; used the piece of shirt to swab his head and body with the cooling water; wet the piece of cloth one final time to drape over his head; and set off.

The following morning, staggering, stumbling and crawling, he emerged

from the rocks to the desert. It was the Der-el-Zor, a true desert with no
foliage or growth of any kind. Its only inhabitants were roving Bedouin
Arabs, people who were not hostile to the Armenians in the sense of the
Turks or Kurds, but were not so friendly that they would share any of their
food and water with the wandering exiles who were dying by the thousands
on the hot sands and rocks from thirst and starvation. The Bedouins were
not cruel, just practical. They were extremely poor, and the food and water
they had was barely enough for their own sustenance. Self-preservation was
imperative. The desert was unforgiving.

Tatios had already approached two passing bands of Arabs, begging for
food and water. There was no response, hardly a look. He was totally spent
as he sat at the base of a towering heave of rock in the simmering heat of the
day, waiting for nightfall and to start walking again, when a band of horsemen and camel riders came around one end of the rocky ledge, so close to
Tatios he could see the expressions on the faces. It looked like a family of
Bedouins, a very large family, with the men riding Arabian horses and the
veiled women in their palanquins atop patient dromedaries, at least twenty
of them. They were thumping slowly along the sand, making swishing
sounds. Everyone in the train was in black from head to foot. Black goat-
hair tents, neatly folded, made up most of the burdens on the camels. Tent
poles, bags of grain for man and animal, and goatskin bags of water completed the 250-kilo loads each dromedary carried. The men were heavily
bearded and had long sabers protruding from beneath their black cloaks.
Children cavorted and ran and played along the way, despite the intense
heat.

The Armenian raised his hand as the leader passed by and observed in
Arabic that "it was a nice day for a ride in the countryside."

The Bedouin was startled enough to break into a wide smile. Whenever
he came upon one of these starving, dying infidels they would end up on
their hands and knees begging for water or a piece of bread. He waved at the
scarecrow with the thick bushy head of hair. Tatios gave him another wave
of farewell as he patted the head of a little girl who had approached him to
stare into his dried up, peeling face. The group was barely past Tatios when
the leader halted the little caravan. The stranger intrigued him. He wanted
to see if the man was out of his mind. If he were, fine—nothing of interest
about someone suffering from sunstroke and he would leave him be. If he
had his senses, then he might be worth talking to. He rode back to the
still-seated Tatios, who didn't get up.

"If you are looking for directions from me, forget it. I'm lost, too."

The Bedouin roared with laughter. He hadn't encountered such audacity
in his whole life.

"And, if you seek bread and water from me, forget that, too. I'm fresh out
and expect not to have any more for some time."

"Who are you?" the Arab asked after he stopped laughing again. This
man might be an infidel—he probably was—but he had a wonderful sense
of humor for a man who looked as if he wouldn't last the day. His voice was
croaking like the rusty hinge on his treasure box.

Tatios tottered to his feet. "I am Tatios Effendi, late of Constantinople and definitely late for dinner, at your service, noble lord of the desert."

The Arab had his own sense of the humorous for certain because even this feeble attempt by the Armenian made him chuckle as he waved toward the caravan, beckoning the adult men over to hear what was going on.

"Aside from being late for dinner, what are you doing here, my friend?"

"Thank you, *effendi*, for calling me friend. I am here, as I usually am once a year, to catch the train for Aleppo."

"But there are no tracks, my friend, and I begin to think you are suffering from the sun."

"I certainly am. It was very unkind of you, *effendi*, to bring up the matter of the tracks. I had hoped the missing tracks were merely a figment of my addled imagination. Now you confirm it, much to my sorrow. Incidentally, if you have any extra water, I . . ."

"Stop. I was hoping you were a cut above the others. I am . . ."

"Let me finish what I was about to say, oh man of no faith. I was to tell you that if you have any water to spare you should wet some cloth and wrap them around your steed's pasterns. I see some inflammation there, and that magnificent animal will be down before the day is out unless you do what I say."

The Bedouin stared at him for a moment. He swung off of his steel-gray stallion and crouched at its forelegs, carefully inspecting them. While he was in this position, Tatios walked over and, with his hand held palm up below the level of the animal's nose, spoke softly in Arabic. The horse nickered softly. Tatios put his hand on the side of its head and patted it. The stallion almost pushed its master over as it stepped forward and nuzzled the Armenian. Arabian horses are never friendly with anyone except their immediate masters. No one can get close to them, not even members of the family. The Bedouin was now in a state of shock. Not only was the stranger right about the pasterns being inflamed but he had never in his life seen one of his horses be friendly to anyone, much less a total stranger. The Bedouin stood up to look more closely at the stranger. Tatios understood his bewilderment.

"It is all right. You have not been stricken by the sun, also, *effendi*. You should know this about your horse. I have not had food or water for three days and I have the smell of the sands and rocks and the smell of death. Your horse understands."

"How do you know so much about my horse? Just who are you . . . *effendi*?"

"I told you. I wait for the train to Aleppo, but I also have raised these fine animals that live in your tents with you. I love them like I would a brother."

"Enough, enough. You must come with us even though I suspect you are an infidel with that name. Do you think you could miss your train just this once?"

"I think you are going the wrong way, *effendi*. I am bound for Aleppo and the coast."

"One thousand pardons, wise one, but I should say to you something that is not courteous. Can a begger choose?"

"Ah, the verities of life. One is confronted with them at every turn, especially in the desert."

"Our Lord Mohammed has written, 'Who can bear a wounded spirit?' I am cheered and pleased to have met you. Please, will you be good enough to share some of our water and bread, eh?"

Tatios had to be lifted onto the back of a horse after he tasted some water. He traveled with Abdoul ben Samir and his family for three days, heading south, before he learned that they were heading toward Damascus. Tatios was seated on carpeting and pillows in Abdoul's big tent after a meal of couscous, sipping acidy, thick coffee served to him and Abdoul and his three brothers by a veiled daughter.

"Damascus . . . I am sure you are not city dwellers?"

"No, we are not." Abdoul stared at Tatios, pondering whether he should say more. The Armenian broke the silence.

"I know about Jemal Pasha, the Turkish governor in Damascus. We heard in Constantinople how he would hang Arabs believed to be plotters before breakfast every morning . . . and he would have the Emir Feisal, son of the Sherif of Mecca, watch the hangings every time."

"Feisal is my cousin."

"Hhmm . . . Something is brewing, eh?" Tatios saw a blankness fall on Abdoul's face again. "I am not prying, Ben Samir. I know just a little about all of this. I was writing daily reports for the French press in Constantinople. I know the Turks do not fully trust the Sherif Hussein."

"He is my uncle, Feisal's father. Feisal was forced to watch a few weeks ago when Jemal Pasha hanged my twelve-year-old brother Zeid who was caught carrying a message meant for me."

"Twelve years old! Those godforsaken . . ."

"My little brother was not heavy . . . and he took too long to strangle on the gibbet . . ." Abdoul's voice was low and intense with control. "Jemal Pasha became impatient—Zeid's slowness to die was delaying his breakfast—so he signaled to have his neck snapped. They did it by yanking hard at his feet."

The silence was heavy. Men could accept most reports of cruelty but rarely those visited on women, children, and animals, all considered defenseless and even more to the point perhaps, all who expected or were supposed to be protected by men.

"You cannot trust anyone too much, I know that, Abdoul. Not in these times when brothers thought to be united by the Holy Book become strangers and strangers could be enemies. I am at a disadvantage here among you. I am as many men as the languages I speak. So you may ask, which one is he, truly?

"It took three days for you to talk about these things to me. Perhaps I have shown some signs that I am who I say I am . . . and not an agent of Jemal Pasha or Enver Pasha or Fakhri Pasha. Yes, I speak Turkish and Arabic and Greek and Italian and Farsi and Hebrew and Assyrian and

German and French, but my mother tongue is Armenian, I am a *High*, and you have seen my brothers and sisters die by the thousands on your sands, victims of our masters, the Turk. What more can I say or do to convince you? I looked very much the victim when you found me. Now that you have given me my life and I look more like a man instead of a picked-over bag of bones you seem to trust me less."

Abdoul smiled. "We will talk again tomorrow, Tatios Effendi. Sleep well tonight, my friend."

Tatios had no idea when it happened that night. In the total darkness of the tent he shared with four tethered colts newly separated from their mares, he awoke to gentle caresses to his private parts and long hair covering his face, almost stifling him. His grunt didn't stop the caresses but removed the head from his face.

"My name is Jamalla . . . take me." The words were whispered in heavily accented Arabic, the breath spiced with a sickly smell of cumin and pepper.

Tatios knew enough about the people he was traveling with to know the woman couldn't be anyone in the family group. "Who are you? What are you doing in my tent?"

"I am Jamalla, a slave of the Ben Samir family . . . bought by them when I was a girl. I am Kurdish . . . Take me . . ."

"How did you get in here?"

"The *hanum* sent me . . . stop talking . . . take me!"

Hospitality covered every aspect of life in the Arab world. So, Abdoul's wife had sent her! Tatios grinned in the darkness. The nocturnal offering could just as easily have been a boy. Oh well, it was all for naught. Jamalla must be very young and very inexperienced or she would not be so insistent, he thought. His ravaged body had not recovered enough to react to anything carnal and he . . . His grunt was a surprise reaction to something she did and . . . She wasn't inexperienced at all. . . .

He joined the four brothers at the campfire at dawn for a breakfast of goat cheese and *pideh* while the women busied themselves taking down the tents and packing the animals. The men were grinning at him and Tatios felt a little sheepish. Then he realized that somehow they had decided to accept him for who he said he was.

"Our tribes are gathering from all over, *effendi,* for something big."

"Against the Turks?"

"The word is out. We are members of the Fetah and we are . . ."

"The Fetah?"

"It is what we call the secret organization for us Bedouins in the Syrian Desert. We await the signal to rise against the Turks."

"Is it going to come from Damascus?"

Abdoul looked at him, appraising every line of the prematurely lined face of the Armenian. "Yes. The Emir Feisal will give the word as soon as he can slip out. He is watched day and night by Jemal Pasha's men . . . but he will get out soon to lead us."

"What can I do to help? Can I join you?"

"You told us you were trying to get to Aleppo in search of your sisters."

"That is true, I still want to but I think I am hopelessly out of reach."

Abdoul pondered the statement. "Our horses would not let you sit on them. You cannot ride a camel . . . and we cannot spare one . . . you cannot walk 50 kilometers in this heat . . ."

"Fifty kilometers! Is that how far away we are from Aleppo?"

"Yes, my friend, perhaps 45 to 50."

"Then, I would like to try, Abdoul."

The Bedouin was shaking his head, slowly. "The desert will kill you. You know not how to recognize direction once the sun comes up. I do not recommend it, my friend."

"If you give me three pieces of bread and six mouthfuls of water, I can do it. Please give me that chance."

"It is your life, *effendi*. I do not wish to be a party to your death but if that is your wish, it is my command. I will certainly help you."

They shook hands and suddenly embraced. "I am not as helpless as you think I am about directions, Abdoul. I will travel by night and use the stars to guide me. I have studied the heavens and I can keep true direction."

"Good, good. I will have the women prepare a sack of food for you." He called to a group of four women who stopped loading the animals to open some large goatskin bags and remove unleavened bread, cheese, a piece of halvah, and filled a purse-sized bag with water. Abdoul spoke again and Tatios was fitted out with a burnoose and a flowing black robe.

Without further ado, he made his farewells and headed westward, leaving a friendship that would be remembered the rest of their lives.

Six hours after he left his friends, a Turkish patrol on horseback stopped him, decided he was a Bedouin, all right, but a Bedouin thief because of his barely recognizable European style shoes. They took his food and water, kicked him in the groin and left him to die. Tatios sat where he was until nightfall before he took up his walk, food or no food, water or no water—he had no choice.

Three days later, without seeing another soul and almost back in the same condition he was when he entered the desert, he decided to give up. He was exhausted, hungry, thirsty, and not quite sure where he was because the sun was so high most of the day. By the time the sun set and he had turned to follow the stars, he knew he had wandered again. He kept seeing mirages and had tossed aside his robe. When he saw an oasis with the walled house, he was certain it was just another mirage. But it turned out to be real. He didn't know he was only 20 kilometers from Aleppo.

He made several attempts to attract someone's attention at the high gate. The inhabitants apparently chose to ignore his pounding, so he began shouting in his cracked, feeble voice as he hammered. The back of his shirt was torn, and the sun had created a giant, festering blister. He weighed less than a hundred pounds, and, with his filthy, matted beard and sunken eye sockets, he looked like a wild man. Literally starving to death, he continued making a racket for several hours, until it was finally opened by a female servant carrying a long cudgel.

She said in Arabic, "Get away from here, you filthy dog. Stop disturbing my master's house."

"Please, in the name of Allah, a piece of bread and some water." He had croaked the plea in Arabic, too.

"We cannot feed every shiftless beggar who comes to the door. Go away."

"I beg of you, one morsel, or some water." Then he added softly, in Armenian, "You cold-hearted harlot."

"What was THAT? What did you call me?" She had raised the stick, ready to strike his cowering figure. She stopped short. "*Aman!* You must be Armenian."

Tatios hesitated to answer since Armenians were given, literally, "the bum's rush" in their fugitive, desperate straits. Then he said something that his father always had said in Turkish if things were in doubt: "It is cloudy today."

The woman screamed with several "*amans*" as she strained for a better look at the tattered, ragged figure before her, then slumped to the ground in a dead faint.

Tatios didn't know what to do at this point so he just sat down beside the sprawled form and waited. In the old country, you never touched a strange woman.

"Tah . . . Tatios?" He stiffened in surprise when he heard his name. She had opened her eyes and was looking at him.

"How, how do you know my name?" he said in Armenian.

"Are you not Tatios, son of *Haji* Hagop?" She was sitting up now, holding his reluctant arm. "I am your sister Ahrussyag."

"AH . . . RUSS . . . YAG!" He couldn't resist the weak roar of recognition, rasping out his older sister's name and embracing her. He remembered later he was so dehydrated there were no tears, but his sister made up for both of them. It had been six years since they had seen each other, and both had been through too much to be recognizable to anyone they had known previously.

Ahrussyag was the cook in the Arab household. She had to leave her brother outside the wall of her master's house, but she fed him and restored his health until he was well enough to travel. Then they both left.

11 CHASE

Mamigon found it extremely difficult to move around freely in the four days after his escape. Turkish military units and the *polis* were everywhere—on the roads and byways, in the towns and villages—everywhere that Mamigon went on his way north. Tallal would be heading north, eventually, to Yosghat and home. At least, that's what Mamigon was counting on. And, he figured Tallal would get there ahead of him, because he would have a horse to make up for the added distance he would be traveling. But there was little chance that he would stay put in Yosghat in these times. Mamigon knew he had to get to Yosghat quickly or possibly lose Tallal once and for all. No telling where the Turk would go once the story of his deed with Mamigon got around and his fellow Moslems began to reject him. Those damned Turks were extremely unforgiving in certain instances. Cutting off hands for stealing a piece of bread or cutting off heads for having illicit carnal knowledge of a proper woman were commonly accepted practices.

Mamigon had collected his meager cache of arms, the bag of gold trinkets, and food (which he found crawling with ants), but he had no horse. He missed his scimitar. He was using his system of running and walking to make up time. He really hadn't invented the system. He had heard a traveling storyteller relate how an Armenian general in the distant past had confounded his enemy by appearing suddenly when the best intelligence had indicated that the general and his army were too far away to be a threat. The general had used the system of run-walk-run.

He was walking and running on what were little better than goat paths over the Amanus range just south of Marash, a city which had more than 100,000 Armenians out of a total population of more than 450,000. He desperately wanted to go through the city, but he was certain the Turks would not only be there in military force but were probably visiting some ungodly horrors on the Armenians. He didn't want to be caught up in that.

The route he was taking would bring him close to that village of Yerebakan. He toyed with the idea of stopping by just to see how the community had fared after he left. Well, he wouldn't plan on it. He had little hope that Baron Dikrahnian or anyone else would be there now, or even alive.

After all the company he had collected going south and then back, he realized he missed Aram and Tatios sometimes. That Tatios was quite a man, but he was too sentimental. That sentimentality had been his undoing. His memories brought up Araxy and the thought that struck him, surprised him: He wondered how many of those poor souls who had been raped repeatedly were pregnant now, if they were alive. Kill the thought, Mamigon. You are becoming depraved and ignoble in your thinking.

The quick change from light to darkness in the mountains almost caught him without a place to hole up for the night. It was too dangerous to walk the steep paths he was on in the dark. He was in luck. Just a short climb to his right, among the rubble of rocks, was what looked like a cave. If it wasn't housing some kind of animal, it would be a good place to spend the night. He slung the Mauser over his one shoulder, the bow and quiver were on the other, and clambered easily to the opening. He peered in, saw nothing; sniffed deeply, smelled nothing that might have indicated the presence of a bear or other mountain denizen; and heaved himself over the ledge and into the opening. He looked around and realized it was a nappe, creating a deep fissure between two crags. But it would provide excellent cover for the night.

Mamigon settled down with his back against the wall, near the opening, and pulled out the cheese, still containing an army of ants. It didn't bother him—he brushed off as many as he could, crossed himself, and chomped into the now brittle stuff. At least the water in his canteen was fresh. The weather was beginning to get cold as fall approached, but he decided not to worry about it. What will be, will be, *kismet*. He sighed and stretched his legs out, marveling at the way his hip seemed to have mended except that he couldn't swing it all the way when he walked or ran, making him limp. No pain, though. Tomorrow the path should be more downhill and . . .

"Get out of here or I will kill you."

Mamigon didn't move a muscle; didn't turn his head toward the treble voice of a boy coming from the back in the total darkness.

"I said, get out of here." The voice had become a bit more shrill.

"Let me share this place with you, boy." He said it softly.

"I want no one here, now get out. I am telling you for the last time." The voice was no longer shrill.

"All right, I will go, boy . . . If you are hungry I will leave you some cheese . . ."

"Just get out . . ."

Mamigon slid over the edge, turned over on his belly, holding his gear in one hand, and groped his way through the darkness to what seemed to be a safe spot. It was just below the opening, but he wasn't going to try to find another place and risk falling. He'd move in the first light.

First light didn't awaken him, however. A shower of gravel did, swept off the lip of the cave above as the occupant attempted to slide over and down. Mamigon was instantly on the alert, wondering what had touched him. It was still too dark to see much, but he didn't have to: a foot descended on his hand, a groping foot that finally settled on his right shoulder. Then the other foot came down; there was a gasp of fear as both feet slid down his chest, and Mamigon found himself holding a small body to prevent him from falling backward.

"Hello." It seemed like the only thing to say.

"Let me go. You were waiting for me . . ."

"I was sleeping on this ledge, thanks to you. Where did you think I could go in the dark?"

"All right, let me go . . ."

Mamigon saw that the path about 2 meters below was now visible and it looked safe enough. He let the boy go. He dropped with a small yelp, his hands pawing Mamigon for a handhold, and crashed on his back. "You told me to let you go, boy."

He was no more than a stripling. He was wearing boots up to his knees, loose britches and loose shirtwaist, and a tight scarf wrapped around his head. The face was not fully developed but there was something about his eyes . . .

"What were you going to kill me with?" Mamigon asked as the boy got up and brushed off, obviously empty-handed.

"I could not trust you wild mountain men so I tricked you, that is all."

"You have quite a bit of tongue for a little whelp. What are you doing up here? Are you alone?"

"Keep to your own business. I have nothing of value so you cannot rob me and I have to be on my way."

"I happen to know you are about 25 kilometers and a good five hours from anywhere, that is why I asked. Are you alone?"

"You would like to know . . . hah . . . so you can murder me and sell my clothes."

"You would not have been in that cave all by yourself if you had had friends along. You are either lost or insane; those are the only two reasons I know anyone your age would be in this wilderness without food, water, and weapons."

"You are wrong, and I am tired of talking." With that, the boy strode off down the trail Mamigon was planning to take. He sat where he was long enough to chew on a piece of dry beef and a couple of chomps of cheese washed down with a nip of water, and he was off himself. He started off each morning with the walking phase for 2 kilometers, shifting to the run after he warmed up. He was about to gear up for the run when a heavy rock bounced off his skull, sending him sprawling to the gravelly path on his face. He wasn't knocked out, only momentarily stunned. He didn't know if his head was cut, but it was beginning to ache and throb. He lay still as the footsteps approached. He lay still when they stopped next to him. He lay still when hands groped for his backpack. When the weight of the pack was gone from his back, he knew the rock thrower would have both hands occupied. He turned on to his side and grabbed the legs, pulling them out from under the body above him. At once, there was a thud, a howl of fear, and a cry of recognition, the latter from Mamigon.

"Are you trying to kill me, boy?"

"I had to do something. You were following me."

"Cow dung! I happen to be going in the same direction you are." He was really irritated at the boy's incursions into his life. First, he had been robbed of a night's sleep and now, a bump on his head.

The boy was aware of a sharpness in Mamigon's voice, which had not been in his previous words. For another thing, the man had sounded reasonable all along. Maybe . . .

"I am sorry, mister, I guess I have been wrong about you. Please do not hurt me and I will never bother you again."

"Not so quick, young man. First, you must answer some questions. What are you doing out here?" They looked at each other as they lay on the path, the man on his side, the boy on his rump, his ankles held.

"I am . . . I am . . . It is none of your business."

"I am making it my business. I do not want to have to keep looking over my shoulder later wondering what fool thing you will do next."

"I do not have to tell you a thing. Now let me go or I will . . ."

"You will do nothing. I have a mind to paddle your smart ass and knock some sense into you. Now, answer me . . ." He yanked at his ankles.

"Stop. I have run away from home. I am on my way to Fekke where one of my older brothers lives. I am very hungry and thirsty . . ."

Mamigon recognized a small ring of truth in the boy's voice—not a lot, but enough to let go of his ankles, sit up, and rummage through his backpack. "Why did not you accept the cheese I offered you last night?"

"I had no idea who you might be. You know how men . . ." He stopped short. "You do not know who anyone is in these mountains."

"Here, eat up. The ants are all right to eat but you can brush them off. I will cut a piece of this beef for you. Eat slowly and do not take water for a while. I am going in the direction of Fekke [it was close to Yerebaken] and we will be company for a while. What is your name?"

"Sadi . . . Sadi, what is yours?"

"You are Turkish, boy?"

"Yes. My father is a poppy grower near Killis. What is your name, mister?"

"Ergun, son of Gokden of Yosghat."

"I have never met such a big man as you. What do you do?"

"I'm on a special job for the *vali* of Yosghat."

"I could tell you were somebody special in the daylight, but I couldn't take a chance. For all I knew, you might have been someone my father had sent after me."

"Why have you run away from home? How old are you?"

"I am . . . fifteen. I cannot tell you why I have run away."

"Have you done something outside the law?"

"Oh, no, nothing like that. It is just a big problem with my father and mother, that is all."

"All right, it is none of my business as long as you do not give me any more trouble. We will share what I have and make the best of things. Agreed?" Mamigon gave him a whack on his butt to seal the unilateral pact he had announced as the boy was in the process of getting to his feet.

The boy whirled around to face him, looking startled, angry and nonplussed, the parade of expressions on his face quickly fading into a forced smile. Mamigon smiled at him. The young today were hard to figure out. This lad was pretty touchy.

They started off down the trail again, Mamigon feigning anger at the knob that had grown on the side of his head. He showed the boy his system of walking and running, but it was no good. The boy couldn't keep up. As the day wore on, Mamigon made a decision. He would let the boy fend for himself; otherwise he would never catch up with Tallal, not if he had to slow down to the boy's faltering pace. At the next rest stop—stops that had tripled in number with the boy along—he proposed the separation.

"You are delaying me, boy. I will have to leave you behind."

"That is fine, Ergun Agha. I will be fine . . ." Mamigon hesitated. The boy looked downcast, and those eyes . . . "I know I have been delaying you. You must be on an important mission."

"I cannot help it, boy. I must move faster. I will leave you what food I have. I can always bag something on the way. I just wish you had something in which to carry water. I have only one canteen and . . ."

"Please, mister. You have been very good about sharing your food and water. Just leave me be and I will manage, really I will."

Mamigon pushed his bag of cheese and dried beef into the boy's reluctant hands, paused, scowled, and handed over his canteen as well. "All right, now, be careful and trust no one on the trail. The next time someone crawls into a cave with you, make no sound. Just hope he will go away."

The boy nodded slowly and held up his right hand in a farewell gesture. Mamigon did the same, whirled and trotted down the mountain path. There was approximately four more hours of daylight, and he was going to make the most of it. He had traveled about a kilometer when he came to a wide open glade with a stand of shrub trees, evergreens, an indication there was probably water somewhere around. He stopped running and walked in among the trees to see what was there. There could be a spring; he was thirsty but not really dry. He was poking around well in the back of the stand he had entered when a high-pitched scream froze him in his steps. Then another scream, followed by loud laughter punctuated by whoops. Mamigon crept back and looked up the trail. There they were, four men with rifles, bandoliers crisscrossing their chest, heavy swords at their belts, all mustached and wearing astrakhans and boots. They had the boy. They had the boy with his britches off, his shirt ripped in tatters. One had an arm locked around his head and neck, two were holding up his bare bottom on either side with the legs pulled up flat against his belly. The fourth man was standing in position in front of the rump to sink his exposed member into him. Mamigon guessed it was the boy because of the remnants of clothes. He could hardly make out Sadi except for a bare behind. The men were Kurds. The penchant for young boys as sexual targets was something Mamigon had heard about over and over again. The Turks and Kurds seemed to go for either huge-bottomed, overblown women or young, smooth-skinned boys. Damnation.

Mamigon strung his first arrow and sent it into the heart of the Kurd who had just begun his rocking motion, making Sadi scream all over again. His second arrow went into the neck of the man holding the boy by the head. Sadi fell to the ground as the two holding him as an offering for their tumescent friend dropped to their hands and knees, scrambling for the trees. Mamigon kept his eyes on the two and picked off the third man who had made the mistake of standing up for a last dash. The fourth man made the cover of the trees on the same side of the path as Mamigon. The big man laid down his bow, carefully unslung his rifle, checked the gun, and watched. There was very little cover and the Kurd and the Armenian aimed at each other almost at the same instant. Mamigon was a hair of a second faster and the Kurd's nose disappeared as the bullet barreled into his brain.

Mamigon dropped back, reslung his bow and rifle, and walked out into the glade to see about Sadi.

They stared at each other as Sadi attempted to cover her breasts with the shreds of her shirt, keeping her eyes on Mamigon, her trembling mouth showing her anguish, her fear.

"You have more than meets the eye . . . boy . . . did they hurt you?"

She nodded slowly, her eyes wide, fear still etched on her face, in the way she held her body.

Mamigon raised his right hand. "I will not touch you . . . Where are your britches?"

"Back, back there somewhere . . . Please do not hurt me . . ."

"Close your mouth, girl! I do not attack girls . . . or women . . . or boys. I shall find your britches and you see what you can do about your shirt. Then we can talk." Mamigon was angry at the implication of her fear of him.

Mamigon found her britches about 100 meters up the trail, tossed them at her feet where he saw her behind a tree and waited until she came out, dressed again.

"Why did you not tell me who you were? Do you think I would have left you if I had known you were a slip of a girl?"

"How did I know what you would do . . . if I had told you?"

"You must have told them."

"I did not." She said it quietly. "They . . . they thought I was a boy at first, like you did. They," she paused, "they were going to do it, anyway."

Mamigon had thought the same thing when he saw them. "Well, who are you and what, in the name of Allah, are you doing in the mountains alone. This time, tell the truth, girl . . . wait a minute, what is your real name?"

"Guzell is my name. I have run away from home. I am eighteen years old and my parents were going to make me marry the *khaimakham*, the police chief, who just lost his wife. My, God, Ergun Agha, he is close to seventy, he has hardly any teeth, his eyes run all the time, and he has the worst breath I have ever smelled. I just had to get away . . ."

"You know you dishonored your parents by what you did?"

"I know what I did, Ergun Agha, but I would rather die in the mountains than have to be in the same bed with that man. You know, my mother actually cried and begged my forgiveness for the match. But, I was eighteen and everybody was worried about me being single. All my sisters were married but nobody wanted me because I was too skinny, they said." The words had poured out.

"Do you think you can walk now?" Mamigon was remembering Rachell.

"I think so . . . I'm . . ." She stopped.

"You are bleeding, are you not?" He said it without looking at her. "I believe it is nothing serious. Women do bleed when they are . . ." He couldn't say it. "Let us walk, woman, but first let us see what those devils had with them we can use."

He picked out the best rifle with matching ammunition for her; picked out a skinbag with water, and collected their food pouches which contained goat cheese and rice balls, and two short wool blankets. Best of all, he picked out a sword for himself.

That night, they spent their sleeping hours among some rocks off the trail, within sight of each other. In the morning, Mamigon realized that his morning toilet the previous day must have caused the woman some minor misgivings because he had thought nothing of urinating among the rocks while the "boy" had stood by, although with "his" back turned. He was more discreet this time and walked down the path to give her private time. She appeared shortly, with a bright smile for Mamigon. The man couldn't help but smile in return—but what was he going to do with her now?

"Were you telling me the truth about going to Fekke to your brother's house?"

"Partly. It is not my brother's house. My mother's sister lives there. I would dare not go to any male member of my family. They would drag me back home. Honestly, I am afraid for my life because of what I did. You are right, it is a matter of honor for my parents, and I have managed to insult that big old lump of a pasha in my own home town."

"Forget it, for now. Let us try to get where each of us is going and hope for the best."

They walked for a good hour before Mamigon started to trot again. He only went a half-kilometer and sat and waited for her. She came up, breathless, as she had been the day before. She had thrown away the 9-pound rifle. They looked at each other and both began to laugh.

"I would carry you, woman, but you are neither my wife nor my sister, and you certainly are not injured in any way that would permit such contact."

She grinned at him. "You have such nice manners. I have never met a man so considerate of a woman's person."

"And, I have never met a grown woman who was able to pass off so well as a boy. Do not become disturbed about this question but I have been puzzled about something. How were you able to hide so much of yourself? You ah . . . ah . . . have . . . oh, forget it!"

She didn't answer him verbally but held out a woolen band about 2 meters long. He nodded and changed the subject. "We will be at the river tomorrow and when we do, I will have a better idea of exactly which way to take you to get to Fekke."

The terrain was softening as they approached the Djihour. When they finally arrived at the river's edge, they were on a bluff about 20 meters above the surface, with no way to get down or cross the water.

"Can you swim?" His question was not really pertinent. He wasn't planning on swimming across the swift current.

"Oh, yes, I can, but do you think I could battle that water?"

"I could not myself, woman. What I think we ought to do is find a bend in the river, go above it and see if we can find something to float us. Then the current will wash us to the opposite bank at the bend."

They found a downed tree, Mamigon heaved the trunk into the water, he piled his weapons, blankets and food on top, they walked in on either side, and floated out. In less than ten minutes they were bumping into the opposite bank.

"It is too cool to leave these clothes on, woman. Take one of the blankets and remove all the wet things to let them dry. I will do the same."

"What is the blanket for?"

"To cover you . . . what else?"

"I would still feel naked . . . we would both be naked under the blankets and it would be improper." Her eyes showed the trouble in her mind.

"Young woman, it is also improper for both of us—unrelated, unattached, and all alone—to be here together. Can we change any of this, short of each going our own way?"

"I will not be marriageable if these things are found out."

"My young girl, you will also not be marriageable if you die of the cold chills."

"I would sooner die than be . . ."

"Camel spit! Stop and answer my questions. Have I seen your nakedness?"

"Yes, I think you have . . ."

"Have I touched you?"

"No."

"Do you believe I will molest you if you and I are naked under our blankets?"

"No, but . . ."

"Enough. Close your mouth. Do as I say."

"You will not watch me when I take off my clothes?"

Mamigon roared. "Move off behind those bushes. Not another word!" Women were certainly hard to understand.

Guzell reappeared in a few minutes, clutching her blanket tightly about herself and sat down a few feet from Mamigon, similarly covered. Both grinned sheepishly at one another.

"Now, is not that better?"

"My body is more comfortable but my mind is uneasy."

"I think all humankind suffers from an overactive imagination. Your nakedness, if you will excuse me for mentioning it, is exactly the same whether you are covered by a blanket or covered by stitched cloth."

"Please . . . you know exactly what I mean and how I feel. I have found you to be a sensitive man and my words are not being wasted."

"Enough, woman. We have said everything about this subject. If you persist in talking about it, I might come to the conclusion that you want to bring attention to your nakedness."

Guzell let out an indignant yelp of protest.

They were in this condition of draped nakedness when the Turkish patrol came upon them. Mamigon had heard them coming but there weren't enough trees and brush to hide their presence. He hid the weapons under a small outgrowth of green. The patrol had come out of the draw and was upon them before the Armenian could slip down and away on the river.

"Guzell?" He hadn't called her by name before. "Guzell, please act as if you are my wife. We are on a trip to visit your aunt in Fekke, all right?"

She smiled. "That is fine for me. My aunt's name is Zora Kucel, in case you are asked."

The horse soldiers rode right up to them, twelve of them, and the sergeant dismounted. Good day, he said. Who are you and what are you doing here? Mamigon said he was taking his bride to Fekke to visit her aunt before he reported for duty in the army. Oh, yes, we are from Killis, over the mountains. No, we did not fall into the river. We thought it would be nice to take a swim and clean ourselves off. No, we haven't met a soul thus far. Things seem fairly quiet. Is there any news we ought to know of? That's good, I am sick and tired of hearing about those crybaby Armenians. It is good that the great Kemal Pasha is cleaning them out. No, I have been out of touch with the news. Thanks, may Allah go with you, too.

"Well, how does it feel being married for five minutes?"

"I thought it was fine." She smiled at Mamigon again and the big man was beginning to feel uneasy at his reaction to her smiles. He liked it.

When their clothes dried, they put them on, with bushes for modesty, and decided to stay there for the night. The next morning they munched on some cheese, rice balls, and beef as they tried to figure out what to do about Mamigon's need for haste.

"My sex should not be considered in your decision. You were able to leave me when you thought I was a boy; your decision should stand now."

"Nonsense. I do not want you on my conscience. I will deliver you to your aunt and we will not discuss it again. Those Kurds were not the only ones in the mountains."

"Look, I was on my own before and I traveled more than halfway before I met you."

"Yes, and then you met others and I do not think you would be here talking to me if I had not come along . . . Ssssh. I hear horses coming."

Mamigon guessed the *chowoosh,* the sergeant, had described him to his captain, possibly, and they probably wanted to question him. He was at least as big as the outlaw they were probably seeking. Mamigon sent Guzell to one side of the trail among the everpresent rocks. He went to the opposite side and waited. Yes, it was the same patrol. It rode by hard and fast and then came back in ten minutes, figuring the two couldn't have gotten much farther. Mamigon was certain twelve men were too many for him to handle in broad daylight. He would be able to kill four, maybe five, before he would be surrounded. These Turks were soldiers, not newly recruited and deputized *polis* such as the unit Tallal had been leading. They stayed on their horses as they looked carefully in all directions, riding by, slowly.

Once they were gone, the two hit the trail, but now Guzell was curious. "I think they were looking for us, either both of us or one of us . . ."

"No question about it."

"Why, do you think? I thought they might be looking for me, but the army wouldn't be bothered with a woman running away from home."

"They are looking for me."

"Why?"

"I am not who you think I am."

"I know not who you are, really. Is Gokden your right name?"

"No."

"Are you an army deserter?"

"No."

"Are you a criminal?"

"The *polis* and the army are after me."

"Are you an outlaw?"

"I must be."

"You did not answer me."

"Questions and answers are useless when you know I lied at the beginning."

"I trust you."

"Why? Because I did not attack you?"

"I trust you because of what I see in your eyes."

"I am a plain blacksmith who has never needed to lie before."

"Why do you now?"

"I have killed many men, some good, some bad, but all in bad blood."

"I have seen you kill. Are the four you killed back there the kind of men you have killed?"

"Many of them, yes. But I have killed army men who could not help being where they were."

"Please tell me, why are you killing? Why are they after you?"

"If I told you who I really am I would . . . would lose you . . ." He didn't look at her. She stopped on the trail and he had to stop too.

"I am so happy to hear you say that. I do not want to lose you, either. Who are you that you think I would shun you if I knew?"

"If you knew, you would be in danger. It is better you do not know."

She didn't respond and began walking, Mamigon following. He was surprised at himself for having said he didn't want to lose her. What was that all about? He hadn't realized until he said it that she had become important to him, and he didn't know why. Sadi the pest had become Guzell the handsome woman and Guzell I-don't-want-to-lose-you . . . all in a period of two days. Oofah, unadulterated cow dung! I am so happy to hear you say that . . . I don't want to lose you, either . . . My mother's *shawlwar*, what drivel! Well, no more of that nonsense—not as long as Tallal was still breathing.

The Sihoun was 50 kilometers away. For the better part of two days they traveled over the rough, mountainous territory, hiding every time they heard or thought they heard someone coming. When they reached the river, Mamigon remembered the exact spot where he had crossed over before, to avoid going near Fekke. The moment that he dreaded most was approaching. He hated to take leave of Guzell and had to admit it. She always smiled at him when their eyes locked and he liked the sparkle in her big brown eyes, eyes that had a hint of the devil in them.

They walked upriver, halfway to Hadjin, before they found a small skiff tied up for someone's special use. They used it, crossed in style and headed for Fekke. It was beginning to get dark when they saw the one minaret that dominated the sky over the town. The two stopped on the river bank they were using as their path.

"This is where we say goodbye. Goodbye." Mamigon raised his right hand, palm toward her.

"Goodbye, and may Allah go with you." She stared at him for a moment, turned on her heel and began to run. Mamigon watched her go, nodded at nothing, and checked the stars to orient himself to the northwest. Sadness was his emotion, bewilderment was his outlook, determination was his drive. He made camp for the night and didn't eat a thing.

He stretched out on the ground on his back, his hands clasped under his head, and stared at the stars, thinking.

He felt more alone at this moment than at any time in his life. Duty. That was it, duty.

Duty to his country that sent him away from home for the first time to study at the academy. His father had patted him on the shoulder and said it would be a great opportunity. He had felt alone.

Duty to his comrades in arms that sent him crawling alone and vulnerable into the face of chattering machine guns and belching cannons to pull out the decimated squad. Loneliness then was an understatement.

Duty to his dead family that sent him pell-mell to crisscross his native land after the killers. The loneliness of self-doubt and doubtful conviction.

Duty to his vow that prevented him from sailing off with Aram and the rest to safety. That moment when the boat sailed off had been a heart tugger. He had been at his loneliest, then.

Duty to the responsibility he felt for Guzell that impelled him to send her away before she was caught up in the maw of blood and terror he was pursuing.

His feelings of loneliness seemed to be permanent. Guzell was the last straw in his imposed series of self-denial that was dominating his life. With Guzell gone, he felt now he had nothing. Nothing but the drive for revenge that had gone awry so many times.

He had lost Tatios in the process. A trace of a smile crossed his face as he thought of Tatios, that spectacular, hell-for-leather character who seemed to know so much of the world and so little of life.

Oh, well, he would make a go of it as best he could . . . Probably die in some dusty path with a knife in his back . . . He fell asleep.

Before dawn, Mamigon was shaken awake. His defensive reaction almost knocked Guzell down as he rolled into her.

"What . . . What are you doing here?" He couldn't help but show his delight, however, with a small smile playing on his swarthy face. He didn't get up.

"I had to find you, whatever your name is . . ."

"A mindless wench, you are! I want you to go right back to your aunt!"

"I cannot go back." She sounded almost elated. "Her husband would not let me stay when my aunt told him the circumstances of my arrival."

"Cow dung! You cannot stay with me, woman."

"Oh, yes I can," she said, dropping to her knees next to him and embracing his head, a breast on his cheek. "I want to be with you . . ."

Mamigon shoved her away, gently, then said, softly: "In other times I would have welcomed you. Now, I must say no." Her arms were still extended at shoulder level.

"I have nowhere to go, now. Can I not stay with you; I promise I will not be a bother. I will run like the wind. I will not talk. I will do anything you say. I will . . ."

"Enough. You can come with me until we find someplace you can be safe. That is all I promise."

In response, Guzell pushed up to him again and kissed him on the cheek. Mamigon jerked away. "You do not know who I am. If you did, you would not be so free with me, woman."

"I care not who you are. I know what you are. You are a kind, gentle, understanding, quiet man who would not hurt a flea off a camel's back. That is all I have to know about you . . . there . . ."

"What would you say if you thought I was not your kind, I was not a Moslem?"

"Oh, I knew all along you were a *giavour*, an infidel. I saw you cross yourself before you ate your cheese in that cave the first night. You were outlined against the fading light. Are you a Chaldaean, Jacobite, Nestorian, Armenian, or Greek?"

"Armenian."

"And, I know you are married . . . How many children do you have and where are you from?"

Mamigon looked at the band on his finger. He couldn't answer. Her questions brought back the past as if a spear had been thrown into his heart.

"I am sorry. What did I say that caused you pain?"

"Nothing, nothing. Let us eat something and get started."

She had a big knit bag full of food that her tearful aunt had given her, and they broke their fast with some soft *pideh,* boiled eggs, and *pahstermah.* Mamigon's appetite was whetted and the food made him feel much better about things once his belly was full.

"I was married, Guzell, and I had three children. They are all dead. They are the reason I am running around the country."

She pondered his statement for a moment. "Was your family killed?"

"Yes. I am after the man who killed them."

"Can you talk about it?"

"There is nothing more to say, really. The man who killed them was a friend. I have vowed to kill him. He violated my wife before he killed her. I have been trying to catch up with him for six weeks now."

"Do you know where he is?"

"I am only guessing, but I believe he is going home to Yosghat. He happens to be the son of the *vali* there."

"Oh. He is Turkish, then?"

"Yes."

"Do you hate all Turks because of what he did?"

"I do not have trust anymore. He was my friend, I thought. He broke bread with me at my table, ate my salt, drank *tahn* that my wife served him. He killed her and her unborn child. He killed my children, my mother and father, and my five brothers. Would you ever trust a man or his nationality if he did it in the name of his government?"

"Government? Are you saying he murdered your family on orders?"

"Of course. He was leading a police unit. He and his men killed nearly 900 men, women, and children, wiping out my village, all because they were Turks and my people were Armenian. Should I trust Turks?" He waited, not knowing what to expect.

"You can trust me." It was said in a low voice with almost a plea in it.

It was his turn to reach for her where they sat and crush her against his barrel chest. He held her without saying a word. He held her, drawing new strength from another human being who seemed to care for him. He held her for such a long time without moving that she finally tilted up her chin to look into his face.

"How do you say I love you in Armenian?"

He placed his scraggly cheek on hers for answer and held her some more. It had turned into a bright, sunny morning and the sound of voices in the distance told them it was time to go.

Mamigon took pity on Guzell and did not press her too hard to adhere to his run-walk-run system. He couldn't, because she didn't have his stamina. By nightfall, they had traveled 30 kilometers and were near a small tributary to the Sihoun, where they camped. The mountains had offered an unrelieved series of obstacles: steep climbs, rudimentary paths that fell away, sheers that brought gasps from the girl, and rock-hard footing every step of the way. Guzell was exhausted and didn't eat anything when they stopped. By the time Mamigon was ready to sleep, she was dead to the stars. He covered her up.

They were off again in the morning, both strangely quiet after the peak of emotions following revelation and awareness. They skirted to the east of Kaisaria and reached Kizil Irmak, the river of the floating bodies. Mamigon marveled at the passage of time and events. It had been only a few weeks, but it seemed like years, since he had been there with Aram and Araxy and the naked couple—what were their names? Oh, well. They found a farmer who paddled them across—he was highly impressed by the gigantic Turk with a hornbow, a rifle, a sword, bandoliers, two pistols in his belt, and a handsome young woman he claimed was his wife. Sure. All Turks traveled around the country armed to the teeth with an unveiled woman being passed off as the wife. Certainly, *effendi*.

Once across, Mamigon figured they were about 100 kilometers from

Yosghat, and he had to make plans. They camped in a small grove of stunted cypress, without a fire so as not to attract unwanted inquisitors.

"If we press tomorrow we can reach Yosghat by night."

"Then what? What will you do when you find this man?"

"I am going to kill him."

"Then what?"

"Then, I am finished."

"Fine, you're finished. Then what will you do;"

"Woman, I have not thought that far ahead. I have nothing to live for, and once I deal with the person who put me in that state, I care not what happens to me."

"You are certain it is that person who has caused you to believe you have nothing to live for? Incidentally, what is his name?"

"Tallal. Yes, when he murdered everyone in my family and destroyed everything I had lived for, I can say that he is responsible for my state of mind."

"Well, big man, I do not know much, but I do know that a person is responsible for the state of his own mind . . . unless there is a sorcerer around. I hesitate to ask you, but do you think you can trust me enough to tell me who you are—your name, for instance?"

Mamigon laughed out loud. He hadn't even thought of telling her after she found him again. "It is Mamigon, son of Magaros of Yosghat Dagh."

She smiled at him for the first time since they camped. He returned the smile. She picked up her blanket, walked over to his side and sat down next to him. "I am not going to freeze tonight like I did last night. I am bundling up with you whether you like it or not."

He didn't say anything but put out his arm and pushed her head down on it, pulling up both blankets to cover them. He pulled her body close up to his with her butt fitting into his lap, his arm circled over her waist.

"Let us get some sleep . . ." They didn't, for a while, a long while. She made barely perceptible backward thrusts of her bottom and his fingers gently pressed at her body just below her breasts. Her movements back and forth became definite, and he allowed the side of his hand to touch the breast closest to the ground. He became aroused and she began to groan softly as her bottom felt him. She suddenly grabbed his hand and placed it on her bosom where it came to life massaging her nipples.

Her voice was low, hoarse. "I do not hurt anymore . . . the Kurd broke it, you know . . ." He hadn't touched a woman since before he went hunting that fateful weekend, and Guzell was finally initiated to the world of the flesh in manner and length of duration and repetition certain to spoil her for the rest of her life . . . if she assumed that this is the way it is all the time . . . and she had no benchmark to go by.

It was past sunup when they awoke, and without a word they were in each others arms again. Finally covered up and truly spent, she looked at him with her big brown eyes. "I suppose I will be bearing your child now . . ."

"I think not, woman. I was careful to spend outside your body. The fourth time I was sorely tempted . . ."

"You *do* care for me, Mamigon," she said, giving him a hard hug.

"I would not have embraced you if I did not have deep affection for you . . . Guzell." It was difficult for him to say her name. "You realize, woman, that you are mine, now. I shall take care of you for as long as I live."

"Oh, yes, Mamigon, yes . . ."

"All right, once I am through with Tallal, we will do what has to be done to correct this illicit situation."

"Illicit? What do you mean, illicit?"

"Just that, woman. We are not married. What we did is only right in the married state. You are not a whore. You are a decent, fine woman who became entangled with me under uncontrollable circumstances, that is all. I will change your status as soon as I can."

"I would like to marry you because you want me to be your wife, not because we did something illegal."

"It is the same thing."

"I should say not, you big camel."

"Please, woman, we are not yet married and you already scream at me like a wife."

"I will not marry you ever if that is the way you think."

"We shall see."

12 EXILE

"I am sorry for you, my son, but there is nothing I can do about it. You have to go."

"I am sorry, too, my father, and I cannot believe that there is no other way."

"There is not, Tallal. You are fortunate that your father is someone in whom the government has faith. If I were not regarded with a good deal of respect I think you would not have been given any consideration."

"Father, the men of the committee of inquiry just refused to believe the facts. I did not lie. I . . ."

The old man with the white chin whiskers held up his palm. "It matters little whether you lied or did not lie, son. The fact remains that two members of that panel were instructors at the academy and knew the Armenian. A third member was a divisional officer at the Cannakale Bogazi and had recommended the medal for that man . . . Mamigon. It was most unfortunate for you, I must admit."

"It does not seem fair. It is ironic that I am being banished because of what I tried to do for my country."

"You are not being banished, my son. And, what is happening now is not because of what you tried to do but how you conducted yourself and what you *did not* accomplish."

Tallal, with growing color on his face, opened his mouth to reply but the old man raised his hand again. "I wish not to confront you about some matters, my son, but I cannot allow you to think for one minute that your superiors and your father are heartless, cruel men who simply ignore your words and to punish you unfairly. You lied, my son. You lied when the simple truth from you would have elicited more favor.

"For one thing, the rebellion at Yosghat Dagh was not led by this man Mamigon. Your men were questioned. He was not there.

"For another, you killed his wife and children, and only Allah knows who else.

"Then, you were defeated by one man, armed only with a bow, and lost thirteen men in the encounter.

"To compound your troubles, you let him escape after losing a dozen men in capturing him. Wait, do not interrupt your father . . .

"What you do not seem to understand, my son, is that this man has become your nemesis. At this very moment he is following you, looking for you, ready to kill you in any way possible. You doubt it?

"Well, do not for a minute. He has been emasculating every man that he kills, no doubt a promise he wishes for you when he finds you. He has left his grisly calling card throughout the central Anatolian Plain, thanks to you. We almost caught him with his concubine at the Sihoun only yesterday. Yes, he is on his way here. If you doubt why he is heading this way, you are a bigger fool than you have shown yourself to be up to now.

"I hope you can see why you are being sent away. You are being sent away to save you from a horrible death at the hands of a relentless killer who once counted you as a friend.

"That is why we are sending you to America. We do not believe he will be able to follow you there. And, once he realizes you are no longer in the country he may soften his terrible rage at the rest of his fellow countrymen. Armenian and infidel though he is, he served his government well in the army. I would have honored him as a son . . ."

The old man indicated he was finished and leaned back on the floor pillows, running his thumb across his *tuzbeh* rapidly, the clicking of the beads the only sound in the room.

Tallal was dumbfounded. Every mother's whelp along the ill-fated line of march southward must have stepped forward somewhere and spilled his guts. Was there anything they didn't know? As if his father was reading his mind, the *vali* spoke up again.

"I forgot to mention something that was really of no great importance among all of your shameful misdeeds. Can you guess? I did not think so. It was the true key to your downfall.

"You lied to the troops about the reward money for Mamigon. When you were driving the exiles past Marash, the provisions corporal took an *araba* into the city to bring back a couple of new kettles to replace the ones that had been shot up in the fighting. Did not you think there would be posters, my son? It is a wonder the men did not harm you when they found out the reward was not one thousand *lira* but five. No wonder you were drummed out by the *yarbay*. Discipline would have been impossible under the circumstances. And, of course, every man was delighted to inform on you. Oh, my son . . ."

"I had my reasons, my father. I will not run away from this man. I must face him and kill him myself."

"You have no choice, my son. You must leave. I would face that man in your place, my son. My heart is heavy that because of him, I will not have the pleasure of your company in the closing years of my life. I would gladly kill him or die in your stead if it would save you."

"Please, my father, I do not want you or anyone else to be in danger because of what I have been accused of doing . . . or not doing." Tallal had tears in his eyes as he addressed the old man. "Please give me one last chance to kill that upstart *giavour*, that camel-spit infidel."

The old man set erect when he spoke again. "I repeat, my son, it is out of my hands, our hands. We must obey or your life will be in jeopardy from your own police. I curse the day I recommended you for that tour of duty to Aleppo. I curse that Armenian son of dung for what he has brought to me and mine."

"Curses will not kill him, my father. I can kill him. Let me stay and do it. I *must* avenge the tears he has brought to your eyes."

"No, my son, you must go to New York."

Tallal sat on the rugs across from his father a full minute before he spoke again. "What is this place called New York?"

"We have had to open consulates in both North and South America to take care of many of our nationals who have gone to both continents to seek work. Near this place called New York are many cities or towns in a province called New England, where they have many tanning factories. At this time there are about a thousand of our fellow countrymen working in these factories.

"You will be an assistant to the consul. You are being transferred from the army reserve to the foreign service. You will, also, no longer have status in the police force. The work will be easy. I understand America is a very progressive country, and I am sure you will like it. For the only time in my life I am glad your mother is not alive so that she would not be exposed to the double pain of leave-taking and the shame you have brought to this house.

"One other matter. You have the prerogative to take along a man servant. I am tired now, my son. We will make our farewells tomorrow morning. If you can find it in your heart, thank Allah tonight that despite everything, you are going to be well off. And try to look kindly into my face. These last few hours are all the time you will have to see me alive, once you leave for America."

13 🙠 IZMIR

Guzell would be his eyes and ears. Yosghat was his territory, and chances of his big frame being recognized were very real. Guzell would go into the city and find out about Tallal Bey. It was agreed. She had done such a good job in fooling Mamigon into believing she was a boy, they decided she would don the same disguise. A woman alone in a Turkish city was not a good idea. Not because she would be attacked or harmed, but because it was not the custom for women to go about freely. Their place was in the home. Mamigon set up camp in what passed for a grove of trees—three of them—in the foothills next to a small spring. Guzell would go into the city in the morning. All she had to do was to locate the home of the *vali* and then make inquiries about joining the *polis*, mentioning Tallal Bey's unit. The rest would be left to chance.

The two had not been friendly after their talk of marriage. Each was reluctant to retreat, and they spent two days traveling without exchanging anything more than essential words. They had been careful not to get involved physically, sleeping almost out of sight of each other. It was going to be the same this night. After they laid out their plans about Guzell's excursion into Yosghat, they carefully separated, acting offhand about it, and settled down against opposite tree trunks.

"Do you happen to know anyone in Yosghat?"

"No, I have never been to this part of the country. It seems much colder in these parts."

"It is because we are on a high plateau. Where you come from the land is flattening out to become desert."

"How do you know so much?"

"I do not know much of anything . . . If I did know anything, I would be able to find words to soften our companionship."

"You just did. I did miss you."

"I missed you, too. Would you care to sit close to me? I know you have been cold the past two nights . . . I will not molest you."

He hadn't finished speaking when she took five steps and was sitting on his lap, her arms around him, her head on his chest. "Molest me, please, if you wish. I would love to be molested by you." Her eyes had the look of the imp. Mamigon hugged her in turn and they sat there without moving, happy to be together once again.

"You know, I feel like a little boy when you are this way. Are all Turkish women as wonderful as you?"

"I do not know about all Turkish women, but this particular Turkish woman feels wonderful when she is with this big Armenian camel."

"There is no such thing . . ."

"What?"

"There is no such thing as an Armenian camel. In fact, I do not know of any animal that could be called Armenian, unless it's the horse. Armenians are descendents of an ancient people called Hittites and the Hittites were the ones said to have domesticated the horse and used them in war."

"Shut up, Mamigon. For a quiet man you have taken to raving and ranting when I am with you." With that, she planted a kiss on his mouth and pushed him to the ground on his back, squirming all over him.

She left for Yosghat in the morning, taking two small gold rings for barter, just in case. Mamigon embraced her, warning her to be careful not to give away her disguise. He murmured something about her not having acted at all like a boy last night. She gave him a hard squeeze around the chest and was gone.

She was back before it got dark, dusty and tired, with a look of haste about her.

"He was gone. He has gone." She was shouting it before she got to the grove. "He left for some placed called Smyrna two days ago."

"How did you find out?"

"It was easy. While I was looking for the *vali*'s house. I came across the headquarters for the *polis*. I asked a man in uniform if this was the place where Tallal Bey was stationed. The man said he had gone to Smyrna to sail for America."

"Do you know how he went? I mean, was he riding or what?"

"I do not know, Mamigon. But I asked another man what was the best way of getting to Smyrna. He told me the fastest way was by train from Angora. He said Smyrna—then he used another name for it that I cannot remember—was on the ocean, not the Black Sea."

"Then, it is off to Smyrna, my girl. What am I going to do with you?"

"I am going with you, that is what."

"Impossible."

"All right. Tell me what I am expected to do while you are gone?"

Mamigon realized it was hopeless to even debate the issue. She was right. They ate and then made their plans. Guzell had a surprise for him. She had gone to an apothecary shop and bought some henna and to a tailor shop for a quarter-inch band of elastic cloth. She mixed the powdery orange stuff with water and rinsed Mamigon's black hair, beard, and mustache with it, wrapping his head in a cloth for the night. She had a needle and some thread, also, and fashioned a patch for one of his eyes.

"In the morning, you will be a redheaded, one-eyed, stooped old man with a heavy limp, escorting your little boy or grandson—it matters not—to Smyrna. How is that?"

Mamigon performed one last rite before they left in the morning. He discarded his weapons, all except his pistols and knife. It was one of the most difficult things he had to do. The wonderful Mauser 98 rifle, the long cavalry saber taken from the Kurd, and the only memento from his boyhood—a longtime friend—the hornbow and quiver his father had given him. He tried to think how he could possibly take it with him, but there was no way he could hide it effectively. It had to go. He had no grease for the rifle and sword to enable him to wrap them up and bury them for possible future use.

He snapped the sword and smashed the rifle with prodigous swings against a tree; he hung the hornbow and quiver on the same tree. If the bow wasn't retrieved quickly by someone, it would become useless because the first sign of dampness or rain would ruin its tensile strength. Guzell removed twenty-five rounds of ammunition from the bandoliers before they discarded them, too.

Mamigon didn't have to disguise himself fully until they reached the outskirts of the big city, Angora, 150 kilometers from Yosghat. As they met more and more travelers on the road, Mamigon stopped alternating from young man to limping old man, and became an old man permanently. In the bustling city, full of uniformed men, they went to the bazaar with the coins Guzell had received in exchange for one of the rings at the apothecary's shop in Yosghat, and ate well from a wide variety of foods on sale—even shish kebab from a street vendor.

Mamigon bought the first newspaper he had read since he returned from military duty last May. The large, folded, four-page paper from Ankara was dated September 24, 1915. God in heaven, it was no more than six weeks since that Sunday in August when he had found his murdered family. It felt more like ten years! The front page was totally concerned with the war being fought on three fronts. The Turkish government had issued a communiqué that the fighting at Cannakale Bogazi was still at a stalemate with the British, Australian, New Zealand, Indian, and French troops—sixteen divisions in all—contained easily on the Gallipoli peninsula. The story said that reports from Germany indicated that the British government was about to boot out the architect of the ill-fated plan to capture Constantinople, a British admiralty official named Winston Churchill. Another story heaped ridicule on the commander of the expedition, Lt. Gen. Sir Charles Monro, who never seemed to have enough artillery shells to press an advantage. The repulsion of the Turkish forces by the Russians on the eastern front at Sarikamish was being treated as a tactical withdrawal and that the Turkish general, Enver Pasha, was marshaling his divisions to smite the Russians a devastating blow, "shortly." The report on the war in Mesopotamia where the British were trying to force their way up the Tigris River and the heavy fighting at Kum was already being described as an ultimate victory for the soldiers of the Ottoman Empire.

Mamigon wondered what the true state of military affairs was. He related everything he read to Guzell. She was deeply impressed with the fact that Mamigon could read, a skill she had not been taught because she was a girl.

"Oh, I have meant to ask you—will water, hot water, wash out the henna?"

"No, never. The dye will grow out with the hair."

"Then, would you please be good enough to go to the railroad waiting shed and wait for me?"

Guzell looked at Mamigon quizzically. "You are not planning to do anything foolish, are you?"

"No, little woman, nothing foolish. By the beard of my father, I am truly embarrassed to tell you because it is a bit of self-indulgence . . . but I must. I want to go to the baths. I have not been to one since I left Constantinople and I may not have another opportunity. Do you mind?"

"I am pleased so very much that you are always so considerate of your woman. I mind not at all. Go. I will wait for you."

Turkish baths, instituted during the life of Mohammed and patterned after the ancient Roman baths found in many an old city, was a luxury Mamigon had discovered when he attended the military academy.

He went into the baths he had noticed on a side street, paid his 2 piasters for a body-length, wrap-around towel, and stepped into the cold water room for a shivering dunking. After he became accustomed to the cold, he repaired to the hot water room and sank into the steaming waters, the initial coldness of his body protecting him from violent reaction to the heat. There were three other men in the 15-meter circular sunken pool and other than a brief nod, words were not exchanged. Once the perspiration broke out on Mamigon's face, he got out and went to the steam room, sitting as long as he could with sweat running from his body. Then the sweating room, where he lolled around until the perspiration abated, before submitting to the expert pummeling of the masseur. In the resting room, he put on his clothes, and left for the railroad shed, feeling like a new man.

It took them two days to get to Smyrna. The route was anything but direct. They boarded a rickety wooden train full of soldiers in Angora and headed west for Constantinople, getting off at Eski Shehr, a little more than 200 kilometers from their starting point. Then there was a four-hour wait before they boarded another rattler on the Constantinople-Adana trunk line south for 150 kilometers to Afiun Kara-Hissar, not much more than a railroad town serving as a junction point. Another six hours' wait here before they could board the one weekly train to Smyrna, 300 kilometers to the west. They were lucky and they knew it.

Their biggest problem turned out to be the cold. The cool air of autumn wafted through the creaky, cracked, and uncaulked wooden boxes that were called passenger cars, hand-me-downs from an ancient French railroad. Other passengers showed no interest in the pair, obviously an old Circassian and his boy, judging from the color of his hair. That mustache was a filthy-looking mess, though. Mamigon and Guzell ate dried apricots and dates bought from vendors at the stops.

Smyrna, called Izmir by the Turks, was a city on the Mediterranean with more Greeks than any other nationality. It was one of the great ports, with a fine natural harbor and a history of tug-of-war over who should control it: the Greeks, Turks, or Italians. The Turks were in possession now, using the seaport as their main channel of communication with the outside world, when they could. After the war broke out, the British navy blockaded everything. The city was full of uniformed men, barbed wire, and road blocks.

"I do not think I should have brought you here."

"Do not make me feel as if I am a burden."

"You are no burden to me. I am concerned for your safety."

"Not as long as I am considered a boy."

"We will have to find someplace to stay."

The army was using almost every available building for billeting. It wasn't until the middle of the afternoon that they found a house in the outskirts where a young widow gladly took them in as boarders, although she was suspicious of them almost immediately. What caught her attentioin was her paying guests' hands. The old man's were huge and tough-looking, but their backs were completely unwrinkled; the young boy's hands were still heavily tinted with the residue of henna, and they were strangely graceful.

The widow Zampara regarded the two as the answer to her prayers. She was close to starvation, without a man in the house. She had been considering using her body among the soldiers to stay alive when the odd-looking pair knocked on her door. Zampara was no fool. Who cared what they were or why they were . . . as long as they paid. The first thing her guests asked about was food, and after Zampara explained her situation, she and Guzell left together to replenish the exhausted larder.

"Zampara knows who we are," Guzell said as they came back in. The big man just stared. "She told me I was a girl and that you were a young man and that we were fooling no one."

"I am not happy about this," Mamigon said, "but it does not matter anymore, I think."

"I told Zampara we were not criminals . . ."

"Did you tell her why we had to run away to get married?"

"N—no . . ."

He turned to the widow. "We made love because we loved each other and were found out. We had to run for our lives. That is why we are disguised, just in case our families are looking for us. You have nothing to fear from us, woman."

"I did not think so, Agha. Your secret is safe with me. I have lost my husband in the fighting and I have no family here. You are welcome to stay as long as you want." Zampara didn't mention that they could stay as long as they could pay. She would handle that easily when the time came. They were in no position to give her trouble.

That night, in a small storeroom equipped with a sleeping mat, Mamigon decided that the best way of finding Tallal would be to find the city's police headquarters in the hope of spotting him there, and then to trail him to where he lived and kill him. It wouldn't do for Mamigon to loiter. Tallal would not be fooled by the red hair or the eye patch. Mamigon was too big not to draw attention immediately. Guzell had to do the work. He described Tallal as best he could, mentioning the man's right hand with the mutilation.

"Probably, he will be wearing gloves on both hands."

"Anything else?"

"Yes, he has a carefully trimmed mustache that stretches to the corners of his mouth."

"You . . . you truly want me to find this man?" Guzell asked in a small voice.

"Why, yes, of course I do. Why do you ask such a question? Do not you know the reason?"

"I do, my man . . . I do."

"Then?"

"I care for you deeply. I do not want to lose you now."

"Why do you think you will lose me?"

"I have a feeling in my bones that nothing worthy of salt will come from this."

"You worry needlessly, my girl. A jackal like Tallal will die as he has lived, cheaply and without honor."

"How can you be so certain? What if you are killed instead of him? Why cannot the two of us start a new life from this very moment and forget the past?"

"That is not worthy of you, Guzell. You are asking me to break my vow to my family. I must keep my vow . . . or die trying."

"That is your final word?"

"Yes."

"Very well, then. I will do as you bid. I will find Tallal." The look in her eyes was something Mamigon had never seen before. Her quiet intensity during the conversation had surprised him. For a slip of a girl, she was extremely headstrong, he thought. But that is what made her so precious, of that he was certain.

14 ⚬ NO EXCUSES

Tallal *was* wearing gloves on both hands, something Guzell spotted quickly on the second day as she waited in the street in front of the police building. She was hawking oranges she had bought at the bazaar and was selling for the same price. My, he is handsome, she thought. She went right up to him and offered him an orange. He told "him" to get lost. She told him she resented his bad manners and would follow him until he bought one. He told her "he" could follow him to hell before he would buy an orange from such a pushy little whelp of a horse bun like "him." She said she would see and dogged his steps.

Tallal went five blocks and disappeared into a big old mansion, not giving Guzell a backward glance. Guzell saw more policemen and others enter and leave in the short time she stayed to confirm her impression that the mansion was being used as a dormitory for government officials.

"I saw several men who could pass for Tallal Bey," she told Mamigon that evening. "I will have to make inquiries to be certain."

"You must be careful, very careful, Guzell. I only wish I knew when he was going to leave for America."

"He could be gone by now, you must realize that."

"I know, but I have to make certain."

"What if you find out he has left?"

"I will have eaten the dung. I do not want to think about it."

"But what if he has?"

"I do not know . . . I do not know . . ."

"Would you give up this madness of revenge you live for?"

"I refuse to think about it until I am certain."

A somberness mantled their evening and neither had much to say beyond the bare civilities, each immersed in thought.

The next morning Guzell was in front of the police station again, waiting for Tallal to appear. She waited until noon and had sold all of her oranges before she came to the conclusion that the police station must not be his post in Izmir.

She bought more oranges and went to the mansion he had entered yesterday to see if he appeared there. He did, toward the end of day, ignored her pleas to buy an orange, and went in.

Guzell gave up on oranges the next morning and simply sat obliquely across the street from the mansion at daybreak. Tallal emerged at seven o'clock and headed west. She followed him to another mansion which had an iron fence all around it, encompassing imposing-looking grounds. It was the house of the *vali*, the governor of the Izmir vilayet.

Guzell took a chance and went to the gate to see if she could enter the grounds as a new servant in the kitchen. She was kicked in the rear and sent sprawling when she couldn't tell the gatekeeper who the cook was.

Mamigon was totally depressed when Guzell reported no luck in any trace of Tallal Bey. He could still be any of three or four men, she told him. Wearing gloves was no help because it was getting cold enough to find more and more men wearing them. After all, it was going to be the first of October tomorrow.

"I think I will take the chance and try to find him myself, Guzell."

"No, never, my man. You would be identified too easily. You would have to post yourself in one spot or roam around in one area. After a while you would be noticed and even questioned. You know that."

"Yes, I know," he sighed. "But I am going out of my mind here, not knowing where he is, whether he has left, whether he is leaving even now as we talk, or whether something terrible has befallen you."

"It should not be long now. Please be patient."

"I have another problem, Guzell." He lowered his voice to a whisper. "That woman Zampara has been paying me too much attention. I try to stay in this hole of a room, but when I go to the outhouse she is always waiting for me with a cup of coffee and . . ."

"Yes, go on."

"Her smile is as wide as the top of her open blouse."

"Oh! Does she not know that I am yours? Oh, I will scratch her eyes out!"

"Sshh. Stop it. I can easily ward her off. My main problem is being cooped up like a wild hawk and you out there doing my work."

Guzell wasn't too sure that Mamigon could ward off Zampara but allowed the matter to pass. She was determined to bring an end to this as soon as possible. Losing Mamigon to that overblown bag . . . ha!

Guzell walked directly up to Tallal Bey the next morning as he came down the mansion's piazza steps.

"You are Tallal Bey, are you not?"

"What? How do you know who I am?"

"I asked around when you would not buy even one orange from me."

Tallal looked down at Guzell, seeing only the street urchin she was acting. "Very well, so you know my name. Now, begone or I will call the police."

"Call them. I will say you exposed yourself."

"You are the son of *Shaytahn*, no doubt about it . . . What is it you want of me . . . Oranges you have not?"

"You are the only man who has not bought an orange from me. I hated you at first but now I have come to respect you and I wish to serve you, to be your servant. You are obviously a person of great position. Who else would treat a lowly street boy in the only way he should be treated? I ask you, Agha?"

Tallal stood shaking his head. He had heard many a plea for alms but this was the best yet. He raised his arms to the level of his chest. "I surrender. You have reached me. Will this *khuroosh* do?" he said, digging out a piaster and tossing it to Guzell.

Guzell had a pained expression on her face as she caught the coin and tossed it back. "Please, Agha, I am not seeking alms. I am sincere in my respect and admiration for you. I wish to serve you, wait on you hand and foot for whatever small reward you wish to bestow."

"You are not from these parts. Your speech gives you away."

"I am from Killis, Agha. My name is Sadi, what is your family name, if I may ask?"

"Very well, Sadi. My name is Kosmanli. I was the *emniyet muduru* in Yosghat until recently. I have come to like you. I like your spirit even if you have a tart tongue."

"Then you will hire me?"

"You are too late, my young friend, I have hired a boy from the police troop. And, I leave tomorrow for America."

"That is a great sadness for me but I insist on serving you without pay, until the moment you leave. You must do me that great favor, Kosmanli Agha."

"I cannot get rid of you, can I? You will serve me, then. Meet me here after supper and you will help me pack my belongings for my sea voyage."

"I am in your debt, master. Thank you, thank you. See you tonight."

Guzell bowed, ran down the steps and left Tallal marveling at so much nerve, energy, and brashness. It was also the inscrutable will of Allah that such beautiful eyes should have been bestowed on a boy . . .

When she returned to Zampara's house, Mamigon was not there. Zampara shrugged her shoulders as to his whereabouts, telling Guzell that he had gone out no more than an hour ago, not saying where he was going or when he would return.

"I am not inquisitive, it is not my concern, but where do you go every day without him?"

"I sell oranges."

"I thought you had plenty of money? Why is not your man looking for work?"

"My brothers are looking for him. It would be easy to recognize him because of his size. If they find me, at least he would be safe."

Zampara nodded. "You will be able to pay me, eh?"

"Without doubt, we will . . . I wish I knew where he went. I have to go out after I eat something. I hope he will be back by then." Guzell was puzzled and uncertain about Mamigon's disappearance. Where could he be? What could have made him leave the safety of the hideout?

She waited until well past the supper hour and left at seven o'clock to meet Tallal. It was dark when she arrived at the mansion.

"Are you Sadi?" A teenage boy with a wart under his left cheekbone addressed Guzell when she reached the piazza.

"Yes, I am." She gasped at the sight of the crystal chandelier in the foyer.

"Good. I am Enver Dash, employed as a striker to Tallal Bey. Come with me." There were men in both military dress and mufti seated about, chatting in hearty tones.

"A striker? What is that?" she asked as she followed him across the front hall.

"I am his personal assistant. I do everything for him that needs to be done. You will be my assistant until we sail tomorrow."

She nodded, following him up a grand staircase to the second floor where they entered a large suite, heavily carpeted, with two divans and a door leading to a bedroom.

Tallal was not there. Enver ordered Guzell around, clearing out clothes hanging in closets and out of drawers, then packing them in trunks and packing cases.

Tallal had not returned in the two hours she worked when Enver told her that the rest of the things would have to be packed tomorrow at the last minute. She could go but should return to finish up tomorrow in midafternoon.

Guzell chuckled to herself once she was outside, heading back. Enver Dash had made her do all the work as he sat around directing her. Her mood changed as she approached Zampara's house. Where had Mamigon gone?

She had to let herself in with the hidden latch key. Neither Mamigon nor Zampara was home.

Zampara returned five minutes after Guzell. "Oh, you are back . . ." Zampara's words were half questions, half statement.

"Yes, I was wondering where everybody was. Where did you go?"

"I went out for a breath of air. Where did you go?"

"I had to go on an errand. I wish I knew where my man was."

Mamigon returned close to midnight, a picture of grim dejection. "I walked everywhere, looking for him in coffeehouses and eating places," he told Guzell, once they were in their room. "I know it was dangerous, but I had to do something. I am beginning to think he has left the country. By the look on your face, I must believe you have had no good fortune either."

"I am still trying to find him, my man."

"I have been able to think much about this. Tomorrow will be the last day I will send you out looking for him. If we do not find him, *kismet*, we will think of other things."

Guzell's face lit up, looking much like the girl who had awakened in Mamigon's arms the first time back on the trail.

"You wait, now, girl. I do not mean I am through with Tallal." Mamigon had realized that Guzell had placed a different meaning to his words. "All I am saying is that I will try to find out where he went and follow him."

"Even if he has gone to America?"

"I do not know . . . We shall have to see. Let us get some sleep, now, and see what tomorrow brings."

The next morning Guzell left later than usual, an hour before noon. Zampara was home during the morning, not visiting the bazaar as was her usual routine. She made Turkish coffee, knocked on Mamigon's door, and offered to share the bitter concoction.

Mamigon sensed something in the way Zampara was acting. He had sat in the corner of the small, barely furnished sitting room, sipping the brew when she asked how his fortunes were progressing. What was different was that she was not trying to be seductive either in manner or dress.

"There is no change, madam."

"Guzell tells me she is selling oranges."

Mamigon's face darkened a bit. It did not sit well with him that his woman should be a common street vendor. "She is doing what she must."

"You have a truly wonderful helpmate to work so hard into the night."

"Yes, Guzell is . . . What do you mean, into the night?"

"Nothing, Agha, nothing. Only that she was out for nearly four hours last night and . . ."

"Last night?"

"Why, yes . . . did she not tell you?"

Mamigon stared at her. What sort of devilment was Zampara up to? What would Guzell be doing out at night. "What are you trying to say, madam?"

"Truly, you did not know? Well, I happened to be taking the night air— it is so lonely for me these days—when I saw her meet a man on the stoa of a big mansion and go in. I happened to be going by again more than two hours later when Guzell came out and reached home before I did. That is all there is to it."

"Where was this mansion?"

"It is the big house on Taurus Yohl, you know, the place where bachelor senior officers and civilian officials are billeted."

"Did you see who the man was she met?"

"No, Agha, I was not able to get a good look because it was dark and they had the light behind them. But he seemed young . . . You seem upset. I hope I do not have your woman in trouble . . ."

"No, I am not worried. I think she has met one of her brothers and is trying to prevent trouble. Thank you, Zampara Hanum." Mamigon was deeply puzzled. What was Guzell thinking of by not mentioning she had met someone? Was she trying to locate Tallal and talk to him? Nothing made sense. It would be perilous to search for her now. He would wait and talk to her when she came home.

Guzell didn't come home for supper. Mamigon waited for her through the hour. At seven o'clock, he fished out his Colt revolver, loaded it, and went looking for her.

He saw her the moment he arrived at the mansion at Taurus Yohl. Guzell was in front, on the street, helping a man heft steamer trunks and several valises onto a lorry. He was still more than 100 meters away when he saw Tallal walk down the steps, get into the cab of the lorry with another man and drive away with Guzell sitting at the back of the lorry.

Mamigon trotted after them. The lorry was heading for the waterfront. Eight long blocks later, Mamigon spotted the lorry on a lighted quay alongside the gangplank of a freighter with the name *Kennebec* on its stern. The trunks were already being carried by porters up to the deck, followed by Tallal Bey in a gray wool suit and gray fedora, Guzell carrying two bags, and a young man bringing up the rear, carrying a small valise.

Mamigon began running as hard as he could for the gangplank. Tallal was three-quarters of the way up when Mamigon let loose with his battle cry—"*Mamigon . . . Mamigon*"—rending the night air.

The wild cry rooted everyone within earshot. Movement on the gangplank froze; deckhands stopped what they were doing; dockworkers brought their shoulders up as if to cover their ears.

"*Mamigon . . . Mamigon . . .*" He was now 30 meters from the gangplank. Guzell suddenly added to the echoes of the battle cry by beginning to scream, her hands at her face. Enver Dash began yelling "*aman . . . aman*" as he floored himself. Tallal Bey, his eyes wide, his mouth open in surprise, began to cringe at what he saw.

Mamigon had gone into a crouch, his legs spread, his arms extended, his fists holding a revolver. Guzell had not stopped screaming.

"Die, Tallal, you diseased dog, die . . ." He roared before he snapped off three quick shots.

Unseen, powerful hands tugged at Tallal's torso as the bullets sent him slamming backward into the opposite gangplank rail and then down to the planking.

A searchlight snapped on from the bridge of the ship, limning Mamigon as he turned his pistol to Guzell. He didn't fire, his mind still grappling with the meaning of Guzell's presence with Tallal. Mamigon could never have violated a trust or loyalty; could Guzell?

In the second or two of indecision, a Thompson began stuttering from the bridge of the *Kennebec*. Mamigon was all too familiar with the sound of machine gun bullets whining past his ears and he dived behind a pile of wooden crates. He watched as the man behind Guzell—by my father's beard, it was the boy who pissed in his pants, the cart driver, Enver Dash—held Tallal's body by the armpits and she by his legs as they struggled to bring it to the deck.

Mamigon couldn't do anything more at the moment except watch. To try to kill Enver Dash or Guzell would have made him a fine, sharply lighted target. Guzell, his lovely Guzell, looking like the boy he had first met. Struggling manfully to carry Tallal's body to the deck. They reached it. Immediately the gangplank was drawn up, the bow and stern lines were cut from the deck since no one on the quay dared step to the waterside to cast them off, and the *Kennebec* slowly inched away under quarter speed, sailing with the evening tide.

Mamigon didn't have time to think about what he had finally accomplished, the fulfillment of his vow, the death of the murderer of his family. Vengeance was his, at last, and he had no time to savor it, to enjoy it, to bask in it, in reality to realize the full impact of what had happened.

The clanging bells of approaching police wagons, not too far away, told him he would have to get away from there in a hurry. The ship's radio must have alerted the police, if not the crashing of gunfire in the night.

He could hear the dockmen scurrying in the long shed to make themselves scarce with the possibility of more gunfire.

Mamigon looked around him. If he hid in the shed, it would be only a matter of time before he was discovered. If he tried to reach the wharf street, he would surely be seen by the approaching police. He was trapped. The ship's radio would have informed the police by now that he had killed a government official. In no time he would be found out as the outlaw being sought across the Ottoman Empire.

He traveled in a stooping crouch to the end of the quay and slipped over the side into the scummy brine, moving back under the quay to hold on to one of the wooden pilings.

After two hours of shouting and orders and muffled conversation overhead, the rays of light cast from the torches through the cracks of the quay's wooden flooring disappeared and Mamigon was alone.

The moon was almost full. Mamigon eased himself out from under, found a ladder to the top and climbed up to look. The shed down the middle of the quay was blocking his view, so he clambered to the top and peeked around the shed corner. At the head of the wharf were three gendarmes, standing around, effectively blocking his escape. Apparently the police were certain he had not escaped and were awaiting daylight to find him.

He slipped back down the ladder and swam to the next pier, staying underwater for most of the trip. Halfway across, he had to struggle to get rid of his boots and jacket. The police were at the head of that pier, also. There was no sense checking the other piers. They would be covered. He swam slowly, under the surface as much as possible, to reach the stern of a steamer tied up three piers away. He hung on to the pilings alongside through most of the night, the water chilling him to the marrow of his bones. His teeth began to chatter uncontrollably. But he waited until the moon was down, and in the total darkness of the predawn climbed up on the wharf and straddled the heavy stern hawser to work his way to the gunwale. He eased himself over the taffrail and stretched out to meld into the deeper shadow of the stern gunwale. He looked around as much as he could. The lifeboats, one on each side at the stern quarters, were visible, covered with tarpaulin. He worked his way to the port lifeboat nearest him, took a chance by standing up and being seen by the night watch, and climbed into the boat, pulling the tarp back over himself.

Mamigon realized the freighter he had boarded was leaving with the morning tide when he felt a rumbling of the screws and the shouted orders to get the ship underway. He waited until the following morning to present himself to the ship's captain.

He found out he was on an American steamer, the S.S. *Nahant Bay*, manned by a Greek crew and registered in Panama. One look at him, no questions asked, and Mamigon was relegated to the boiler room as a stoker. Seven days out of Izmir he learned the freighter was bound for Brazil to unload its tin vats of camphor oil and pick up coffee for North America.

Mamigon didn't care where he was going, what he was doing, nothing mattered to him. Tallal had managed to dog his thoughts even in death. First his family and the horrendous betrayal of a friendship, and now Guzell's duplicity even as Tallal had died at Mamigon's hand. How could any of this have happened? He had saved himself on the Izmir docks because he was not a quitter but life held no special allure for him now, no goal, no future, just a simple existence until he could join his past at a place and time his uncaring God would decree.

BOOK II

Boston

1   ENVER DASH

Enver Dash felt much like the willing horse these days, much like the horse that kept getting all the work because it was willing. It was shine the boots, do the laundry, iron the collars, buff the brass plates at the front door, sweep the front steps, wash the three company limousines, help the chef in the private dining room, wash pots and pans, and replace the flowers not only in the waiting room, but also in the tiny automobile vases . . . by Allah, life in the army would have been easier back home than here in Boston, Massachusetts, U.S.A.

Worst of all, he was asked to—no—told to accompany the bookkeeper and the cook to the market merely to carry back the foodstuffs. A common carrier, a donkey, that is all he was as far as they were concerned. He remembered the words of his old grandfather who had told him when he was a little boy to stop crying when his cat died. "You will survive distress, my son, but not disgrace." Enver Dash was certain he was not going to survive the disgrace of being a woman's servant. Only the unstated promise in the eyes of the bookkeeper that something more than a worker relationship was in the offing had mollified his inner discontent. She was a full-bodied woman in her early forties whose husband had fallen overboard from the ship bound for America years ago. She seemed to have found physical solace where she could among the staff of Euphrates Export-Import Company. Enver was probably one of the last of the consenting if not eager males who had yet to embrace her opulent charms . . . truly a Turkish delight.

Ever since that fateful trek to Aleppo with the Armenian exiles, Enver always felt a certain amount of trepidation commingled with a sense of gleeful adventure when a new sexual tryst was in the offing. His fears had to do with his penis. He had been castrated and the lack of an expected sac at its base had prompted him from the very beginning to establish his virility immediately with a consenting woman. He would plunge right in without giving his partner the slightest chance to find out what he had or didn't have. His deep sense of loss and woebegone outlook five years ago after he had been shorn of his testes had disappeared about three weeks after the horror when he had awakened one morning during the march to find he had an erection. He couldn't believe it, and kept the fact to himself for fear the perpetrators would think the job hadn't been done. But it had happened again and again in the mornings. In the dark of the night he had masturbated, finally. Not only was the feeling no different from what he had experienced before, but, miracle of miracles, he had actually ejaculated gobs and gobs of fluid. To test the miracle completely, he had found a young girl straggler from the main body among the *arabas*, ready to drop from exhaustion and hunger. She was no more than ten or eleven, Enver had guessed.

He had lifted her on to his *araba*—the same one in which the Armenian outlaw had been held captive—and raped her repeatedly with great ease and gratifying results. She had not made one outcry or movement after he slugged her into submission and Enver had not been sure she wasn't dead when he dumped her in a motionless heap from the cart the next day. He was a man after all!

The first year in New York City had been his best year of sexual activity. He had even been accused in a paternity charge by a desperate consulate worker. Enver always smirked when he recalled how he had shown his shorn privates to the accuser's brother to scotch further talk that he was responsible. He sensed he was losing interest in women with the passage of time but he liked the attention he received from them. Allah knows, he received very little attention from anyone. What he liked best about his romantic escapades was that after the participants had spent their lust, and activity had ceased, the woman never failed to "ooh" and "ah" at the unfamiliar sight of a penis without the usual pendulous appendage, a penis that looked much longer because of the missing sac. The major surprise was that Enver was able to have a solid, highly useful tool despite the fairy tales associated with such a situation. When he went further and explained to the ignorant that he couldn't impregnate them, he became a veritable darling.

The one element in all of the exchanges that left him and his admirers unsatisfied was the explanation of how he had come to be that way. He would always become mysterious and vague. The real explanation was too shameful for him to admit: The commander of his military unit back in Turkey had had him denutted as punishment for allowing a prized captive, who would have brought much bounty money, to escape.

His face would go into a deep frown when he thought of that wild Armenian strongman, Mamigon. That whore-licking, cock-sucking bastard had been his downfall from the moment he had caught Enver after the sacking of Yosghat Dagh.

That was all in the past now—let's see, it was after the Sabbath had ended at sundown that fateful evening, a Saturday, October 4, 1915, when he had left Smyrna in a hail of bullets from that wild man—it was now May 6, 1921, exactly five years and seven months, give or take a day or two.

He was in Boston now, where the civility and polish of that old city's residents had made Enver forget much of the past. There were no reference points, no sights, to bring any of his early youth back to him. He was a short, stocky, swarthy man of twenty-two years whose major problem was how to be helpful to the office staff and still do as little work as possible. The men had found out long ago, from talkative women who hadn't kept Enver's secret secret, and made Enver the butt of their barnyard humor. But, that was ever thus.

Enver's single room on Tremont Street over an antique store, rented from the suspicious Armenian owner who accepted Enver as a Turkish-speaking Yugoslav, had been the scene of many trysts, wonderful trysts, marred only by the necessity to go down a flight of steps to the rear of the store to use the toilet facilities.

In the private, untouched world of the shipping company, Enver had found it easy to become accustomed to his new life. Everyone around him spoke his mother tongue, he rarely had to fend for himself when he left the office building on Boylston Street around the corner from Park Square, facing the Public Gardens, and the oasis of an Armenian coffeehouse was always within short walking distance. He found it almost as natural to go to an Armenian coffeehouse as a Turkish one. The customers were more apt to speak in Turkish since there were enough Armenians who couldn't speak Armenian to make Turkish the lingua franca. Enver couldn't understand any of the politics—all the conversation was political, it seemed—but he was always amused at the sudden and often roaring diatribes against Tallat Pasha, the interior minister; or Sultan Hamid, the Terrible; or Fakhrit Pasha, the Butcher; or Enver Pasha, the Executioner.

He didn't know of many Turks who lived in Boston. Most everyone he knew of was living in a place called Peabody, a little city north of Boston where many tanning plants were located. This type of work had drawn the Turks to that area as well as to Brockton, a shoe manufacturing city to the south of Boston. Since the war in Europe had deeply eroded the work base of most Balkan and Mediterranean countries, the Turks were one of many nationalities who had sought economic, political, and social refuge in the Americas, mostly in the United States and Argentina.

He had liked New York but fell in love with Boston from the day he set foot on its narrow, cobbled streets. It had reminded him of some of the cities in Asia Minor he had visited.

Enver had scratched his head in wonderment at how quickly he had taken to his new way of living, just six days after leaving the shores of Anatolia. It had been an uneventful crossing. Nothing could have been as eventful as the moments of sheer terror he had felt on the gangplank as he lay flat to escape the bullets of that wild Armenian.

Carrying Tallal's bullet-torn body onto the deck of the *Kennebec* had been the last thing he had wanted to do that night, but that goat-headed Sadi had insisted on it. He couldn't worm his way by so he helped him get Tallal's body up the rest of the gangplank.

Wonder what happened to Sadi, he often thought? On the fourth night out, with things nice and peaceful, he had tried to stick his little roommate. Sadi had kept very much to himself. Enver had never seen him in a state of undress, although he himself had walked around a few times without a stitch on in preparation for a saltwater shower on deck, pumped up from the sea. Sadi had kept his back to Enver on those occasions. On that fourth night, Enver had climbed up to the upper bunk with a stiff member to get some relief from Sadi's unexplored rump. A sharp elbow in his ribs had been his first reward. A side-swinging fist in his face, sending him back to the deck on his behind had been his second. Hampered by the darkness as he made one more determined, snarling attempt, his chest had cleared the rim of the bunk and his hands were on Sadi's soft bottom facing him when Sadi's heels came slamming across into his shoulders, knocking him senseless to the deck. When he regained consciousness, he had begun to vomit and was sick for the rest of the trip. He never once said a word or looked at Sadi again. The ship's doctor had said he had suffered a mild concussion and should be careful where he walked around the next time. Decks are not meadows, the doctor had admonished.

Once the ship had docked at a South Boston pier, Sadi had walked off and disappeared, never to be heard from again. The *Kennebec* had gone on to New York and Sadi—no one knew his last name—had been forgotten after inquiries about a homeless Turkish boy went for naught.

Today, Friday, was shopping day and he dutifully followed the cook and the bookkeeper, Ismet Hanum, on the long walk to Cross Street near the market district to do the shopping, mostly from pushcart vendors. Whenever the cook's back was turned, the bookkeeper turned long, unwinking stares on him, certifying to Enver that she was ready for him whenever he liked. He licked his lips at the thought of parting her legs and nestling in her warmth. He would have to let her know where to meet her, that would be all the arrangements needed. He wondered if she knew about his special lack. Perhaps she did, perhaps she didn't, but if she didn't it would turn out fine if he could mount her before she found out. He had learned quickly in his young life that breasts and balls had little bearing on ultimate sexual enjoyment once the preliminaries were disposed of. Both were superficial appurtenances whose initial importance seemed to fade as intimacies developed. Only one of the women had mentioned that she had missed the bouncing of a man's balls against her crotch as she was being serviced, even though she had climaxed repeatedly under his ministrations. Enver had walloped her with an open hand across her jaw and left her crying.

The bookkeeper had arrived after supper to meet Enver waiting at the street doorway to his upstairs room. He had left the office earlier than usual to fix up his bare room. Fixing up had meant finding a clean pillowcase and smoothing out the bedsheet even though it hadn't been washed for weeks. She didn't look around the room when she entered. She simply pulled the cord to douse the light from the one hanging bulb in the center of the ceiling. When Enver heard the rustling of her clothes as she undressed, he did the same. She pushed him down to the bed and began fondling his member. Not a word had been exchanged. The activity became hot and heavy and Enver wanted to cry out at times at the fierceness of her embraces and the almost uncontrolled use of her teeth on parts of his body. She seemed to be climaxing all the while, even when Enver wasn't sticking her. He was wondering who had the male role in this encounter. She initiated everything, but he was finally left breathless and steaming when she suddenly rolled over on her back and quieted down with a small sigh.

Enver was a happy man, but he couldn't help but remember what he had heard his father say one day in a discussion about a widow in their village: "A buxom widow must be either married, buried, or shut up in a convent." Ismet Hanum was certainly the type they must have had in mind . . .

He was startled when the bookkeeper spoke up for the first time that evening, still lying naked beside him. "Tallal Bey wants to see you first thing in the morning."

2 🙰 REUNION

Mamigon had too much time to think. He was leaning with both elbows on the taffrail next to the port poop ventilator staring at nothing and at everything as the S.S. *Nahant Bay* swung at anchor in the Boston Harbor channel. The left side of the harbor front was a solid mass of fishing trawlers, seiners, and yawls, their short masts heavily festooned with lines and sheets, jammed together to avail themselves of every inch of pierage. On the right of the huge harbor was the navy yard, full of four-stacker destroyers and two-stacker cruisers, all of them still in their wartime gray and some with the zigzag white stripes that were supposed to have confused enemy submariners. Dominating the harbor and landscape was a single, tall, pointed tower Mamigon learned later was the Custom House, the tallest building in New England, soaring in lonely splendor above the slate-gray rooftops of the city. The only other structure clearly discernible was the gilt dome of the State House, sitting atop Beacon Hill in close juxtaposition to the Custom House, giving the casual surveyor of the cityscape the unacceptable thought that some sort of phallic symbolism had been the intent.

Mamigon's work was totally manual and it had left his mind free to dwell or roam. If it had not been for the constant and demanding physical effort he had had to put into the work of stoking the two boilers with coal the first week he had joined the ship's crew, he probably would have meditated for days without moving a muscle. The exercise became his saving crutch. His inability to speak Greek had limited his relationships, although a quarter of the crew spoke Turkish. None of his fellow stokers spoke it, and his contacts with deckhands were rare. He had become the seventh man in the stokehold and had become instantly acceptable because he never worried about the changes in the watch, shoveling through his time consistently, his great strength never seeming to be exhausted. Eight days after he had stowed away on the *Nahant Bay*, the rusty, dun-colored 15,000 tonner had dropped its hook in the harbor at Recife. Mamigon never left his bunk in the crew quarters in the bow during the three days in port, going topside only as the freighter steamed out with its new cargo of coffee.

The captain, a tall, blond and blue-eyed man by the name of Nicholopoulos, could speak Turkish. He had called Mamigon to the bridge, now curious about the giant stowaway who had not attempted to jump ship. No, Mamigon had answered the direct question, he was not a Turk, he was an Armenian. No, he had not stowed away to escape conscription. He had served in the army. Yes, he was wanted by the police . . . yes, for murder. No, he had fought Turkish soldiers and police and killed some of them. No, it was a personal matter and it was now all settled. No, I cannot go back to my homeland. No, I have no family. Yes, I would like to stay on board, I have no place to go. Twenty-two American dollars a month? That is kind of you . . . what is that in real money . . . nine pounds Turkish? That is good but not necessary. I do not have need for money. Thank you, can I go now?

The freighter's home port was Boston. The *Nahant* had a regular route: coffee to Baltimore; cutlery, cordage, and boots to Smyrna; camphor oil to Recife; and coffee to Baltimore. Boston was visited once a year for the dry-docks where the *Nahant*'s barnacles were scraped and the boilers relined. The advent of war changed the steamer's itinerary. She stopped sailing across the Atlantic and shifted her trips from Baltimore to Boston with coffee, and wool cloth and boots to Recife. The change was safer for the steamer and, as it turned out, far more lucrative for the owners.

As for Mamigon, he had become a virtual monk aboard ship. He had had many opportunities to leave. He could have left permanently with the bless-ings of the ship's captain. He could have stayed ashore as long as the ship was in port. He chose neither. It was as if he were condemned for life to be a prisoner on board, a prisoner without shackles one could see. The bars and shackles were there. He had decided that since there was little reason to have faith in his fellow man . . . and certainly no reason at all to have faith in such a savage, cruel, uncaring God . . . there was little need to traffic or consort with anyone. It had been easy to renounce his God and seek redemption, unconsciously, in self-imposed slavery on a modern-day trireme. It was harder to turn away from the company of men. Mamigon was one of those males whose libido was aroused only if he cared for a specific woman. One-night dalliances had never been for him. He had never been able to understand the Tallals of the world. The natural biological reflexes had been taking care of his pent up drives. Mamigon was persev-erative, never letting go of an idea or thought once it was implanted in him.

The belief that two human beings he had thought were close friends had betrayed him had become an obsession. Tallal had been like a brother; Guzell had been like a good wife and friend. Both had torn asunder his sense and concept of loyalty and fidelity. With his entire family gone with the sword, both his deep sorrow and his deep rage had been banked much like the fires in the ship's boilers.

With the captain's permission, he had established his own little forge in the engineer's quarters where he painstakingly cast molds of worn down or rusted fittings, recast them, furbished them, and reset them all over the steamer. He worked with brass fittings at first, re-creating couplings, grom-mets, sleeves, and stanchions. When he had exhausted all possibilities in brass, he turned to iron fittings. He had started the work about a year after he had stowed aboard. The S.S. *Nahant Bay* was the best-fitted vessel on the high seas after five years even though she had been launched at the turn of the century.

Every day the cargo ship was at sea, Mamigon worked one watch as a stoker and assigned himself two watches as a blacksmith-turned-machinist to occupy his physical and mental needs. Otherwise, he seemed to be a man totally devoid of additional interests. He didn't seem to care about anything, certainly not enough to discuss a single topic with anyone. He never asked where the *Nahant Bay* was heading, he had no interest in the news when the ship's complement returned from shore leave . . . no interest in women . . . no interest . . . no interest in anything . . . until a September night in 1919—four years after he had slipped aboard in Izmir—when the *Nahant Bay* was battened down and ready to leave Boston in the morning.

Mamigon was at his usual place on the ship's stern rail looking at the lights across the harbor when he heard a rising commotion behind him on the waterfront. He strolled to the bows to see what was going on down below in the street. Captain Nicholopoulos and the first mate, standing back to back, were on the main avenue that served all the wharfs. They were surrounded by a yelling, howling crowd carrying torches and brandishing everything from pokers and knives to cudgels and baseball bats that to Mamigon seemed like special weapons for mayhem.

The two from the ship were holding the crowd at bay with their drawn pistols, weapons they carried whenever on shore carrying money and drafts to the ship's offices.

One look and Mamigon had run to the gangplank at the well deck, picking up a huge winch spanner along the way, yelling "Come on" to the crew.

When he reached the quay and began sprinting for the mob, he let go with his almost forgotten battle cry, drowning out most of the mob's cries and grabbing everyone's attention.

The three-foot spanner in his hands weighed at least 6 pounds as he held it high over his head like a toothpick and bellowed his cry again. The mob, several hundred young hooligans from the looks of them, maintained its ring around the captain but at least fifty or so squared away to face the onrushing lone attacker. The ship's crew had not followed Mamigon at that point.

In the flickering half light of the burning torches Mamigon couldn't see if any of them had small arms but he noted that the spanner in his hands was just as long but heavier than anything the mob had in front of him.

Mamigon began a wide-arc swing of his weapon as he got closer. In hand-to-hand combat, the German officers had drilled into him at the academy that only three opponents could be simultaneously effective against a single enemy when firearms were not involved . . . gauge the three closest to you . . . seek out the most dangerous appearing of the three . . . dispatch him swiftly . . . and move in to the stronger one on either side . . . in one quick movement.

His forged steel spanner hit the iron poker held up by the center ruffian to parry the blow, tearing the poker from the hand and sending it winging into the mob where wild cries of pain arose. The spanner continued its deadly arc, thudding into the poker man's temple, continuing on to the right to smash an upheld piece of wood and slam into a shoulder, continuing on, as Mamigon moved forward into the mob, to elicit a howl of surprised pain as a knifer ready to stab him in the back felt the prongs of the spanner rip across his nose, continuing on to smash into a head again, almost lifting the body attached to it and sending it into three others, continuing on to smash a jaw as its owner was bringing down a bat to Mamigon's head, continuing on . . . unopposed, as the mob finally parted, giving him a wide passageway to the side of the ship's officers. Moans and cries became the sound of the night. Defection from the mob became rampant as a dozen or so armed members of the crew were seen running to the scene. Suddenly the mob dispersed, leaving the street in almost total darkness with the loss of light from its torches. The captain kept slapping Mamigon on the back in speechless appreciation. Mamigon had been baffled. Was this the way Americans acted? No, no, the gendarmerie of the city had left their posts. They were in some kind of a dispute with the city government. It looked as if the entire city was unprotected now that the police had left their duty to protest their grievances, while rioting, looting, and general lawlessness prevailed.

Mamigon had gained unwanted but added stature as the result of his actions. The captain had raised his pay to thirty dollars, retroactive to the day he came aboard. Mamigon had refused any recompense and the captain had been holding it for him, shaking his head at the likes of such a man. The captain wasn't sure about the man's past but he could find no fault with the taciturn giant who was still a stranger to him despite the passage of years on board.

After the incident in Boston—years later Mamigon had determined that it was the police strike that Governor Coolidge had squelched—Mamigon was asked by the captain to take dinner with him in the officers' ward room, which the Armenian had politely declined. He had agreed, however, to play a daily game of backgammon with the captain, the only relief from the austere life Mamigon had allowed himself. It was a turning point for Mamigon. He slowly began to open up and exchange small observations with Captain Nicholopoulos. By the time the *Nahant* had reached Recife, Mamigon had agreed to accompany the captain ashore for the paperwork the officer had to do. On the return to Boston, now the quiet and sedate city it always had been, Mamigon went ashore again to have coffee and later supper before the two returned aboard. Mamigon never said much but Captain Nicholopoluos found the relationship easy and undemanding. And nothing could persuade Mamigon to leave the stokehold and take duties topside. The captain eventually gave up trying to change his mind.

Mamigon had asked some questions at their first visit to the Boston waterfront that had brought smiles to the captain's face as he had answered them. No, those women were not streetwalkers. Yes, that is the way they dressed in America. Certainly, the legs were visible and their backsides were clearly outlined since petticoats were not worn here. Honestly, they were unapproachable, modest, proper ladies, some married, some not. Do you want to get together with a woman? Excuse me, Mamigon, I thought your questions were leading up to that. No, I understand. I didn't mean to embarrass you. (Phew, what a hard head!)

That's the way it had gone for five years . . . almost to the day he had left Izmir that fateful night in October, 1915. Too much time to think, too much time to exist, too much time left before death. Perhaps he should go ashore when the *Nahant Bay* is berthed and walk the strange city without the company of the captain.

That is what he did, walking slowly in his slightly limping gait, wearing trousers given him by the captain that were just barely long enough and a jacket that was very tight around his shoulders, and sleeves that were so short he attracted smiles from passers by. His shirt collar couldn't be buttoned but he wore a black tie to complete the picture.

Mamigon was fully bearded, not having shaved since the day he went on that hunting trip in 1915. The ship's barber had trimmed the hirsute growth up short. It had taken nearly eight weeks to get rid of the henna dye Guzell had applied to his hair and facial growth.

His first walk had taken him directly over the spot where he had charged to the captain's side that dark night with the howling mob, then under the elevated rail tracks, up the street to the Custom House tower's gray granite facade, and then the slow, gradual incline up narrow streets to the top of the hill where the imposing sprawl of the gold-domed State House dominated the sky. The dome reminded him of the dome of the Aya Sofia, the great mosque in Constantinople. He slowly retraced his steps, not venturing into side streets, to return to the ship.

It was a Saturday. The captain met him at the gangplank as he was leaving the ship for a night of dinner and drinking.

"Why do you not wish to come along? It is not good for you to continue renouncing the world."

"I do not wish to, captain. Thank you."

"If it is because of money, you have plenty, Mamigon Agha."

"No, many thanks, it is not the money."

"It is your badly fitting clothes, then?" Captain Nicholopoulos was very conscious of clothes, always dressed in the latest fashion when stepping out on the town. He always sported a heavy, gnarled cane, a memento from his father.

"I am poor company, captain. I do not wish to become the object of your pity. I recognize your kindness and thank you, again, for it."

"It is not kindness, *bahbahm*! I like you."

Mamigon paused, unable to say more but deeply irritated at the persistency of the captain. "Let us go, then . . ."

They walked in the deserted darkness of the waterfront for 10 blocks before entering a doorway and going upstairs to a Greek restaurant complete with a bouzouki band. Mamigon had little to say, but that didn't stop the captain from growing ever more expansive as the ouzo took more and more of his senses and Mamigon ended up having to help his staggering companion back to the ship.

The brisk October night air helped the captain revive. "It must be Sunday morning now, my friend. If I am ever in port on a Sunday, I go to church and pray for my family back home in Greece . . ."

Mamigon grunted assent, so the captain continued, "I find it helps me, my conscience, when I do this. Are you a churchgoer?"

"Once I was. It has been nearly six years since I have attended services."

"There must be an Armenian church in Boston. Why do you not find out where and go tomorrow . . . this morning, I mean?"

"No, not I."

"Very well. I just thought I would mention it . . ." The captain knew enough not to pursue the thought from a certain finality in Mamigon's voice.

Mamigon didn't sleep well that morning and was on deck watching the sun's first rays cracking the solid blackness to the east. It was barely light enough to see when Mamigon left the ship and retraced his steps of the day before toward Beacon Hill and the State House. The heart of a big city could not be more deserted than on a Sunday morning at dawn, but he almost bumped into a policeman sauntering clear of a building corner.

"Armenian," he said to the quizzical policeman, pointing to himself. "Armenian," he said again, hoping his English pronounciation of what he was told meant Armenian in English was good enough.

The policeman nodded emphatically, looking up at the huge, bearded man. "Yes . . . ?"

Mamigon held his hands in prayer and then opened them as if in question.

"Of course . . . You want to go to church. Let's see, now . . . turn down the next street and walk about twenty blocks . . . twenty," he said, sticking his ten fingers at him twice and crossing his wrists to indicate intersections.

Mamigon patted the officer on a shoulder and walked on. It had never occurred to him that there could be an Armenian community or even a church in this American town. The captain's talk had aroused his curiosity and it might be good to see some fellow Armenians if such existed here. The policeman had not hesitated about it . . . perhaps there was a church. In any event, it would be a nice walk.

He found it on Shawmut Avenue. He recognized the Armenian script on the plaque even though he couldn't read it. It was a tall, red brick structure and it was not open. Across the street in the next block was a park with benches along the paths that crisscrossed the treed and bushed scape. He walked over and sat down to wait. He noticed that the park was duplicated in the block beyond, a street with elevated rail tracks separating the parks. Only the chirping of sparrows broke the stillness of the morning. His clothes were tight and his discomfit was aggravated by the coolness of the morning.

People finally started arriving, some walking past him as he sat on the bench. He could tell immediately they were Armenian from their eyes and the bulbous nose tips of the men. Mamigon had always marveled how he could distinguish an Armenian from the Greeks, Turks, Arabs, Persians, Nestorians, Lebons and all the rest of the Middle Easterners who populated that part of the world. Only a rank outsider would mistake one for the other.

He didn't stay long once he entered the edifice and climbed the handsome circular stairway to the upper floor where Mass was going to be celebrated. The long morning prayer was being chanted. Mamigon was appalled. He stood at the back of the church for about ten minutes, did not cross himself, and walked out quietly. What had bothered him . . . shocked him . . . was to find the congregation seated in family groups. The men were not worshiping together as had been the practice for centuries. Their wives and children were with them. The change was too much for him to swallow. In the old country, the women and young children occupied a section to the side or rear or the balcony, if there was one.

After nearly six years, the jolt of smelling incense and the chanting of the morning prayers in the ancient minor key had evoked memories and senses long forgotten or buried. The bitterness of that harsh, utterly cruel Sunday morning in Yosghat Dagh and his plea for a sign from his God had not faded. He still crossed himself before he took a meal but that was almost a reflex action that he found impossible to counter with his will. He had been surprised at his inability to eat the one time he had not remembered to make the sign of the cross before he started.

He hurried back to the ship, ravenously hungry now, ate the heavy, greasy breakfast the galley always cooked up in huge quantities, and went back to his bunk for sleep. He was deeply troubled about something and it hit him while he was eating: He had not a penny in his pockets and had to ignore the beckoning collection plate sitting in expectation on the vestibule table. It was another reflex he could not help.

The *Nahant Bay* sailed at evening tide the following Tuesday and it was three weeks before Mamigon was back in Boston. He had a suit of clothes now, purchased in Recife, complete with a black derby, high-button boots, and a camel's hair overcoat. Mamigon still had a small fortune in gold, silver, and gems in the small bag he had kept around his waist, his share of what had been distributed among the women after the *polis* unit had been routed and the survivors rescued.

It was a Tuesday when the *Nahant* docked and the four-day turnaround for unloading and loading permitted Mamigon to find an Armenian coffee-house where he spent several hours sipping Turkish coffee and listening to the talk around him, mostly in Turkish. It was an extreme pleasure hearing his native tongue again. The *Nahant* sailed Saturday in a snowstorm for its three-week roundtrip to Recife. Mamigon was back in Boston the last Saturday in November as a howling storm he learned later was called a nor'easter, dumped rain on the area.

It was bright and sunny with a snap of cold in the air Sunday morning when Mamigon decided to take a stroll to the church he had visited more than seven weeks ago. It was early again and he sat on the bench closest to the street corner near the church to wait, this time bundled up in his handsome coat, complete with derby. The church doors were not opened until eight o'clock for morning prayers. A sad commentary, he thought. In the old country, the church doors were never locked and morning prayers began at five. His idle gaze had noticed a large five-story building facing the twin park on the other side of the elevated tracks. It must be some kind of an inn, he thought, or a school of some kind . . . and definitely for women. The only sex that entered or left was female . . . he shook his head at his imagination . . . a dark-haired woman who left the building had all the manner and walk of Guzell from a distance. Guzell . . . he had shunted her from his mind . . . he had not wanted to come to grips with her defection . . . accept it in any way . . . and had relegated her to the dead. He sighed and went to church where he stayed through the morning prayers and left before the Mass started.

One of the pleasant surprises of the new land he visited every three or four weeks was a simple mechanical device called a shower bath in *fresh* water, indoors. Being drenched with saltwater on the deck of the *Nahant* was not the best way to keep clean, especially in hot weather when the briny residue itched all over. In the old country, the customary practice of taking a bath on Saturday night to prepare for church on Sunday morning involved the bothersome chore of filling tubs. It was a happy day for Mamigon when Captain Nicholopoulos steered him to a public shower maintained by the city. He would put his clean underclothes in a paper bag and walk for nearly an hour to take a luxurious shower every evening he was in Boston.

He was back again in Boston two days before what the Americans, he found out, were celebrating as Christmas, a Saturday. The *Nahant Bay* stayed in port over the holiday week, leaving the third day of the new year on a Monday. Mamigon had attended morning prayers on both Sundays he was in port, spending some of his spare time during the week, after his shower bath, in the one coffeehouse he frequented, a former storage loft over a store, operated by a tall cadaverous man who went by the name of Koko. Koko, with a white apron around his middle as the only indication of his role as owner-manager-coffeemaker-waiter, shambled among the twenty or so tables with a small tray, setting down demitasses of Turkish coffee, the only item available. Nothing else. No whisper of food, absolutely no liquor since Armenian men rarely drank. The price was tailored to his clientele, the majority of whom were poor: a demitasse cost five cents or more, depending on the customer.

There were three types of customers in the coffeehouse. The majority were card players, devoted to the game of *scambil*, a form of poker, who filled the room with raucous shouting when someone made a score. Koko extracted an extra dime per demitasse from each of them for the use of a table. In addition, the big winner—enriched by as much as two or three dollars—would give Koko a tenth of his winnings. The second group of customers were the former political activists who would gather as many as five or six to a table, not including bystanders, arguing about the circumstances surrounding the massacres in Turkey, the politics that had caused them, the perfidy of the Turks, the French, and the English, the unreliability of the Russians, and the future of the Armenians. Some of the discussions threatened to conclude in blows as the Dashnaks, the Hunchaks, the Rahmgavars, and the nonaligned had at it. Koko charged ten cents for each demitasse at these tables because the men were so busy talking they rarely ordered second and third rounds, limiting his profits severely. Then there was the third type of customer, two old friends who would come in one at a time, acknowledge one another with a small gesture and sit together in silence, occasionally nodding as if in response to each other's unspoken

thoughts, but mostly lost in sad reverie. This would go on for two, sometimes three, coffees before one or the other would sigh, say it was good being
there, and take leave. Koko charged a nickel a cup to this type.

Mamigon fit in this latter category, except that he had no companions.
He would sit alone, take two unsweetened cups, pay his dime, and leave,
having stared at the table top the entire time he was there. Attempts by some
to start a conversation always failed. Mamigon would simply shake his
head, regardless of what was said or asked. The men learned to leave him
alone, even though he had become the object of much conjecture. Who was
this big, taciturn, antisocial man? Someone said his name was Mamigon,
but he never spoke to them. They had heard he only spoke Turkish, which
all of them could speak, of course, but he seemed to have no friends, no
family, no one they could seek out to establish a reference point.

It was a cold January day, New Year's Day, and Mamigon had decided
he would warm his bones with a spot of coffee. He felt chilly after his
shower. When he climbed the stairs to the coffee house, he found all the
tables taken, the place loud with voices and heavy with cigarette smoke. He
turned to leave.

"MAMIGON!"

He whirled, startled at the roaring shout of his name. My God, it
was . . .

"TATIOS! It *is* Tatios?"

Tatios extricated himself from a tight group around one of the tables
across the room and ran to the big man, dodging tables and bodies.
Mamigon did the same, and they embraced without saying a word. Tears
rolled down the thin man's cheeks.

"My God in heaven, man, I thought you were dead!"

"I was sure *you* were. I cannot believe it!"

Everyone in the room had stopped what they were doing or saying, transfixed by the tableau unfolding before them.

"How long has it been?"

"It must be five years . . . at least."

"How did you get away?" Both said exactly the same words at the same
time.

They had pulled back from their embrace, but still held on to each other's
arms, Mamigon towering over Tatios.

"They shot me and thought they had killed me," Tatios said. "How about
you?"

"It is a long story, but I slipped away from the *araba* with the knife you
left me. Oofah, I cannot believe it. I did not think for one minute you were
alive, much less in this part of the world. Before we say another word, is
Tatios your real name, or do you still think I am a goddamned Turk?" The
place erupted in laughter, joining the two.

"My name is Tatios, son of *Haji* Hagop of Gurin, but tell me who you
are. I only heard you shout your name when we were riding down on the
Turkish column."

"I am Mamigon, son of Magaros of Yosghat Dagh. Tell me . . ."

A gasp went up from their captive audience, followed by cheering and clapping as the men rose to their feet. The two friends were astounded.

"Mamigon Agha, the Avenger! Mamigon the Eunuch Maker!" The men began crowding around the two, slapping Mamigon's back and seeking a handshake.

"Oh, for Christ's sake, let us go!" Unsmiling, Mamigon pushed his way through the room and down the stairs to the cold air, Tatios behind him.

"Where did they get all those horse buns about me, anyway?"

"You are famous, man. You are one of the few heroes we Armenians have. Those women and your brother that you led to safety. They got to Crete and then to Athens, where your brother and one of the women told the story. It was published in Athens, then the *Times* of London, and it got to this country. All the Armenian papers printed stories about you . . . and one of them had a copy of the wanted poster. It was marvelous reading in 1917. You caused a heavy upsurge of support for the campaign the Americans were conducting here to 'Feed the Starving Armenians.'"

"I cannot believe it . . . What was all that hollering about me being the eunuch maker?"

"You . . . do not know?"

"Would I be asking if I knew?"

"Your brother Aram told the newspapers how you left your mark on all the soldiers you killed."

"How did he . . . what did . . . how do you get eunuch maker from that?"

"He said you cut off the private parts and placed them in each dead man's right hand."

"Cristos!"

"What is the matter, man?"

"My brother is crazy . . ."

"Why, what does that mean?"

"I never once did that . . ." Mamigon saw the look of disbelief on Tatios's face. "I swear."

"Araxy, one of the women with you out there, says she slipped back once to one of the battle scenes and saw the dead men exactly as Aram described . . ." Tatios didn't feel like calling his friend a liar.

"Hmm . . . Was Araxy with Aram when she saw this?"

"I do not know."

"Was anything else mentioned?"

"No . . ."

"Was any mention made of a mark on the forehead?"

"By God, yes! Looked like the sign of the cross, Araxy said!"

"That is right. That is the mark I made on the forehead of each man I killed in battle. That is the only mark I left."

Tatios kept looking at Mamigon as they walked along, slowly.

"I wanted to make sure they knew that one man, and only one man, was responsible and that that man was a Christian. Verily, I had thought of decapitating each man but that seemed too much."

"Then, who did . . . ?"

"Must have been Aram himself, that is who." Mamigon looked as if he were a man talking out loud to no one in particular. "I thought something was eating at him. He was the youngest and Mama had doted on him. I remember, now, his howls of pain when he saw her dead . . . had to hold him to quiet him down . . . never cried again as far as I could tell . . . must have gnawed away at his senses, though . . . It must have been Aram, though I cannot believe it."

"He never said anything? Gave no indication?"

"Nothing . . . nothing, but I recall now that he was never exactly where I had expected to see him. It was not a conscious expectation, though. You know what I mean . . . Something or someone is not exactly right but you think nothing of it until other facts or events place it in perspective."

"What happened to Aram, do you know?"

"Have no idea what happened to Aram or the women until this business of Araxy and Aram came up. Thank God, they escaped to safety. Did the news stories say anything about them staying in Athens?"

"No. Apparently they had just arrived and were the center of attention. Wonder why Aram said you did it instead of taking the credit for himself?"

Mamigon shook his head, perplexed. "Must have made me look like someone out of his head . . . cannot believe it . . ."

"After what the Turks did to us, that sounded like small retribution. It gave all Armenians a lift!"

"Camel dung and bull dung!"

"It was purple reading, I can tell you. By the by, did you catch up with Tallal?"

Mamigon looked down at the sidewalk as they walked. He finally nodded.

"Did you send him to hell?"

He nodded again.

"You seem not to relish the thought, Mamigon . . . something wrong?"

"He turned out to be a fly."

"A fly? What are you saying?"

"I lowered myself. There was no joy in it."

"Why was Tallal a fly?"

"My father told all of us, his sons, that our thoughts and actions should soar like an eagle. I had forgotten his words: An eagle does not hawk at flies."

"Perk up, Mamigon, death was too good for Tallal."

"I know that now. I have been wandering about at sea without ambition, without desire, without a flint-spark of grace."

"Mamigon, the rest of us are gathering up the twigs and chips of what has been left to us and making the best of life. I am married now, and . . ."

"That is good news. Who did you marry?"

"Do you remember when I tried to get you to leave the *araba* with me? Do you remember the shots fired just as I left?" Mamigon was nodding. "Those shots were being fired on my instructions by a woman from my village whom I met again here in Boston. It is a long story but I married her five years ago. We have two children, a girl and a baby boy."

"Good, good . . . I am happy for you. What was your wife's family name?"

"Her name is Eksah Drevanian. I attended college with her brother who was butchered . . . you remember . . ."

"Yes, yes. What do you do for work? You must be a professor or something."

Tatios paused before he answered. "I sew buttons in a men's suit factory. My education is classical and I cannot speak English well enough yet to get the kind of work I want. I am a failure."

"Come, come, a man of your intelligence will find something better soon. Keep up your spirits."

Tatios laughed outright, shaking his head. "Look at who is telling me to keep up his spirit. You seem to have surrendered yourself to your past."

They walked for a long time in silence until Mamigon asked where Tatios lived.

"I live in a part of the city called the South End. We have a church organized only three blocks from our street. We are heading in that direction, now."

"Oh. That must be the church I have attended in the past few months."

"You . . . you have been at our church?"

"Yes, if your church is the only one in these parts."

"But, I have never seen you, and I go every Sunday."

"Tatios, I only stay for the morning prayer and . . ."

"Enough. You will come home with me tonight, meet the family, and we will go to church tomorrow morning."

"No, thank you, Tatios. I will meet you tomorrow morning at the church."

Tatios couldn't shake Mamigon from his resolve and the two parted after a long handclasp.

3 ❧ ALARM

It should be very important to be called into the office on Saturday, the Moslem Sabbath. Enver was perspiring by the time he arrived in Park Square after his mile-long hurried walk. It was a cool May morning and he had not thought much of the idea that a bath was in order after his activities of the previous evening, but he had little choice but to sponge himself with a wet, wrung-out undershirt in the cold of his room, shivering all the while.

Ismet Hanum had left in the dark of the night and the fatigue she had caused in Enver almost made him late for his appointment.

Tallal Bey was pacing back and forth in his carpeted office that had heavy damask drapes shrouding the windows that looked out on Boylston Street. From the look on his thin, aquiline face, Enver could tell that his master was in a foul mood. "Sorry I am late, your Excellency. My watch stopped."

"Sorry does not help. A bad workman blames his tools. I have serious business to discuss with you. Sit down."

"I am honored, *effendi*."

Tallal looked steadily at Enver Dash. So this was the type of person he would have to count on to help him. Hhump. His life was becoming one stupid mistake after another, he thought, rubbing his left arm—his badly mended left arm—in reflection. Tallal was all but convinced that the heavy curse the Armenian most certainly must have laid on him was taking its toll. His father had been right. It had been a cursed day he had been assigned to command the unit ordered to escort Armenian exiles to Aleppo. Everything had gone wrong. Even as he was boarding the steamer for America, that berserk Armenian had almost killed him. Only the expert surgery of a Canadian doctor on board the *Kennebec* had pulled him through. In the process, he was now without a kidney and a lung, and had an almost useless left arm, the humerus shattered by Mamigon's bullets. If his wounds had been sustained on a battlefield, he would have been left for dead.

He didn't take his eyes off Enver. For some reason not clearly explained to him, Enver had brought that smart-mouthed boy, Sadi, aboard and Tallal had been forced to pay for his passage as well. Only, the boy had vanished once the ship had docked in Boston before they sailed on to New York, and he was personally out of pocket for the boy's fare. If those beginnings were not auspicious, things had become worse. The consulate in New York City was closed in 1918 when the Americans broke off relations with Turkey. The Americans had not declared war on Turkey when hostilities were declared against Germany the year before. But the situation in the Middle East "deteriorated," as the diplomats were apt to say, after the victorious English, French, and Italians began to press more claims on the remnants of the Ottoman Empire. Tallal had been quietly sent to Boston to head up the Euphrates Export-Import Company, Ltd., there. His real job was to be the eyes and ears of the Turkish government in the New England area.

What was now giving Tallal fits was information in two separate reports he had received from his field staff. It was routine for his people to infiltrate among communities of Armenians, Bulgarians, Arabs, Syrians, and Lebons to pick up news and information to be fed to the mother country in packets forwarded by Turkey's American go-between, the Swiss Embassy in Washington.

Tallal had gasped for breath when he read in the report that the Armenian outlaw, Mamigon of Yosghat Dagh, was seen on several occasions the past few months at Koko's coffeehouse on Tremont Street. So, the mad, relentless Armenian had followed him to Boston! Tallal felt certain the Armenian had not located his exact whereabouts yet. Otherwise, Tallal would have felt the sting, of that he was certain. It is more than five years, he thought. Won't that bastard ever give up? Or, was the whole thing a coincidence. Well, it is written, a danger foreseen is a danger half avoided. So be it, *kismet*, he will get Enver on to the task.

"I have a job for you, Enver."

"Thank you, Excellency, I am honored to be able to serve you."

"You may not be so thankful when you find out what the job is."

"Anything, *effendi*." Enver had learned long ago that a fawning, obsequious lackey was better thought of than one who reacted as a man.

"Do you remember that wild Armenian, Mamigon, we captured and you let escape back in Anatolia?"

That man, again! Enver Dash groaned. "I was castrated by your *yarbay* after . . . after you left on account of him."

"I know, I know."

"I thought the police had caught him that night in Izmir and hanged him! By Allah, is he still alive after all this?"

"Yes, Enver, alive and right here in Boston."

"How do you know this, sir?"

"He has been seen several times at Koko's coffeehouse. I believe that is close to where you live, is that not so?"

"By Allah, yes. The coffeehouse is only a block away!"

"Good. You will keep close watch on the coffeehouse and try and find out where he lives, what he does, who he sees. Is that clear?"

"That is all?"

"For now, Enver. Once you find out those things, then I can make plans."

"I will let you know the minute I learn anything, Excellency."

Tallal sent him away as he went into further reflection. He couldn't expect any help from the American authorities. When it came to Turks and Armenians the Presbyterian and Congregational churches in Boston had managed to wash the image of the Armenians clean and establish the adjective of "Unspeakable" for the Turk. As an Unspeakable Turk, Tallal had managed well despite it. His infinite, darkly handsome charm and suave manners did it for him. The few Americans who worked in the export-import house were agreeable and generous people, but they seemed reserved in their relations with all the Turks. Tallal never allowed his chagrin and deep resentment to surface, always maintaining a delicate air of smiling approbation when he was among them. He realized soon enough that his features and deportment, not to mention his fancy automobiles, were more than enough to beguile the women—women who dressed in such revealing fashion that he was constantly swallowing his spittle at the sight of each female rump leaving his office.

It wasn't too long after he had arrived in America that he gave up going to brothels. There was no need to pay for it. The liaisons with initially shy but vivacious Irish servant and cleaning girls were many and often. They were magnificent creatures, by Allah! They weren't too fat nor too skinny, with smooth complexions, funny upturned noses, blue eyes and light hair. Their only drawback seemed to be the lack of sexual imagination. They loved copulation, once they were seduced into it, but rarely assumed more than one or two positions. He remembered the first experience he had with Mary.

She couldn't have been more than eighteen. She spoke with such an accent—different from the other "Americans" Tallal had come in contact with—that Tallal had used it to open a conversation with her when she reported to the offices at five o'clock each afternoon for her job as a cleaning woman. She had emigrated to America from Ireland only eight months before to find work and a husband—both in scant supply where she came from. She had blushed mightily through the brief conversation, cut short by the appearance of her co-worker Sheila. Tallal had made a mental note to pursue the girl, bedazzled by her fresh, young looks, the swell of her bosom, and the elegant ankles visible below the calf-length skirt that encircled a flat belly and rounded hips. But it was her shyness that had intrigued him the most. After successive days of casual "hellos" he talked to her again when Sheila wasn't around, learning that she lived with highly protective relatives in South Boston and rarely went out except to Sunday Mass and novenas. Tallal had commiserated with her, telling her he was lonely too, not knowing anyone in the city and having trouble with the language. Two weeks later he had treated Mary to a truncated dinner—the necessity to get her quickly home the governing factor that night.

Three days later, he had kissed her hand. Two days after that he had kissed her on the cheek when she appeared for work, causing a blush so deep Tallal feared she would drop to the floor. He had suggested dinner again instead of the novena she announced she was attending that evening. She accepted. When she appeared later at his office door to say she was ready to go, he had kissed her on the mouth, holding her weakly struggling form as he continued bussing her until she relaxed and responded. He did not let her go, kissing her soundly as he moved her to his leather divan, and eased her down to sit next to him. She fought off his searching hands repeatedly and Tallal had wisely taken her to dinner instead of forcing the issue.

Mary didn't fight too hard the next time when Tallal had hooked a chair under the door knob, pulled her down to the divan, and ended up with her camisole and bloomers rearranged, her initial shyness and embarrassment blown away by the bellows of passion, the vestiges of her virginity staining her underclothes and the fly to his pants which he had not removed. She had cried and had pleaded with Tallal to say he loved her. A puzzled Tallal had complied, not knowing that the American words were the only payment demanded (initially) or required for services rendered by women who weren't in the business of peddling their bottoms. Mary had been fired from her job a month later when Tallal realized that her talk of marriage was serious and expected.

Sheila, in her early twenties, was his next conquest, the seduction executed in almost the same order and manner as Mary's. When he was through with her—tired of her mewling and whimpering about being used and betrayed—he threw her out for "stealing" a worn-out mop that had already been replaced. Help wanted notices in the *Boston Post* brought all the new blood Tallal needed to keep his offices clean and his libidinous drives assuaged. Tallal basked in the warmth and passion of his succession of wonderfully naive sexual partners. His only frustration in the liaisons was the consistent reserve demonstrated by the women through their shocked reaction to his cruder carnal suggestions. Tallal still had to visit the street walkers to satisfy his baser desires. Oh, for those nights on the banks of the Bosphorus. He missed them when he remembered to compare. But Tallal was seeding a good portion of Boston's future harvest of young citizens.

4   GUZELL

"Are you the friend of Mamigon Agha?"

"*Evet*, yes," Tatios replied in Turkish as he turned around to look at his questioner. He silently appraised a young woman with long black hair, beautiful brown sloe eyes accented by long lashes, and the clearest complexion he had ever seen on a living thing. She was absolutely beautiful in aspect, carriage, shape, and form. He couldn't help but break into a smile.

She had watched him as his appraising eye had swept her but did not feel the need to retreat inwardly. He did not possess the usual male leer. "I need your help, *effendi*." Her language was Turkish, with an inland dialect.

"A creature of Allah cast as handsomely as you should not have need for anyone's help, my young *hanum*, but perhaps this mortal might serve." Tatios was being carried away even though the setting was a drab South End street in Boston two blocks from his home on a sunny May afternoon.

"Please be serious, *effendi*. I have seen you walking to church with Mamigon Agha and I seek you on a matter which may be life and death."

"Well, by all that is sacred and true, I shall be serious. But this is not the place to talk about serious matters of life and death. Would you care to go to my place?"

Her face fell at his last question. Tatios noticed the change. "Please, Miss Whatever-Your-Name-Is. I am suggesting you talk to me in the presence of my wife. Incidentally, what is your name? My name is Tatios, friend of Mamigon . . ."

"My name is Guzell, also a friend of Mamigon, son of Magaros of Yosghat Dagh."

"Well . . . I am surprised my friend has never mentioned someone as lovely as you. I do not believe he could have forgotten you once he met you. Have you known him long?"

"Yes."

"Since he came to Boston?"

"No."

"I see you do not wish to talk. What is it you want of me?"

"I *do* wish to talk. Only I do not know where to begin . . . I am . . . afraid."

"Afraid? Of what?"

"You may not understand me, the same as Mamigon Agha may not understand. I am afraid to approach him and I am beginning to have the same fears about you."

"Obviously, unfortunately, I am not anything like Mamigon Agha, my dear. Why do we not go to my house. It is Saturday afternoon, the twenty-eighth day in the month of May and my wife will welcome you without dismay . . ."

Guzell grinned broadly. "Your Turkish is beautiful, *effendi*. Thank you. If you truly are not being intruded upon I will accept your very kind invitation."

"You are most welcome, my dear. Now tell me, how do you know Mamigon and . . . wait. So you will not have to repeat everything twice, let us go home first and have something to eat as you tell both of us."

They walked a block to Harrison Avenue, turned down one block and went to Sharon Street, a short block of three-story brownstones that once were the townhouses of the wealthy. It was a totally Armenian immigrant neighborhood now, and in seconds the entire block was aware that Tatios Effendi was in the company of a strange and beautiful woman, not his wife.

Diggin Eksah was surprised at the visitor her husband introduced but recovered quickly enough to smile warmly at her as she sneaked quick glances at her husband.

"Well, this *is* a pleasant surprise. A friend of Mamigon Agha is very much a friend of ours," Eksah said. "Have you eaten?" It was the usual question asked of any visitor to an Armenian home.

"Yes, please do not bother. I am not hungry. I approached your husband because I saw him with Mamigon Agha several times and . . ."

"Have you talked to Mamigon Agha?"

"No, Diggin Eksah. That is why I wanted to speak to your husband. I am afraid to talk to him."

"Afraid?" Eksah's question was answered by Tatios who told his wife that Guzell had mentioned life and death and that it was a serious matter. "What are you afraid of, my dear?" Tatios asked.

"I was with Mamigon Agha in Anatolia when he was trying to find a certain man."

"Tallal Bey!"

"Yes. We met on the trail—I was running away from home—and he saved my life."

"Where was this?"

"Somewhere between Fekke and Yosghat, where we were bound. Mamigon Agha was certain Tallal Bey would be in Yosghat."

"Ah, you found him, then . . ."

"No. He had gone on to Smyrna and we followed him by taking the railroad train." She saw Tatios's eyebrows knit. "I had dyed his hair with henna and had him wear an eye patch to disguise him . . ." Tatios began to smile.

"You caught him in Smyrna, then?" Tatios had a tinge of impatience in his voice.

"Yes." Now her voice had dropped.

"I believe there is more . . . ?" Tatios looked at his wife for a moment. "Do you wish to talk alone with Eksah Hanum?"

"That would be easier for me but it is you, Tatios Effendi, who might be of help. May I be frank?"

"You may, certainly, but I cannot promise you anything until I know what it is you ask of me. If it is within my power, yes . . ."

"Mamigon Agha and I became very much attached to each other. He wanted to marry me once he had disposed of Tallal Bey."

Eksah let out a small yelp. "Oh! Was that the man leading the exile caravan? The one who had captured Mamigon Agha?" Tatios gave her a quick sketch of the facts so that Guzell could continue.

"We felt certain Tallal Bey would recognize Mamigon Agha in Smyrna on the streets if Mamigon Agha went looking for him, so I disguised myself as a boy and did the looking. I found him the first day."

Tatios nodded in triumph. "Ah, the scene was set, eh?"

"Yes, I found out that he was leaving the next day for America."

"That left Mamigon with little time. What happened?"

She stared with wide eyes at both man and wife, almost with a plea in her look. "I did not tell Mamigon Agha I had found him." She let out a long breath of air as if a huge burden had been taken off her back.

"You . . . told him nothing?"

"I could not bring myself to." Her eyes welled with tears. Guzell was being torn by the same thing again. Should she tell them she had seen Tallal in Boston?

"I understand . . ." Eksah was nodding slowly with her eyes closed.

"You understand what, my wife? Tell me, Guzell Hanum, is this why you are afraid to talk to Mamigon Agha? He does not know about this?"

"Oh, yes, he does know." She was sobbing now. "Somehow he found out and caught us as I was helping Tallal Bey carry his bags up to the steamer."

"Ah, hah! What did he say to you?"

"No, no, he was too far away. He let out a yell and shot down Tallal Bey in front of me. I am sure he would have killed me, too, if someone on the steamer had not fired an *altipawtlah* at him." She continued to sob.

"How did you get here?"

"The steamer people pulled up the walkway before I could get off and I had to sail to America."

"There . . . there," Eksah said, placing an arm on her shaking shoulders. "You were trying to save Mamigon Agha from possibly getting killed, I know."

"May I die this instant if that is not the truth. I hoped to see Tallal Bey off and never tell Mamigon Agha he had been found and lost. I just could not bear the thought of losing him, that is the honest truth."

Tatios was sitting quietly, pondering, shaking his head. No wonder Mamigon never mentioned her. He must have felt totally betrayed . . . especially if he had discussed marriage with her. "How is it that you have a Turkish name, my dear?"

"I am Turkish." Guzell saw the look of utter shock cross both faces.

"Did Mamigon know that?"

"Oh, yes, yes. That is what is bothering me the most, Tatios Effendi. He told me about his close Turkish friend Tallal and how the man had betrayed him in the most devastating way possible. He told me how he could not trust Turks anymore. Then I come along, he puts all his faith and trust and love in me and I turn right around and betray him, too. At least it looks that way. I . . . I . . . only meant to save him from possible harm."

"There is an Armenian saying: A confessed wrong is half redressed. Let us see what we can do about this."

"Where is Mamigon Agha? I watch for him every Sunday since I saw him sitting on that park bench last fall, but he appears only rarely."

"Where do you watch for him? Do you live around here?"

"Yes, I have a room in that building facing the park, the Franklin Square House for single women."

"Why, you are only a block away from us and two blocks from the church. We have to go by your place to get to church."

"I really cannot believe in the ways of Allah. I am taken halfway around the world to a strange, foreign city and I am a stone's throw from people who are friends of my greatest friend, my love."

"What happened when you arrived in Boston?"

"I walked right off the ship as a crew member. After two days of wandering around, some men and women in blue uniforms blowing musical instruments on the street took me to their place, fed me and cared for me for a week and then found work for me at this place where I now live. I have been here for the past five years, waiting on tables and cleaning up afterwards."

"Enough for now. The reason you do not see much of Mamigon Agha is because he works on a steamer. The boat comes back every three or four weeks to Boston. He only comes to church when the boat is here with a Sunday in the layover."

"Do you know when he is expected again?"

"Hhmm. He sailed last Thursday . . . we cannot expect him back until June 16 or 17. That should have him here for that weekend."

"You know Mamigon Agha better than anyone, Tatios Effendi. Having told you my story, do you think I should see him first, myself?"

"I am not sure, Guzell Hanum, not sure at all. I have seen him with a controlled fury unlike anyone I have known. He has been on that steamer for five years and has not really associated with anyone until we stumbled upon each other."

"What does he do on the steamer?"

"Shovels coal."

"Oh . . ."

"Yes, for five years. He has had much time to think, much time to remember, much time to forget. What he has chosen to remember and what to forget is locked in his head."

"What would be his reaction when he sees me, I wonder . . ."

"We can only guess. How close were you two?"

"We . . ." Guzell's face reddened. "We . . . Mamigon Agha said our relationship had become illicit and that he would have to marry me." She kept her eyes on the floor, her voice low.

Tatios had a small smile on his face, looking at Eksah. She was frowning at him before she spoke: "A man like Mamigon Agha does not offer his name lightly. He must have felt deeply about you. I feel he will want you back once he knows the full story."

"Do you really believe that?" Guzell's eyes were alive again.

"I believe it, without a doubt. What is your feeling, Tatios?"

"I think it best I feel him out about you, Guzell Hanum. There is no need for further hurts for both of you. I will have to think of some way of mentioning you, to get him to talk before I let him know you are here. Did he know where your steamer was going that night?"

"I have no way of knowing whether he did or not. But he did find us at the docks. I really have no way of knowing . . . except that he was limited in where he could go and who he could talk to. I have a feeling he simply followed me and found us at the dock. Of course, he could have asked afterwards. But there was so much gunfire that he probably had to run. We heard police bells as the steamer pulled away."

"It must have been frantic. Well, I am going to assume he knows nothing about you being in Boston. You must be careful not to show yourself the weekend of Saturday and Sunday, the eighteenth and nineteenth. If things develop favorably, my wife or I will get in touch with you. Now, let us have something to eat before I take you back."

Tatios came to the conclusion he would have to see how conversation developed with Mamigon in reference to Guzell. He practiced a hundred different approaches, always being the winner in tricking Mamigon into providing the opening gambit on the topic.

When he met Mamigon at Koko's for a game of backgammon—Mamigon's ship had docked Friday and he would be in port until Wednesday—they didn't play. Mamigon wanted to talk.

"Tatios, my friend, I have been thinking about myself and the way I have been existing."

"It is about time that you give some thought to the way you are wasting your life. How old are you now?"

"I will be thirty-three before the year is out."

"You are three years older than I . . . and thanks to the Turks, you have nothing to show for it. But you cannot blame them forever."

"I have shut the Turks from my mind. I have been thinking of leaving the *Nahant Bay* lately, but it is difficult."

"Difficult?"

"Yes. It has become my home. I work, eat, and sleep, and worry of nothing."

"And women?" Tatios had found his opening.

"That is private, Tatios Effendi."

"It is private, most certainly, but I ask you not that I wish to pry but to bring to your attention a fact of life you have been locking up in your boat."

"It is private . . ."

"Grant you it is private, but unless the Turks did to you what Aram did to them, you are still a man who needs female companionship."

"Oofah, I say it is a private matter."

"It is not a private matter to me, your closest friend. I have expected you to ask me about a woman for companionship ever since we met in Boston. You have acted like a monk . . . if not a eunuch."

"It is private matter."

Tatios grinned. "I cannot imagine that you have shifted your affections to men."

"No, I care not for that kind of sex. It has been offered on shipboard and I have refused the kindness. No, I promised myself I would never become entangled again with a woman."

"What kind of a promise is that? What do you mean, entangled?"

"The story is long and it is a private matter."

"I have the time to listen and your privacy is sacred to me."

"Oofah. I did not expect this tonight."

"Talk to me, *bahbahm!*"

"On the trail of Tallal, I lost my proper conduct with a slip of a girl."

"Excellent. I believe you mean you slept with her."

"Yes."

"Fine. You had sex with a woman. You did not force her, of course . . ."

"No. We developed mutual feelings of admiration and affection, deep affection."

"She was attractive, no doubt . . ." Tatios had used the Turkish word "guzell" meaning attractive or fine.

Mamigon's usual impassivity was broken by the word. His eyes widened as he said, "By Allah, that was her name . . . Guzell!"

"Wonderful. So you were in love with her. Knowing you, you proposed marriage, of course, because you do not take such actions lightly. Correct?"

"Yes."

"Ah. She refused to marry you so you renounced women forever. Correct?"

"Your imagination is almost as big as your fancy words, Tatios. No, we were to be married once I got rid of Tallal."

"You did get rid of Tallal. Why did you not marry her?"

Mamigon stared off into space for a long moment before he answered. "She was Turkish."

"You did not know she was before you asked her, before you took her to bed?"

"No, Tatios, not that. She found Tallal before I did and was leaving the country with him when I found them. I should have known. She was Turkish and you cannot trust Turks."

"Pshaw, Mamigon. There could easily be another explanation. You do not seem to be a person who could have been misled by a skirt."

"I was."

"Have you given any thought to another explanation?"

"I tried, but the evidence was overwhelming. She was on the gangplank with him when I shot him down."

"So you renounced your whole life . . ."

"Tatios, Guzell's actions took the spirit out of me. I thought I had found someone to fill the terrible loneliness, allay the deep bitterness I had been feeling since I found my slaughtered family. She stepped on the last shred of spirit I had left in me."

"Mamigon, the least you could have done for yourself was to have demanded an explanation from her."

"I could not ask for anything. She sailed out of my life to God knows where."

"If you met her by chance in Recife, for instance, or Boston, would you give her a chance to explain?"

"It is too late, Tatios. Explanations would be useless. You know what they say: A woman's strength is in her tongue."

"I think you are wrong, my friend. I think you prefer, also, to fool yourself about her. You would rather think the worst than face facts that might change your life."

"There is nothing I can do about it."

"Are you saying, Mamigon, that if Guzell were here you would listen to her, treat her kindly?"

The big man sighed. He stared away again for a long while, then began to nod in assent. "Yes, I remember her more with kindness and love than I do with bitterness. I have thought about her a good amount. She turned away from me only at the last instance."

Tatios struggled within himself. Should he spring Guzell's proximity on Mamigon, or wait. He decided to wait. He had talked Mamigon into talking and perhaps time would eradicate some of the subtleties of his extraction of the facts from Mamigon's mind. He changed the subject. "You have refused to visit with us, to honor my home, Mamigon Agha. I now extend a formal invitation to have Sunday dinner after the Mass."

"I politely, with great regret, decline, my good friend," Mamigon said, getting up. "I will meet you in the park tomorrow morning for church." With that, he left.

Tatios realized that the big man had uncharacteristically talked at length about himself and had to leave for a psychological regrouping.

On his way home, Tatios stopped at the Franklin Square House lobby and asked to have Guzell meet him in the reception room.

5 ✥ DISCOVERY

"I found him, Excellency."

"Good! You spent nearly two months looking for him. Where?"

"In the coffeehouse, near my place."

"Did you learn where he lives?"

"Yes . . . but . . ."

"Did you or . . . what is the problem?"

"He went back to a boat in the harbor."

"I could learn more by talking to myself in the mirror! Is he a passenger? Is he leaving the country?"

"I cannot tell, Excellency. He went aboard near midnight. It is a freight boat of some kind. I think he must be a crew member."

"You think? You chestnut-brained son of a goat. Find out immediately."

"How . . . how would you do that . . . Excellency?"

Tallal Bey groaned. "You simply walk up to the gangplank officer and ask the man if an old friend of yours is still a member of the crew, that is all. If the answer is yes, fine. If the answer is no, then you ask if he is a passenger. In either case, you have your answer."

"Should I go now?"

"What, at two o'clock in the morning! Of course not. Wait until a decent hour tomorrow morning, about ten o'clock. It is Sunday and a friend calling would not be out of place."

"What if he is on the boat and recognizes me?"

"He would not be standing there waiting for you or anyone at such an hour. Enver, you are undoubtedly a squash head. I told you when you grew that beard that it creates lice, not brains. But it will give you a small degree of protection from instant recognition. Go and do what I say."

"One thing more, Excellency. He was at a table talking with a man. I could not follow both of them. Do you think it important I find out who the man was?"

"Your first and only task is to find out exactly what Mamigon is doing and where he is living or working. Is that clear?"

"Yes, Excellency."

Enver Dash was on Atlantic Avenue Sunday morning turning into Rowe's Wharf where the S.S. *Nahant Bay* was berthed, its bow pointing to the city. He asked about his "big friend, Mamigon" and was told that his friend had left very early that morning for church services. He should be back by two o'clock. Thank you, I do not wish to leave my name. I want to surprise him, thank you. Leaving port Wednesday, eh? That gives me plenty of time . . . He is a hard worker, eh? Five years with this boat! No, he never told me where he worked. That sounds like him, all right. Thanks, again.

He walked the mile or so back to the office and called Tallal at his home in Peabody to tell him what he had found out.

"That is good enough for now, Enver. We will make plans for when he returns to Boston. Go home and enjoy yourself. You did well."

Enver kept snarling to himself "you did well, you did well, you did well," as he walked home. That Tallal was a ball buster, a cock licker, a boy sticker. Why did he always make Enver feel like an idiot? Someday, he would get even.

6 ✧ MOVING PICTURES

It was the first night in port, Boston, a little over three weeks after Mamigon and Tatios had talked about Guzell. As was customary on the first night in port, Mamigon accompanied Captain Nicholopoulos to dinner, a routine established after the street mob incident the previous September. The clothes Mamigon now wore, matching jacket and pants, a vest with a shirt and tie around the stiff, detachable collar, were almost as confining to him as the uniforms he wore in the army. The high shoes were more comfortable but were exactly like the army boots he once wore, except that he could lace the upper part with six pairs of hooks instead of grommets. The black derby sitting on his head, the vogue in 1921, made him feel decidedly overdressed and foppish, especially since he viewed the captain, the man who had picked out his clothes for him, to be on the vain side. Mamigon had drawn the line at one item he discarded after two experiments: garters below his knees to suspend his socks. Enough! He had also eschewed a cane that Captain Nicholopoulos had recommended on the basis that it would draw attention to his slight limp. He really felt it would have been the final dandification of Mamigon of Yosghat Dagh.

Captain Nicholopoulos was late returning from the shipping company offices with the first mate, and by the time he cleaned up and was dressed for dinner, the sun's light was being shielded by the hills west of Boston and the harbor was gathering the gloom. The two were well suited to each other as company. Neither engaged in or required chitchat as they walked silently up the pier to Atlantic Avenue and turned downtown on the deserted street, the tapping of the captain's cane the loudest sound within earshot of the pair. They were between the separated cones of light from adjacent street lamps when they stopped.

Four burly men were ahead of them, blocking the sidewalk, their hands behind their backs. A slight sound made Mamigon slowly turn his head to look back. There were four men behind them, walking up, making no attempt to hide baseball bats in their hands. Steel pull-down doors featured the stretch of closed stores on their left. Two casual figures apeared on the street, abreast of Mamigon and the captain. They were in a trap.

Mamigon pulled the captain to a storefront and whispered to him to keep his back to the wall. He relieved him of the heavy cane, standing flat against the same wall to the right of the captain.

The four on each side stopped advancing on the pair when they were fifteen feet away. Faces were barely discernible. One of the pair out on the street spoke up.

"We want to talk with the big one holding your cane. You can go." The speaker pointed to Captain Nicholopoulos. His voice was thick and his English heavily accented. Mamigon understood the import of the words.

"You go," Mamigon whispered. "I do not die easily, GO!"

The captain did not move. The men with their hands behind their backs now produced window sash weights, short and heavy lethal weapons if wielded by strong hands. They looked strong now, as everyone closed in, an air of quiet assurance in their solid step and manner—no hurry, no fear.

The captain's right ear almost went deaf as Mamigon suddenly bellowed his battle cry—MAMIGON! MAMIGON!—lunging and swinging the cane at the four with the sash weights. His speed, coupled with the wild sounds he was making, caught them unprepared: The oaken stick cracked across their shins with Mamigon flattening out on his belly, well out of reach of their short weapons. He was up in an instant to face the onrushing four with the ball bats, his back now to the downed and howling foursome who were trying to cope with one of the most painful superficial injuries inflicted on a human. A shot rang out.

The cane shattered in two as a bat caught it in its first swing. Mamigon didn't utter a sound as he went down under a flurry of blows to his head and shoulders.

As he hit the sidewalk, another shot rang out, followed by two more, then a fifth. Captain Nicholopoulos stood with a smoking pistol over Mamigon's body as the attackers scrambled off into the darkness, pulling and carrying two of their comrades with them.

He could make out blood on Mamigon's head. He tried to talk to him but there was no response. He touched his jugular and felt a pulse. He looked around. He didn't want to leave him alone in the street. Those human wolves might return. So he fired a shot into the night sky. Two of his crew ran out from the pier to the street. His shout attracted their attention to the scene.

The police were called. The captain described the events, shaking his head at the speed with which things had happened. He always carried a gun

ashore, but did not have time to make use of it before Mamigon was battered. He was certain it was part of the same gang of ruffians that had
attacked him and his mate when the police went on strike. They must have
waited for a chance to get revenge because this same man had attacked the
whole mob with a spanner and rescued him and his mate. He felt helpless
that he couldn't describe the attackers. He accompanied his unconscious
friend to the emergency room at City Hospital on Harrison Avenue.

Mamigon was wheeled into the operating room after a session with a
roentgen machine that a nurse told Captain Nicholopoulos provided inter-
nal pictures of the body. It was past midnight when a white-gowned doctor
came into the waiting room to see the captain.

"I'm Dr. Fenton. Are you the next of kin?"

"I am Captain Nicholopoulos of the S.S. *Nahant Bay.* No, I am not kin.
He is a member of my crew."

"Well, the man . . ."

"He is an Armenian from Asia Minor. I have never heard him talk of
family. I think he has Armenian friends here in Boston."

"The man has multi . . ."

"I will pay his medical costs. I want the best care you can give him,
doctor."

"Look, the man will . . ."

"I want him in a room all by himself. I have left my name and office
contact in Boston, the Wellington Shipping Line."

"Captain, I am not . . ."

"Your bills will be honored, sir."

Dr. Fenton stared at the dapper man, wondering if the hospital would be
sued if he kicked him in the balls to shut him up. Then he saw how moist the
man's eyes were. The captain was afraid to hear what the doctor was about
to tell him.

"He'll be all right . . ." Dr. Fenton touched the captain's arm as he said
it in a soft voice.

"Thank God . . . I feel I am responsible for his hurts, doctor. I was so
scared I forgot about my pistol."

"Your friend's constitution is strong but he's been hurt in the one area
that's most vulnerable, the head."

"How bad is he hurt?"

"His skull is fractured, broken, in two places. We had to go into it and
take some pressure away from his brain. The oc . . . the bones around his
left eye were smashed. He has a broken jaw and both his upper arms, his left
shoulder and blade are broken. Another blow to his head would have finished him off. Did you see what he was beaten with?"

"Four men with ball bats, you know, those 2-pound sticks you Americans
play ball with."

"Hhmm. I'm a Londoner myself and I've never bothered to find out how
much a cricket bat weighs. How do you know that a baseball bat weighs two
pounds?"

"One of the crew picked up a bat that was dropped by a mob that attacked me in 1919 during the police strike. We did not know what it was meant for. We are all Greeks on the ship. We were certain such a fine piece of tapered wood was not meant for use against humans. Out of curiosity the cook weighed it . . . ha, ha, ha." The laugh was strained. "He saved my life at the time," the captain said, waving his hand in the direction of the operating room.

"Well, he'll be all right, old chap. Are you in port for long?"

"No, doctor. I will be taking her out next Wednesday. Should be back in three weeks. Will he still be here?"

"Definitely. When he's able to amb . . . walk, we will be conducting some tests to see how his motor ba . . . brain is functioning with his reflexes."

"In that case, good-bye, doctor. Hopefully, I will see you when I return. Take good care of him, please."

Dr. Fenton shook his hand and nodded. "Get some sleep, old man. I'm going to do the same."

When Mamigon did not appear Saturday night at the coffeehouse, Tatios thought the freighter must have fallen behind on its schedule. It had been due the previous Wednesday. Sunday, after the services, Tatios decided to take the long walk to the harbor to see what news there was of the *Nahant*. He had awaited Mamigon's return with great anticipation. He was going to produce Guzell, for better or for worse. The steamer was there at the pier. When he found out the steamer had been docked since Wednesday, he asked about Mamigon, all the conversation in Greek.

Tatios almost collapsed from exhaustion as he walked and ran the 3 miles back to his house. Mamigon was at City Hospital only 3 blocks from his house, had been there since Wednesday. He ran up the granite steps to his home, told Eksah the news that Mamigon was badly hurt, cleaned up with a change of clothes, and took his wife to the hospital with him.

They found Mamigon in a private room, his head and jaw completely encased in bandages, his left eye nearly closed shut from the swelling around the temple, and his shoulders and arms in a heavy cast. Eksah let out a gasp of empathy. Tatios smiled at his friend and asked the classic question: "How do you feel?"

Mamigon nodded ever so slightly. He obviously couldn't talk. Eksah pulled up a chair beside the bed and held his hand. Tatios stood on the other side, baffled for the first time in his life. He was a talker but a talker needs responses to keep going—and in this case, needed answers. He thought of a solution. He told Mamigon to squeeze Eksah's hand once for "yes," and twice for "no." That way, they might be able to talk, is that suitable? He squeezed once.

"Firstly, do you want to talk now?" One squeeze.

"Do you know who did it?" Two squeezes.

"Do you know why?" Two.

"Are you in pain?" A pause, then one squeeze.

Tatios said that was enough. He would talk to the doctor and see if he could do anything. They sat with Mamigon until eight o'clock when the nurse said they had to leave.

The captain met Tatios and Eksah the following evening at Mamigon's bedside. The conversation slipped from Turkish to Greek and back to Turkish when Tatios's Greek was too classical for the captain to catch all the words. The rapport was instantaneous and the captain had supper on Sharon Street the next evening before the men went to visit Mamigon again. Eksah decided to stay home with the children since she couldn't understand Greek. It was the captain's last night ashore as he would be sailing the next day. After the visit, they talked.

"Do not worry, captain, we will look after him. I knew him in the old country, as I told you, and he is a special man."

"I know nothing about him, Tatios. Have you ever met such a close-mouthed man?"

"Never. He is worth knowing, however, as you have probably found out."

"He has saved my life. He was hiding on my ship in Smyrna when I first met him. Do you know why the police were looking for him?"

Tatios told him the whole story, accompanied by much shaking and wagging of the captain's head, punctuated by several ahs and gasps. Tatios was a consummate storyteller.

"I wish the crew could have heard this tale. Well, good night, my friend. I shall see you in three weeks, God willing."

The wires were removed from Mamigon's jaw the following Saturday. Eksah fed him some *mahtzun* with only a small demur from Mamigon, who referred to the food by its Turkish name, yogurt. The puffiness around the left eye was greatly diminished although the entire area was livid. His headache was not as pronounced and even though he spoke very little, he enjoyed the visits. Tatios was a font of information, gathered entirely from the foreign language newspapers he read. He was making a valiant attempt to learn English as quickly as possible but was not adept enough to be able to fully comprehend the news in the Boston newspapers.

Tatios carried on with the news he had been reading, giving Mamigon a series of highlights that only a bedridden man could appreciate. That first Saturday, with his jaw unwired, Mamigon heard about America's need for "a return to normalcy," a need that had ousted the party of that great man, Woodrow Wilson. Wilson's name may have never reached Anatolia but Tatios assured both his listeners that his plan to create an American Protectorate of Armenia in the Caucasus would have meant the final and eternal salvation of the Armenian people. After more lamentations, Tatios went on to the man who had wrested the presidency from Wilson, Warren Gamaliel Harding. He was going to return the United States to the good old days of 1913. No more entanglements in European affairs. The point had been made that the billions of dollars the French owed the United States after the war had been reduced by what the French said the United States owed France for the cost of the land where the American soldiers who died in the war were buried.

Most exciting was the change in the American constitution that now allowed women to vote, a change that was cited as the main reason for the handsome Harding's election.

Did you know, Mamigon, that a new law makes this country almost like Turkey or any other Moslem land? Yes, you cannot buy or drink intoxicating liquor anymore. The women had their way, it seems.

And, what about this piece of news: There were more than eight million passenger cars in the country right now . . . that is almost as many people as live in Turkey.

Or, they have something here called the cinema—the picture of people moving about on a flat wall, just like a stage show and thirty million Americans go to see them once a week!

Amazing country. I will let you sleep now and we will talk again tomorrow . . .

The next day, it was news from the old country. The Greeks, who had captured Smyrna, now called Izmir by the Turks, in 1919, had been repulsed as they drove toward Ankara earlier in the year but 1921 proved to be a series of small victories for the Greeks. They were faced by the military tactics of Mustapha Kemal Pasha, the hero of Gallipoli, and things didn't look good. The British Reuters wire dispatches said the Greek army was poorly equipped and the British, who had instigated the whole adventure, were not being too generous with military assistance for fear of antagonizing their new found Moslem allies in the Middle East. We shall have to see how the Greeks make out, old friend. I hope an avenging God smites those Turkish bastards, once and for all . . .

As the visiting hours waned the following Saturday night, Tatios halted his long dissertation on domestic and foreign news to become personal. Eksah was home taking care of the children.

"I hope you feel well enough to accept a visit from a long lost friend tomorrow."

"Long lost friend? Who?"

"Someone you will be very happy to see again."

"Who?"

"I want to surprise you."

"I am not well enough for surprises. My head still aches. Who?"

"You are also not well enough to force me, my rugged friend, into telling you. Wait and see. Good night." Tatios chuckled all the way home, seeing the look of frustration on Mamigon's face. It would be absolutely impossible for Mamigon to guess who the visitor would be . . . *Sacre bleu!* He hoped it would turn out well.

Tatios appeared with Eksah after Mass let out at half-past twelve. They had brought the usual collection of delicacies for Mamigon who was losing weight from the hospital diet. His head was still swathed in the pressure pack; his shoulders and arms were still encased in plaster; his left eye and jaw were still livid and misshapen by the swelling. His beard had been shaven off; only his mustache remained intact, now scraggly and unkempt.

Eksah went directly to him, as she always did, and kissed him lightly on the cheek. Tatios held his hand for a moment before he sat down. There was an air of expectancy, finally broken by Tatios. "I have brought a visitor to see you.

Mamigon nodded. "I know who it is."

Tatios was standing up again to leave the room when Mamigon's words stopped him. "You are not disturbed?"

"Perhaps I do *not* know who it is . . . if you believe I will be disturbed."

Tatios left the room and Eksah got up from her chair to stand by the wall. Her husband came into the room leading Guzell by the hand behind him.

Mamigon gazed with unwinking eyes at Guzell who stood at the foot of the bed directly in front of him, her head cast down slightly, her hands folded in front of her, her eyes, however, looking fixedly into his. Neither said a word although a slight tremor was noticeable around the woman's mouth.

Eksah tilted her head toward the door and Tatios joined her outside. They didn't hear a sound as they walked away. Tears were streaming down Eksah's face.

"I did not know . . ." Mamigon uttered the words, softly.

"I am hoping you . . ."

"I did not believe I would see you ever again."

"Nor did I. I am hoping . . ."

"Are you well?"

"Yes."

"One cannot ask for more in this life."

"I see you have been hurt."

"Yes. I seem to attract violence."

"For a gentle man, you . . ."

"Guzell?" The name was uttered in a small puff of impatience, as if to stop the small talk. "Why are you here?"

"I . . . I do not know . . . I am . . ."

"Why did you come?" It was hurled in a low voice.

"To ask your forgiveness!" She hurled her words right back at him.

Mamigon didn't reply, not taking his eyes away from her defiant ones. The silent seconds seemed like hours before he spoke again. "I expected wails and the gnashing of teeth, the pulling of hair . . ."

"That never crossed my mind."

"You expect me to forgive you, simply because you ask?"

"Yes."

"I am not Allah, I am an ordinary human with feelings and . . ."

"You have been *my* Allah. You were my whole life. I was your scabbard in more ways than one. Do you remember what you said to me once on the trail? A sword does not cut its sheath? I have clutched that to my bosom. I am here now to, at least, make you realize that I was not betraying you. I was trying to protect you . . ."

Mamigon had listened intently. "Protect me?"

"Yes, protect you, you big camel. You were so intent on killing Tallal you were not thinking. It never crossed your mind that *you* could die instead of Tallal in a confrontation. Well, it crossed my mind and often. If I could have died for you, I would have. But it would not have stopped you. When I learned he was leaving the very next day, I helped him go."

"You were going with him . . ."

"I was not. I was helping his striker get the luggage aboard when you came storming along and shot him down. You would have shot me, too, if they had given you a chance."

He looked away for a moment. "I do not know that. My blood was dictating my actions. Tell me, my girl, what do you want of me now?"

"I told you. I want your forgiveness. I never should have stood between you and the vow to your dead family. I realized that after all these years of thinking about it." Her eyes were cast down.

"That is all?"

"That is the only thing I can ask of you."

"Would you ask . . . have you thought of asking me other things . . . ?"

She said yes without hesitation.

"What, as an instance?"

"That you not hate me anymore."

"Woman, I forgive you on one condition . . ." She waited. "That you forgive me, in turn."

Guzell began to cry, quietly, as she moved from the spot where she had been rooted since she walked in to hold Mamigon's raised hand. She held his hand in both of hers, rubbing and rubbing it, staring into his face through her tears, seeming to regain some of the lost years through the simple act of touching.

That's how Tatios and Eksah found them when they returned, a bit anxiously, to see how the reunion had prospered. Mamigon freed his hand the moment the others entered.

Mamigon shook his head at Tatios. "I was certain you had found my brother Aram. Tell me how you found her."

The story was told. As the visitors arose to take leave, Mamigon asked Tatios if he could talk to him privately for a moment. After the women stepped out, Mamigon motioned to Tatios to come closer.

"Something has been nagging at my thoughts since the attack on me, old friend."

"Yes. Please tell me about it."

"There is not much to tell, but I believe it is important."

"Yes . . ."

"The men who attacked me were not ruffians from the streets of Boston. They were not seeking revenge for that night I broke a few heads myself."

"How do you know?"

"I brought four men to the ground when I cracked their shins. It sounded natural to me then, but now I know what was wrong."

"Yes?"

"They were swearing and howling in Turkish . . ."

7 ﹠ DEATH WISH

"It is difficult to believe but he is alive!"

"Alive? The Armenian is alive? Impossible!"

"But, true, your Excellency. I saw him myself. I was not too sure, at first. His beard was gone. But you cannot mistake the height and the carriage. It was Mamigon, truth to say."

"Where did you see him, Enver?"

"He was walking in the company of a young woman and that man I have seen him with in the coffeehouse. They were in front of the hospital. I followed them to the other man's house."

"How could it be possible that . . ."

"Your Excellency, excuse me. I watched our men hit him on the head with those ball bats. Verily, it sounded like bludgeons hitting a watermelon. Afterwards, I saw the ship captain lean over him and cry . . ."

"Enough. I will have to find a trained assassin to send this man to hell. Ordinary methods do not seem to get the results. Do you know when his ship gets into port? We will have to get rid of him before he leaves for another three weeks. I do not want this matter to go on forever."

"Your Excellency, the ship was back August 10, last Wednesday, and will be leaving tomorrow afternoon, after church services. The captain is a Greek."

"There is not much time to plan anything. We will bide our time, Enver. Remember, young man, death keeps no calendar."

8 ﹠ MEMORIES

By the time the *Nahant Bay* was back in port on August 10, the decision had been made. Mamigon would not return to the ship. He would take up life in America. Guzell had visited him in the hospital every possible moment she could get away from her duties at Franklin Square House 4 blocks away. It was almost as if they had never parted. He was talking about correcting the illicit nature of their past; she was talking about forgetting the whole thing if that was the reason he wished to marry her. In between there were long periods in the hospital of rapport expressed in total silence, broken only by an occasional sigh from one or the other.

The Saturday came for Mamigon's release, a little over a month after he entered the hospital, apparently none the worse for his experience. Everything had mended properly but Dr. Fenton did warn that he might suffer occasional dizzy spells if he moved too quickly the first week or two after release. Captain Nicholopoulos had already visited with Mamigon and had paid the hospital and doctor bills which totaled, for thirty-one days, $257, the high cost due to the private room. The hospital safe disgorged its bag of gold and gems found on Mamigon's body when he had been carried in, and the captain insisted on paying Mamigon for seventy full months aboard the *Nahant,* amounting to $2,100 dollars American. Mamigon had a small fortune.

Mamigon announced he was going to marry Guzell after one problem had been settled between them. They were seated in Diggin Eksah's kitchen on the sofa, with Tatios and Captain Nicholopoulos present.

"My future wife will not be seen on the streets in American clothes," he announced. He had not commented before about Guzell's dresses, the first he had seen her in.

There was general silence. Everyone had become acquainted with Guzell enough to know that she could handle Mamigon. "I am so very happy you feel that way, my man. I feel uncomfortable walking around on the streets with my ankles and calfs exposed."

Mamigon looked at her, trying to find even the smallest element of mockery. "And I feel that you should wear some sort of a shawl or coat over your shoulders and dress."

"I have to agree with you, again, my man. This country is so uncivilized, compared to the old country. A woman would not be safe walking around exposing her shape to every leering brute."

He was taken aback. American women *did* wear clothes that revealed their ankles, their bosoms, their hips, and their necks—clearly—but they never seemed to be molested, jeered at, or talked to on the streets. "I would not go as far as to say that, my girl . . . perhaps I should leave that to your good discretion."

"Thank you, my man. Now, when do you want to take me to a church clothing store?"

"A church store?"

"Yes, a place where they sell those floor-length gowns the nuns wear."

"Nuns? Gowns? What are you talking about?"

"My man, if you want me to dress so that my ankles do not show, I will have to dress like one of those nuns, that is all I mean."

Mamigon looked around at the others, all of whom were trying to suppress smiles and laughs. He smiled broadly. "I see, I see. Very well, dress as you wish. I will not speak of it again."

Mamigon was recovering from some mild cultural shocks. The bold stares of the hospital nurses had unnerved him initially when they had bathed him time and again, looking directly into his eyes many times. And all American women looked straight at him when they talked to him. A woman just didn't behave like that with a man. In the old country, she would have given the man a quick passing glance and then talk with her eyes looking down or away.

The women here also tended to smile broadly, revealing their teeth! That just wasn't done. The mouth should be covered by a hand when one had to laugh.

The clothes women wore were a problem in another way. Mamigon had found himself struggling not to stare at them as they walked by. It had startled him at first until he became accustomed to the phenomenon and trained himself to ignore the compelling urge to look at the clearly defined rump passing by. He was ashamed he had such compulsions.

The rules were set for Mamigon and Guzell without need for anyone to tell them. She would remain at Franklin Square House until a marriage date could be fixed. They would meet in the company of others, always, until they were married. Tatios would be best man and Eksah would wait on the bride-to-be. The only real question was delicate. Should the marriage be performed in the Armenian church, since she was a Moslem? Would she be offended or even understand and accept the ritual?

Mamigon solved the whole problem without realizing a problem existed.

"Captain Nicholopoulos will marry us on the ship once I have some means of providing for Guzell and myself," he announced the following Saturday at Tatios's house during supper.

"Why not in church where such vows are exchanged before God?" Tatios asked the question more in puzzlement than as a remonstrance.

"I am not a believer, old friend."

"I find that difficult to believe."

"But true . . ."

"Since when did you stop believing?"

"Since I found that my God was so lacking in mercy, He allowed even the innocent to die in screaming agony."

"You have no right to judge Him."

"I am not judging Him. I am saying there is no God."

"If all of us who suffered and saw our dear ones killed or die in front of us felt the same way there would be no basis for right and wrong, for good or evil, for . . ."

"Verily, you speak the truth, Tatios Effendi. There was no right when I came upon my burned village, there was only evil."

"Does Guzell Hanum feel the same way?" All eyes turned to her, except Mamigon's.

"I am not schooled in such things. I should not speak."

"Say what you feel, my girl. It is fine with me."

"I prayed every day to my Allah—who is also your Allah—to bring Mamigon back to me. He did. I must believe in Him."

"I asked Him for a sign that day, that day of the slaughtered innocents. One small sign that He knew what He was doing. That there was some higher meaning, some grand design for all that mayhem. The skies were as empty as my faith is now."

"You seriously believed that God would do as you commanded?"

"I asked for very little."

"I am sad, Mamigon Agha, that you have such emptiness. It is an emptiness that weighs much upon your shoulders. But let us change the subject. Zakar Agha will be coming over after supper to discuss a work possibility for you."

Baron Zakarian had an idea. Armenians, forever the tradesmen, had opened up butcher shops, grocery stores, fish markets, fruit and produce markets, and shops everywhere in the metropolitan area. For these merchants to invest in a truck to haul what they needed from the wholesale markets once a week was not sound. Now, if Mamigon were to buy a truck and offer to haul their goods to their stores for a small delivery charge, wouldn't they leap at the service? Mamigon's first reaction was that he didn't know how to drive a truck. Nothing to it, Zakar Agha said. When you buy one, the seller will show you how to run it. We will ask those merchants first, before you buy a truck, to see if they would give you their business.

Baron Zakarian did the asking, the service was considered a good idea, and Mamigon bought a used Pierce Arrow flatbed truck with solid rubber tires for $300. He learned how to drive it in one day and on the last day of August, 1921, Mamigon was collecting all kinds of foodstuffs from the commission merchants in the wholesale market district around Faneuil Hall and delivering them for ten cents for each item to a string of retail stores.

"Mamigon's Express" was born, his name emblazoned across the front of the truck body. He took another important step. Mamigon found a place in a heavily Jewish section of the city called Roxbury, on Blue Hill Avenue at Grove Hall. It was a six-unit dwelling over a Chinese laundry and an automobile service store with a gasoline pump on the edge of the sidewalk. Except for the Williams family over the laundry, the units were rented by Armenian families. Mamigon furnished the place with a double bed, a three-piece living room set posted around an oriental rug, a couch and table and chairs for the kitchen, and several boxes of kitchen utensils picked out by Guzell and Eksah.

The only thing left to do was for Mamigon and Guzell to get married. The *Nahant Bay* arrived back in Boston the following Tuesday and the nuptials were set for Saturday afternoon on shipboard. The captain had told the owners that the *Nahant Bay* had had some work done on the screw and needed to take her out for trials before she took on cargo again. The wedding party, including half the residents of Sharon Street, boarded the ship and the captain performed the ceremony when the *Nahant Bay* passed the 12-mile limit. Tatios and Eksah stood for the couple. The ship's crew had outdone itself in cleaning up the wardroom. The food was totally Greek, which was to say that it was exactly what the Armenians were accustomed to, as was the music and much of the dancing. Mamigon did not dance nor did he kiss his bride. It would have been unseemly for him to do either, he felt. In any case, he didn't know how to dance. He thoroughly enjoyed watching the dance of the men, however.

Truth to tell, it was a bad day for Mamigon. He had to force a smile much of the time. Standing beside Guzell during the brief rite had brought his mind back to another time, a far-off place where once he had stood for hours in front of Father Vasken with a slip of a girl, only sixteen, standing beside him . . .

9 ⚜ SURVEILLANCE

Tallal Bey was certain his intelligence apparatus was breaking down. He had sent someone other than Enver Dash to meet the *Nahant Bay* and the man reported that absolutely no one even faintly resembling Mamigon had debarked the two days he and his cohorts watched the ship. Where was that big bastard?

"Get back to that house where Mamigon's friend lives and see if you can learn where our friend is."

"Our friend?"

"Mamigon, you dolt!"

"Yes, your Excellency, yes, *effendi*. Do you want me to do anything more than find out where he is?"

"No . . . No, first we will see what is happening . . . where he is . . . or even if he returned with the ship. You know, Enver, we assumed he left with the ship when it sailed. Perhaps he did, perhaps he did not. Perhaps he sailed and left the ship in another country. Find out all you can."

"How should I do this, Excellency?" Enver had a touch of fear in his voice. Tallal did not like questions. He was right.

Tallal opened his mouth to speak, his face reddening. He realized that he wasn't sure himself how Enver was to gather all this information about a man who knew what Enver looked like and might be proximous to his inquirer. He said, finally, "Do the best you can but, above all, do not be obvious, be sly like the fox."

"If I get the chance and he and I are alone, should I shoot him?"

Tallal hit his own forehead with the heel of his hand. "Do not even think of it! Do not take any action until I tell you to, is that plain and clear?" He was shouting.

"Yes, Excellency, yes, yes . . ."

"And take Ali with you. Between the two of you, there might be enough brainpower to get the job done. Now, go."

Enver bowed out, smiling on the outside, dripping with venom on the inside. That man made things difficult. Why was he treated like some kind of a jackass? And now, Ali. That miserable slob who always had drool at the corners of his mouth was the last person Enver wanted to associate with. Ever since Ali had learned that Enver was a eunuch—that's what Ali called Enver—he had wanted to see what it looked like. Enver wasn't about to parade his privates as an exhibition but Ali had been determined. They had struck a bargain. Enver would show it to Ali in the privacy of his room if Ali would relieve him with his mouth. Ali had been greatly impressed by what he saw and followed through with the promise. But he had added a final touch to the event Enver had not counted on. Ali turned out to be an accomplished wrestler and Enver had found himself suddenly in a choking hold and Ali's member embedded in his sphincter . . . a most painful conclusion to what Enver had expected to be at best a dubious adventure.

Now the bugger was to be with him on assignment. Ali had escaped the cane and bullets that night on the waterfront when Mamigon was beaten senseless. He would relish the new assignment having announced loudly to his comrades that he could have eliminated Mamigon by himself, if given the chance.

Ali always had a smirk on his face when he met Enver, and he always inquired if he was ready for another session. Enver would growl a string of obscenities and ignore him. Now he had to seek him out and associate with him on business. He found Ali in the storeroom in the basement, taking inventory.

"Tallal Bey wants you to help me on an assignment."

Ali's face was in a smirk the moment he laid eyes on Enver. "At your place or down here . . . "

"May a thousand camels shit on your face, you whelp of a whore. Close your ugly mouth and get ready to go with me."

"I will go anywhere with you, lovely man," Ali said, and burst out in loud laughter as Enver grabbed a crowbar and swung it at his head. "Put it down, put it down, Enver. I promise to be good. What is it the chief wants us to do now? Attack some children? Sends ten against one man . . . hah!"

Enver liked the derogatory reference to Tallal enough to soften his attitude toward Ali. "We have to find out where that big Armenian is we failed to kill that night. We thought he was coming off that boat but he was not seen. Tallal thinks that if we shade his friend on Sharon Street in the South End we may learn something. We are to start now."

"Fine with me, but if this goes on into the night I will lose a tryst I have arranged with . . . you know who."

"Ismet?"

"The one and only. She is a ball buster . . . I am sorry, you would not know what that means."

"Bull shingles, Ali, bull shingles. I got into her bloomers a year ago."

Ali looked impressed but said otherwise. "Well, if I miss getting her tonight, I shall simply knock you down and get into yours."

"Bull shingles, again, you filthy, hairy ape."

They learned nothing loitering around at the corner of Harrison Avenue and Sharon Street on Friday, and it was only curiosity that made them scrutinize the big truck with the swooping headlights that turned onto Sharon Street late Saturday night to disgorge about thirty well-dressed men and women from its back. The light wasn't very good from the gas lamps on the street but they had no difficulty spotting the huge frame of the man they sought helping people off the back, then climbing back into the driver's seat and leaving.

Both men were dumbfounded. They had seen their quarry and lost him before they could find out a thing. What was that truck all about? What was that crowd in the back of the truck? What was going on? They had no answers. Ali felt they should not tell Tallal of this development until they could learn more. If they reported what they had seen without additional information he was liable to hand them their heads.

Two weeks went by. They were at their post on the corner of Sharon Street continually during reasonable hours. They never saw the truck again in that time. A check at the waterfront revealed that the ship had sailed the week before.

Enver finally reported to Tallal that following Mamigon's friend had revealed nothing about Mamigon. He was nowhere to be found. The ship had sailed September 12 and wasn't due back until October 3 or 4.

Tallal told him to cancel the surveillance for now. It would not do to have Enver and Ali become too noticeable a fixture in the neighborhood. The weather was turning and a cold rawness was beginning to dominate the air frequently enough to render useless a proper clothing forecast for any particular day. The spring would be time enough when loiterers would not be unnatural.

Tallal was feeling expansive. The news from home was good. Mustapha Kemal Pasha had halted the steady advance of the Greek armies into Turkey at the Sakarya River. Respect for the new Turkish republic was growing as its army's counteroffensive showed signs of success.

10 TALES

For the first time since that never-to-be-forgotten Sunday in mid-August of 1915, Mamigon was experiencing a sense of well-being. He worked six days a week in his newfound business, still the tall, dark, taciturn man whose humble work did not detract one iota from the instant respect he commanded among the men with whom he came into contact. It was, perhaps, his steadfast gaze into their eyes, or his choice of few words in necessary conversations, or his dour visage, or, perhaps, his height and massive proportions that made men hold him in the esteem rarely evoked by one who is seen most of the time in blue denim overalls and a cloth cap. He was out of bed at four in the morning to break his fast with a straight shot of *rahki*, that hundred-forty-proof alcoholic dynamite distilled from raisin mash, and was back at his flat by six or seven o'clock in the evening to be greeted by his bride.

Guzell, whose upbringing had trained her to be a dutiful, loving housewife, was being just that and loving her new existence with a man she considered fortunate to have as a husband. She had felt lonely, at first, among all the Armenians—much more than she had been when she was with all those women at the Franklin Square House—because she had felt the hostility expressed in a myriad of subtleties of word, expression, and glance. But that had faded within weeks as she became known as Diggin Guzell, Baron Mamigon's or Mamigon Agha's new bride. Since Mamigon spoke only Turkish she did not have any adjustment to make there. She realized quickly that she had special standing in the Armenian community because of Mamigon. Aside from his prestige and stature he was also a man of relative wealth. He was the first in the community to buy an automobile, a huge, four-door convertible Studebaker for the astronomical sum of $550.

The automobile was a wondrous thing, but so many things in America had been wondrous to Mamigon, who tried not to show his delight and surprise in front of Guzell, the veteran in such matters because she had already been introduced to the wonders five years ago. Wonders such as electric lights in each of the rooms, water available simply by turning on a tap *indoors*, and no need to go out into the cold or the heat for your toilet. You simply used a funny-looking bowl standing on the floor with a source of water constantly replenished by merely pulling a chain attached to a box above. The device was better than the small hole in the floor over which one squatted in fancy homes in the old country, and certainly a far cry from an outhouse. And there was no need for porters in America to carry away the buckets of offal each morning as was the system in the old country. He had come to the inescapable conclusion, however, that the water in the bathroom taps was unclean and only drank from the kitchen faucets.

There were some major bafflements that took longer to resolve.

First was the language which he was in the constant process of learning from everyone around him. What bothered Mamigon was that the words didn't mean the same thing even though they sounded exactly the same. There was no lilt, no softness to the tongue either. The words all seemed to run together, sounding to him a little like German.

As for the Americans themselves, where in God's name were they? He had come to America expecting to be a stranger among English-speaking people basically of English extraction. Instead, he was surrounded by people who spoke everything, it seemed, except English. Oofah, these so-called Americans were all foreigners, just like himself, with the exception of the supervisors and managers at the market. They spoke English the way it was meant to be spoken, he was sure of that.

Mamigon's conversations with Tatios about things American were entertaining. The two would meet Saturday nights at Tatios's home since Mamigon had a car. It was cozy during the winter months. The men would play a few sets of backgammon in the front room of the small, four-room flat, and the only contact between the men and women was when Eksah or Guzell served Turkish coffee and sweets. Mamigon commiserated with Tatios's disclosure that he ate his meals with his wife. Another breakdown of good custom, Mamigon had thought. In the old country, the men ate alone, first, while the women ate in the kitchen or cooking area with the small children. When the boys reached the age of seven or so, they joined the men. Men shouldn't be bothered with the chitchat and constant bickering inherent in the female character, no question about it. Of course, Tatios and Mamigon were the only males in the house, and it would have been a bit silly for them to eat in lonely solitude.

Mamigon had told his friend most of the story of his search for Tallal; Tatios dragged it out of him by constant pleas for details. And without prompting, Tatios told how he had finally gotten out of the clutches of the Osmanlis, relishing most the fantastic coincidence that had saved his life when he found one of his sisters near Aleppo. He had learned also that his brother Harootune, whom the Turks had classified as an intellectual agitator, was hanged in Istanbul—kind, gentle Harootune who had welcomed the revolt of the Young Turks as a hopeful sign that the government had returned to the policy of reform and tolerance of Armenians that had been abruptly abrogated by Sultan Hamid II.

"As soon as I got my strength back, my sister Ahrussyag stole some clothes and I dressed to pass as either an Arab or a Turk. We left before midnight, a week after I got there, and walked the 20 kilometers to Aleppo by daybreak, traveling as husband and wife.

"We found the German mission and, sure enough, my American friend, Harry Sears, was there. He passed us off as Turkish friends of his and made us stay in his room while he made arrangements. In two days he had papers for us and we were in the seaport of Iskendaroun on an American steamer headed for Boston with a cargo of pickled lambskins that would be used for hat bands. We were listed as retainers for the Sears family and did not go through Ellis Island.

"Mamigon, I am unable to find anyone in Boston who knows of Harry Sears. He mentioned a place that sounded something like Chester but I am not able to find it. I have given up. The least I wanted to do was to thank him for saving my life twice, but . . ."

"If it is to be, it will be, my friend. Do not worry about it. Your friend Sears seems like a man of many parts, much like you."

"I may be a man of many parts, but the parts seem to be of tissue paper and rusted metal—some of them are too flimsy and the others are weak from disuse."

"You know, my friend, what you just said is what impresses me about you. You have the ability to string word pictures that makes it easy for plain people to understand. It is a gift that few have. With such a gift, you will be able to make your mark in America. Listen to me, do not lose sight of who you are. A man is measured, in the end, by what he overcomes within himself."

Tatios looked hard at Mamigon for a moment, then jabbed him lightly in the arm for reply.

Mamigon's big truck became a familiar sight in Sharon Street, parked in front of the brownstone row house where Tatios and his family lived. He never came empty-handed—a crate of fancy navel oranges one Saturday, a bushel box of Thompson seedless grapes the next, a 5 pound loaf of cream cheese packaged in tinfoil, or a 2-gallon tin of jelly—all were accepted with great protestations of insincere regret that he had gone to so much expense and that it wasn't necessary. Mamigon knew it wasn't necessary, but he also knew it was a good thing to do. Tatios was earning about $6 a week in the suit factory.

Eksah's husband chose to ignore the fact that she was taking in wash. He was deeply embarrassed that his wife had to work to assure the family of food and shelter. Tatios became more and more irritable at home as his despair deepened.

Mamigon didn't know how bad things were for Tatios until one Friday night, when he stopped to drop off a shank of lamb for the family because he didn't want to keep it a whole day without benefit of an icebox. Tatios was not home—he was apt to disappear on Friday nights and give no explanation when he returned around ten o'clock—and Eksah poured out a tale of woe.

She said that time and again Tatios would quit his job for real or imagined insults to his pride. And, time and again, she would make a clandestine trip to the factory and beg Mr. Kondazian, the owner, to take him back. And Mr. Kondazian would send for Tatios Effendi with an apology and a plea to return. Tatios would say, See, they know they were wrong, their conscience bothered them. And he would return, none the wiser that his wife had paved the way again.

"He is a highly educated man, Mamigon Agha, and this life is not for him. I know that, but he cannot find any other work. He walked all the way to someplace called Cambridge, to a university, but his English was not good enough. He is learning quickly, though. You know, he spoke to them in French, German, Greek, Latin, Italian, Arabic, Turkish, and Armenian, and it made little difference. He was crushed. He was so despondent that week that he even canceled the story hour."

If not a success as a breadwinner, Tatios had quickly become a social success as a storyteller among the Armenians in the ghetto. On Sunday afternoons there was standing room only as he held forth in the middle of his parlor, spinning tales. Having read a Victor Hugo or a Flaubert or a Homer in the original, he would retell the story in successive Sundays, much as was done in the old country, where the storyteller was the major source of entertainment for the entire village. Chairs would be carried to his house by the men of the neighborhood. The story hour was limited mainly to adult males. The only exceptions were women well into their sixties and seventies who were treated as peers: they were even allowed to smoke cigarettes with the men and exchange small talk as they sipped wine or *rahki*. Once it began, story hour was definitely not a time for small talk or wine sipping, though. It was serious, satisfying business. The females sat in the rear of the gathering, the chairs usually in a double row, with two rows of cross-legged listeners on the floor almost up to the feet of the storyteller. Tatios was completely surrounded and stood during the usual two-hour session with barely a square yard of space for himself.

He was a consummate actor as well as a raconteur, using his hands in a variety of sets; his head in a variety of cocks; his shoulders and torso for the telegraph of suspense, dejection, or other emotions; his legs and feet for subtle stances and slight pirouettes for physical action to supplement his words.

But it was his voice that carried his audience. The loudness, the softness, the drawn out whine of pain or swoon of delight, the guttural sounds of passion or death or despair, the lightness in the voice for the female character and the variations for the various male characters. He was a master without question.

As the storyteller he relied on the license of his position to allow him to talk about and describe facts and situations and problems written by the author that ordinarily would have been taboo in conversation if it had concerned the real world—at least taboo in public. But the author had written it and who was to question words printed in black and white?

Consequently, Tatios could and did express concerns absolutely foreign to those of his listeners, such as that of Dostoevski's strumpet who worried whether her transitory lover would be gentle with her and not treat her as a side of beef. For this last phrase Tatios would hold his hands wide and puff his cheeks to show that she truly was a side of beef to begin with. Many of his male listeners would nod their heads knowingly.

Or, describe the lactation period of a pregnant woman by cupping his hands upward and shaking them as if he were weighing two objects in his hands to give his audience the sense of heaviness. This was too close to home and a silent squirming would be the listeners' response.

Or, rattle off Flaubert's scandalous observations on the relative merits of certain women in bed, describing German women as "vaporish" as he imitated a swoon, French women as "licentious" as he adopted a leer, and Italian women as "passionate" as he breathed heavily. Tatios, of course, gave the undeniable impression that these were obviously his own personal observations.

Or, Plutarch's lines about Alexander the Great that led the listeners to believe that the young Macedonian king had run amok at sacrificial and celebratory rites totally naked to exhibit his sexual wares . . . something Tatios's Armenian listeners felt was the wont of most Greeks anyway.

Or, assuming the total celibacy of Sherlock Holmes, with his utter disregard of women as sexual objects, to be the epitome of male strength—leading one listener to question Tatios afterwards as to the possibility that Holmes might be Armenian.

Yes, Tatios was able to be gross while erudite, to pander as he was being literate, to excite while he was enchanting—providing a total though temporary escape for his listeners from the drab, dark, dreary dullness of the daily scramble for bread in a fearfully foreign environment.

For sheer drama and consistent suspense, Tatios relied on Dumas. Thus, when Edmond Dantes was victimized and thrown in jail, the audience moaned; thus, when the Abbe Ferrari died in Dantes's arms, the tears in the eyes of the audience were mixed with everyone crossing himself when Tatios, in a cracking voice, said, "He died peacefully with a small sigh." Tatios, of course, did not say another word for a good thirty seconds to milk the full sadness of the episode.

As is the case of an audience at a stage play attributing the words of the writer to the actor, Tatios's audience did the same thing with him. Long ago the community had come to the conclusion that Tatios Effendi was the most intelligent, most educated, most sensitive, most accomplished, most sophisticated man in the world. If the culture of the community had not been strict, not been so cohesive, so incestuous in a way, Tatios Effendi would have been offered a variety of acceptable daughters as a means of gaining him for the family . . . and to Hades with that smart, high-nosed Eksah.

Mamigon never sat in on any of these story hours. He was being taught Armenian by Eksah in the kitchen, with Guzell learning as much as she could without seeming to interfere with the important task of teaching the man first.

Mamigon had worried about the mysterious Friday night disappearances of his friend, although he did not say a word to Eksah. He was more worried than curious, because he knew Tatios to be a sensitive man and wondered if he were up to something stupid or rash. He didn't like to do it, but he decided to ask Tatios and did so the following night over backgammon.

"You seem to be unhappy, my friend."

"I am beating you, why should I be unhappy?"

"I am not talking about games, I am talking about life."

"Life is a game, my friend, and I am temporarily losing."

"It is good that you say temporarily. I am glad. Now I have no worries about what you have been up to on Friday nights."

Tatios cocked his head in surprise, then tilted his head toward the kitchen. "Girl, Miss Drevanian!" His wife appeared with a look of concern on her face. Her husband didn't call her in that manner unless he had something urgent to say. "Have you been bothering Mamigon Agha with your silly gossip?"

"Please, my man, I said nothing to Mamigon Agha I would not say in front of you."

Mamigon stood up. "Tatios, this matter is between you and me. It has nothing to do with Diggin Eksah. Please excuse her." She left with a fleeting smile for Mamigon, without a by-your-leave for Tatios.

"This is a small community, Tatios Effendi, and your Friday disappearances are well known." Tatios seemed mollified. He lowered his voice.

"If you do not make it public, I shall tell you and only you, because I am ashamed I spend time away from my family and worse—I spend money we desperately need." Mamigon girded himself for the terrible truth. "I go to the cinema on Cobb Street."

"The . . . cinema?"

"Yes. They show motion pictures of American *chobans*—cowboys—and I pay ten cents for a ticket and see the showing twice."

"But your English is not good enough for you to understand . . . What is the attraction in seeing cowherders?"

"The horses, Mamigon, the horses. They ride beautiful American horses. I saw the posters in front of the cinema house one day and I could not resist. It must be a special American breed because they are not like the English thoroughbreds I saw racing in Paris, nor are they Arabs. But those horses are almost as good as the Arabs I bred. And what riders! I made out the names of those cowboys and I only wish I could meet them, especially a fellow by the name of Tom Mix. He calls his horse Tony—I know not if the horse's real Italian name is Antony—but he is no doubt the greatest horse-back rider I have ever seen. He is better than I am. Oh, if you could only see him ride. He brings me back to the old days . . ." Tatios had tears in his eyes. Mamigon sighed and wondered about people like Tatios. His own stoic temperament could not fathom the Tatioses of the world. Crying about horses? Oofah!

Tatios's two children were always present in the kitchen, playing on the floor with wooden blocks or coloring books, the boy Hagop dominating and cheating his older sister Mary at every turn.

Mamigon had heard Hagop, only three years old, call his mother on occasion with the same command his father used when irritated: "Girl, Miss Drevanian!" The whole family had chuckled at first at the little fellow's precociousness, but his repeated attempts to elicit the same reaction later had met with decided coolness by his mother, who announced that one tyrant in the family was enough.

It was the third Sunday in March and the weather was showing signs of spring. Mamigon had driven to Sharon Street as was usual these days and had walked to the Sunday services with Tatios more as a nice thing to do than because he wished to worship. Tatios was the choir director, taking up the chores he had abandoned in Constantinople. His tenor was a thing of beauty as he chanted the responses during the Mass.

As the two left the church, Mamigon said casually, "Do not turn to look, but I am certain we are being followed."

"Followed? What do you mean, followed?"

"I noticed a man in a new brown suit standing across the street from the church when we left. We have turned down three streets and he is still behind us. He seems to wait until we turn a corner before he comes into view."

"How do you know this? I did not see you looking back."

"The first time I turned my head to look at you, I saw him from the corner of my eye. I am watching him now as I talk to you. If he is not following us, he has all the marks, the actions of doing just that. I know."

"Should we stop and ask what he wants?"

"No, my friend. It is better that we part. You go straight for the trolley stop and go downtown. I will follow. I will circle two or three blocks and take the next trolley downtown. Get off at the next stop and go home. I will see you at your house for my lesson. Do not look back, whatever you do."

They split up and Mamigon continued walking to the next corner and went down the street. As he approached the end of the block, he looked sideways at the trees across the street as if something had caught his attention. Ah. He was being followed for certain. He felt at a disadvantage, completely puzzled, so he decided not to collar the fellow until he could figure out what the attraction was. After he turned the next corner, he had one more block of three-story homes to go before the trolley stop . . . and he wasn't at all sure there would be a trolley ready for him to board. The hell with it, I'll act as if I've changed my mind, he thought, to throw off the fellow. So, he suddenly stopped as if he had thought of something, snapped his fingers, and headed for the trolley stop. He didn't try to see if his follower was still around.

The trolley came after a ten-minute wait, and, as Mamigon climbed aboard and dropped the nickel fare in the box, he realized his shadow was getting on, too. Mamigon went all the way to the rear and stood to look down the length of the interior. There were few Sunday riders, and he was easily able to pick out the back of the man who had followed him aboard and who was now staring straight ahead, knowing that Mamigon could exit only by passing by him.

Mamigon would have to go downtown and take the subway back to the South End. He left the trolley, walked casually down the ramp, took the stairs, and ended up on the subway platform. He didn't look to see if he were still being followed. The subway train arrived to take passengers from both sides of the split platform. Mamigon stepped aboard, waited until he was sure the doors were about to close, snapped his fingers again as if he remembered something, and stepped back on the platform as the doors slid shut. He was alone as the train rumbled off with its familiar whine and screeching wheels on the curved track ahead. He didn't once look at the cars to see if the man was aboard. He knew he would be, and he wasn't about to be seen checking to see if his ruse had worked.

Mamigon did some thinking. It was obvious to him that the fellow had followed them to the church from Tatios's house. Mamigon was certain he would have noticed if anyone had followed him to Sharon Street from Roxbury. Oofah, the whole thing was getting a bit silly. There didn't seem to be an explanation for it, but there probably was a simple one. He should have stopped the fellow and asked. Oh, well . . .

He took the next train, which emerged from the subway onto elevated tracks on Washington Street in the South End, got off and walked with his distinctive whisper of a limp to Sharon Street.

Tatios asked the question. "What happened after I left?"

"Nothing, my friend. I was right. We were being followed, but it was me he was after. He got on the streetcar when I did, but I managed to lose him at the subway station. I still do not know what it is all about. Any ideas?"

"Did you recognize him?"

"I never did get a good look at him. I did not want him to know I knew he was following me. I did not recognize the back of his head. He had black hair, a beard, and big ears. That is all."

"Well, I think we must be careful from now on to see if we are followed again. I really do not know what I would do if I found I was being followed."

"Do nothing. Act naturally and continue to where you were going, that is all."

Mamigon was pensive as he drove home with Guzell that evening. He was remembering again what he had dismissed from his mind as imagination—the howls of pain and the curses uttered in Turkish that dark night in July.

11 &&SUPPOSITIONS

"I suppose we will have to use one of the company automobiles."

"I suppose so, but Ali will drive. He has a license from the authorities."

"I suppose he must, but I am able to drive, your Excellency, you know that."

"I suppose you can, but Ali will drive."

"I suppose you will let me drive one of these days."

"I suppose I will . . . but I believe we have supposed enough today. How do you propose to find out where he is living now?"

"We shall have to wait until next Sunday, Excellency, when he completes his visit to the church and drives back to his house. I was unable to follow him, as you know, when he drove off in his automobile with a woman yesterday."

"Our quarry is not aware of us, is he?" The moment Tallal asked the question his heart sank. The look, though ever so fleeting on Enver's face, had answered his question. "Well!"

"I think not, Excellency . . ." Enver imparted total lack of conviction when he said it. He was quivering inside.

"*Think* not!! You big brown horse's sphincter. He spotted you, DID HE NOT?"

"I . . . I . . . I am not certain . . ."

"Tell me what happened." Tallal was rubbing the lump on the upper left arm Mamigon's bullets had created.

"Well, when the two left the church they boarded separate trams heading downtown. I stuck to Mamigon and boarded the same tram he did. When . . ."

"They boarded *separate* trams going in the same direction?"

"Yes, *effendi,* separate. When we arrived at the subway station, he walked directly by me without looking, went aboard the train, seemed to remember something, and jumped off just as the doors closed. I was unable to follow him."

"An old trick to shake off a shadow, you dolt."

"I decided to go back to Sharon Street and wait to see if he returned there. That is where I saw him get into a big automobile with a woman heavy with child and drive off." Enver felt exhausted after he finished the portion of the report he had neglected to mention earlier. The little prick Tallal had a way of finding out everything!

"Next Sunday, then, you and Ali will try to discover his den and provide me with as much detail as possible. Now, have you conveniently left out anything you might want to divulge?"

"No, nothing, your Excellency."

"Very well, Enver, please get out of my sight."

Tallal was certain Mamigon knew of his whereabouts now. If he saw Enver following him, then he just as easily must have followed Enver. That crazy could be waiting for him outside the office building this very moment . . . by Allah, would he ever be rid of that Armenian? He had called off the surveillance almost six months ago, last September, and now, at the end of March, he had found him, he hoped . . . or Mamigon had found *him*.

12 ❧ BROTHERS

Mamigon felt as if he had been married to Guzell all his life, although it was only six months—six months and two weeks, to be exact, as it was the last week of March. The Boston winter had been cold, slushy, and uneventful, a perfect period for the two to become totally reacquainted without the need for too much socializing with friends because of the weather. Mamigon's new home was a good 5 miles from the South End, which was directly on his way to work, though not a casual walk.

The past had become distant, the scenes of death and destruction that had been so real for so long had become infrequent though heart-stopping nightmares. Guzell was making it easier for him to forget. What he never remarked on or hinted to Guzell was the complete change that had come over her. Gone was the spontaneous eruption of emotion that had been the hallmark of their relationship on the mountainous trails of Anatolia. Gone was the mad abandonment of body and self she had exhibited on the hard ground they shared as they had held each other. Gone was the small whoop of joy when she had managed to bring a grunt of response or a deep sigh of contentment from her consort in those bygone years.

What was it, he thought, that caused Guzell to change the moment she had become his wife? She was, from their first marriage night, sedate, demur, shy, and totally passive, much like his first wife, his "little baby girl." He would recall Guzell in their first physical responses with a small grin. Marriage certainly seemed to have a stultifying effect. But she was his darling, his second self, and he found a creeping impatience toward the end of each day as his work wound down to rush home just to be with her.

They would spend the evenings trying to understand the English in the *Boston Globe* for which he paid two cents each afternoon. The most troublesome aspect of it was that there were too many words and expressions that didn't seem to have a Turkish counterpart. What was a "three-decker" or "the El" or an "ice rink" or a "department" store or "cellophane" or "ketchup" or . . . the list was infinite and provided good-natured banter as they attempted to guess what the words meant through the context of their usage.

Guzell was pregnant. She had been since the second month of her marriage. She had blushingly confided in Eksah about some sudden changes in her body functions two months after her wedding day and was horrified when she had to submit to an examination by a man, the monocled Dr. Yardume, to learn she was with child. Women attended women in the old country, without benefit of a physician. The news had prompted, of course, the usual finger counting by the women to establish the fact that she had been married on September 10 and was expected to give normal birth about June 30—a month's leeway—very proper and upright.

Mamigon's reaction to the news when he had stopped at Sharon Street to pick her up on the day Eksah took her to the doctor's office was distant and cold until they arrived home. The moment he had shut the front door he pulled her to him and held her close and tight to his chest for what seemed forever. Then he held her away and kissed her on the forehead.

"My anger is gone."

"Your . . . your anger?"

"Yes. Though an ass may be ladened with gold, it is still an ass . . . and I have been that ass." She was still perplexed by his words, so he continued. "I railed at God. I scolded and scorned Him for taking away what He had given me in the first place. He has chosen to ignore my faithlessness, my anger. He made me do penance for more than six years before He answered me."

"Allah is all powerful, my man. Never lose your faith. It is all we have in facing the trials of life."

Mamigon had nodded. She was noticeably with child now in late March, almost six months into her pregnancy, and a neighbor, Diggin Odabashian from across the hall, visited with her most of the day. Diggin Odabashian had lost her four children as well as her husband in the Exile and had remarried in Boston to a quiet man who had lost his family also. No one in the community became too excited about births, marriages, or deaths. Sack cloth and ashes dominated attitudes; practically every woman from the old country wore black constantly, and the three stages of life only managed to bring hard memories to the surface.

It had not crossed Mamigon's mind before Guzell's pregnancy but now he liked the realization that there would be a renewal of the Magaros bloodline. It probably had been too hard for him to grasp that the massacres had literally wiped out all but two of his family, and he wasn't at all certain of what had become of Aram. The fact Guzell was born Turkish and that their progeny would be an admixture of *High* and Turk, Christian and Moslem, was inconsequential to Mamigon. The infant would be theirs, his and hers, and would carry his name. For the sake of his forefathers, he liked that idea very much. It would be nice if the newcomer would be a boy, but it was not all that important. He would certainly father more children. He remembered something from the past and grinned. The sponge diver's wife . . . Theodora? . . . would be interested if she knew that her stitching work had not been in vain.

But he was now certain that he had to protect Guzell above all else if Mamigon, son of Magaros of Yosghat Dagh, was to have, and continue to beget offspring to carry on the proud old name from Anatolia.

He confided in Tatios.

"Someone is trying to kill me, old friend."

"Are you talking about that beating you survived?"

"Yes and no. Tatios, I never mentioned something that could have meant something or nothing at the time. But it has meaning now. My attackers that night were Turks."

"Ah!"

"I am asking myself who could it be and I do not know."

"You have discounted new acquaintances or enemies here?"

"I know not of any."

"It must have something to do with the time we were followed last March."

"Undoubtedly."

"There must be Turks living here."

"There must be. Where?"

"We will have to find out."

"No, my friend, I will find out. I am not seeking help, my good friend. I am telling you this should something happen to me that may be unexplainable. You should know. You will look after Guzell if anything happens to me?"

"My friend . . ." Tatios stared at the big man. "Of course . . . He that loves the tree, loves the branch."

No more was said. Mamigon had stopped at Sharon Street on his way home on Saturday. As he stepped out of the front door of the brownstone tenement to walk down the eight granite steps to the street, a huge figure of a man wearing a soft gray fedora, suited in sharkskin gray, smiled up at him from the sidewalk, a perfect row of teeth lighting up a swarthy, handsome face.

"Remember your little brother!" The words were in Turkish.

Mamigon hurried down the steps without a word and grabbed Aram's shoulders, staring into his face. "It *is* my little brother . . ."

They clasped hands, still staring, but now both had huge grins. The brothers were veritable giants.

"You have developed a belly," Mamigon said, poking a finger at Aram's midriff.

"And, you have not changed a bit, big brother."

They finally embraced, eyes glistening with tears, the shock of seeing each other having receded slightly.

The "wheres," "hows," "whens," and "whats" came tumbling too fast from both their lips for intelligible conversation. Mamigon pressed him into his truck and they went to Koko's coffeehouse to talk. Driving to his home would have taken too long.

Armenians are generally people of small stature and the appearance of the brothers at Koko's caused a stir. Everyone knew Mamigon by sight and reputation. The giant look-alike with him was too much to ignore.

Koko rousted three customers away from a table in the corner, ushered Mamigon and Aram to it, and shuffled off to bring them coffee after Aram was introduced to him. Koko felt very important at this point, responding to questions from the other tables with an air of impatience as if they should have known—as he certainly did—that the other chap was Mamigon's brother Aram. After bringing the demitasses he hovered at a respectful distance from their table, making sure no one approached them and neglecting his other customers to boot.

Aram recounted how Panagos, the sponge diver, had brought his boatload of survivors safely to Crete where the group hired a boat to take them to the mainland and eventually to Athens. Armenian families took in most of the women by the time Aram bought passage to America. At Ellis Island he was told that a motorcar company in Michigan was hiring workers. He was living in a place called Dearborn and making automobiles on an assembly line. He was told by compatriots in Detroit about an Armenian in Boston purported to be his brother and decided to investigate to see if it were really his long-lost brother Mamigon.

"So, here I am."

"So, here you are. Are you married?"

"Are you joking? Me, married? I get all the bottoms I need without a ring." Aram laughed.

"I am so happy to see you again. I could not imagine what had happened to you. How long can you stay with me? We have much to talk about. You realize we are the only ones left in the family?"

Aram didn't answer right away. Mention of the family, all butchered, seemed to darken the reunion. But not for long.

"I must get back to Detroit, big brother. They gave me special leave when I told them you might be here."

"How long can you stay?"

"I must go back tomorrow . . . Please do not look like that. They will not hold my job for me. I need the money, big brother. I am in bad trouble and need every cent I can lay my hands on."

"What kind of trouble, Aram?" Mamigon had become aware that his brother had yet to ask one question about him other than the fact that Mamigon was doing well in the trucking express business.

"Not the kind of trouble we had in the old country, big brother. Just a matter of money I owe, that is all. It would be nothing to a man like you."

"What kind of man do you think your brother is, incidentally. I am still in wonder about the story you told of me and what I was supposed to have done to the Turks back there."

"Good, eh? The newspapers paid me for the story so I laid it on thick, I thought the Turks would be after me if I admitted what l did, so I said you did it. Made you famous, big brother."

"Did you learn nothing about honesty and truth in the family, little brother?" Mamigon was getting impatient.

"Do not be angry, old man. You were having all the fun knocking off those bastards. You were treating me like a little kid. I had to prove something to myself."

"A man should own up to what he does, that is all I am saying. I am not passing judgment on what you did."

"You are always passing judgment, just like father used to do. It was like you to pass up all that cunt that was ready for you on the trail. I could see it in their eyes, the way they were looking at you. I took care of them for you, big brother. I screwed Araxy and Anahid and . . ."

Mamigon raised his hand in a signal to stop. It was the expression on Mamigon's face that halted Aram's outpouring.

"Save it, Aram. I do not think we have anyting further to talk about."

"Oh, yes we do. You are a big man on account of me. The least you can do is help me out now. I have been gambling and need a heavy purse. What can you do for me?"

Mamigon stuck his hand into his overall pocket, took out a folded wad of bills and tossed it across the table. Then he put down a fifty cent piece on the table for the coffee and stood up.

"That is all I have. You can have it, Aram. Let us say good-bye for now."

"Wait. You must hear my proposition. We can both be rich if . . ."

"Good-bye, little brother." Mamigon left Aram as the latter began to rise from his chair and strode out to the street.

Aram would have been impressed. Mamigon was sniffing back the tears.

13 ⚜ INDEMNITY

Ali stomped down the stairs two at a time, showing amazing agility most people would not associate with a frame as simian as his. When he reached the street he gulped in huge quantities of cool air, reveling in the sudden freshness of the atmosphere in sharp contrast to the stuffy dankness of Enver's room. Walking back to his place, an alcove in the basement of the importing house, would be just right to clear away the slight skim of sweat that clung to him. He liked the way he smelled, a smell that reminded him of his latest triumph over Enver. The two had settled down during the winter into a once a week session of give and take, exchanging sexual roles as their desires dictated. Ali had had to coax Enver into the situation but the shoe was now on the other foot. Enver was the pleader, the persuader, and Ali liked his role as the reluctant one. He could dictate at every turn and tonight had not been different. He had obtained relief from Enver and then had casually knocked him down and left without the slightest attempt to satisfy his raging companion. Actually, he might have done it but he was not going to take any chances with his prowess in bed tomorrow. Tallal Bey's secretary was going to be in the building tomorrow afternoon for something and on Sundays the place would be deserted. Ali was licking the corners of his mouth at the thought of Mirvet. He had given her a gentle, tentative pat on her backside only last week and she had responded with a smile. Now, if that wasn't a signal, Ali didn't know what signals from women were!

Ali was ten steps from the coffeehouse on Tremont Street when his eyes bugged. There he was, the big man, the Armenian shit, stopping as he came out the door of the coffeehouse. The man looked in Ali's direction trying to make up his mind, then turned and walked in the direction Ali was going. He was now only six paces ahead of Ali, heading downtown.

Ali's breath came a little shorter, not from fear but from the adrenaline that began pumping into his system. He had proclaimed to everyone and anyone that he could have taken the Armenian that night without the need for ten men. Only the gunfire from the captain had stopped him.

Now he had his opportunity. This was going to gain much favor from Tallal Bey, no question about it. He carefully pulled out the 8-inch dagger he always carried in a sheath snapped on to his belt. He wore a belt instead of the generally worn suspenders because of his knife.

It was about nine o'clock, the street was dark with little traffic on it. Ali tailed his prey who walked in a steady pace ahead of him. Ali watched for the place up ahead where a service alley was located. As the figure ahead was within two steps from the alley entrance, Ali broke into a lope, caught up at the mouth of the alley, grabbed the unsuspecting man by the arm on the alley side, yanked him into the alley, and as the big man turned into an involuntary dance position with Ali, Ali's knife sank into his heart. Not a sound was uttered by either killer or victim.

Ali looked down at him, looked around to make certain he wasn't being observed, kicked the dead man's soft gray fedora deep into the alley, and sauntered away after cleaning off his bloody knife on the dead man's coat.

14 ⚜ NO FAMILY

The police were at Mamigon's door near midnight. Mamigon had said nothing to Guzell about his brother Aram being in town when he had arrived home that evening. The two bluecoats asked Mamigon to accompany them downtown to answer some questions. No, they couldn't say what it was about, but would he come, now? He was driven to police headquarters on Berkeley Street, leaving a frightened Guzell behind.

Koko was sitting on a bench against the wall of the station house when

Mamigon walked in. Mamigon was led directly to the desk where the sergeant on duty made a call and a man in a suit came through a door to size up the man who had been brought in.

The plainclothesman turned to Koko and asked him if this was the man. When Koko nodded, he was told he could leave. Koko waved a tentative hand at Mamigon and walked out.

That's when Mamigon was told that a man, identified by Koko as his brother, was found dead, knifed through the heart, in an alley near the coffeehouse.

The police were certain robbery wasn't the motive. Aram had more than $400 on him, most of it in a folded pack. A check of the area had brought Koko to the scene and he immediately had identified the body as that of Mamigon's brother. Since Aram had left within ten minutes after his brother's departure, the police were curious. They took Mamigon to the morgue for positive identification.

"Yes, that is my brother."

"What was he doin' here? His papers say he's from Detroit."

"He come to see me. He need money. I give him what I have."

"How old is he?"

"Twenty-six before year is out."

"Does he have a family?"

"No, I am last of family."

"You don't look as if you give a damn about your brother, mister."

"What . . . ?"

"Did you have anything to do with this?" The detective didn't like the coldness he was sensing in Mamigon's reaction to his brother's death.

"What?"

"You heard me."

"I think maybe you think I kill my brother."

"Yeah, somethin' like that."

"Civilized men do not kill their brothers. Turks might, but not civilized men."

"What the hell are you talking about . . . what Turks?"

"Never mind, but do not say I kill my brother. I loved my brother."

"You sure have a lousy way of showing it, mister."

"Men do not wear feelings on their sleeve."

"Listen, you. You're a bit too cool and collected about this for my taste. Was there bad blood between yuh?"

"No."

"Do you know who killed your brother?"

"No."

"Do you know why he was killed?"

" . . . No."

"You hesitated there. Why?"

"If I knew why he was killed, I would know who . . ."

"Did he have a girlfriend here?"

"This first time he come to Boston."

"I didn't ask that. Did he have a girl here?"

"I do not know. I believe not."

"Do you have a girl?"

"I am married man."

"Did your brother know your wife?"

"He did not know I was married. I met him first time today in six years."

"Well, you sure don't impress me as giving a damn about him."

Mamigon's voice lowered and the detective heard a new tone in it. "I am now last of seven brothers. Turks killed five in the old country. I have done with crying long ago. Aram understands. He laughs now because of foolish questions I must answer."

The detective bit at his lower lip for a second or two, shrugged his shoulders, and took Mamigon back to the station for contact information before he was driven home.

After reassuring Guzell that everything was all right, he told her about Aram's murder.

"Who could have done such a thing if robbery was not the reason?"

"I know, but I have no proof."

"You know? Did you tell the police?"

"I know something, woman, but not enough to tell them."

"Please tell me."

Mamigon pondered an answer, then decided that since he didn't have good facts, there was little good reason to bring up the subject of Turks with his wife. She might feel bad about it; it was the third of May with eight weeks left to go in her pregnancy. She should be placid about things.

He gave her a long hug instead of an answer. Mamigon couldn't tell her what was really bothering him, bothering him so much that he wanted to be alone, to be able to vent his emotions. His last words with Aram had been unhappy ones. He had walked away from his brother, not realizing at the time that his good-bye was going to be his last. If only he had embraced him again . . . if only . . . The sons of Magaros of Yosghat Dagh were now reduced to one.

15   AT LAST

Tallal Bey had to wait until Sunday afternoon to celebrate the news. Ali had to wait for his secretary at the office before he obtained the telephone number to call him at home. It was difficult for him to believe, at first. From September, 1915, to May 7, 1922, was a long time to wait to get rid of a nemesis, a nemesis that had cost him much, including almost his life. He sat in his easy chair in the room he had furnished as a smoking room where he did his reading and almost felt sorry for himself. He had no one close to him so he could share his final triumph. So, Mamigon was dead. May he turn slowly in the fires of hell. Perhaps now he could go on living without having to look back over his shoulder, an almost spontaneous reflex he had acquired in the years since that day he lost his head and put Yosghat Dagh to the sword.

He would have to reward Ali in some special way. So, he had been spending the evening at Enver's room. The slight catch in Ali's voice when he had explained why he happened to be in the vicinity of the coffeehouse had been enough for Tallal to guess what the two had been up to. Gross, such grossness. Ali had reported in his flat, expressionless voice what had happened. How fortunate Ali always carried that pig sticker with him, his *yataghan,* the evil-looking two-edged knife he had found so handy when he had met Mamigon.

No, Ali had assured him, there was no question about who it was. Ali had seen him before, remember? At the fight when they had tried to eliminate him with sash weights and ball bats? Yes, it was the same big dung eater, dressed up for the night, and, oh yes, when he slammed the knife into his heart he could have kissed him, he was that close to him. No question about it, *effendi,* it was Mamigon.

Yes, there was no one to share his joy. He had been disgraced in his homeland and had arrived in the new world almost a physical cripple because of the Armenian. He couldn't exert himself too much physically or he would find himself panting for breath with only one lung. He rarely took off his shirt in the company of female companions unless he was certain the affair could be conducted in total darkness. He was ashamed of the badly mended, lumpy left arm. Only one woman, Mirvet, his secretary, had seen his arm. She had become his steadiest companion through the years although not his only one. Tallal found variety the pepper of his life and had no difficulty finding willing companions for the weekends in his Peabody home, a former farmhouse sitting by itself in a lightly populated area outside the city.

He wondered when, if ever, the government would open the promised consulate in Boston and eliminate the masquerade of his export-import company. The United States government certainly knew what was going on but chose to ignore the operation. Why not? The United States had not declared war on Turkey when it did so against Germany back during the war because of all those American missionaries running around Turkey. The Americans must have had close to $20 million tied up there. They certainly weren't planning a military effort against the Turks. So, let them be, but break off relations later when the English and the French raise pointed questions about neutrality with an enemy of the Allies.

He was almost thirty-four now and it was about time to make something of himself. He wasn't the marrying kind but, perhaps he could entice Mirvet to live with him. There were no close neighbors for anyone to talk about them and he was in charge of the office. There could be no censure for such illicit goings-on. He would give it some thought. She could keep house for him, cook meals, and give him the pleasure he required when others were not available. He could always toss her out if things didn't work out.

Ali was having the time of his life. Now the favorite, the special man at Euphrates Export-Import with perquisites bestowed on him by the general manager—perquisites that included use of one of the company cars. He still drooled at the corners of his mouth, mostly because of his filthy habit of chewing Egyptian tobacco leaf. Despite this drawback to personal relations he had acquired new status among the company employees because of the obvious standing he enjoyed with Tallal Bey. He had his own little office now on the main floor even though his paper duties seemed to be nonexistent, and his major assignment was to accompany the general manager wherever he went—as his driver. Enver had almost suffered a stroke when first a gleeful Ali and later a derisive Tallal Bey had informed him that it was all over—Ali had taken care of the matter of Mamigon. Enver had been detached and ordered to a listening post in Peabody.

Ali had to keep quiet about the reason he had achieved such sudden favor, but he had allowed broad hints with arched brows and simultaneous caresses of the hilt of his dagger, really almost a short sword, to get across the message that it had been a deed of arms and valor. He looked the part with his ponderous wrestler's build, a head that was beginning to bald despite his youthful years, and a quickness of step that marked the athlete. His main drives were eating huge amounts of lamb and rice pilaff, undressing and servicing women of any age and build, and making a few side forays into the realm of homosexuality to keep his appetites whetted. He lived his own concept of life to its fullest.

Ali's newest delight was driving the coupe assigned to him around town when his services were not required by Tallal. He ranged far and wide, seeing areas he had never ventured to before or even suspected were there. He had no eye for architectural or arboreal beauty but he savored the green of the suburbs and the sight of western clad women undulating along, causing him many a near mishap on the road. Both the green of the land and the sharply delineated pulchritude of the women were still new to Ali, having come from a land that was basically sere and dun with women wearing shapeless clothes with *shawlwars* and *yashmaks*.

He had never driven northward along the sea and he thought it would be a nice diversion to see the area as spring was in full bloom and the weather was better than anything he had experienced in Anatolia. He took the route through Faneuil Hall down to Atlantic Avenue to make the crossing at the Charlestown Bridge.

Ali's command of the English language was poor, but not poor enough that he could not make out what seemed like a familiar word to him— MAMIGON—emblazoned across the front top of a truck backed up at the fish markets on Atlantic Avenue. It was ten o'clock in the morning. Ali drove another two blocks before he braked his car at the curb and pondered. The man he had killed was supposed to be a truck driver and it would be an unthinkable coincidence that there could be two truck drivers in the city

with that rare name. The business must have been taken over by someone
else was the conclusion Ali arrived at. But his wit was not without imagination. He was curious. He left his car and strolled back to see if he could
see the man who was now driving Mamigon's truck.

Ali had no trouble discovering who the driver was. He was huge, heavily
mustached, a hawk nose . . . BY THE BEARD OF THE PROPH-
ET . . . IT IS THE MAN I KILLED . . . or his ghost!
Aman . . . Aman! What is happening? Ali was unable to move, staring
thunderstruck at what he believed was an apparition. Luckily, the object of
his concentrated stare was too busy to notice Ali, otherwise the fascination
certainly would have produced some sort of reaction.

Ali finally recovered and retreated to his car, his equanimity in shambles,
his thought processes scrambled.

Who was it he had killed?

Was this a ghost or maybe his brother?

Had he not killed him that night, after all?

OH, PIG DUNG. THE MAN HE KILLED DIDN'T HAVE A
MUSTACHE! *AMAN!*

What am I going to tell Tallal Bey! He is going to kill me, no doubt about
that! What am I going to tell Tallal Bey?

I cannot tell him, I cannot tell him. I will lose everything . . .

Enver will have one big last laugh on me.

Ali's thought of Enver and his own reaction suddenly made him remember something. He calmed down immediately. He remembered back then
when he and Enver had lost track of Mamigon and had not reported it for
two weeks to Tallal. Good. Everything is not lost, then.

As long as no one knows about his mistake he will correct it before anyone
finds out. None will be the wiser. But he would have to take care of the
matter immediately.

Ali forgot all thoughts of a sightseeing tour of the North Shore. He concentrated on following Mamigon's truck for the rest of the day to find out
the best way to eliminate him from the face of the earth, once and for all.

17 ✄ DELIVERANCE

"If Dr. Yardume is right, we will have a son in about two weeks."

"Allah willing, Guzell."

"We will name him Mesrop, son of Magaros, after your father, as we
agreed."

"Yes. If it is a girl, we will name her after your mother, Jehan."

She smiled at him. He had insisted on her mother's name when she knew
he would want some memory of his own dead mother. "You will be unable
to stay with me tonight when the doctor arrives, you know."

"I know. I will stay across the hall and send Mrs. Odabashian over."

"I must laugh, my man. The doctor says it is necessary for one last examination to make certain everything is all right. He says that because it will be my first child there might be something unforeseen. For the life of me, I do not know what. I feel fine."

"I am glad. Did he say seven o'clock?"

"Yes. We have an hour until he arrives. Supper is ready. After we eat, we should spend some time with the newspaper before he arrives. I am beginning to understand more and more each day."

"I am, too. You make learning much joy, my woman."

"I care for you, too, my man." Guzell's eyes were beautiful, her face radiant, her slim body in the awkward pose of someone with a watermelon under her clothes.

After they ate, Mamigon waited until she washed the dishes and put them away. Then he led the way into the front room, carrying the newspaper with him. He snapped on the overhead lights and went to his easy chair that backed into the bay window facing the street to switch on the standing lamp. They would need plenty of light.

He turned his back to the window to ease down into the chair.

Guzell was three feet behind him carrying a small tray with a demitasse of coffee and a tall glass of water for the man of the house.

He settled down into the cushion at the instant the window glass behind him shattered.

A small hole appeared in Guzell's face, just under the left cheekbone.

She leaned backward for a millisecond as the tray and contents crashed to the carpet, then fell backward, dead before she hit the floor, a bullet in her brain.

Mamigon leaped up, took two steps toward her slumped figure, turned to the window, took three steps toward the shattered glass, then stumbled back to the lifeless form. He fell to his knees beside her; there wasn't even a drop of blood.

He didn't touch her, just stared at her in a stupor, his eyes wide, his mouth working furiously, just staring until a pounding on the door brought him to reality. "GUZELL," he roared. "GUZELL . . ."

His stentorian cries made the door pounder, a foot patrolman, break in the door, with five or six neighbors behind him. Mrs. Odabashian, in the forefront, began to scream hysterically. "What have you DONE! What have you DONE! Wild man . . . wild man! I know about you!"

Mamigon didn't get up. Tears were streaming down his face. The patrolman surveyed the scene quickly, pushed everyone out to the hall, used the Odabashians' phone, and forced his way back into the flat. Mamigon, now dry eyed, was still on his knees beside Guzell's body.

Before the patrolman could say a word, an agitated voice called out from the doorway: "What is going on here? What is the matter with Diggin Guzell?"

It was Dr. Yardume. He walked quickly to Guzell's side, held Mamigon by the shoulders and eased him up and out of the way to examine the body.

He finally placed a stethoscope on the bulging belly, listened for a few seconds, and leaped to his feet.

"Officer, get one of those women to help me! The baby is alive and I am going to take it! Clear the place and get me some sheets or something, hurry!"

Mamigon was pushed out with the rest, uncomprehending, uncaring, in complete shock. A calmer Mrs. Odabashian was called in to help the doctor. The patrolman didn't leave Mamigon's side after he found some sheets in the bedroom. Even though the doctor didn't ask for it, he also got one of the women neighbors to heat up some water.

Mamigon stood in the hallway, not much more animate than a tree trunk. Two policemen in plainclothes arrived. One of them recognized Mamigon from the inquest in Aram's murder. He tried talking to Mamigon since they had to wait to examine the murder scene.

"The crowd outside says a shot was fired from a parked car across the street. What do you know about it?"

"Uh . . ."

"Come on, speak up, man."

"Uh . . ."

"You'll have to talk, mister, this time you'll . . ."

He was interrupted by a crying Mrs. Odabashian who came out of the front room carrying a small bundle of cloth, a tiny face visible. She wasn't too certain about it but she finally handed the bundle to Mamigon, barely able to utter through her gasping voice that it was a boy.

Mamigon held the tiny figure in the swaddling clothes for a second or two. Then his face lit up, his eyes began to sparkle and he almost shouted, "She is not dead? She is alive?"

Mrs. Odabashian was unable to accept that twist. She burst into renewed wails, shaking her head as she held on to Mamigon's shoulders, and repeating and repeating: "She is gone . . . she is gone . . . she is gone!"

"What is . . . this?" Mamigon had not understood a thing that had transpired since the doctor had arrived. He was looking at the infant in total bewilderment. The patrolman tried to help.

"The doctor took him from your dead wife, mister. Come on, sir, snap out of it."

Mamigon understood command. His shoulders squared ever so slightly, he looked about him as if for the first time to see what was going on, and looked at the baby in his arms. His eyes veiled for an instant at the sight of the tiny little form, his mind racing backward in time to a dusty, hellish street in Yosghat Dagh, kneeling beside his ravaged wife, gently, carefully swabbing off the wrinkled little thing lying next to her—that would have been his fourth child. Time had not healed that well. He asked Mrs. Odabashian to place the infant in the crib in the next room that had been made ready for his arrival. Then he faced Dr. Yardume who just then came out of the parlor. The plainclothesmen had gone in when the baby had been brought out.

The good doctor was evincing disgust with the policemen who had accused him of disturbing evidence in a murder case. He said he would wait for the coroner to discuss what he had done. He certainly wasn't going to permit the death of another human being in the interests of evidence.

"She is dead, doctor?" Mamigon's voice was calm, matter of fact.

"Yes, Baron Mamigon. She died instantly without feeling pain in the slightest."

"Thank you, doctor. I see you were able to save the child."

"Yes, there were no complicatons. Thank God I was here, almost when it happened. Otherwise . . ." He shook his head.

"Is the baby going to be all right?"

"Healthy for certain. I would say he weighs over eight pounds."

"You have done well for me, doctor. I am eternally in your debt."

"I wish it were for other reasons, my son. Do you want something to calm you?"

"Thank you, doctor. I am in control, now. Thank you."

The interrogation was conducted in the kitchen. The officer in charge established that Mamigon and Aram were brothers, that Aram had been murdered only five weeks ago, that this sort of thing just couldn't be a coincidence, that he must surely have some very strong enemies.

No, he didn't know of any enemies. Yes, the bullet was surely meant for him. No, there had been no other attempts on his life. No, no suspicious accidents. No, he wasn't a revolutionary of any kind. No, he wasn't a Communist (you mean, Bolshevik?), and no, he had never been one or belonged to the party. No, he had never fought with his wife. No, not once during their ten months of marriage. No, he didn't know anything that could shed light on the shooting. No, he didn't know who had lived in the flat before he had moved in. No, he had no girlfriends. No, she never left the house, she couldn't speak English too well. No, she had no boyfriends (are you crazy or something?). Before she married me? No, definitely not. She lived at the Franklin Square House. No, there was no life insurance (what's that?). No, nobody owed him money and he didn't owe anybody money. No, he wasn't a citizen yet because he couldn't speak English too well. Yes, he wanted to be a citizen. No, he really didn't know anything. He was just a poor truckman. Yes, he had worked for a steamship company as a stoker before he came here. No, the army didn't want him because of his bad hip. Yes, he had served in the Turkish army as a first lieutenant before he came here. No, he had no guns or other weapons in the house. Yes, of course, he knew how to use a pistol or rifle. Yes, they could search the house if they wished, as long as they didn't disturb the baby . . .

"Looks clean to me," the plainclothesman said to the sergeant. "I wonder if it was case of mistaken identity?"

"Sure is missing a motive here, at least on the surface but, you know lieutenant, you never know about these foreigners."

"Yeah, did you notice he didn't cry? He's some big sonovabitch . . ."

The body was taken for the usual autopsy in cases of violent death.

18 &NO STRIKES

Mamigon returned to work a week after Guzell was buried. There had been no question that Tatios and Eksah would take care of his infant boy. The only thing that seemed to matter to Mamigon now was the baby. There was general agreement that the big man would have drifted off, probably signed on to the *Nahant Bay* again if it weren't for Mesrop. What none realized, however, was that the fires of vengeance had been rekindled in Mamigon, fires so carefully banked that it required a major cataclysm to reveal them.

Mamigon carefully scrutinized everyone he saw to make sure the person wasn't Enver Dash. It was difficult for him to grasp that the teenager whose life he had spared in Turkey could be the cause of all his present grief—but with Tallal dead, who else could care enough about the past to pursue him? To try to kill him? To kill his brother, probably in error?

He was certain Guzell had died in error. Enver Dash knew her well enough, but as a boy. But, no, the shot that killed her would have entered his head if he had remained standing . . . would that he had. The gunman could not have been aiming at Guzell. He wouldn't have been able to see her when he was pulling the trigger.

He was in the unfortunate position now of being the hunted. He knew that the constant upheaval in the mind of the hunted only served to dull the senses and slow the reflexes. The necessity to be constantly alert required responses to a multitude of false alarms. Energy is sapped, the will flags, the icy nerve becomes boiled noodles. Mamigon recalled the story of the man who sought the magical hot stone on the seashore and decided to toss all the stones into the sea, one by one, until he isolated the special stone; except that he became so engrossed throwing stone after stone into the brine that when he picked up the hot one, he tossed it away before his senses had a chance to signal him not to. He was afraid he would get caught in just such a frame of mind in a Turkish trap. But, when, how . . . ?

Mamigon didn't have long to wait. A week later, he was making a delivery near Codman Square on a street where the trolley lines on Talbot Avenue prevented a vehicle from parking at the curb in front of the store. He always used the back alley, a narrow, one-lane access to the rear of all the stores facing the street. He backed up his truck, climbed into the back, and was busy stacking the tailgate with boxes and bushels marked for the store when a black coupe drove up the alley and stopped behind the truck. Mamigon stuck up an index finger signaling "one minute" and jumped off the tailgate to pile the boxes on the store stoop. This sort of thing happened often and Mamigon knew he could move the truck in less than two minutes.

Not wasting a second, he began sweeping the boxes two and three at a time off the tailgate and onto neat piles on the stoop when he felt, more than heard, someone behind him. Perhaps it was intuition, but as he pivoted to see what was behind him he was clutching three boxes of grapes in close embrace. The huge knife in the fist of the man behind Mamigon slammed off the boxes into a flying arc.

"I think you dropped something, mister," Mamigon said, staring into the now startled face of his attacker. Still staring, he dropped the boxes and grabbed the knife wielder, a stocky, medium-sized man, by both upper arms, and lifted him off his feet.

"Who are you?"

The man didn't utter a sound. He spit a spray of tobacco juice into Mamigon's eyes, jerked up his arms and slipped out of the Armenian's grip. The blinded Mamigon succeeded only in ripping off a sleeve, as his assailant slipped away. Mamigon heard the coupe slip into gear and then the throb of the engine as it receded down the alley.

The big man was almost helpless, rubbing his tearing eyes, trying to see through the quivering slits of his eyelids, waiting for the tears to irrigate the bitter nicotine and salt that was blinding him. When he could see well enough, he went into the store and got the proprietor, Baron Avedesian, to let him use the wash bowl. He went back to the truck and was finishing his unloading when a young policeman appeared from the side of the truck.

"You're blocking the alley, mister. Move your truck."

"Okay, sir. I move out right away. You let me take off boxes, eh? Ten only left."

"Right now, mister. I want this alley cleared right now."

"Okay, sir, I move out but I get ticket if I park on the street to unload."

"You'll get a ticket right now, if you don't move. I mean it, mister."

"Okay, sir, I move right now. I no have money for bakshish." Mamigon had referred to the two dollar "donations" he made occasionally to policemen who ticketed him for moving through a stop sign at two or three miles an hour instead of coming to a complete stop. When the truck was loaded, a complete stop would have meant starting up in low-low gear, a veritable crawl. It was a game and Mamigon played it after learning the hard way. No one had warned him about "paying the two dollars."

"No money for what?"

"I cannot give you a tip for letting me unload, sir." He turned his back to the cop and walked to the truck cab to move the vehicle. The policeman took two steps to the rear of the truck, picked up an ear of corn from an open bushel and flung it. It hit Mamigon hard directly on the back of his head, knocking off his cap, making him stumble forward a step.

Mamigon turned very slowly and said with great deliberation, "I told you I go. Why did you hit me?"

"I'm going to ticket you right now for attempting to bribe an officer of the law." The policeman, slightly shorter than the 6-foot 4-inch truck driver, was producing his pad.

"I not give you money. Why did you hit me?"

"Shut up, and let's see your driver's license and registration."

"I ask you one more time, sir. Why you hit me?"

"One more time, hey? Who in hell do you think you are, you goddamn foreigner?"

"I am American. I citizen now. You should not talk like that. I take you to chief."

The officer was laughing now. "You kill me, mister . . . citizen . . . you silly bastard," and he gave Mamigon a slight push to the right shoulder to emphasize his derision.

First, a knife attack, then tobacco juice in his eyes, and now a sneering cop. That was more than enough for Mamigon. He gripped the policeman's arm, yanked him completely off his feet in a flash, and tucked him under his left armpit. The policeman struggled mightily to free himself, his legs thrashing in the air, but Mamigon carried him like a doll, making his way to the end of the alley and out to the street.

Once out on the main thoroughfare, Mamigon simply stood there, holding the officer like a sack of potatoes, looking up and down the street. A crowd began to gather, but no one came to the policeman's rescue.

It seemed like hours before a police car and a motorcycle officer finally appeared on the scene, simultaneously. Three plainclothesmen and a uniform pushed through the now huge but good-natured crowd, and one of the officers ordered Mamigon to let the man go.

Mamigon swung his catch upright to his feet and stepped back, saying "I want to talk to the chief. This man is no good. He hit me."

"You'll talk to the chief, all right, mister. You're under arrest."

He stuck out his hands for the manacles, saying, "What I do with truck?"

"What the hell happened?" the officer in charge asked the policeman Mamigon had just released, ignoring the Armenian.

"I tried to get him to clear the alley. He was blocking it with his truck. You can see that. Without warning, he grabbed me and dragged me out here."

"That is not the whole story, officer," Mamigon said. "He hit me on the head with ear of corn."

"Bullshit. I didn't have a chance. All I wanted him to do was to clear the alley. He gave me a lot of lip, tried to bribe me, and then grabbed me."

"You are not telling the truth . . ."

"That's right, the officer is not telling the truth!" It came from the crowd.

"Whoa, hold it. What's going on?" It was the officer in charge asking.

"I witnessed the entire incident from my second-floor kitchen which faces the alley. This officer should be reprimanded for his conduct." The voice belonged to a woman, about thirty or so, trim and purposeful in her bearing.

"Who are you, lady?"

"My name is Hartnett, Miss Hartnett. I am a schoolteacher, and that officer is not fit to wear a uniform."

"Thank you, lady, but I go to police station and see chief. He will fix him."

"Don't you believe, it, sir. They'll get you so confused you will end up in jail."

"Enough of this," the head plainclothesman said. "Let's get to the bottom of this at the station."

"Make sure they book you, sir, so that you can sue them for false arrest, and I'll be your witness," Miss Hartnett yelled.

"Wait a minute, wait a minute. You seem pretty sure of how this is going to come out, lady."

"I certainly am, unless we've thrown justice out the window. This officer told the driver the truck had to be moved out of the alley right away. The driver was very polite, he sirred the officer, but asked if he could take off the last few boxes. The officer said no . . ." She told the story in every detail.

"You forgot to mention he offered me a bribe."

"I did not forget because a bribe was not offered. It was exactly the opposite. The driver specifically said he had no money for bakshish."

"Bakshish?"

"Bakshish."

"Bakshish. What's that?"

"Bakshish. That's a widely used Middle Eastern word for tips or gratuities. Certainly not a bribe. You should know that, inspector." Miss Hartnett had fun using the word.

"Yes, yes, of course. Well, Landry, what do you have to say about all this?"

"She's got it all wrong, inspector. She's in cahoots with . . ."

"Oh, for Cris . . . Listen, are you saying that Miss Hartnett and this truck driver worked up this cockamamy story just to get you in trouble? Miss Hartnett, if you give us your address I think we can conclude this matter without any more fuss. Perhaps the best thing to do is to forget the whole thing."

"I want to see chief, sir."

"Ooooh, no. What are you, a troublemaker?"

"I do not make trouble before. I want to make trouble for corn thrower," Mamigon said, rubbing the back of his head.

"Mister, sir." It was Miss Hartnett. "I know it's not right, but please forget it. It won't be worth the trouble you'll get into pursuing your principle."

Mamigon thought it over, then walked to where Miss Hartnett stood, took off his cap and made a slight bowing motion. "Thank you, thank you, miss."

Still rubbing his head, perhaps for effect, Mamigon went over and shook hands with the inspector and went back down the alley where he finished unloading the truck, coming out of the back door with a package. Then he carefully scanned the windows, found the one with Miss Hartnett, who had returned home and had been watching, and motioned to her to raise her window all the way. She did, smiling a bit quizzically, but gathered herself quickly enough to catch the carefully tossed box of candy Mamigon neatly dropped into her window.

"Bakshish," he called out, waving. As he drove off, he realized that no one had seen the attack on his life. That was good. There was no need for explanations to the police. That was bad, too. Enver or his pals could attack in broad daylight and get away with it, even though the attempt failed. He wondered who the barrel-chested ape was who had surprised him with the vile antics of the camel—expectoration.

Mamigon made weekly deliveries to his customers who owned stores that dealt in perishable commodities. The very next week, in the same alley, as he left the store after a ten-minute wait for an item check before payment, he found his truck ablaze. The canvas tarpaulin covering, heavily treated with resin to make it waterproof, was burning gloriously. A quick look up and down the alley showed the thoroughfare was clear. Mamigon jumped into the cab and drove the truck out into the main street to prevent the flames from torching the rear of the alley structures. As he braked the truck, there was Miss Hartnett again, running for a red box on the curb, only a few yards from the burning vehicle. Mamigon scrambled out and began slapping at the flames with his jacket. He was almost at the end of his delivery run and he didn't take the chance of going into the truck to pull out the remaining boxes. The burning canvas could drop on him.

"The fire trucks should be here any minute, mister."

"Thanks, lady. Is that what red box is for?"

"Yes, it's a fire alarm. All you do is break the glass and pull down on this lever."

"I very lucky to have you around, lady."

"I may be lucky for you but you're just about the unluckiest man I've ever seen. What caused the fire?"

Before he could answer, the roar of the American-LaFrance fire engines and pumpers became discernible. Three of them screamed down the street, spilling men and hoses when they stopped, and the fire was out in two minutes. Most of the canvas was gone and the stakes and roof arches were badly charred. Everything had the pungent smell of a doused fire. Twice, now, in a week's time, Mamigon had provided the main attraction for the neighborhood.

The fire captain and one of the firemen were going over the truck body with special care. The captain turned to Mamigon. "Do you know how it started?"

"No, sir. I came out of store in that alley. I find truck burning. I pull truck out to save buildings. This lady call you."

"What's your name, mister? Hey, Bill, get that cop over there to take a statement. And, check the alley."

Mamigon went over his story again for the policeman's notes, casting an eye occasionally in the direction of Miss Hartnett, wondering what was going to happen now.

"Mister, this fire was set with a blowtorch. Someone went around both sides of the truck, spotting the canvas every foot or so. You can see where the flames were started."

Mamigon shook his head, not understanding. It didn't seem like anything Enver or his henchmen would do. If he had been trapped inside the truck, then burning the truck would have been a logical Enver move.

"Do you have a helper? No? Do you know why anyone would want to burn your truck?"

Before Mamigon could answer the last question, there was a yell from one of the firemen who was inspecting the underside of the truck bed. The captain and most of the squad ran over. The captain emerged from the group, holding four sticks of dynamite, complete with detonators and two long fuses.

"Here it is mister. Here's what all that fire was about. The fuses were strung out to each side so that the fire would touch them off. Whoever did it was kind of stupid. The canvas burned upward, away from the fuse ends, and it would have taken the fire to burn through the wooden truck bed to get at the fuses. I guess it was meant to go off while you were fighting the fire. No chance, lucky for you.

"OK, let me ask you again: Do you have enemies? Who wants to kill you this badly?"

"I do not know . . . I don't know, sir." He glanced quickly at Miss Hartnett's direction and thought she was looking at him rather peculiarly.

"Well, you'll have to come downtown to the station. We'll have to check you out, mister." It was the policeman talking.

"What can I do with my truck? I have some undelivered stuff in the back that is burned but the storekeepers will be looking for it . . ."

"Sorry 'bout that. Just follow us to the station."

It got pretty ugly for Mamigon at the station. There it was, in black and white: Less than three weeks ago, on June 14, your wife was killed by a shot meant for you. Now, what the hell is going on? Are you going to talk or not? You know nothing? Oh, yeah? Somebody takes pot shots at you, kills your wife, and then tries to blow you to kingdom come, and you know nothing? You'd better talk. Who's trying to get yuh?

A veteran cop knows when the subject of his interrogation is without fear, without any inclination to talk. They let him go because he really was guilty of nothing they knew of.

Enough was enough. He garaged his truck, drove to the market and asked his friend Carpenito to handle his business for him for two weeks, with an open end on the agreement in case it took longer. Then he began a tour of every business establishment on Tremont Street, beginning with Koko's coffeehouse, giving as good a description as he could of what he thought Enver Dash looked like today. He remembered the bearded shadower on the streetcar that Sunday long ago so he added a beard to the description. The wart on the cheekbone was an important characteristic except he wasn't sure the beard would not be covering it. He threw in a good description of the tobacco spitter for good measure.

It was the most successful search ever launched. Within an hour after he started, the antique dealer on Tremont Street, a block from Koko's, told Mamigon that a man who certainly could have been Enver Dash had occupied the room over the store until early last May when he suddenly left without a word. No, he did not know for whom he worked. Why, yes, that's the description of the other fellow who came around at times. No, he had no information about either of them. They are Turks? Ah, he had had suspicions but the man seemed harmless enough and a rent was a rent. What can I do to help you?

There it was. Enver Dash had been living within a block of the coffeehouse and now he was gone. Mamigon did not know which way to turn. There was only one thing to do: Continue to be a target and hope to survive long enough to exact payment for Guzell and the trouble in his life.

19 ✣ PEABODY

Tatios, though he was thirty-one, felt like a fifty-year-old man looking back and wondering what he has accomplished during his life. He had arrived in America in 1916, and six years later he was still working in the suit factory, all because, he felt, he couldn't speak English the way it should be spoken. He was painfully aware of snickering looks he provoked when his forays into the language betrayed him as the foreigner he was. He was constantly bemused by the reaction to his name, usually in the form of "What are you?" and the follow-up question, "What's that?" He never really knew what to say and resented it when the venturesome persisted by asking whether he was an "Ay-rab" or a "Jew of some kind." He developed a boring lecture about his ancient nationality, which went something like this: His land, according to the Bible, was where Noah's Ark had come to rest on Mount Ararat; Armenia was the first Christian nation on earth when St. Gregory the Illuminator had converted the Armenian king, 1,700 years ago; after more than 3,000 years as an independent nation with its own warlike kings, Armenia finally disappeared with the invasion of the Seljuk and then the Ottoman Turks in the eleventh and fifteenth centuries; and the Armenians survived as an identifiable people with their own language and church mainly because they were hardy dwellers of the Armenian Plateau bound loosely by the Araks, Tigris, and Euphrates rivers.

He would point out that it was easy to spot an Armenian because of his surname—it ended in "ian" or "yan," meaning the son of, like the English names Richardson or Thompson.

He had scant opportunity to expound the litany, however, and had to be content with exasperating his wife and family and friends. However, because of his storytelling ability and his command of languages, he was frequently addressed as Tatios Effendi, *effendi* being a Turkish title of respect meaning "master." The title pleased him immensely.

Tatios was given to tossing off phrases that no one understood. When his son pleased him in some way he would say something that sounded like "ek sehgee mohnoomentoom ih reh pehreneeoos." He never explained it and the boy, who thought it was another Armenian phrase, learned years later that it was in Latin—*exegi monumentum aere perennius*—meaning, I have raised a monument more lasting than bronze.

When Tatios wanted to stress his sincerity, he would touch his heart and say *ex animo*, another Latin phrase meaning "from the heart."

At the coffeehouse, in the midst of an argument, when someone tried to change the subject, he would invariably pipe up with French: *Revenons à nos moutons* for "let's get back to the subject."

Being a bit longwinded in his dissertations, Tatios had a ready phrase in Italian to cover the reluctance of impatient listeners: *da tempo al tempo* for "some things can't be rushed."

He never tried any of his demonstrations of erudition or learning on Mamigon. Somehow he knew that it would not go over well and, anyway, he had too much respect for the man to be affected or precious with him.

Thank God, he had an uncomplaining wife. A shrew would have been the last straw. Eksah had taken in Mesrop as if he were her own. Mamigon had stayed in the flat on Blue Hill Avenue, paying $16 a month rent. He had been unable to bury Guzell in the strict Moslem tradition—in a plain white shroud directly in the earth—because the law in Boston required burial in a casket. But Mamigon had arranged for a burial plot that was north and south in direction and made sure that Guzell's face in death was turned to her left shoulder. Thus, with the casket placed in the earth with the head to the north, she would be eternally facing the east, the direction of Mecca from North America. He had presided over many a burial of his own troops in Anatolia not to know that a Moslem was buried facing the direction of Mecca. He had been unable to bury her next to his brother because of the lack of room to position the casket.

Mamigon would have become a recluse had it not been for his friend Tatios. After the burial, they had talked.

"It must be the Turks, but why? Who?"

"How can we find out?"

"I do not know, but I will, my friend. I have decided that it could be only someone called Enver Dash."

"And who is that?"

"He was with Tallal most of the time. When I killed Tallal, Enver was with him and Guzell on the gangplank."

"Guzell, may she rest in the light, told me the ship she left here was going on to New York."

"How far is New York from here?"

"About 200 kilometers."

"Perhaps Enver Dash came to Boston."

"It could be the answer, Mamigon. Who else is there that could know or would care? But, how could he have found out you were here?"

"I am fairly certain now that my presence became known from the day we met in the coffeehouse and all that fuss was made about who I was. It all makes sense, now."

"If it is Enver Dash, how do we go about finding him?"

"Tatios, do you think we could talk to the men who gather for your story hour Sunday? Why not ask them if they know of any Turks living or working in the area? It might give us a direction."

There were about forty-five men gathered on the Sunday just past the forty days of mourning. Tatios explained that Mamigon had to find any and all Turks in the Boston area and if any of them knew of any, it would be of great help. Most of the Armenians were shopkeepers but there were musicians, bookkeepers, tailors, cobblers, rug dealers, antique sellers, and ordinary factory workers, like Tatios. None was unemployed.

Tatios had taken down fifteen leads, some with addresses where the Turk worked, some with addresses where he seemed to live, some with nothing more than a suspicion. The main thrust of the answers to the general question was that if you wanted to find Turks you should go to Peabody, a town north of Boston. Mamigon decided to follow up the local leads. Since Mamigon had insisted on contributing eight dollars a week toward the baby's keep, Tatios now had enough money for small nonessentials, such as travel. He didn't tell Mamigon. He traveled by streetcar and subway and commuter rail to Peabody, looking for some sign of a vague Turk called Enver Dash who was attacking his friend.

His first trip to Peabody had found the coffeehouses closed—it was a Saturday afternoon. By six o'clock the coffeehouses opened their doors, and Tatios was beside himself with excitement. The clientele was totally Turkish. Crowded with Turks, all speaking Turkish, all looking like the Tatars they were, all slurping their bitter, scalding, wonderful coffee exactly as the Armenians and the Greeks did. Tatios had no problem fitting into the scene, with his impeccable Turkish, and his hawk-like features. He only lacked a mustache, which most of them sported; he had not regrown his after he had scraped it off to pass as a woman in the convoy. In no time he had new friends, albeit former farmers and tanners with little or no education.

He returned home that night, resolved not to tell Mamigon anything until he had a good lead. He felt he was not as conspicuous as his big friend and, therefore, might be able to get a line on the mystery that would help bring the bloody events to a conclusion.

He returned the next Saturday and visited the other coffeehouse. He made new friends there but mainly listened and kept his eyes open. Repeated visits for another three months on successive Saturdays brought nothing more or new. In fact, he found himself in the midst of a wild celebration in September at the news of Kemal Pasha's smashing of the Greek forces, the capture of Smyrna, or Izmir as the Turks called it, the sacking of the city, and its Greek inhabitants put to the sword to eliminate that cancer on Turkish soil once and for all.

He didn't know it, but his wife was beginning to wonder about the flimsy excuses he made about his absences, always with the strong admonition that she was not to mention anything to Mamigon for reasons he would expalin later.

It was a cold November Saturday on one of his trips to Peabody—on the Saugus Branch of the Boston and Maine—when he walked to the end of a queue in North Station to get his round-trip ticket. The line usually moved up quickly but that day the woman traveler at the window seemed to be mapping a trip to the moon. Tatios shifted his weight from foot to foot as minutes dragged by.

"It seems like hours when there's a delay in a ticket line." The tall young man in front of Tatios had turned slightly sideways to voice his own irritation. Queues seem to create instant camaraderie, bred by feelings of shared frustration.

"*Deus gubernat navem,*" was the best Tatios could think of for a non-committal reply. He trusted his Latin one hundred percent—he felt his English was worth only twenty-five percent.

The man in front of him turned around completely, a smile playing on his wide mouth. " 'God steers the ship?' Why, I haven't heard that since my schooldays. I . . . say, don't I know you . . . ?"

They stared at each other for a minute, then Tatios grabbed the taller man firmly by the shoulders. "You're Harry Sears! You're Harry Sears!"

"And, you're Tatios, the Armenian who speaks every language except English! How are you, my friend?"

"I am fine, fine . . . How are you?" The two repeated themselves, expressing the inanities that total surprise wrings from the mouth when the senses rule the mind.

"Wait, wait, let's go sit down over there and talk, my friend. Tell me everything. I've wondered a thousand times whatever became of you and your sister once you left on that ship for America."

Tatios filled him in on the details of what happens to penniless immigrants who find themselves in a new land, the feelings of security they derive from the close-knit intercourse of a ghetto, and the nostalgia and deep sadness they experience at being separated from the land they had loved—the only land they had known—and forced to live among strangers.

"But we no longer worry about policemen or soldiers at the door. We no longer worry about the safety of our women. We no longer worry about footpads and cutthroats. We only worry about making a living and making sure we are acceptable citizens."

"What do you do for a living?"

"Oh, I get along. I write for newpapers. I do a lot of translating. I'm doing very well. What are you doing;"

"'Oh, I finished med school and I'm an intern now at Mass General. But, Tatios, your whole manner has changed. What's the matter with you? Are you in some kind of trouble?"

"Yes, my friend. I am in trouble because I find it so easy to lie to a friend who has saved my life, not once but twice. I have done none of those things in America. I could only find work as a tailor. I sew buttons on men's suits six days a week. My wife taught me how to sew buttons so I could get the job."

Harry shook his head. "Why didn't you look me up when you came here? I told you where the family home was. You repeated it and I saw you write it down. I was so sure something terrible had happened to you when I never heard from you again. What happened?"

"I lost the paper and I thought your place was somewhere called Chester . . ."

"Manchester-by-the-Sea! That's what I told you. Manchester-by-the-Sea. I was in line to buy a ticket to go home just now. Say, if you live in Boston, what are you doing here? Where're you bound for?"

"Oh, I was going to Peabody to visit with some friends. I can't tell you how glad I am to have seen you again, finally."

"I'll say! Let's exchange addresses. We've got to keep in touch. I'll write to you real soon."

They parted, Harry going to the now deserted ticket window, and Tatios deciding to head back home instead of another futile evening in Peabody.

20 ❧ EMILY

"Please, lady, I do not remember your name even, and you want to know all about me."

"I'm sorry I'm such a busybody. My name's Emily Hartnett and I'm a schoolteacher."

"Miss Hartnett, I do not understand you . . . your English . . . well. I speak German and Turkish and understand Armenian a little, but . . ."

"What are you, Turkish?"

"No, I was Turkish citizen but I am Armenian, a *High*. Now, I American citizen, but I speak English not too well."

"You are perfectly understandable, but would you be kind enough to tell me how you pronounce . . . say your name? It's painted on your truck, but . . ."

"My name is Mah-mi-goan. It old Hittite name and also name of old Armenian king. People say 'Mammy gone,' but that is wrong."

"Mamigon," she repeated, then. "Look, I interrupted you, stopped you in your work. Will you find time to come to my place for a cup of tea . . . or coffee?"

He was surprised—for the second time. The first time, he had been startled when he had finished making the alley delivery to Baron Avedesian's store to find her waiting by the cab of his truck. She had smiled and held out her hand to clasp his, which he had done, after a flash of hesitation and the swift removal of his cloth cap. What did *she* want? What a good-looking woman . . .

That's how they got into conversation. She had asked him if he was feeling all right since he had not made any deliveries in the alley for two weeks. He had said he had not been feeling well, but he was feeling fine now.

"That man with the knife didn't hurt you, did he?"

"Oh? You saw knifeman who spit in my eyes?"

"Yes."

"Why you not tell police about me? I saw you watch me when they ask me about enemies, after my truck catch fire. Why you not tell them?"

"Because I think you are a good man. I . . ."

"Do you know about me?"

"No, only what I have seen going on in the alley. I don't understand why you don't seek the help of the law, unless you are a criminal, too . . ."

Surprised or not, Mamigon knew he had to talk to her. It would not do to have someone know about him and not understand who he was and what was going on. He would have to be agreeable to anything she said until he could reach a decision best for everything and everyone concerned.

"I have one more delivery to make, lady . . . Miss Hartnett. I like to come to your place very much, but I am dirty. I need bath. My overalls, it smell."

"You're OK the way you are, Mr. Mamigon, but if you will not feel comfortable, we can meet some other time."

"Tomorrow, Saturday. If you are free Saturday in afternoon, I come then?"

"Fine, Mr. Mamigon. I'll see you Saturday afternoon . . . and you really don't have to dress up."

After taking care of his morning deliveries the next day, Mamigon stopped at the public showers, washed up, put on his Sunday clothes, and drove his car to Codman Square and Miss Hartnett's place. The tree-lined street was residential, his big car stood out where he parked it. He figured out which house it was from his count of houses in the alley. She was on the second-floor piazza of the two-decker, and beckoned him up with a wave. He entered her apartment and was overcome with the aura of femininity, both in decor and odor. She was in a plain beige dress with a prim Peter Pan collar and brown and white saddle shoes.

Mamigon was nervous and found it hard to breathe. It was totally improper, what he was doing, he thought. A lone man did not enter the apartment of a young woman who was also alone. He had struggled with the thought since he had accepted her invitation the day before, and only the specter of Enver escaping because this woman might inform on him to the police, drove him to appear.

"Sit here and I'll be right back with the coffee." She returned with a tray bearing a small pot, two cups, and a plate of sugar cookies.

"Well," she said with a big smile that dazzled Mamigon, "what shall we talk about?"

"Miss Hartnett, you want to talk to me. I have not much to say . . ."

"All right, why does someone want to kill you . . . or hurt you?"

"I want to kill them, that is why."

"You . . . you want to kill *them*?"

"Yes, lady, I want to kill them. The man who is trying to kill me is a young man, a Turk, called Enver Dash. He worked for a man called Tallal, a man who was my good friend, a comrade-in-arms, a friend of my family. Tallal kill everybody in my family."

"My God, when . . . how did this all happen?"

"In the old country . . . Turkey." He stopped, but she didn't say a word, just stared at him. "It is a long story. I tell you this much. I follow Tallal all over Turkey and kill him. His men still try to kill me. They have found me and tried to kill me. They have killed two more in my family in America. I cannot go to the police; they cannot go to the police. We both are doing what we believe we have to do." Mamigon gave a brief description of what happened and the long pursuit with the frustratingly dangerous situation he was in now.

The woman shook her head. "You know you can't go on like this. You need help of some kind. They have the advantage of you. They probably know right now that you are here visiting with me, do you realize that?"

"I do realize that, but I think you will be in no danger as long as I stay away and they do not think I have friendship with you."

"I'm not worried about danger to me, only the danger to you. Maybe I can help you, find him for you." It was more a question than a statement.

"Please stay away from this. Every time someone gets close to me, the person has died at their hands. You are not to get close to this problem I have. You understand?"

"All right, Mr. Mamigon. I won't get involved, but I want you to come to me if you need help of any kind. Is that understood?"

"Fine, that is fine. I do that," Mamigon said, thinking that was as good an answer as any to fob her off. He stood up, not having touched either food or drink and held out his hand. She shook it, solemnly, and walked him to the door.

"I will be watching out for you when you make your deliveries," she said. "I am home by four-thirty every day. That's why I always seem to be around when you enter the alley. Please, Mr. Mamigon, let's be friends. I'm very much interested in you and what is happening."

"You should not have interest, Miss Hartnett. I am poison to everyone around me."

"I see you have married, again. What does your wife think of all this?"

"Married? Oh, no, not married. I wear old ring from two weddings. Turks killed both my women."

She gasped. "Both of them?"

"Yes. I marry woman only last year here in this country and I have a child. They tried to kill me and bullet kill my wife by mistake."

"Oh, my God!"

"I think I go now. You take care of yourself, pretty lady."

She reached up on tiptoes and gave him a quick peck on the jaw, tears in her eyes. He backed up, startled at such a demonstration of affection, and banged into the door frame, hard. She burst into laughter at his obvious discomfit. After a second or two, Mamigon joined in the laughter, made a slight bow, backed out of the door, turned and went down the stairs to the outdoors. He crossed the tree-lined street to his car and drove off.

A week later, again on a Friday, he was in the alley making a delivery when he spied her form outlined at the window and waved. She opened the window and gave him a cheery hello. "Why don't you come up for that coffee you never touched?"

"It must be cold by now."

"I'll warm it up for you if you promise to drink it this time."

"Are you sure it's all right to come up?"

"Oh, for goodness sakes, get up here." She almost barked it with a trace of impatience at his need to be coaxed.

"All right, all right." He went back into the store, bought a box of chocolates, drove the truck around into her street, and went to her house.

She was in the same attire he had seen her the week before. Must be her only dress, he thought, or maybe she wore it weeks at a time, who knows? He caught himself thinking he should give her money to buy extra dresses. It made him catch his breath. What the hell is the matter with me? She's almost a total stranger and a woman who hasn't even been formally introduced!

She brought out only coffee, this time, in two cups. He took one, still standing, not knowing where to put his other hand or what position of nonchalance to assume. He didn't feel like sitting on any of her furniture. She sensed that.

"Please sit down on that chair, Mr. Mamigon. It's old and your work clothes won't matter."

"Thank you, I'll stand. It is very nice to see you again . . ."

"It is nice to see you, too. What have you been doing with yourself. Have you had any more trouble?"

"Nothing new, lady. No, no trouble. I like to ask you question . . ."

"Certainly."

"Are you lady with dead husband?"

"Why should I be a widow—a lady with a dead husband?"

"You are very pretty and I no think you not married."

"No, I'm not married. I've never been married. You can't be a married woman and have a job as a schoolteacher in Boston."

"Ah, you are married to job."

"You could say that."

"You never want to get married?"

"Now look at who's getting nosy! Anyway, I can't say whether I ever wanted to get married or not. I never met a man who gave me such thoughts. I never did have much of a chance to meet men, though. I'm an only child and I had to take care of an invalid mother for years before she died. I don't worry about marriage, now."

"You did not answer my question. You do not want to get married?"

"Well . . . yes . . . if the right man comes along."

"What is the right man?"

"Someone I could respect, love, and share my life with."

"I had an old friend in Turkey who asked the widow of his best friend to marry him so that he could take care of her. She was handsome, strong-willed woman. She say, not now. He say, when? She say, some day, maybe. He say, some day soon? She say, some day, not too soon. He say, some day, maybe in year? She say, some day, maybe in year, two years. He say, some day, in year, two years, too long. She say, some day, maybe or never. My friend wait six months, sees that she does not need anyone to take care of her, so he marries a young girl who needs someone to take care of her."

"Did the widow know anything more about the proposal other than that your friend wanted to take care of her?"

"What do you mean, anything more? Is it not enough that the woman be cared for?"

She shook her head slowly, looking down at the floor. "My dear man, there is more to marriage than simply 'taking care' of someone. There is more to it than giving her money for shoes and clothes and food and a roof over her head. There is more to marriage than simply having children. Do you have any idea what I'm talking about?"

Mamigon let out a big sigh. Women were all the same. It didn't matter whether they wore *yashmaks* and *shawlwars* or immodest western dresses, they were all the same. Shades of his darling Guzell. This woman was talking about something that really had nothing to do with the serious, pragmatic, demanding, stultifying condition called marriage. One's emotions were a poor foundation for the marriage state. Emotions waxed and waned but the institution called marriage persisted. It was forever and it could not be based on quicksands of physical desire or physical beauty. It had to be founded on carefully considered reasons, pro and con, as to why this person and not that person was a more suitable mate for the long haul. Hah!

"Yes, I have good idea what you are talking about. But, you must understand me, too. I like the way you look—excuse me, Miss Hartnett—but that is small reason to marry you. I like you very much, but I do not have right to think of you in close way. You are at age—I think about twenty-eight—when it is too late for you to have children. If man does not marry with purpose of having children, there is no good reason for the marriage, don't you agree?"

"Marriage? Babies? What in God's name are you talking about? I was talking about the real reason, I believe, that the woman you would want to marry would not want to marry you. She would want to be loved . . . loved . . . wanted . . . desired . . . cherished . . . not regarded as a fancy horse and buggy that must be cared for!"

"I think I go now. It is getting late . . ."

"Sure, run away, Mr. Mamigon. If you can't be right, don't accept it, just run away and hide."

"You are nice lady, but I no like way you treat man. I am not boy. I go now. May the light of life shine on you."

She didn't say a word, didn't attempt to follow up or keep him there.

21 ❧ ATTACK

Tatios was back in Peabody a week after he met Harry Sears, grumbling to himself about the cold November evening and the feeling of growing futility in what he was trying to accomplish. He couldn't tell whether Mamigon was telling all, but he had said he had been the target of a knife attack in a Dorchester alley by a man who was not Enver. Apparently Enver had an accomplice. That could be the only explanation at this point. Tatios felt hopeless and he was becoming disenchanted with all the acting he had to do in his conversations with his newfound Turkish friends at the coffee-house.

He had thought the exuberance he had displayed last September in the Turkish massacre of the Greek inhabitants of Izmir was bad enough, but he had to dance with the men when the armistice ending the war with the Greeks at Mudanya was another excuse for a wild celebration, the Greeks having been soundly trounced. Then, dancing again last month when Mustapha Kemal Attaturk Pasha, the *Ghazi,* had abolished the sultanate and established a republican form of government in Turkey. *Sacre bleu,* would celebrations never cease!

If he didn't love that friend of his, he would have given up these trips long ago. He had been at it now for, let's see, four months. The conference with the neighbors was on a Sunday, July 30, and here it was November 25 and the best results to date had been more attacks on Mamigon and a faint feeling about one of the frequent denizens of the coffeehouse, a bearded young man who never failed to be there on the Saturdays Tatios was there. The man never joined his group but Tatios had the feeling that the man was looking at him when his back was turned. Oh, well, it was obviously a case of too much snooping around on his part and what that Vienna psychiatrist had described as paranoia.

It was back to the same boring dung with these lead heads: sipping coffee and kicking around the Armenians and Greeks and that stupid head, President Wilson, who had tried to set up an American Protectorate of Armenia on Turkish soil. Can you swallow such gall? Thanks be to Allah, the American Senate had thrown out his ideas, all fourteen of them. President Harding and now, President Coolidge had not revived any such fool notions. The Armenians were a rebellious lot and had to be handled in the only way rebels could understand, the rope and the knife.

"Absolutely," Tatios chimed in, "but I believe we should not have been so harsh on the women and children. Killing off the uppity, smart ass men sure made sense, but I must draw the line at women and children. It is against the word of the Holy Book."

"I agree, but what were we going to do with the women and children? The boys will grow up to be men and their mothers will have poisoned their minds against us. We would have had to knock them down all over again in another generation. I think we did the right thing for the good of the country."

"Logic, always logic. It is the basic clear thinking of the Turk and his training under the precepts of the Koran that has made us great. I cannot fault your answer." Tatios was gagging but he was an excellent actor. He turned his head to gather his thoughts and his eyes caught those of the bearded man, who turned away a bit too quickly to be natural. Tatios did not let on to a thing. He ordered another coffee, dawdled with it as the conversation continued, yawned mightily, and said it was time for him to leave.

Outside, he went down the street a few doors and stepped into a store's recessed door to see if anyone was following. He waited almost ten minutes and was about to give up when the bearded man came out, and, without looking to his left or right, walked in the opposite direction into the darkness, punctuated by streetlamps. Tatios hesitated, then decided not to follow him. He had a train to catch, anyway. It was getting to be nine-thirty.

There was a letter from Harry the following Monday. How would he like to work for Harvard University at its Peabody Museum? The curator of the museum—one of the finest museums of anthropology extant—needed a full-time translator, a language expert who would help with foreign and ancient language transcripts and manuscripts relating to artifacts and treatises that were constantly arriving from expeditions and scholars all over the world. If Tatios were interested, he should visit with a Dr. Sprague as soon as possible. The Peabody Museum was a block from Harvard Square. Tatios had visited the university years ago looking for a job. He was elated.

Dressed in his one good black suit with a new starched white collar buttoned on, Tatios visited the old red brick museum, sat down with Dr. Sprague in the latter's sparsely furnished second floor office, and trumped the curator with a pedantic display of languages. German being the language of science, it was decided that Tatios had the job and could translate and mark everything into German. This saved him from the task of translating into English, his weakest language. Tatios walked tall when he left, having used his French as the language of the interview and Latin and classic Greek for his humorous asides. He had the job and would be reporting for work the following Monday. His pay was to be twenty-two dollars a week, a quantum jump from the eight he was earning at the suit factory.

He felt he had unfinished business, though. He gave notice to Mr. Kondazian at the factory on Saturday and took one more trip to Peabody to visit the coffeehouse.

Sacre bleu, the bearded fellow showed up within ten minutes and took a table behind him again. Tatios had to ignore the man because of the physical setup. Then the break occurred—a crack in the wall of darkness that let in the light he had been seeking for so long.

One of the Turks at his table was talking about the perils of visiting the big city, Boston, and how he always got lost. The city was so big, so crazy in its street patterns that he rarely found his way back on the route he had taken. "Eh, Enver, you lived there for years, do you not agree with me?"

Everyone interested turned to look at the man behind Tatios, including Tatios who took his cue from those around him.

Enver looked decidedly uncomfortable for a moment, averting his eyes from Tatios's gaze, mumbled something, then spat out a "yes."

"Say, are you not Enver Dash, Tallal Bey's man?" Tatios grabbed the straw.

Enver stared at Tatios without answering, stared at him for so long that Tatios heard at least two voices say "Sure, that is the man" and "What is the matter, Enver?"

"It is a pleasure to know you. I have heard so much about the great Tallal Bey, anyone connected with him deserves a salute," Tatios said, saluting the now bug-eyed Enver Dash. Enver didn't say a word and slumped back into his seat, staring down into his demitasse.

So, the man behind him was Enver Dash! The Turk must have known who he was all along. Why else would he be watching him? It was a dangerous game and it was time to tell Mamigon, no question about it. Between them they would work out some kind of strategy and bring the matter to its end, whatever the result. He wrote something on a piece of paper and stuffed it into his vest.

Excited about the information he had, he was impatient to leave. Perhaps a bit too abruptly he got up, excused himself, grabbed his coat from the hook on the wall where he had left it and went out into the darkness. As he had done so many times before, he headed straight for the railroad depot even though he would have to wait about twenty or thirty minutes this time. But this time he was followed. He didn't realize it until he arrived at the depot which was deserted as usual, and sat on one of the long, dark solid-wood benches in the small station. The door opened to his left, a cold breeze swept in. But it wasn't the wind that sent a chill to his heart. That bearded fellow who Tatios thought had been watching him walked in, sauntered toward him and stood squarely in front of him, about 6 feet away.

"I heard you mention Tallal Bey." He spoke in Turkish.

"Yes, so what?"

"What is your interest in Tallal Bey?"

"It is none of your business, but I worked for him once."

"I think you lie, *giavour Ermeni*." He couldn't have been more than twenty-five years old, Tatios guessed.

"My honesty or dishonesty is not the question here, my young Turkish brave mouth. Who are you? What do you want?"

"I have a score to settle with your oversized friend, but right now I want your life, you skinny dog," and he moved toward Tatios. The door opened and the stationmaster looked in to see if there were any passengers for whom he needed to flag down the Portland to Boston express. Tatios's pursuer relaxed briefly.

Tatios looked at the stationmaster and waved a greeting, since he had a nodding acquaintance with him. The man waved back and left. Tatios arose from the bench, muttering something in Greek.

"What did you say?"

"I mentioned my Greek friend Homer in answer to your stupid desire: 'It lies on the knees of the gods.' What is your problem with my friend?"

"My master wants him dead, that is all, and you will not get away to warn him. Do not move . . ."

"You are doing this for Tallal? He is not dead?"

"Fuck Tallal. I have my own score to settle."

"What has my friend done to you? Is Tallal still alive?"

"It matters not to you—only that I have to kill you, and now."

"Wait, wait another minute. It will not make that much difference to you. What has my friend done to you that you want to kill him?"

"I was blamed for his escape back in Turkey. I was driving the *araba* after we captured him. He slipped away, and the army officer was sure I had cut him loose. I told them earlier the story of how the big guy had not shot me and everybody thought I had repaid him. They were not really sure, so you know what they did? You know what those bastards did?" His voice had become shrill, with deep anxiety tingeing the treble notes. "They cut off my balls, that is what they did . . ." He was breathing heavily now.

"I am sorry for you, but Mamigon is not responsible for what your own people did to you. Wait, wait. How did you find out Mamigon was here?"

"That was easy. All you smart-ass *Ermenis* were boasting about him after you two met in that coffeehouse. Some of us drop in there the same way you come to our places. I almost got the big whoremaster. I will cut off his cock and balls when I get him if it is the last thing I do. That is why you die."

With that, the young Turk leaped at him, producing a long butcher knife from under his coat. Tatios did a fast sidestep, tripping his attacker, and the knife stuck in the top of the bench. The man screamed as his hand slid down from the handle at the jolt of impact and the blade sliced through his clenched hand. Tatios had now braced himself and delivered a heavy kick to the man's belly. The Turk fell away from the blow, pulling the knife with him, blood dripping everywhere.

Tatios tried once again to use his feet, this time to kick the arm holding the knife. He missed. The knife came to rest in Tatios's abdomen, the Turk deftly twisting it up and out in one quick motion from his sitting position on the floor. The Armenian had never felt cold steel in his guts before. He felt as if all the air in the world was suddenly there as he shuddered, gave a guttural cry, and collapsed.

The stationmaster, who had heard the initial cry from the Turk, came running in just as the knifeman reached the door; the trainman thudded to the floor, knifed in the throat. The Turk wasn't going to leave witnesses.

Tatios tried moving to the door, in excruciating pain. My God, it felt like ten thousand stomach cramps. He arched his back repeatedly as the pain racked him. He was feeling much colder; a heavy sweat broke out and he began to shake uncontrollably. His hands pressed against his belly, but they were losing their strength. I wish someone would come, he thought. He had to tell Mamigon what he knew . . . God, it hurt . . . God . . . help me . . . Girl . . . Girl . . . Miss Drevanian . . .

22 &CERTAINTIES

"The devil takes a hand in what is done in haste."

"If you say so, Excellency, but I know everything will be all right." Enver's voice had a tinge of pleading in his sullen voice.

"I do say so. It is difficult for me to believe that you took it upon yourself to kill that man, regardless of your reasons."

"I tell you, he found out about me."

"And that was enough to kill him? A man in a coffeehouse, who happens to have been a friend of Mamigon, mentions your name and you leap to the conclusion that he means you harm, so you kill him. Wonderful! Will wonders never cease!"

Enver started to speak.

"Oh, close your stupid mouth, Enver. Tell me again, you are certain no one will be able to trace the killings to you? Are you certain you left nothing traceable to you?"

"Nothing, *effendi*, nothing. The man died and the only witness, the station man, died also. There was not a soul around when I left the place, and I went all the way to another city to have my cut hand treated."

Tallal turned to Ali. "What do you think? Will anything come of this in your opinion?" Before Ali could answer, Tallal interrupted, "What is on your mind, Ali. I detect something."

"Nothing, Excellency, nothing, really. I think Enver did no harm to us."

"Hhmm . . . Do you have something you wish to tell me?" Tallal's intuition was ringing bells and he never ignored them.

Ali gambled on throwing Tallal off the scent. The man was incredible in his sharpness. "Excellency, I have been thinking that I could be of greater service to you if you brought Enver back from Peabody and the two of us shared responsibilities."

"Oh, you miss Enver?" Tallal had a leer on his face.

Ali looked down, scuffling his shoes. How did Tallal know about them? "It is just that two can serve you better than one, Excellency . . ."

"The man is the mind, Ali, and your friend joining you here would not mean another whole man, I am sorry to say."

"If that is your wish, Excellency, *kismet*."

Tallal looked long and hard at both of his now silent minions. "But, you may have struck on something, Ali. Perhaps if Enver was to return you could keep an eye on him to save him from himself. Very well, it is done. Enver will join us next week. Now go."

Once the pair was outside Tallal's office, Enver began snarling, "I am going to kill him . . . I will kill him, I swear . . ."

Ali looked at him, laughing. "In good time, my friend, in good time. I asked for you because I have put one over on Tallal and I need your help to continue it."

"You what?"

"Yes. Our grand master, our general manager, our superior dung heap thinks I got rid of his enemy Mamigon."

"Well, did you not?" The look on Ali's face was enough. "By Allah, by all that is sacred, you are not lying! What have you done?"

"I became tired of his raving and ranting about not finding him, not killing him, not having any brains, not worthy of our pay . . . so I killed someone who looked like Mamigon and got Tallal off both our backs."

"I cannot believe you could take such a chance! What if he found out?"

"How could he? We have been his eyes and ears. We have been his hired killers. All we have to do is to go about our own sweet way and kill the Armenian in our own good time."

"We?"

"Why not? We worked well together before. We both seem to be regarded as swine by Tallal Bey, even if he has been extra nice to me because of what he thinks I did. Time is watering the gratitude, my friend, and I do not think I will be in his special graces much longer."

Enver thought it over, looking sideways at Ali. It would be good to have Ali back . . . for other reasons. His proposition could be turned into a deal whereby he could get what he wanted and . . . "All right, Ali, it is a deal, but I will exact certain payments for this cooperation. You can see that one word from me to Tallal about you and all would be over for you."

"Let us not *bazaar* about it, Enver, and no threats. We will work together and reap whatever rewards there are."

"Do you know where he is now? Has he moved from Grove Hall in Roxbury?"

"No. He is still there. I have much to tell you." Ali recounted the stabbing attempt, the dynamite attempt, and, the most delicious item of all, the killing of his wife. "I wanted to make him suffer for all the trouble he was causing me, so I potted his pregnant wife the first chance I got." Ali liked the little change he made in the facts. He still remembered the surprise he had felt when the woman's face appeared in his sights just as he had pulled the trigger.

Enver was looking saucer-eyed at the smiling, self-satisfied killer. "You have done all that?" He made a mental note never to trust Ali. The man was too cold-blooded for him. Rape her for sure, hurt her some for sure, but kill her for the fun of it? Not much fun in that.

23 ⚜ HOSPITAL

At first, the Peabody police had thought the two they found in the train station had fought with each other. But the drops of blood on the bench, the gouge in the wood, the distance between the two, and a trail of blood out the door helped establish the presence of a third person.

The stationmaster's body was easy to identify but the bushy-haired one with the stomach almost gutted was not. There was no wallet in his clothing and the initial conclusion had been that it was a botched robbery attempt since dollars were found in the pants pockets of both victims.

The arrival of passengers for the nine-thirty train had brought the police and ambulances to the scene. Tatios was rushed directly to J.B. Thomas Hospital and operated on despite the massive loss of blood, low blood pressure, deep shock, and erratic pulse. The doctors took the chance on the premise that he would die in any case. He survived some wholesale resections of the intestinal tract and patching of the stomach wall. It was not until Tuesday morning that he was able to speak and identify himself. The problem of how to get in touch with his family was solved by the Peabody police who contacted the Boston police who had a patrolman knock on the door of his home.

Mamigon arrived with Eksah that day. Harry Sears arrived the following day after he had read a brief account of the trainman's murder in the *Peabody Times*. Harry took care of Tatios's nonappearance on the job at Harvard.

Tatios was too wan and weak to do more than nod and say yes or no to his visitors the first two days, being as comforting to his wife as a man could be in his condition. On Thursday, he asked Eksah to go buy some candy for the nurses while he talked with Mamigon.

"It was Enver Dash."

"I was sure."

"He frequents the coffeehouse with the green door near the town square."

"Good. I will find him."

"Be careful."

"Have no worry about that."

"One more thing. He did not say so in words but . . . are you sure Tallal Bey is dead?"

"Why?" Mamigon's eyes widened ever so slightly.

"I am not certain of it in the slightest, but Dash mentioned Tallal's name in a way that sounded as if he were referring to the quick rather than the dead."

Mamigon nodded. "I will find out before I kill him. He tried to kill you because of me."

"Do not kill for me, Mamigon."

"The list grows longer, Tatios Effendi."

"I care for you, brother of mine. Watch for yourself."

"Tatios, the first blow is half the battle. I shall strike the first blow, for once."

"I will see if my friend Harry will escort Eksah home. I can see you are impatient."

"That is not proper. I will take Diggin Eksah home first. I insist." He drove the twenty miles to Boston and was back by nightfall to take a loitering position in a doorway across the street from the coffeehouse with the green door.

Near and Middle Easterners ate early suppers and by six o'clock the men began arriving singly and in pairs to the macho atmosphere of their social hall, rife with heavy tobacco smoke, a thousand different blended smells of stale coffee and unwashed bodies, and the shouts and calls of card and backgammon players. A big, black potbellied stove cooked the trapped air.

Mamigon watched Enver Dash go in with two others. He left his post and walked to the square where he ordered a bowl of soup and coffee in a diner. It was going to be a long night but he didn't tarry too long for fear Enver might have other plans and leave before the usual two or three hours the men stayed in such places, if they had a family. If not, they would close the place.

He waited for nearly two hours, then walked into the crowded place. It had about thirty square tables, four to a table, a dark, oiled-wood floor, dingy brown leather curtains on six large windows, no coverings on the tables served by wooden, spindle-backed chairs, and a door opening into the small kitchen where the coffee was being constantly brought to a boil in small, four-cup quantities.

He filled the entrance to the place, tall, huge, unsmiling, his hands hanging loosely at his sides. He didn't move from the doorway, looking slowly around the room. The conversation, the playing, the sipping, began to abate until there wasn't a sound after a minute following his appearance. Everyone was looking at Mamigon. His manner and mien seemed to telegraph a foreboding.

His searching eyes stopped in the middle of the sweep and riveted on Enver sitting at a table in the back. Mamigon began moving toward Enver's table, hardly looking where he was going, not taking his eyes off him.

Enver was staring back, his eyes wide, his mouth open, as he slowly began to rise. The three men sitting with him recognized the fear that was growing on Enver's face and pushed back their chairs and crowded away. There still wasn't a sound in the place. Enver was rubber-kneed and shaking by the time Mamigon reached the table.

"Have you killed anyone lately, my pants-pissing lion?" Mamigon's voice was low but could be heard throughout the hushed room, the icy tone removing any doubts about how serious the intruder's intentions were.

"I have not harmed you . . . leave me alone!" The querulous, tremulous voice was barely above a squeak.

"You have killed for the last time."

"Grab him . . . he is an Armenian outlaw!"

"*Massabi bohglu schun,*" Mamigon snarled in his best Turkish obscenity. "You would hide among your friends, eh?" He raised his right hand and delivered a lightning-fast backhand that caught Enver on his right cheek and sent him spinning into the wall and sprawling to the floor.

"I will be waiting for this piece of dung. Any of you who think you want to help him, do . . ." He turned toward the door. Half the men between Mamigon and the door stood up, blocking his way. None had his height but their solid phalanx more than made up for it.

"Who are you, mister?" A short, bandy-legged man near the center with a heavy mustache asked the question.

Mamigon looked around, a slight smile around his mouth, seemingly unperturbed and unafraid, a psychological telegraph that easily reaches a doubting antagonist. "*Sic dirr,*" was all he said, throwing down the gauntlet.

A growling murmur rippled through the room. The big bastard wasn't giving an inch. "Who are you? What do you want of that man?" It was the same man speaking.

"*Sic dirr*, all of you." Mamigon's voice was still low, icy, but his teeth were not visible as his jaw hardened.

They rushed him. Mamigon brought his elbows up, his fists clenched and touching at the knuckles across his chest and swung them out in one prodigious sweep. Five in front were slammed backward among the others and the tables and chairs. Two tables collapsed, chairs splintered, and the crowd began to roar.

They closed in again. Mamigon took a step forward this time for momentum and bodies were tossed like matchwood, one slamming into the stove and knocking it down, its glowing coals spilling out on the oiled floor.

Mamigon, panting, stepped back, again, his arms at the ready.

Enver Dash leaped at his back, slamming a knife into him.

Mamigon staggered forward from the impact, braced his legs, and turned slowly, the knife in his back.

He seized his whimpering attacker with one hand grabbing a shoulder and gave him a mighty whack on the jaw.

Enver dropped to the floor like a loose bag of bones, unconscious to the world.

Fire leaped up from the floor and spread rapidly.

A mad scramble ensued as the erstwhile contenders struggled to reach the outdoors through the entrance as well as through the back door in the kitchen.

As the flames crept up two walls, Mamigon, still on his feet and watching the last of the customers pushing their way out to safety, bent over in a spasm of fitful coughs and staggered out through the now clear front door, dragging Enver behind him.

The police left the scene in care of the firemen and rushed Mamigon to the hospital. Mamigon's feeble attempts—he was fighting ever-growing shock—to have the police hold Enver, was fruitless. The admitting nurse recognized Mamigon immediately as the man who had made arrangements to pay for Tatios's care. The police were fascinated.

While Mamigon went into surgery, a detective, the only one on the Peabody force, went to Tatios's room to find out the connection. Two Armenian nonresidents of Peabody found knifed within a week of each other. One knows the other well enough to pay for his medical care, and the weapon taken from the back of the latest victim could easily have been the knife used in the first attack. What's going on?

Since Tatios had no idea what had happened he wasn't much help. Mr. Hastings, the detective, wasn't interested in discussing the relative merits of inductive and deductive reasoning, expounded with a sprinkling of French to help the thought along. He was trying to learn why two Armenians who knew each other were knifed in Peabody and probably by the same man. Did Tatios know who knifed him?

Tatios wondered what the result would be if he said yes. He couldn't figure it out, so he said "perhaps."

"Perhaps?"

"Yes, perhaps I know."

"Do you or don't you, never mind perhaps."

"I do know the man's name but I don't know who he is or where he's from."

"Well? What's his name?"

"Enver Dash."

"What kind of a name is that?"

"Turkish."

"Ah."

Tatios didn't respond to that reaction other than to stare.

"The Turks and Armenians, of course."

"Of course, what, officer?"

"You don't like each other, and that's putting it mildly."

"That may be so."

"All right, what's going on? Did you see this Enver Dash kill the trainman?"

"Yes."

"I think I am going to arrest you for not coming forth with that information."

"When was I supposed to have come forth with it, officer? I have been conscious and have been receiving visitors now for four days. This is the first time a member of the force has been here."

Hastings scratched his head. "Nobody's been around to . . . ?"

"No, no one."

"I can't believe it. We had a man here Sunday and Monday to question you when you came around. Wonder what happened . . ."

"Probably a mixup at your office. My problem about Enver Dash is that I don't know where he lives or works." Tatios described how he was followed from the coffeehouse, yes, the same coffeehouse that almost burned down tonight, to the station and set upon because he said he knew me to be a friend of Mamigon. Yes, the man you say was knifed tonight. Really, he is going to be OK, isn't he?

Mamigon's luck was with him. The knife had slipped off the shoulderblade and penetrated the chest cavity almost in a direction perpendicular to the ground. Nothing vital was touched but he had lost about a pint of blood that had to be drained out.

Four days later he was in Salem District Court under police guard. He pleaded guilty to all charges and was fined $100 for disturbing the peace, $700 for damages sustained by the coffeehouse, and $25 court costs. Ten days in jail was suspended after a lecture from the bench that Mamigon should try not to socialize in Peabody again, especially among people who don't like you, and that all you Turks should learn to comport yourselves as law-abiding citizens of your new country. Heavy drinking and bad blood do not mix. The name of Enver Dash was not mentioned. Baron Zakarian, escorting Eksah, paid the monies to the bailiff and Mamigon, his left arm in a sling to immobilize the shoulder, walked out.

The court episode had a deeply interested spectator who reported the affair to Tallal Bey.

24 ACCOUNTING

"Our Lord Mohammed said that the true pleasure of life is to live with one's inferiors, and, by Allah, I have tried mightily, and verily, true pleasure has been bitter vetch.

"Both of you have lied to me about official duties and results. Both of you have displayed incredible ineptitude in the performance of your duties. Both of you have conducted yourselves in a manner that brings shame to your manhood.

"But, most devastating of all, both of you have exhibited such stupidity, such a lack of judgment, such total ineptness that if this were the army I would have you shot before I would let you stumble about in the civilian world.

"Did either of you truly believe that I would not learn that you had not eliminated Mamigon?

"Did either of you think for one moment that I could not have taken care of your mistakes if you had admitted them?

"No, perhaps I deserve what has happened because I overestimated your ability to think and act. Both of you are confined to kitchen and cleanup duties for the next month without pay. You will live in the basement and will be watched constantly. I will decide on what to do with you later. Get out of my sight!"

25 MOVING

Harry Sears would not take no for an answer. Tatios and his family were to move into the vacant caretaker's cottage on the family estate in Manchester-by-the-Sea for a month of convalescence before he reported to Professor Sprague. If, somehow, arrangements could be made for an automobile, Tatios could make his home there permanently among the trees, the green, and the sea in exchange for tutoring the large Sears family in any of the languages Tatios knew.

When Mamigon was apprised of this development on the last hospital visit he made to see Tatios, he immediately volunteered the use of his own car for as long as Tatios needed it, and he indicated that that could be forever and he wouldn't mind.

Tatios's angry reaction to all this giving without being able to respond in kind brought the pointed observation from Mamigon that it would be totally impossible for him to ever repay Tatios and Eksah for taking care of his baby boy. "I am forever in your debt, my friends, and using my machine is so slight a payment that I am embarrassed to even mention it. I will miss my boy, but I will salve that pain by the knowledge of where he is growing up and who is seeing to it that he grows up properly. God, in His infinite wisdom, gives and takes in bewildering ways."

So it was done.

26 REVISITED

He was back with Emily six months after he had been with her last. When he was unloading in the alley, he had carefully avoided looking up at her windows, acting as if she never existed. His avoidance of her had taxed his will and he could not erase her calm face from his mind. Finally, on a bitterly cold Friday in January, he said to hell with it all, he would do what his heart dictated. He bought a fancy box of Whitman's Samplers, brought the truck around to her street and knocked at her door.

She opened the door, looked up at his face with a big smile, and waved him in with a grand, sweeping gesture of her right arm. He bowed, handed her the candy box, and stepped in to stand stiffly, both not having said a word.

"From my limited knowledge of the Near East, I think I remember that the men prefer the buxom to the blithe or debonair. Am I to assume something from this gift?" she said, patting a slim hip for emphasis.

"I do not know of such things, Miss Hartnett. I bring candy because an American friend told me once that people in America bring candy when they go to other people's homes."

She got up on her toes again and managed to reach his jaw in a light kiss. "I missed you, Mr. Mamigon."

"I missed you, too," he said, embracing her small frame and holding her to his chest. Her face rested on his rough clothes, barely reaching his shoulder. They stood there, rocking gently.

"I want you to know that I am not twenty-eight, I'm thirty . . . and . . . and I've finally . . ." She stopped and didn't continue. The pause was resolved by Mamigon's sudden grunt as he swung an arm under her thighs, swept her feet out from under her, cradled her surprisingly insignificant form in his massive arms, and carried her to the easy chair she had once told him he could sit in, sat down, and held his face close to hers. He could reach her lips with his in that position, and he sought them out. She turned her face away: he brought his hand to her head and nudged her face back to his, and they kissed, her face disappearing under the foliage of his massive mustache. Their lips were hungry and searching and the kiss was hard and prolonged. She eased back and tried to look into his face at close range, and Mamigon noted that the eyes looked almost crossed at that distance. Her face was beet red.

"I not going to let you go, lady."

"Please," she whispered, "my name is Emily."

"Emily, I not going to let you go . . ."

"I don't want you to . . . Mamigon." She kissed him this time, and the touch was softer, less urgent. They pulled back again, and looked steadily into each other's eyes.

"Well, here we are," she said with a bit of flippancy in her voice. "What next? Why don't we talk, Mamigon?"

For answer, he sat her up on his lap and helped her to her feet.

"I do not ask pardon, Emily. You are wonderful lady and I hold you close to me because I . . . I . . ."

"Sshh, don't say anything. There is no need," she said, smoothing out her dress.

"I go now. I have to think. No time for talk." He stuck out his hand, clasped hers, and let himself out with Emily standing in the middle of the room shaking her head.

Mamigon began arranging his deliveries on Friday so that his last stop would be at Mr. Avedesian's store in Codman Square. He was a happy, yet troubled man. His warming thoughts about Emily were constantly salted and cooled by his deteriorating self-image; deteriorating because his thoughts seemed to concentrate on the memory of her soft lips and soft body and his unabashed desire to touch her again. A good man did not have such propensities for a good woman who wasn't his wife. She wasn't even his fiancée and there was no one to speak for her or protect her from what he regarded as his dubious encroachments on her person. Nevertheless, he found himself daydreaming and waiting for Friday to come around each week for the excuse to see her. It never occurred to Mamigon that he could simply drop by after work on any day or on a weekend. He had to have an excuse. A man just did not pursue a woman; he could never seem to be directly interested. It was downright infantile and absolutely undignified, he thought. It was so much more civilized in the old country. Intermediaries would take care of such preliminaries and the aura of disinterest was maintained, eliminating the danger of losing face if the suggested match was rejected.

When he saw her at the window the week after he had kissed her, he stood as close to the second story window as possible and invited her, in a low whisper, to meet him at Piscopo's, a restaurant around the corner. She nodded quickly and disappeared from the window.

Piscopo's was a long, narrow eating place that served everything from steaks and chops to soups and sandwiches, dished out in generous portions by a generously porportioned Greek who glared at customers who left anything on their plates. "People hungry all over world," he would say with stentorian abandon, "and Americans waste food." This pronouncement usually washed over the back of the departing culprit or culprits. The place had a counter and anchored stools stretching the entire length on one side and four-place tables on the opposite wall. There was little privacy for conversation in Piscopo's because of the white-tiled walls and floor, the white linoleum on the counter and table tops. Sound absorption was nil and the breakfast and lunchtime clientele dined in a hubbub. At first sight, the whiteness also gave the eatery the appearance of a surgical dispensary, but the effect was quickly dispelled by the olfactory senses.

They reached the restaurant simultaneously and had the place almost to themselves at four o'clock in the afternoon. Mamigon ushered Emily to a table near the rear and repeated her request for "just coffee." The proprietor, who knew Mamigon as a taciturn, no-nonsense truckman who collected his ten cents for each crate delivered and never exchanged pleasantries, couldn't believe his eyes when the big man entered, escorting a pretty, little, obviously "American," lady. Mamigon didn't give Piscopo a second glance, and came right to the point with Emily.

"I no think it wise to visit you in your place, Emily," he said as quietly as possible. He had noted that Piscopo had not returned entirely to his place behind the cash register. He was hovering halfway, no doubt hoping to hear what his Armenian friend could possibly discuss with an American woman, who certainly was not a tramp.

"Why not?"

"I think you know. I no act as gentleman. You have no—what you say—guardian?"

She almost laughed, but said with a grin, "You mean chaperone? Mamigon, if you are bothered by what happened, you've got to remember that I did not resist. I did not stop you. I was very happy. You showed that you liked me."

"A grown man should control himself, Emily. I had no right. That is why you must not be angry with me if I don't visit with you anymore."

"All right, if that's what you want. Would it be too much if we met here for a cup of coffee on Fridays?"

Mamigon realized he was suddenly disappointed that she had agreed so readily to confine their relationship to antiseptic meetings in a public place, but he certainly had asked for it.

"That would be very nice but people will talk about you . . . people will not understand, and you have your name to protect."

"Mamigon, this is America and it is perfectly all right for a man and a woman to meet in public as often as they wish and simply talk. I'm not the least bit worried about my reputation." She grinned, her blue eyes sparkling, as she waved in the direction of Piscopo. "You aren't worried about people like him, are you?"

"No, I'm not worried about him and what he thinks. I guess I don't know who it is I'm supposed to protect you from."

"Let me worry about that, Mamigon, please. Let's talk about you. Anything new about Enver?"

"No, nothing much has happened other than more trouble. I cannot believe Enver has the brains to have done what has happened, though."

"I wish I could help you, Mamigon. I wish there was something I could do . . ."

"You are doing enough, Emily. Knowing there is someone like you in my life right now is important to me. At least, if I am killed, someone will know the truth of the matter."

"Don't talk like that. I want to be more than a passive bystander. I want to do something about it."

"We will see, Emily. We will see. Finish your cup, please, and let's be on our way before Piscopo loses his mind. You know, he's been trying to hear what we've been saying. If we keep on this way, he's going to fall over the counter trying to get closer."

They laughed as they stood up. Piscopo straightened up and walked to the register to collect the two nickels Mamigon left for the coffee. They walked to her house, where Mamigon shook her hand and promised to meet her again next Friday.

"I would like to make dinner for you, but if you don't want to come to my place, I guess I can't . . ." She was grinning again.

"I know. I go home now. I come back tomorrow at five o'clock and we have lamb chops at Piscopo's. Is that alright?"

"Wonderful, but can we eat a little later, say six o'clock?"

"Why not? Why not? I meet you in front of Piscopo's at six o'clock."

He wondered why she wanted to eat so late in the day, but then, American women and their ways were strange to him. Despite his stenotopic inclinations, he was positively elated at the turn of events, and also a bit nervous at the thought of eating a public meal with a woman. America was changing his conduct in ways he would never have envisioned in the old country. He had no Tatios with whom to play backgammon on Saturday nights anymore and had become an avid reader of American and Armenian papers in the evenings to help him to obtain a better grasp of the languages. Supper with Emily was going to be a most welcome break from the hermit-like existence he had chosen to follow. He never went to the coffeehouses because of the attention he attracted.

He arrived in Codman Square after he stopped for his shower at the public baths, dressed in his Sunday clothes. He had even given his highbutton black shoes a shine and felt totally self-conscious as he stood in front of Piscopo's glass-fronted establishment, five minutes ahead of time. The lights had been turned on for the sign across the front of the place. He waved at Piscopo who had signaled him to come in. Mamigon figured he might have to spend as much as two dollars for the two meals, but it was worth every penny of it, just to be with Emily. He had to park the truck on Emily's street, and walked past her two-family dwelling to get here. It was twilight of an October evening and he didn't pay any attention to the two men walking up the street toward Piscopo's. The street was practically empty—after all, everyone would be home finishing supper. Ah, there was Emily, just a block away, well behind the two men now approaching him. Hmm, they were trying hard not to look at him, he noticed . . . Holy Saint Gregory! It was the knife man from the alley! He couldn't mistake the pongid frame . . . and the other one? Enver!

Mamigon bent over in a crouch, much like a Greco-Roman wrestler. The heavy man came at him with his knife high; Enver held his knife low. They were no more than three steps from him now. Mamigon calculated he couldn't disarm one without the other getting him. He braced his feet and lunged backward, bent over. His rear smashed through the plate glass of the storefront. He sprawled on his back in a swirl of glass shards on the tile. Blood from his back smeared the white floor.

Mamigon was on his feet in an instant. The heavy man's attack was slowed down by his need for care as he eased his bulk through the shattered window. Enver came rushing through the door.

The place was a hubbub of screams and yells from a score or so of men and women in the restaurant who upturned tables and chairs in a mad rush toward the rear. Piscopo was howling like a nutted bull.

Mamigon grabbed a chair and held it in front of him to ward off Enver's rush through the door. The blood was dripping down his legs.

At the last second he thrust the chair viciously into his attacker's face, slamming him to the floor.

The window entrant was now almost to him, his knife high in the plunge position.

Mamigon flung the chair upward, catching the man with a glancing blow on the chin. He staggered back, momentarily stunned, but he didn't lose the knife.

"Mamigon! Here . . ." Piscopo shoveled a heavy butcher knife, handle first, toward him.

The Armenian grinned now at his attackers, regrouping for another attack. He had the chair in one hand and the knife in the other.

They approached him with greater care, watching his eyes. Mamigon suddenly slammed the chair toward Enver on the left and slashed at the heavy one.

Both retreated but Mamigon lost his knife in a deft parry by the heavy one.

They had him now. The pair leaped toward him just as a shrill blast from a police whistle pierced the bedlam of the restaurant. The whistle stopped them short. They whirled for the door to get away, the outraged howls of Piscopo in their ears. He was charging out from behind the counter, butcher knives in each hand.

The two were out the door by this time and turned to run in the direction they had come. But the whistle blasted again—it was Emily's—and that was all the hesitation Mamigon needed.

He grabbed one of the huge knives from Piscopo as he ran out the door and flung it mightily at the heavy-set man's running form, only 6 or 7 yards away. The scream was primal as the blade reached his upper back and sliced through, the tip protruding from his chest.

Heavy One collapsed to the sidewalk and lay still. Enver continued his mad gallop to get away, never once stopping to see what happened to his friend.

Mamigon was bleeding heavily from his backside, sliced open on the right cheek by the shattering window. He could feel the blood squishing in his shoes and for the first time felt waves of dizziness. He kneeled to the sidewalk, holding the wall of the storefront.

Piscopo was beside him in an instant. Emily was still running to the scene, screaming all the way.

"They wanted my money, Piscopo. Thanks for saving my life . . . That was fast work, dropping that man with your knife."

"You hurt, Mr. Mamigon. He is hurt," Piscopo reported to Emily who arrived at the moment to kneel beside Mamigon.

"Please call a doctor," she said peremptorily, taking command of the situation. "It looks like a flesh wound, Mamigon. Did they cut you anywhere else?"

"No, I think I'm alright. Piscopo got one of them with his knife . . . "

"Mr. Mamigon, you . . ." Piscopo couldn't finish what he was going to say.

"*Please,* Mr. Piscopo, please call a doctor!"

"Awrite, I go call doctor . . . I go call doctor. I call police, too." He strode into his restaurant purposefully, muttering in Greek and then yelled at his customers to remember to pay before they left.

The police arrived before the doctor. Emily pressed a large cloth napkin from the restaurant to Mamigon's wound, not moving him until a doctor took over.

Passersby and Piscopo's customers began crowding the scene: two men on the sidewalk, bleeding heavily; a red-headed young woman ordering the police to leave the big man alone until he could be treated; and a fat, aproned man telling anyone who wanted to know that he had foiled a holdup attempt. The tableau was swathed in yellow light from the restaurant.

Emily did most of the talking: No, officer, this man was waiting in front here for me. No, we're just friends and he and I were going to have something to eat. Yes, I saw the whole thing. They drew knives as they talked to him. No, I didn't hear what they said but he told me they wanted his money, and he refused. They began to fight and Mr. Piscopo came out with a butcher knife and struck one of them and the other ran away after wounding this man. Is that right, Mr. Piscopo?

The restaurateur apparently accepted the role of rescuer thrust upon him. He confirmed Emily's story but wanted to know who was going to pay for his broken plate glass. Of course, Mr. Mamigon will, Emily said quickly.

The doctor arrived, checked the wound through the torn pants, and announced the laceration was superficial, requiring only a few stitches. Far more attention was paid the other knife victim, who seemed to be dying, if not dead. He was pronounced alive, finally, and the ambulance carted him off. The doctor said he didn't need to take Mamigon to a hospital to treat him if there was a suitable place available. Emily volunteered her apartment, which was less than two blocks away. Mamigon said no. Emily's jaw hardened; she directed the police as they wrestled him into the squad car, with the doctor now pressing the wound. They carried him upstairs to her bedroom. The police said they would be back tomorrow and left. The doctor placed Mamigon prone on the bed and applied a batch of gauze with ether to his face. While the anesthetic was taking effect, Emily put the suture needle in a pan to boil and then helped the doctor remove all of Mamigon's clothes, including his bloody pants and underwear. She brought in two floor lamps and placed them opposite the doctor's side of the single bed so that he would have good light. Once the ether took effect, the physician stitched up the 7-inch fissure while Emily swabbed away the welling blood. The sewn-up wound was bandaged and taped, and he was covered up.

"He's a very big man and he shouldn't be allowed to turn over at least until morning. Do you think you can manage?"

"Of course, doctor. When will the bandage have to be changed?"

"Well, first of all, he shouldn't walk around for twenty-four hours. Then change the bandage every day—you saw what I did—and have him come to my office a week from today so I can remove the stitches. Here's my card."

"That's fine, doctor. How much do I owe you?"

"Four dollars, if you have it. Luckily, the glass penetrated only two centimeters at the deepest. He didn't lose too much blood. There was hardly any subcutaneous fat, the man is all muscle."

"Thank you, doctor," Emily said as she handed him his fee. "I'll bring him to you next week."

After the physician left, Emily looked at the torpid figure of her friend, gathered up his bloody clothes, threw his underpants in some cold water in her washtub, and soaked up as much of the caking blood on his torn blue serge pants as she could with cold water. She thought of mending them but realized it was a lost cause. The repair would be noticeable. It was probably the only suit he had . . . and he had worn it to take her to dinner. She put aside his money and papers.

Morning light in the cheery, robin's-egg blue bedroom found Emily dozing in the easy chair she had dragged in and Mamigon groaning.

"How do you feel?"

"Huh? I have a big pain in head . . . I am . . . where . . . where are my clothes?"

"It's alright, Mamigon. The doctor had to remove them to stitch you up. How do you feel?"

"My head is . . . Can I have my clothes now?"

"Please, Mamigon. The doctor says you've got to stay in bed until tomorrow morning or else you'll start bleeding again. You've been cut in a place that will stretch and pull if you try to stand up or walk."

"I take care of myself, Emily. You get my clothes and . . ."

"You're going to stay there, Mamigon. The police said they would be back sometime today to talk to you, so you can't leave, at least until they see you."

He pondered over her words for a while, then, "All right, I stay, but I put on my clothes. Did you . . . were you with the doctor when . . ." He had a pained look on his face. He had been sensitive about his private parts ever since that day at the military academy in Constantinople when the German medical staff had examined the new cadets. He hadn't thought anything about standing naked with the other men until his innocent question a few days later when he asked his fellow cadets why they insisted on "Horse" as his sobriquet. At first he thought they were referring to his giant frame, but leering allusions made him realize otherwise. Funny . . . his wife hadn't mentioned it, but then she certainly hadn't had another man; and neither had Guzell . . .

Emily knelt beside the bed and kissed him on the cheek. "Stop worrying about everything and just get well, you big horse!" She was startled at his sudden groan of anguish as he brought his arm up to cover his face. "I'll . . . I'll make some coffee and toast for you now and see what you want to eat later."

He was on his back, the coverlets up to his chin, when she returned to the bedroom with coffee and buttered toast. He averted his eyes when she entered.

"All right, Mamigon, what's really bothering you?"

"I should not be here."

"Why not? You need someone to take care of you, and . . ."

"You are single woman and I should not be here."

"Why do you keep bringing that up? If I weren't willing—sincerely willing—you wouldn't be here."

"Unmarried young woman and unmarried man do not . . ."

"All right, Mamigon, all right. Eat this toast and stay where you are until the police come and go. I'll get your clothes ready—your pants are torn— and you can leave tonight. I don't know how you'll be able to drive your truck. You won't be able to sit for long without breaking open that wound. Why don't you let me take care of you until you can drive that truck? Until you're able to, I'll concern myself about you, OK?"

"Thank you, Emily, I will leave as soon as police go."

She threw up her hands and stamped out, leaving a glum Mamigon to his confused thoughts.

The Sunday morning watch sent a young policeman to take Mamigon's statement. Someone hadn't done his homework at the station, probably because Saturday nights are disconcertingly busy; there was no mention of Mamigon's previous escapades.

As the cop was about to leave, Emily spoke up. "How's the man doing, the one who was stopped by Mr. Piscopo?"

"He died, ma'm."

"Who was he?"

"We don't know. There was no identification on him. His fingerprints aren't on file, either. He's a real John Doe. We've got him on ice." He sounded very professional.

"Did you catch his partner, by any chance?"

"Naw, he vanished. Must have got away in a car."

"Well, thank you, officer, and good luck." The cop left.

"Who John Doe? What is fingerprint?"

After Emily finished explaining, Mamigon reminded her that he needed his clothes. She nodded, went to the kitchen, and returned with them, tossing them on the bed.

"I washed the blood out, but your pants are ruined; they can't be mended."

"That's all right, Emily. I can't thank you for all you have done."

"Don't bother thanking me, Mamigon. I can't stand a stubborn man."

"What is stubborn?"

"Stubborn . . . a donkey is stubborn."

He didn't say another word. Left alone, he rolled over onto his naked belly and eased himself onto his feet as a sharp pain tugged at his backside. He found he couldn't bring up his right leg to slip on his shorts and he couldn't bend over to try it from the floor. He tried three more times before he noticed drops of blood on the shorts. He was in a predicament, and Emily had warned him. He didn't want to get back into the bed and ruin it with his dripping wound, and he couldn't put on his shorts. He stood on his underclothes to stop the blood from dripping on the carpet, unable to dress.

"Emily."

She came to the door and looked in to see him standing naked beside the bed, his hands covering his genitals. There was anger in his eyes.

"I . . . I . . ."

She didn't utter a sound as she flitted to the bathroom and came back with a bath towel to wrap around his waist and a smaller one to press against the oozing wound.

"You big, stubborn baby. Why don't you do what's good for you, just for once!" She made him turn to the bed and eased him back down. "Lie on your back, now, while I keep this pressed against you and I'll go when you are lying on top of the folded towel . . . there."

"I sorry I make so much trouble, Emily . . ."

"Sshh, it's all right, Mamigon. It's just that you don't know how to let people who care for you do things for you. And I'm going to say something and I don't want you to get angry: Please stop worrying about being naked in front of me in these circumstances. They could have killed you last night; you could have been dead all this time and, really, what difference would it have made if I had ever seen you naked. You're alive and you are going to live. The only price you seem to be paying is that a strange man, the doctor, and a good friend, a woman, have seen your nakedness. Come now, Mamigon, is that too high a price?"

"You have words for everything, Emily. I keep quiet from now on and do as you say, OK?"

She leaned down and kissed his forehead. "If the bleeding doesn't stop I'll call the doctor, but I don't think you tore any of the stitches."

The bleeding did stop. She replaced the bloody bandages before they dried to the wound. There wasn't a murmur from Mamigon. Then she picked out some clothes from her closet and announced she would be going to the eleven o'clock Mass if Mamigon didn't mind being alone for about an hour. He waved his hand in acceptance. Mamigon heard her making her ablutions in the hall bathroom, and she returned to the bedroom looking radiant in a smart black frock. Mamigon was fascinated by the sound he had heard from the bathroom.

"Excuse, please, but I hear running water in bathroom and it sound like shower. Could it be?"

"Why . . . yes, what of it?"

"You mean you have shower bath in your own home?"

"Of course, Mamigon. I pay twenty-four dollars a month for this apartment. What do you expect? Don't you have a shower bath?"

"No. I have tub. I take shower Saturday nights in place near Dudley Station. I have shower yesterday before I meet you. Tell me, Emily, how long did it take to heat up water? It take me half hour to heat tank at my place."

"My goodness, Mamigon, I don't have to heat up the water. It is always hot from a tank in the basement of this building. You poor man, you must be living in a cold-water flat . . ."

"How do you keep water from spilling all over floor when you take shower?"

"The tub has a curtain. Look, when you're able to get up and around, you'll be able to see for yourself. Now, you get some rest and I'll see about feeding you when I get back from church. See you later," she said, giving him a peck on the forehead again.

Mamigon awoke to find her sitting in the chair next to the bed, looking at him. "Well, sleeping beauty, I'm glad to see you back in the world again. Feel OK?"

He nodded, looking at her smiling face and held out his arms toward her. She went to him and was engulfed in a long embrace, her smooth face pressed against his stubbly cheek. Neither let go and Emily finally moved her knees off the floor and stretched out beside him on top of the covers. Mamigon began rubbing her back, gently, and they began kissing. They were warming up when Emily murmured that he wasn't well and should lie still. He didn't respond to that; his arms tightened about her. She murmured something about food; he didn't let go, kissing her with greater fervor. She began squirming to break his hold. He held her captive until she whispered she wanted to take her dress off before it got all wrinkled. He let her go. Emily pulled her dress off over her head and came back to him in her slip, kicking off her shoes. Mamigon shook his head, tugging at her slip. She stepped back, turned her back, unsnapped her stockings from her garterbelt, and came back to him, still in her slip. He held the covers open for her to get in. She squealed as she snuggled up to him and they held on to each other, Mamigon rubbing her back again. He noticed that the throbbing of the wound abated as the blood in his body shifted its concentration elsewhere.

"It not fair that I naked and you are dressed," he muttered in her ear. That was all she needed. Under the covers, with much movement and with some assistance from him, she squirmed out of her underclothing.

"Mamigon, I . . . I . . . haven't done this before. I . . . it might . . ."

For answer, he covered her body with his and silenced her with a long kiss, their lower organs rubbing against each other on the outside. They went at it in this manner for about five minutes, her tension growing rapidly until her eyes closed, her teeth ground, and she finally let out a long, low moan, her hips moving violently. "Put it in, put it in, I need you." She was gasping. Mamigon, who was straddling her legs, slipped between them and gently sought entrance in the wet orifice. She burst into renewed frenzy, moaning as she climaxed again. Despite her shoving motions to engulf his member, Mamigon held back. He didn't want to end the experience with sudden, deep pain for her. He had never forgotten his clumsy, inexperienced efforts on his wedding night with his child bride, and also Guzell's guttural screams when the Kurd had ended her virginity.

"Please . . . please . . . Mamigon . . . please . . . if you love me . . ."

Mamigon still held back as she gyrated and heaved under him, resulting in two more explosions for her, his member now at the hymen, but not pushing. Even there, she was tight, a combination of her unused vagina and his size. He had no trouble holding back his own release; he had always been able to exhaust Ahgavni and Guzell, not climaxing for as long as two or three hours, if necessary. She experienced one long climax, finally, her moans easing into sighs and she seemed to collapse, her face now drained of color. Mamigon broke off and held her close, stroking her hair, perspiration gleaming on her brow and covering her body. She fell asleep in his arms. Mamigon felt at peace with the world, but was suffering mightily as his cut began throbbing with double vigor.

"Am I going to be pregnant?" was the first thing she said when she opened her eyes three hours later, smiling at him.

He grinned back, shaking his head. "I did not leave you with seed." Mamigon didn't know American words of endearment for women, so he resorted to German as the closest foreign word she might understand: "*Mein Liebling,* I didn't break your *Jungfernschaft.*"

She gasped and laughed: "You mean all of that happened to me and I'm still not a fallen woman? I'll have to teach you English so I won't be guessing at what you're saying in German."

He kissed her and they began to warm up when she suddenly sat up, covering her breasts, and announced she was ravenously hungry and would get them something to eat. "Close your eyes until I put something on," she commanded.

Emily was in her slip and slippers when she returned from the kitchen with a cup of chicken broth and two ham sandwiches on a tray for him. She wouldn't let him sit up, but propped him halfway to spoon him the broth. Then she returned with her own tray of broth and a sandwich and they munched in silence.

She collected the trays, returned, sat on the edge of the bed with her back to Mamigon, pulled off her slip, and crept under the covers again, warming herself against him.

"I didn't hurt you, did I?"

She kissed him and gave him an extra squeeze. "I didn't realize how wonderful sex could be. I was brought up very strictly, you know, and my mother constantly warned me about being a bad girl and how terrible boys were. Boys became men, and I never really separated the two. I've had suitors, Mamigon, but I think I scared them away because I was more educated than they were, and I wouldn't let them kiss me."

"Why did you let me?"

"I was really at the point in my life where I had shifted from hope in finding the right man to resignation as an old maiden lady. Then, about a year ago, I saw you unloading your truck in the alley, saw your big, strong body carrying those boxes like playthings, and I wondered what kind of a person you were. Frankly, I had naughty daydreams about you, Mamigon. I've really 'known' you for a long time. Then, that incident with the police. I liked you instantly because you were so direct and yet . . . so quiet . . ."

"You think I am right man?"

"Yes, Mamigon, from the moment I realized you had old country manners and you didn't look at me as if you were undressing me . . . as most men seem to do."

"I am only truck driver. You are schoolteacher . . ." He pronounced teacher as if it were spelled "titcher."

"In this country, that sort of thing doesn't matter. It's who you are that counts."

Mamigon thought she was convincing herself about that, but he let it go. He kissed her at length, his hand cupping a breast, gently massaging the nipple a certain way to erect his member, not that he needed any excitement. She rolled over on top of him and began a rapid rocking motion, trying to force him into her, forgetting his wounded backside. Mamigon gently did a reverse roll, and he was on top again, between her welcoming legs. It was the same series, all over again: First on the outside, climax; outer entry, climax; desperation moves on her part to gorge her crotch with him, climax, climax, climax, climax . . . then total collapse on her part. Mamigon still had held back. He found it took most of his will power not to break into her, in response to her craving movements, her pleas, her warm wetness. She was curled up on her side now, her bottom fitting into his lap, with allowance made for his tumescence fitting across her vulva. When her breathing became quietly regular in sleep, Mamigon carefully moved to the edge of the bed, brought his knees to the floor without rousing her, and stood up, using his left leg for leverage. He found the bathroom in the hall and took time to examine the wonders of a shower tub. He crawled painfully back into bed, assumed the cradle position with her and fell asleep, too.

He was awakened by the tender ministrations of a warm bathcloth on his private parts. She was in a bathrobe.

"I took a shower and I thought you would like to be cleaned up a bit. I didn't think you would allow me to sponge you down if you'd been asked."

Mamigon was surprised at himself: He wasn't embarrassed; in fact, he liked the attention she was giving him. What a woman! Were all American women like Emily? He smiled at her. She had him turn over and washed his back, changed his bandage, and covered him. She sat in the chair and they looked at each other for several minutes before words were necessary.

"Technically, I'm still a virgin, is that right, Mamigon?"

"Yes. You would feel pain and there would be blood if you lose . . . virgin?"

"Virginity." She smiled. "I don't know how Father Mulvaney is going to take it when I tell him."

"Tell . . . ? Tell Father?"

"I'm a Catholic, Mamigon, and I have to confess my sins to my priest."

"You have to tell him you were naked with a man?"

"Of course. After all these years, I'm afraid the good Father is going to be in for a real shock."

"Why you have to tell him about nakedness? I make confession to my priest, too. All we have to say in Armenian church is 'I have sinned' and priest asks for God's forgiveness. It is private business between me and my God."

"This is private, too, Mamigon. You only tell the priest. He never tells anyone else. He has to know so that he can decide what one must do to atone for the sin. We pay different prices for different sins. We call it doing penance." She was enjoying his puzzlement.

"But, priest is man."

"He's God's man on earth. I have some shame when I make my confessions."

Mamigon shook his head. "I felt I was wrong in my passion with you. Now I know I wrong. I hope you forgive me."

"Oh, for goodness sake, what an idiot you are. You have more inhibitions about life than my maiden aunt in Chicago. Keep talking like that and I won't ever kiss you again."

It was Mamigon's turn to grin. "That is big price that I no pay now."

27 &. PLOTTING

"Enver, I'm going to send you home. You are an incompetent bungler."

Enver Dash shrugged his shoulders, looking at the Sheraz on the floor.

"It's impossible for me to believe that the two of you could not dispatch one unarmed man."

"Excellency, you know he is not an ordinary man."

"Camel shit! The reason he escaped was simply because neither of you had heart, that's all."

"I wounded him badly, sir. He was on the ground when I left. The police were everywhere."

"Why didn't you finish him?"

"I don't know that I didn't. I couldn't wait around to do anything more. Before Ali and I even got to him, a policeman was blowing his whistle . . ."

"Well, be certain that you didn't kill him. One of my acquaintances has a policeman friend who said the attempted robbery victim was only slightly cut. So, you didn't even hurt him badly, as you claim."

"Please, your Excellency, please. This man must have a genie for a friend. He has escaped every time any of us have got close to him. I wonder why there was nothing in the newspapers about Ali?"

"I had great hopes for him," Tallal said in a softer voice. "He shouldn't have died the way he did, bleeding to death in a gutter in a foreign land. We can't claim his body, of course. There would be too many explanations."

"You'd think the police would have told the newspaper people about him to see if he could be identified."

"Enver, the one thing you don't seem to realize in 1923 Boston is that people like us, with names that are not English and with Mediterranean looks, are considered foreigners, even if we are citizens. Ali Souroglu certainly had the 'foreign' look, and our man Mamigon has the look as well as a name to go with it."

"So, we are considered foreigners. What has that to do with the newspapers?"

Tallal smiled, indulgently. "Foreigners here in Boston are treated the same way the Irish are treated—like camel shit. If one Irishman kills another Irishman, the newspapers don't bother to report it unless a landed Bostonian is involved. The same treatment is extended to anyone who looks Mediterranean. Ali's death would mean nothing to the people who read Boston newspapers. Thus, the papers don't print it."

"I guess the Americans are treating us the same way we treat infidels in our own country."

"Not quite. They insult us by ignoring us, treating us as less than human."

"Exactly, Excellency . . . the same way we treat infidels in our country."

"Shut your dumb mouth, you unschooled donkey. What you don't understand makes you unfit for conversation. Now, what am I going to do? Give you one more chance to redeem yourself or send you packing back to a job in Yosghat cleaning stables?"

"It may take more than one more chance, your Excellency, and I am willing to try as many times as it takes to kill that big pile of swill."

"Good, good, that is what I was hoping to hear from you—a little dedication and enthusiasm. All right, where is he now?"

"He's holed up with that red-headed whore at her place for the past four days, ever since they carried him there."

"He hasn't left at all?"

"No. His truck has been sitting where it was down the street, exactly where he left it last Saturday. I marked the front tire and the curb, and it's never been moved."

"Then we must assume he has not left her place because he is recovering from the wound you gave him. I'm sure he would have gone to work if he could have."

"She's been going and coming, but I don't know if she has a job or not. And I don't know if there is anyone else living at her place. Twice, she has brought bundles of food from the store, and that's all."

"I've a plan for you, Enver, a plan that can't fail, unless you botch it once again. Now, tell me honestly, do you think you inflicted more than a flesh wound?"

It was an uncomfortable moment for Enver Dash because he knew, from vivid, stark memory that he couldn't have even scratched Mamigon as the big man fought him off that night. He admitted to Tallal that that could very likely be the case. Tallal scowled.

"All right, good. We know that flesh wounds take no more than four or five days to heal. I predict that Mamigon will be driving his truck away some time between today and Saturday, no later. This is what you will do . . ."

"I think I go home tonight, Emily."

"Tomorrow's Friday, Mamigon, and you might as well stay here until Saturday, when I'll walk you to the doctor's office. You know Saturday is the day he said he would remove the stitches."

"Emily, you can see I'm OK now. I walk, I sit, I stand, I put on my own clothes, I . . ."

"All right, go, if you want to leave so badly. Go ahead, go . . ."

"Please, *mein Liebling*, why you so angry, so quickly? I only go to stop being big bother to you."

"You're no bother. You just want to be reassured that I want you to stay. You are such a dumbbell. Don't you have any idea by now how much I care for you, how much I like you . . . how much I love you?"

"I care for you too, very, very much, Emily. But you know this not way for two grown people to act. You know what we are doing is wrong. I know it is great wonder, great feeling, great liking, great what-you-say, love."

"Mamigon, you look like a big, wild animal, a savage, to me, but you are the most gentle, most thoughtful, most considerate human being I've ever known. But you are so full of it, sometimes. Why can't you accept life as it is without creating so many obstacles to your happiness and to mine?"

"What you mean, 'full of it'?"

"I mean you are up to your ears, almost drowning in your sense of what is right and what is wrong."

"Do you have sense of right and wrong?"

"Mamigon, I've thrown away thirty years through what I thought was right and wrong. Now, I've invested my senses, my thoughts, my very soul, in you. I've given you my total self to do with as you please. Do you know why . . . ? I thought you didn't. I'll tell you why: You've awakened the true woman in me. You've made me recognize true feelings—no, not only of the body—but who I really am. I revel in it because I trust the person who has awakened me and who is holding my heart in his big hands. You caught me as I was about to slip into the abyss of self-righteous goodness and purity. I would have become the hypocrite that one becomes when life passes by and its joys are the specters of what might have been. No, you big dumbhead, I don't have any sense of wrong anymore. I just know, I am certain, that what I am doing now is the *rightest* thing I've ever done."

Mamigon was sitting in the chair next to the bed where the conversation had started. She had settled on the corner of the bed and was staring into his solemn face, waiting for his reaction to her storm of words. She finally had to say, "Well?"

"Emily, you know I want to stay here. But you know I must go, too. All right, I stay until Saturday. Would you like to go to Piscopo's for supper Saturday night?"

"Only if you bring a gun along to match my police whistle. How did you like that whistle, incidentally? I've carried it for about ten years and last

Saturday was the only time I used it. You know, when I blew on it the first time nothing happened other than a big puff of bits of thread and dust." She was laughing in the way that gave Mamigon a start of pleasure. She was beautiful, no doubt about it, fit for the harem of any sultan. The outburst of sexual activity Sunday afternoon had leveled off. She had insisted he keep the bed for the night to pillow the bandaged backside. She slept on the sofa in the front room and in the morning made a breakfast for him of orange juice, four fried eggs, a batch of sausages, and a pot of coffee, and told him to stay put until she returned from work. He didn't have the heart to tell her he never ate breakfast. But he ate everything and slept through the day until Emily returned in midafternoon with two bags of groceries. She changed his bandage as evening approached, took off her schoolteacher dress, shoes and stockings, and was under the covers with him "just to warm up a bit," she had said. It was a repeat of Sunday, with two sessions interrupted by food. It was the same timetable on Tuesday and Wednesday, the removal of her working dress becoming the signal for what she explained to Mamigon was "intercourse" or "copulation"—words, she said, that were exciting but academic for her until now.

Emily hadn't been able to get her school clothes off Thursday evening before Mamigon had started the conversation about going home.

"That police whistle could have saved my life, you know, Emily. I owe you so much I no know where to start the counting. I have money in my pants. Did you find it?"

"Yes, it's on the dresser. You were carrying more than two hundred dollars on you, Mamigon. I counted it . . . I hope you don't mind. Why do you carry so much on you? That's about a month's pay for me."

"That's all the money I have, Emily. I need money when I drive truck. Sometimes I must pay C.O.D. at wholesale house where my customer has no credit. Anyway, I no have place to leave money at home. I carry around."

"You shouldn't carry all you have. If you are robbed, you won't have a cent."

"I no carry all that anymore. I leave half with you to take care of all the money you spend on me."

She turned white. "You keep your money, you big swellhead. I didn't do a thing for you that I expected money for, and . . ."

"I know that. You know that. That is why sharing the money is right." He caught her by the wrist and pulled her onto his lap, wincing slightly at the pressure on his wound. He kissed her hard and kept it up to prevent her from talking. She finally relaxed in his arms, only to suggest more comfortable "attire" and bed.

"Do you think you could be a swell guy and go all the way this time?"

"Go where?" He understood before he finished asking. "I no want to talk about that, please."

"I'll make you do it, Mamigon. I'll make you . . ." She was face to face with him, pressing against him as they stretched out on their sides. She wiggled upward until her breasts were covering his face and swung her nipples back and forth across it. He averted them with little success and managed to mutter something about "breasts are for babies." She didn't relent and he took a nipple and used his teeth to bite and nibble gently. Emily squealed and positioned the other one for similar treatment. The nascent desire for more was denied as Emily wiggled back to his face to kiss him with new abandon and then move her face to his bullet-scarred chest, surprisingly sparse of hair, where she nibbled on his pectoral protuberances. It was Mamigon's turn to move his hips with desire, but she would not be deterred from licking his chest, his navel and then his flat, hard belly. She moved closer and closer to his pubic hairs and, when her cheek first touched his erect member, he firmly pulled her back, turned on top of her, and started what, for Emily, ended after about an hour as a total ataractic.

Mamigon held her tightly after her moans and sighs abated. She had almost screamed at him, constrained by her constant fear that neighbors would hear, when he had deftly foiled her attempts to make him go in "all the way." She didn't fall asleep this time.

"Don't men need to relieve themselves? I've read about reproduction and you are supposed to ejaculate . . . spit out semen . . . seed, as you say. You . . . you haven't, have you?"

She *would* have to bring that up! Its articulation forced him to face up to another inhibition he had not been able to overcome: Ejaculating in the presence of this American woman outside of her body. It would be crude, sloppy, totally embarrassing. He wasn't about to indulge himself even though he had successfully overcome his aversion to being naked in her presence. In fact, he found a certain amount of pleasure in walking around in the buff, totally reassured by Emily's own growing immodesty—she had gone to the bathroom naked once—coupled with her words of affection and her ingenuous glee at the sight and feel of his massive chest and narrow hips. He hadn't realized until Emily that a powerful male physique was attractive to the female.

"I can't do it."

"Do you mean you are unable or simply you won't?"

"I no want to do it."

"Oh, Mamigon . . . why not?"

"I no want . . . I don't want to say."

"Please tell me, talk to me."

"I not sure I can . . ."

"I've been completely yours, Mamigon. I have no secrets from you. Why can't you be the same with me?"

"All right. I am . . . afraid . . . that not right . . . I am in shame."

"Shame? What are you ashamed of?"

"You know. I no . . . I feel shame if I make seed in front of you. I dirty your bed."

"Oh, you big dummy, you overgrown boy, you . . ."

"Please, you no . . . don't fun with me, I . . ."

"I'm sorry. I wasn't poking fun at you. I'm just relieved, that's all. You are so complicated, Mamigon. I wonder if all men are like you."

"You not . . . you are not like other women, Emily. I know only two other women in my life this way. My child wife and Turkish girl I married. The mother of my dead children in old country never move or make sound when I . . . do this with her. Guzell open my eyes to woman's feelings, needs, but we had little time to know each other well before she die . . ."

"Did you love them?"

"I want to die when Tallal kill my bride. She everything to me, my life, my children. She trust me, she like me. I now kill for her. She not like me for that if she alive, but she is not here anymore to stop me. Turkish girl, Guzell, like me, too. She trust me, give herself to me, and I marry her, but she die. I no say . . . I don't want to tell you how."

Emily felt a bit left out by his recitation and could only hug him and hold him without words. After a while, they put on their clothes—Mamigon in a pair of pajamas she had bought for him—had something to eat silently, and gravitated back to the bedroom and bed.

Emily thought that what had been happening between them since he was carried into her apartment was what happened during honeymoons. Neither could get enough of the other's body. This time, Mamigon was surprised when he felt her hand on his member—the first time she had ever touched it.

"I have been ashamed of something, too, Mamigon."

"Tell me, Emily. Have no shame with me."

"Look who's talking about not having shame. I . . . I, oh, I can't say it."

"Tell me, trust me. I like . . . I love you, Emily, *mein Liebling*."

"I want to kiss you there." She squeezed it to let him know what she meant.

He closed his eyes, unable to look at her. It was Guzell all over again and he had not been able to accept it. Guzell's ferocity and unswerving determination had accomplished it, however. He didn't say anything. He couldn't find it in him to expose himself further as being boylike. Emily moved with hesitation at first, finally touched him there with her lips, before he jerked her back and mounted her.

It was the same sensuous, soaring, searching series of climaxes for Emily. But this time, as she began her final, overwhelming climax, her right hand left his back to grope under the covers and push a bath cloth into his hand. As her hips sank into repose, he covered himself with the cloth and, shortly, his breath whistled through his distended nostrils. She was fascinated by the pulsing of his organ, which she touched to see what was happening. It seemed to pulse forever. He sagged over, next to her, a small smile on his face.

They fell asleep and did not awake until morning light. The narrowness of the single bed had not bothered them during the night, the first night they slept together. Their legs were entangled and his arm was still under her head. Emily pulled back as they kissed, and announced she would be hopelessly "dead" in the classroom if they did what they wanted to do again.

Friday was a repetition of the day before and Saturday morning started off, and ended, with Mamigon using a succession of four bath cloths. Emily showered first, then removed his bandage and he took his first shower after a week of sponge-downs. After breakfast they left the apartment for the doctor's office, she in a tweed suit-dress, he in his former Sunday best, sewn together both in the rear of his pants and the flap of his jacket.

The doctor removed the stitches from his backside which sported an inch-wide red welt paralleling the cheek line, pronounced Mamigon in good shape and took his two-dollar fee. The pair returned to the apartment, each with an armload of groceries.

"I hope the neighbors no talk about you, Emily."

She grinned at him as they sat in her front room—she called it a parlor—relaxing with coffee. "My neighbor downstairs is a seventy-two-year-old widow who's visited about once a month by her son. She's stone deaf, poor thing, and I get the feeling that her son visits with her only because he collects the rent from me. Other than that, I have no friends in the neighborhood. It's really funny, Mamigon, how people tend to shy away from schoolteachers. Maybe they think we know more than they do and would rather not find out, for sure."

"I like smart woman, Emily. Smart woman makes man smart man. She also save man from beating his chest too much . . . like big monkey. I am thinking of asking you to do me big favor."

"Anything, Mamigon, anything that I can do for you."

"I ask that, maybe, you make my English right. You make me speak in way you speak."

"Wonderful, wonderful, Mamigon. I've been going crazy wanting to correct you when you talk. I don't know how you were able to learn as much as you have, and it's pretty good except for the German construction you give most of your thoughts. All right, from now on I will interrupt you when you talk and try to correct your language, OK?"

"OK." They sat smiling at each other, a man and a woman in complete accord.

Piscopo's restaurant had a new front glass. After the effulgence and volubility of Piscopo's greetings subsided, Mamigon handed him eight dollars for the glazing before the two sat down. Emily eschewed lamb for pork chops, and she had to restrain her big companion when Piscopo refused to accept money for the meals. She literally pushed Mamigon away, leaned over the counter, and kissed the beaming Greek on the cheek.

"He sincerely wanted to do that, couldn't you see?" she said as she dragged Mamigon out the door. "He was happy to see you well again, that's all."

She tried to hold his hand as they walked. He pulled away with a jerk. "Please, Emily, not in public place . . ."

"Mamigon, you act as if I tried to take your clothes off. Really, it's done here as a simple sign of affection . . . love."

He shook his head and they went back to her street in silence. The sight of his truck made him announce that he would be going back home that evening.

"You will come up for a little while, won't you, dear? It's early yet, it's only seven o'clock."

"Sure, Emily, I am sad that I will be leaving you."

"I'm sad, too, Mamigon . . ." He swung his arm, held stiffly down, toward her and found her hand. When they reached the openness of the porch steps, he let go and followed her up to the apartment.

She made coffee and they talked about her school work; about how heavily most Irishmen drank; about her surprise at his lack of interest in alcohol; about his knowledge of Shakespeare—learned at the military academy in German through Goethe's translations; about his friend Tatios and his fourteen languages; about her great admiration for the president, Mr. Harding, whom everyone in and out of Washington seemed to like so much; and the vice president, Silent Cal, who, it was claimed, was silent in sixteen languages; talked about language idioms; and it was time to go, he said.

"Sweet sorrow there is, in parting," he said, first in German, then in the translation.

Emily hugged him mightily, laughing in delighted giggles. "Shakespeare wrote in English that 'Parting is such sweet sorrow,' but I don't know that I don't prefer the German construction better."

Mamigon shrugged at so much delight over "nothing" and gave her a long squeeze. He wanted to push her down and make love to her but he was ambivalent about it. He let the urge pass, kissed her at the doorway, and left. If he had looked back before she closed the door, he would have seen the tears in her eyes.

He walked to his truck, strolled around it to see if everything was intact and climbed into the high cab-over-engine seat. After setting the magneto on the wheel, he climbed down, cranked the handle twice to start the engine, got back in, and headed home.

One of the many "Washington Streets" in Boston was the one that connected Codman Square in Dorchester with Grove Hall in Roxbury, and Mamigon pooped along in his rattling Autocar, humming a Turkish jig for the first time since he left Yosghat. It was totally out of character for him, and he knew it . . . as it was out of character for him to be despoiling American virgins, he thought. He really hadn't "despoiled" her, though, since he hadn't really entered her . . . Cow dung! Who are you kidding, Mamigon? What the hell difference does it make how deep you go? The fact is, you had intercourse with her, you used her and you are clinging to technicalities and telling yourself how wonderful you are because you didn't "despoil" her. Cow dung, again! Just how much more could you have done with her, short of impregnating her? And parading around naked as if God hadn't intended you to keep covered. Hhmmm . . . neither the Bible nor the Koran said nakedness was bad . . . only that it covered original sin. Emily's was certainly original sin. She'd never been serviced before, that was certain. But, she helped level off and balance the guilt he had harbored when he had seduced Guzell. Guzell had been an *altipawtlah,* a machine gun, in breaking down his inhibitions. It hadn't seemed too horrendous, perhaps because everything had transpired, at first, under trees and sky . . . human nature seemed less gross in such settings. It was different, almost lascivious, in the bedroom. Emily had emulated Guzell in her breadth and scope of desire. It sure felt good to realize, once and for all, that he hadn't been taking advantage of his darling Guzell. And now, Emily, glorious Emily with all the trappings of education and upbringing and grace, and yet, no different than that slip of a woman reared in the hills of Anatolia when it came to her natural instincts. If only one could accept and be at ease under circumstances that demanded passivity from the male animal. Oh, well, time would . . . Damnation, watch out for those dogs!

He slammed both feet to the floorboard, the left hitting the clutch pedal, the right squashing the brake, to stop the truck. It was heading directly for three large dogs, two following one across the street—spotlighted suddenly in the glare of the truck's arc lamps.

The screaming of the rear tires as they grabbed cobblestones did not cover up the sound of the Luger as the pistol spat flames twice through the backlight of the truck cab and the smell of cordite permeated the air.

Both slugs winged harmlessly through the left-side opening of the cab, the aim radically deflected by the sudden stopping motion of the truck. The mouth of the pistol had jammed against the back of the window, the trigger squeezed accidentally. Someone had been riding in the body of the truck, waiting to kill the driver.

The truck came to a stop; the dogs ran off, unhurt; Mamigon slid out the side to the ground under the truck. Two legs appeared from the back of the truck as the gunman lowered himself from the platform. He made the mistake of trying to finish what he had started instead of running.

Mamigon yanked an 8-inch double-edged knife from between the floorboards and the cross braces where he had secreted it after the dynamiting incident.

In the few seconds it took the gunman to come out the back, jump down, and squat to see where Mamigon was, the huge knife was slicing across his knees. The gunman ran, howling, into the night. Mamigon didn't chase him, totally drained from the series of unexpected events. He sat on the running board for a minute until irate motorists impelled him to drive on home.

His mind was racing now. If he hadn't cared for dogs, he surely would have been a dead man now. What a fantastic coincidence! Perhaps he was meant to get Enver after all. He's had plenty of good shots at him . . . and missed every time. But, what cost! The gunman certainly wasn't lucky. It had to be Enver, the hapless knife wielder at Piscopo's, the pathetic trembler who knifed him that night in the Peabody coffeehouse. What made Enver so persistent, determined? He wondered if he should tell Emily about what happened. My God, Enver must have been sitting in his truck for hours waiting for him to leave Emily's place. Hours? How would he know what day, what time Mamigon would leave? He must have been sitting in the back for days. He would check when he brought the truck to the garage on Geneva Avenue.

When he pulled in, parked, and went to the back, he had his answer without climbing aboard. It smelled like a latrine. He'd have to clean it up before he could cart food in it, that's for sure. He walked, in deep reflection, to his flat and went to bed.

29 & DISCHARGE

"The plan was foolproof. Either I have been sending a fool on a man's errand or the Armenian leads a charmed life."

Enver rearranged his crutches and simply shook his head, saying nothing.

"That's it . . . that's all. It's ended. I'm not going to pursue this anymore. I'm done with you . . . and I'm done with Mamigon."

"What will you tell the government?"

"Fuck the government. I'll take care of that. When will you be able to walk without those things?"

"In about two or three days, the doctor says."

"Good. Next week, you'll be gone from here."

"Where . . . where are you sending me? Please, your Excellency, I've tried very hard to do your bidding. I . . ."

"Shut your big mouth, and stop sniveling. I've decided I no longer require your services. I don't want to worry about Mamigon seeing you or tracing you by chance to this place."

"Where are you sending me?"

"I've found a job for you at the fish pier unloading the fish trawlers. Here's the address and the man's name. I don't ever want to see you again, Enver."

30 & WORDS

Emily wanted to see where he lived. She had mentioned his place on several occasions during the past two months but he had never taken the hint. She gathered that Mamigon simply slept there, had his clothes washed downstairs in the Chinese laundry once a week—no starch, please—and ate one meal a day around the noon hour at the Bay State Lunch in the market district near Faneuil Hall. Every Saturday, without fail, they took supper at Piscopo's, and only once in the past two months—and that was only last week—had they succumbed to their pent up physical desires, sneaking up to her place at midnight after a Harold Lloyd comedy, *Safety Last*, the title requiring an explanation from Emily.

She was startled when she realized she had the recurring thought that the closer the relationship the less she seemed to know about him. Or, was it that the more she knew about him the less she realized she *did* know. The first time she saw him was more than a year ago when she had arrived home about four-thirty in the afternoon from school and caught a glimpse of him as she did the usual thing: open the curtains in the kitchen windows looking out over the back alley. Then she had realized one day that the truck always seemed to be there on Fridays, like clockwork, and she had begun to play the game of whether the truck would be there or not at four-thirty.

The size of the driver had not made an initial impression but as the weeks and months rolled by her attention began to focus on the driver rather than the truck. It had dawned on her eventually that when the delivery happened to be the last stop, the truckman would not drive off immediately. He would stand leaning on the tailgate and light up a cigarette, smoking about half of it in three minutes—she had timed it—staring downward, apparently deep in meditation. The cigarettes seemed more like fat toothpicks to her at first until she realized it was the hand, the huge hand and fingers holding the smokes, that made them look so ridiculously small.

The foreshortened view she had of him from her second floor vantage had not given her a true idea of his height or facial details—other than his mustache—until the day she had spoken up for him in the fracas with the policeman in the alley. He was *tall*. He was massive around the shoulders. He was terribly handsome in a dark way. His eyes were black and piercing, with lines at the temples that crinkled when he smiled on rare occasions.

It was Mamigon's voice, low and modulated with a timbre that had stirred her when she heard him for the first time that day. The tone of the voice, its quality, seemed to verge on the border of a suppressed laugh, a touch of humor, although his words and thoughts were rarely humorous. That was it!

Emily had begun to fantasize about him. She had watched for him after he had tossed her the box of candy, being careful to stay behind the new sheer curtains she had installed just for that purpose. She wondered what he would be like as a man friend. She realized that if it had not been for the brief encounter that day with the police she would probably not have developed a personal interest in the big truck driver. Now, she could recall his eyes, his voice, his easy, sure moves, and the slight limp that imparted a degree of mystery, of heroic deeds unstated.

Her fantasies were vague, at first. She would test his reaction at seeing her by chance . . . and he would smile broadly when they met. The setting was always ethereal at first but began to take more definition in successive "meetings." They met on a sidewalk, on a sidewalk in front of her place, on the piazza in front of her door, at her front door as she let him in, in her front room . . . she had stopped there. He had always smiled and she had smiled back. No words.

Then she began dragging him persistently into her own world, molding him to fit her tastes, ascribing to him her own cultural attainments and values. Her mental excursions into his world took sharper, clearer definition. He would be dressed in a handsomely tailored suit, complete with vest and a gold chain across his front that dangled the square silver medal of Phi Beta Kappa which he would absently pull out and twirl as he viewed the Winslow Homer collection at the Fine Arts Museum; or expound on the Egyptian treasures from the Valley of the Kings displayed in subtly foreboding splendor on the lower floor.

Or imagine herself decked out in evening gown and corsage at Symphony Hall—opened she remembered when she was seven years old—bathed in the music of Bach and Beethoven by the Boston Symphony, listening in rapt adoration later to his observations on the verve and attack of the orchestra in playing the Third Symphony in E Flat or the symbolism evoked through the elegant pianissimos of the Italian Concerto in F Major.

Or seated fifth row center at the Old Howard to catch the great actor, John Barrymore, emote and shape Macbeth to new and grander depths of tragedy, and relive the highlights later over coffee and cake as her escort repeated lines with his own interpretations.

Emily's fantasies had even taken Mamigon on long walks through the Public Gardens to admire the flowers and fauna, but those flights of fancy had not worked too well. But, was he any of these figments of her imagination? Could he be? Very probably not! But she had had her dreams and she had reveled in them.

Was he Catholic? Most of the darker Mediterranean types seemed to be, but this man with the funny name didn't quite fit the mold. His name didn't have an "i" or an "o" at the end of it. Come to think of it, she didn't know if Mamigon was a given or surname. My God, what if he were a Protestant? But, wait Miss Hartnett, what do *you* care what he is? Or do you? No, certainly not! He is a big mountain of a man who drives a truck. He seems to be interesting, that's all. After all, aren't truck drivers crude, coarse, uneducated, given to belching, toothpicking, and scratching? Aren't they given to wiping their noses on their sleeves, tracking up carpets with dirty boots, smelling peculiarly, and all in all, BOORS in capital letters? This big guy probably drank himself into a drunken stupor before or after he beat his wife and slept in his underwear.

Emily had straggled along with such thoughts and fantasies, never crossing the threshold of physical contact in her mind until the day she had invited him up for a cup of coffee and had pecked him on the cheek. She had been appalled afterwards at the spontaneity of her action and his ungainly retreat. Self-dismay would instantly slip to a smile at his awkwardness.

Mamigon, for a big man, seemed so shy and retiring, so quiet, yet so startlingly intelligent and totally unlike what her imagination had evolved for him.

Perhaps he *was* different from what she had imagined truck drivers to be. Perhaps he wouldn't paw at her body or tear off her clothes. She had a new picture now of the two of them together: first a close embrace, then a slow-motion removal of her clothes and . . . and . . . she had never been able to complete the picture. The whole thing was truly impossible to contemplate. She felt revulsion at herself at times when she thought of going *that far*.

She recalled Bryan Kelley, the handsome accountant whom she had been seeing for several months until he announced that he was going to Washington to take a job in some government statistical bureau. Bryan had made the rash assumption, without consulting her, that the friendship should be sealed for posterity with a good-bye introduction to her never-never land—a place he had yet to visit even on a digital foray. Her shock had been exceeded only by an unpremeditated and resounding slap to his jaw, followed by a punch to his midriff when he had suddenly materialized behind her in the kitchen, where she had gone to make tea, wearing *only* a broad, stupid grin.

After seeing Bryan in such total exposure—the first man she had ever seen thus—it had taken her uncounted months to regret that her action had been so violent and final. If only he had not approached her so unexpectedly, so crudely, so . . . if only he were back now . . . if only she had . . . He had been so nice, so undemanding, so . . . ah, so undemanding. That was it. Bryan had been totally acceptable as long as he had not acted the part of a male. Now, she had been having thoughts about this wild-looking "foreigner" who couldn't even speak the language properly and was certain to be twice as much the animal as Bryan had proved to be and certainly would be more like those primates she had viewed at the Franklin Park Zoo.

Her daydreams had become fairly specific by the time he was visiting with her. Yes, she would sleep with him if he wanted her. She would sleep with him and keep it quiet from her family and friends. He wasn't the kind of man her family or friends would be quick to accept, if to accept at all. After all, she was educated and had a good job. He was an immigrant and definitely "not one of us." But she was certain he was going to be her very last chance at some kind of real male-female relationship before she slipped into total spinsterhood, a word that made her shudder. So many in her family, especially back in the old country. No, sir, she was going to have her fling and to the devil with precepts, concepts, church, mother, the school committee, and her prissy friends who never went beyond the fantasy stage.

Emily had shocked her family when she had insisted on living alone. None in the family had dared state what they were alluding to. Emily was the tough one in the family. She had already broken some of the rules that governed the conduct of young, unmarried women in her day. She had learned carpentry from her father before he died when she was seventeen, and she had won a unique job as a saleswoman in, of all places, a hardware store when she had demonstrated to the owner that she knew better than he what the various tools were and how they should be used. She had worked her way through Boston Teachers College and remained in Boston when her mother had to move to Chicago to consolidate the family and its economics with her unmarried brother.

The terrifying event at Piscopo's that night had provided the opportunity she had hoped for. In retrospect, she had marveled at her forwardness with the man—slipping into bed beside him while he was patched up and ready to bleed at the drop of a bandage. She had gasped at the first sight of his bare body. Bryan had not prepared her for this. She had given little thought about a naked Mamigon and the fact Mamigon had skin as smooth as a baby's with delicate growths of black hair on his chest and calfs did not register much reaction. His pubic hairs were black, of course, and surprisingly silky to the touch. The one and only negative reaction to Mamigon was the first kiss they would exchange at any time. The smell of his Camels seemed to be entrapped in the foliage on his upper lip. But even that was offset by the lack of a stubble that had reddened her face when she had prolonged an embrace with Bryan or Joe Crowley, a previous friend.

She still marveled at his gentleness, his desire to please her, his control, his combination of little boy and powerful man. But the most marvelous development was her realization that he was a totally acceptable human being. It was difficult for her to remember that he was still "foreign-looking" to others, that he still spoke with an accent, that he still seemed outwardly like a rough-hewn truck driver, and that he certainly wasn't Irish, not even Black Irish.

She realized now that once Mamigon had recovered enough to leave her apartment, both had become skittish and wary of their liaison. Hang propriety, was Emily's initial reaction—it was the threat of losing her job if the school committee found out that made her less bold.

After their tryst following the Harold Lloyd movie that night, Mamigon left at dawn, hoping the neighborhood was asleep. Emily was still the technical virgin. Mamigon had made it plain that they would not take full pleasure until they were wed. But, she would not discuss marriage with him, she said, until the horrible business with Enver was resolved, one way or the other.

"It's out of my hands, Emily. Even if I was . . . were . . . (thank you) . . . to call the whole thing off, I have no idea what Enver will do. He hasn't moved against me since that night when I left you to go home. Maybe he's done with me."

"Would you end your vendetta if you knew he wasn't going to try anything more?"

"If it means that you will . . . would . . . (thank you) . . . marry me, of course, *mein Liebling.*" He preferred the German to the English word for darling.

She sighed. "Oh, Mamigon, what are we going to do? We can't get married until we know what's going to happen to us . . . and I feel uneasy about us coming here. I haven't mentioned it before but I can lose my job as a schoolteacher if the school committee finds out I'm having an affair with you—with a man."

He nodded. So . . . Americans weren't as free and easy as one would believe on the surface of things. They just did things a bit differently. It *was* wrong, what they were doing, and she would have to pay the consequences. He felt that Emily was trying not to hurt his feelings by not stating one more drawback to their relationship. If she married him, she would have to resign her job. It was a wonderful job and it would be a big shame to give it up unless the man was a good wage earner.

"Could . . . could we stay at your place some Saturday?"

"My place not fine . . . is not fine (thank you) and I ashame to take you there . . . am ashamed (thank you)."

"Mamigon, please. Is it more important to save you embarrassment than to have the shame ultimately fall on my head?"

That convinced him. "Let's go there as soon as we finish eating, OK?" Mamigon wondered if her heart had suddenly speeded up, as his had, the second he had mentioned going somewhere where they would be alone. Mamigon paid Piscopo—a benign Piscopo these days—the flat dollar-and-a-half he charged them no matter what they ate, and walked the four blocks to his truck which he had parked as far from Emily's street as possible.

"I am getting my car back next week, Emily. My friend, Tatios, has been able to buy one. We won't have to ride around in stupid truck anymore."

Emily hugged his arm. "Riding in your truck was fun the first few times, dear boy, but that big pile certainly wasn't meant for pleasure trips . . . I love you . . ." After the announcement by Mamigon, she didn't mind the cold wind whistling into the cab through the roll-down flaps that constituted the side "doors" to the compartment.

He parked the truck in the cavernous one hundred-vehicle garage and they walked the short block up the hill to the six-intersection, sprawling square known as Grove Hall, pushed open the building entrance door, and walked up a broad flight of oil-rubbed interior stairs to the first landing and his flat. He opened the double door and waved her in ahead of him into a large square foyer containing a round-topped Frigidaire.

"You look around first to satisfy yourself," he said quietly. "I no . . . I didn't make up the bed . . ."

She checked the first room on the left, a bedroom with a baby's crib in it; the second door on the left, the front room or parlor with a fireplace and a bay window overlooking the square; the door directly in the center, the bathroom; the first door on the right, the kitchen, with a table, a sofa, and a coal-burning stove with an oven and three gas burners; and the second door on the right, obviously a dining room with a fireplace converted into a bedroom with a plain dresser and a brass double bed. Except for the bed, it was neat as a pin.

She walked back to Mamigon, still standing in the foyer, took him by the hand and walked him to the kitchen, looking up at his face, whispering, "What in heaven's name is the matter with you? How could you believe in what you said to me about being ashamed? It's perfect. Mamigon, what's that funny looking little brass pot with the long handle?"

"I make Turkish coffee with it. It's called a *jazzveh*."

"Would you make some now for both of us? I've never tasted Turkish coffee."

"You will not like it, Emily—too strong, but that's good idea, I'll make some. First, I make a fire. It's cold in here."

He kindled wood in the bedroom fireplace, piled some anthracite over it, and then made the coffee, pouring the thick brew into two demitasses. It was the first time in his life he had made coffee for a woman. They sat at the table, still with their coats on, and sipped at the hot liquid, Emily making faces at first. By the time they were finished, the kitchen and bedroom had warmed up enough for them to take off their coats.

"I tole you . . . told you, you would not like it. Next time I'll make it with a little sugar for you." She didn't say anything but kept looking at him with wide, expressive eyes, and he didn't have to be asked. He took her hand and guided her into the greater warmth of the bedroom.

Sunday morning, he didn't have to get up at dawn. They luxuriated in the newly appreciated expanse of a double bed, doubly attractive now because the fire had gone out and the room was cold for a March day. She missed Mass for the first time in years and years. Emily asked him how old he was.

"Let's see, it's 1923 . . . I am thirty-five. Why?"

"Just curious, dear. You're five years older than I but I feel as if I've been reborn again and am only sixteen."

"Emily, you should know this: I was never ashamed to bring you here. I lied to hide something. I did not want to bring you to my bed until we were man and wife."

"I knew it had to be something like that the minute I stepped into your flat, dear boy. I wouldn't call this the Presidential Suite at the Statler, but it's very comfortable. How does one wash up here?"

He leaped out of bed, naked, trotted into the kitchen and lit the gas burner under the hot water coils for the big stand-up tank in the far corner of the room. Then he performed another first: He drew the hot water for her in the tub, carried her to it, bathed her as if she were one of his children, bundled her in his oversized terrycloth bath coat, and dried her tenderly on the bed. While she dressed, he used the same water to wash his body, and the two became irreproachable humans again, fully dressed, dignified. He had very little to eat in the flat, so they went out and ate at a Jewish delicatessen a block away and then he drove her within a block of her street.

Mamigon's business kept improving during this period, and he bought a second truck and hired a new driver.

The weeks slipped by into summer with hardly a variation in the weekend routine except that Emily cooked for them in his flat. They never visited her place together again. He taught her how to drive and she kept the car on her street, joining him only on weekends. No one knew, of course, about Emily. On a few occasions on a weekend when there had been knocks on his door, Mamigon had never answered. It would have been the end of his reputation in the Armenian community, he knew, if it were learned that he was entertaining a woman. Women were not playthings. They were meant to be housewives and mothers. Sex was not considered something to be enjoyed and, certainly, never out of wedlock. He had broken every taboo, and he grinned as he realized he didn't much care. Not anymore . . . not when there was such a creature as Emily around who loved him for everything he was . . . and wasn't.

Enver seemed to have faded as a nemesis in Mamigon's life, and he was inclined to leave it at that. He suggested marriage again. It was June, President Harding was planning his three-week trip to Alaska, Secretary Hoover was reviving the Commerce Department into a helpful adjunct for business, and the country was doing fine.

"Do you really believe it's all over between you and Enver?"

"I don't know what else to think, Emily. It's been six months now. I don't know whether he's even in the country, much less looking for me."

"All right, darling. What do you say if we wait until the end of the next school year. We can get married then and I'll be able to leave my job gracefully instead of walking out during the term."

"That's fine with me, Emily. And we can make plans to visit your family in Chicago, if you wish. I don't want them to worry about who your husband is and whether you are all right."

"That's thoughtful of you, dear. I'd prefer to go to Niagara Falls in New York."

"Anywhere you say, Em, just as long as you're happy."

31 ❧ FROM THE GRAVE

They talked about moving into one apartment right away to save money. It seemed like a good idea and her apartment was decided upon because it had central heating, hot water, and a shower bath, even though it cost eight dollars more a month than Mamigon's flat. She decided to go through the flat to see what should be moved and what thrown away. There wasn't much in the house except for the furniture.

"What are in these shopping bags?" She had pulled out two stuffed bags from the kitchen closet. They were both still in their bathrobes, having discussed their decision over breakfast.

"Oh . . ." he had to think. "Oh, those bags are the clothes and belongings of my . . . of Guzell's. Diggin Eksah collected them for me to go through. I just didn't have the heart, Em, and I forgot all about it. You know, it's been over a year, now."

"I think you ought to look through the stuff to see if there's anything you might want to save as a keepsake."

Half-heartedly, Mamigon began pulling things out, mostly clothes, when he came across two thick bundles, wrapped in newspapers with twine. They were Guzell's things. He tore open the first one: shoes, a cloche hat, stockings, underthings . . . all that she had possessed on earth pressed together in one package. What was in the other? He opened it: bloodied clothes, the blood black and caked on the white blouse and dark skirt—the clothes she had worn when the baby had been taken from her. My God! The police morgue must have sent them back to his house and he had not opened the package. What the hell was he supposed to do with the things? He was washed by a wave of sadness.

"What *is* it?" Emily had come back into the kitchen to see him with his head bowed, unmoving.

"They're the clothes she had on when she was killed, Em. I didn't throw them away."

Emily said nothing. She sifted through everything, putting aside this and that for possible keepsakes for him. "What's this?" she said, holding up a writing pad covered with scribblings in Turkish, Armenian, and English.

He stared at it. Guzell had been practicing, apparently. She had Mamigon's name in block print in three scripts, her name in like manner . . . and . . . *Tallal* spelled out over and over again with *Euphrates Export-Import Company, Ltd., Boston, Massachusetts, United States of America.* In three languages, President Harding, the vice president, the mayor, and the governor were also not neglected. She had practiced with every possible name including the residents of Sharon Street.

"Wonder what this means?" Mamigon asked, picking out immediately the one name that shouldn't have been there.

"I don't know. It's his name, all right. Why should she have used his name? You said he was dead."

"This has been in my house for over a year and my sadness kept me from finding out. First thing Monday, I'll see about this . . ."

"See about what, Mamigon?"

"Well, I'll want to find out if Tallal is really at this company, or was there, or where he is now. Don't you think it smart to find out so we'll know what might come from where?"

"Swell! The minute you get a line on Tallal, you'll be after him like gangbusters. I know more than you think I know about you, Mamigon. You did not come all the way to the United States because the ocean air was good for your health!"

They had their first fight. Mamigon was not about to relinquish his position as head of the house. If he wanted to pursue the matter, he would pursue it. No, it was not a violation of his promise to forget about his oath to kill. He wasn't suggesting that. Then why should he want to find out if he were still around? For his own peace of mind, that's why. He still looked over his shoulder at unexpected sounds or cars that followed his truck or auto too long. Why was it too much to ask to see if the Turk was in Boston? No, I'm not a liar, and I resent being called one. Of course, I won't do anything if he is still here. I am a man of my word, Miss Hartnett.

"*Miss Hartnett?*" She burst into laughter. "My, but you can become formal all of a sudden, you big horse."

"I'll show you what kind of a horse I am, Miss Hartnett," and with that, he picked her up off the floor. carried her to the bed, and fell on top of her.

Her fists beat a puny protest on his head and shoulders as he parted her robe and wiggled and shoved to get himself between her surprisingly strong, resisting legs. His weight proved too much for her and she tried to protect her vulnerability by pushing herself upward. He threw an arm under her head, stopped the movement with pressure on her shoulders, and jabbed at her sex with his probe. She went limp and lay still, not moving a muscle as he moved against her for several minutes, thrusting against her virginity. She was lubricating but did not provide a quiver of response. As it became evident to him, after nearly ten minutes of labial friction, that she had no intention of reciprocating, he stopped, covered his front quickly, and got off.

She didn't move from her position of forced surrender, her legs in a wide spread on the bed, her red pubic hair etching her cleft, her eyes sparkling defiance. "You're no better than a dirty Turk . . ."

"Dirty Turk?" His hand went back, palm open. He hesitated, then dropped it.

"Go ahead, hit me . . . That's the only thing you haven't done!" She was sitting up now, her neck extended, daring him.

"You are uncommon slut, Miss Hartnett. You make a trial of my manhood. I cry inside. I don't know who I am anymore. I attack your flesh and even think of hitting woman . . . woman I think I . . . love."

He didn't quite know whether he was more angry or more ashamed. Emily did nothing to abet his shame or anger. He couldn't believe the turn of events. Less than an hour ago, they were planning a life together. Now he was at a loss as to what to do: beg her forgiveness or throw her out. He was reluctant to test her anger. If she said anything else as devastating to him as her previous remark he was sure he would end their relationship.

Emily dropped her robe, calmly dressed in front of Mamigon and, without looking at him, asked if he would give her a ride home. He nodded, put on his clothes, and drove her to the front of her house without a word exchanged between them. She said good night, slammed the door, and went in.

The next morning, he went about his business as usual until he found a lull in the work at midmorning to look in the phone book for the number of Euphrates Export-Import Company. He was at the public phone outside the Bay State Lunch. Amid the drone of the wholesale market he asked for Mr. Tallal Kosmanli. Just one minute, please. I'll see if the general manager is in. Who shall I say is calling?"

A wave of blood surged to his brain as he hung the receiver back on the hook and steadied himself. Tallal! Alive! Alive!

He thought it over as he walked back to his truck, completely detached from his surroundings, awash with emotion. What should he do now? He was desperately and deeply despondent about Emily. He was afire with the thought of Tallal once again. Another thought glimmered briefly. She was probably right about his ultimate intentions. Should he succumb to his emotions . . . or should he make his peace with Emily and forget all about Tallal as he had promised her he would? Guilt dominated his thoughts when he thought of her. Mamigon, how could you have lost control like that? You spoiled everything. You did the unforgiveable. She'll never come back to you. You'll have to seek her out and beg her forgiveness. Beg her forgiveness! Does a man . . . ? His racing thoughts leaped illogically. Must tell Emily that Tallal is still alive. I'll wait for her on her front porch. She'll be . . . Good Lord! She'll spit in my face! The Turk's name would be anathema . . . The sight of me would be . . . I must tell somebody . . . If only Tatios was close by . . ."

The rest of the week was the same. Mamigon took no action whatever about Tallal. He wrestled the pros and cons of his vendetta, his word to Emily, his loss of Emily, his total indecision.

Saturday morning, he was knocking on Emily's door.

She opened the door halfway. "Yes?" Her face was expressionless.

"Can I talk to you?"

"*May* I talk to you. What about?"

"Thank you. May I talk to you about Tallal?"

"There is nothing to talk about, go 'way," and she shut the door, firmly.

He stood for a moment, staring at the white paint of the door, 6 inches from his nose, anger and shame flooding his senses. Then he turned slowly, and went down the stairs as softly as possible and out to the street. He would never, never, see her again, that's for sure, he thought. Who, in hell, did she think she was? To hell with her . . . By God, he would go ahead and do what he had to do with Tallal. To hell with her . . . good riddance. No woman had ever insulted him before . . . twice. Dirty Turk, eh? Slam the door in my face, eh? All right, Miss Hartnett, you'll never see me again, no . . . never.

He sat behind the wheel of his car, not starting it as new determination and decision brought back wild scenes of the past, pumping him up: his wife, raped and butchered in the dust of the street . . . his little children with their heads smashed in . . . Ardavast gasping out Tallal's name with his last breath. You almost forgot, Mamigon . . . you almost forgot. They're waiting in their grave for you to keep your vow . . . and he added Aram to the list, poor, misguided Aram . . . and darling Guzell . . . my darling Guzell . . .

32 ❧ THE END

Euphrates Export-Import was in a row of attached buildings on Boylston Street, near Park Square, facing Public Garden. It was a narrow, four-story, brick edifice that had no back entrance, as far as Mamigon could determine. He had limited his afternoon deliveries so that he could return downtown every day to check the building and Tallal's movements after work hours. His vantage was a park bench across the street, behind the tall castiron spiked fence of Public Garden.

On the Saturday Emily rejected him, Mamigon had checked other entrances to the building. None. Monday through Friday he determined that Tallal left at five o'clock on the button and walked to Park Square. The first time he saw the Turk he wasn't too sure it was him. Only the walk seemed familiar; but Mamigon made certain by standing in the stationery store next door to get a closer look when Tallal went by on Wednesday. It was Tallal, all right, the sonovabitch, with only a few more pounds on him and a slight puff to his face, mustache and all.

The next Monday, Mamigon positioned himself in Park Square. Tallal appeared on the far side, across the street from the statue of Lincoln in the square, and dodged cars as he crossed over, headed for the B & W bus station and the parking garage next to it.

On Tuesday, Mamigon went to the bus station waiting room to check the cars and occupants coming out of the garage. Tallal did not emerge. After a half hour, Mamigon went around the garage to Eliot Street and found another entrance/exit.

On Wednesday, he was unable to get close enough but he was still able to detect Tallal, in his black fedora, driving out of the garage and turning left, heading further downtown into Stuart Street. He was driving a black Buick coupe, the same car that had been in the alley when Mamigon had encountered the tobacco juice spitter. Mamigon watched the Buick as long as he could, moving along Stuart Street toward Atlantic Avenue and South Station . . . perhaps. He lost sight of it after the coupe crossed the crest of Tremont Street, where Stuart becomes Kneeland Street.

On Thursday, he stationed himself at the intersection of Harrison Avenue, the next block beyond Washington and Tremont. Tallal drove by, remaining on Kneeland, going under the tracks of the el until he reached Atlantic Avenue, where he could turn only to the left, still under the elevated structure.

On Friday, Mamigon mingled with the crowds of commuters at South Station to see if Tallal continued up Atlantic Avenue, or turned off to the right on Summer Street. Tallal drove straight ahead, under the elevated tracks.

On Saturday, Mamigon drove the length of Atlantic Avenue, under the elevated tracks and decided Tallal would be crossing the Charlestown Bridge over the Charles River to City Square in Charlestown. He'd wait for Tallal there on Monday.

He was sure Tallal would take Rutherford Avenue from City Square, and he proved to be correct Monday afternoon.

Tuesday, Mamigon was at the towering Schrafft's chocolate factory building to see if Tallal's car turned off Rutherford to cross the bridge over the Mystic River for Everett. He didn't spot the car.

He was at Sullivan Square, near the Schrafft building, again on Wednesday. This time, he saw the black Buick sail by, heading across the flat bridge on Broadway, and into Everett.

No question about it, now, in Mamigon's mind. Tallal was heading for Peabody. Thursday found Mamigon in his car on a side street, just off

Broadway at the Melrose-Malden-Saugus line to pick up Tallal's car, as he hoped it would be, getting on to Route 1, heading north.

He was right, again. He followed the coupe, with two or three cars intervening, until Tallal turned off to the right in South Lynnfield at Lynnfield Street. Mamigon didn't follow him. He turned around after a brief interval and went back home. He didn't want to be behind Tallal that long a time and run the risk of being noticed by the Turk.

On Friday, he missed him. The following Monday, he waited for the coupe at the first major intersection on Lynnfield Street, at Summit Street. The coupe turned left at the intersection. Mamigon waited until the car disappeared around a bend on Summit and followed. In six minutes he was at Forest Street, and the coupe was nowhere in sight.

Tallal had either stopped on Summit or had turned either left or right on Forest Street. He backtracked on Summit, a street with hardly a house on it. It was almost dark, but Mamigon made out the Buick parked in the gravel drive of a lonely house. He drove by and stopped his car out of sight of the house and walked back. When he made certain the car was Tallal's, he went back to his car and drove home. He needed to make a few plans, collect a few items before he confronted his erstwhile friend. He was so preoccupied in tracking down his old enemy he didn't notice he had picked up a tail on his last trip.

He made one final preparation. He retrieved his double-edged, 8-inch knife from beneath his truck, cleaning off the heavy grease and giving it a new edge.

It was now Wednesday, the second week in July, 1923, and Mamigon felt that if he didn't take care of Tallal now, once and for all, it wouldn't be because he hadn't tried. He drove his truck to work, as usual; worked through the day, as usual; drove to his garage, as usual; put on his patched suit, not as usual; stopped at the public showers for a bath and clean underclothes, not as usual; and then headed for Peabody and Tallal.

He surprised himself by thinking more about Emily than about the immediate task at hand. His preoccupation with tracking Tallal and finding him had softened the impact of Emily's insults—to the point that he was now convinced that his mission would help him get back into the good graces of his great love. Yes, he loved her beyond words. If only he could communicate that feeling without the need for words . . . words, he felt, he could not master nor muster in her presence.

He reached Tallal's street in a little over an hour. It was close to eight o'clock and it was getting dark. He stopped beyond sight of the house, walked to the gravel driveway, which he avoided, and crept carefully to the three-story frame building covered with gingerbread trim. There was a porch across the entire length of the front. There was a barnlike structure on the right side about 100 feet away. The front door had glass in the upper portion, curtained, with a light behind it. There was a light in a left corner room on the second floor in front. There was also a light at the back of the house on the first floor.

Mamigon went to the back of the house, treading carefully so as not to be heard or to kick some unseen object in the dark, alerting the inhabitants. He was able to look into a window in the rear. It was the kitchen, and it was empty. He wondered if Tallal was married, if he had any kids. That would complicate things, but the chances were he *was* married. He waited. He really hadn't thought the thing out, he realized now that he was so close to Tallal. A man in his late thirties ordinarily would be married and have children, too. Why hadn't he thought of that possibility? Damn. He waited. After a good hour, someone walked into the kitchen. It was Tallal, in a wine red dressing robe. And he was alone. Come to think of it, children would have made noise. It was too early for anyone to be in bed.

Tallal was sporting a light mustache, and his brown hair had receded on each side of his head, leaving a broad arrow of hair on top. Mamigon was fascinated at his own reaction to seeing the man he had hunted for over eight years with a passion that knew no quenching. He was almost without emotion now, simply looking at someone who was about to feel the consequences of some of his youthful, savage actions. Mamigon wondered how the man could look so ordinary, so innocent. He should have sprouted horns by this time. He should have had the look of the heartless snake he was. Mamigon couldn't work himself into the frenzy he had imagined he would experience when he met Tallal, the butcher.

Mamigon waited some more to see if anyone else came. Tallal was busy preparing something to eat. Good! A wife would certainly have done that for him. By God, the man was totally alone, he must be. He decided not to wait anymore.

He went up on the back stoop, tried the knob—it was locked—and smashed in the door with one kick. Tallal was standing near the table with a cup and saucer, his mouth agape, eyebrows arched, transfixed at the sudden crash and appearance of . . . of . . . the crazy blacksmith from Yosghat! Mamigon was standing about 10 feet away, a knife blade glittering below the clenched fist of his right hand.

"You have no soul so there is no need saying your prayers," Mamigon snarled, advancing a step.

"I am to die now without a chance?" Mamigon liked the fear he saw in Tallal's face.

"No. You *are* going to have a chance. The same chance you gave my wife and children and my mother and father and brothers. The same chance you gave the two you killed here . . . no more, no less. Is that enough of a chance?"

Tallal swallowed hard but didn't retreat as Mamigon took another step toward him. "It's been seven . . . eight years and we are in a new country. I haven't done anything wrong to you here. The Americans will hang you if you go through with this."

"You never did know the difference between right and wrong, did you, Tallal?" Mamigon had spat out the hated name. "You stand before me and say you never did anything wrong here. I guess, in a way, you're right. What you have been trying to do to me here is simple children's games compared to your savagery in the old country. Tell me just this: What made you hate me and mine so much that you had to kill and violate my family personally? Tell me, you bloodless shit from a maggot!"

Tallal's eyes shifted momentarily to the floor, then he looked back at Mamigon with a slight sneer playing around his mouth and nose.

"Because I knew you broke a dinner plate after my visits at your home and laughed because I was a lowly Turk."

So. That was it. That was the real, ultimate reason the Turks butchered the Armenians. They felt all along that their conquered subjects were really superior to them . . . the master felt inferior to his slave!

"You Turks are more stupid than I realized. Your poor, empty soul did not cringe from your brutality because you thought we wore two faces? You thought I despised you because you were a Turk? Do you think I would have been a friend of someone I despised?"

"All you Armenians are the same—hypocrites. You took me hunting with you because I was the son of a powerful magistrate, the son of the head of the vilayet. That's the only reason."

"I am glad, now, to know that I am not the only one who has a low opinion of you. Your own opinion of yourself is such that I would hate myself if I felt as you."

Tallal was still holding the cup and saucer but he had begun to inch toward the sink where a paring knife was visible. "You have no choice but to let me live, otherwise the Americans will kill you, too. Tell me, how did you find me? Who told you where I was?"

"A friend of mine told me, a friend you killed a year ago . . ."

"You . . . you waited a year to . . . ?"

"She came back from the grave to tell me."

Tallal laughed. "I know you're lying, you devious Armenian clod. You've been talking to our mutual friend Enver, that's who. So . . . he couldn't keep his mouth shut."

"Enver told me nothing."

"Sure, sure. Once I get rid of you, I'll have to go down to the pier and feed that donkey's ass to the fishes. I was hoping he'd get killed in the crash when he shot at you while you were driving the truck." With that, Tallal dived for the knife in the sink, the cup and saucer in his hands crashing through the window pane behind Mamigon's head.

Mamigon easily dodged the crockery and didn't move, allowing the Turk to grab the knife and square off against him. "I was hoping you would reach for that knife . . ."

Tallal lunged at him. Mamigon did a bullfighter's sidestep and slammed the back of his assailant's head as he guided the Turk's body past him with a leg hoist. As Tallal scrambled to his knees to get up, Mamigon caught his jaw with a knee, sending the man back to the floor again, against the wall, unconscious.

Mamigon sat down beside the inert form. He had the power of life and death over Tallal right now—a moment he thought he had lived for. He lit a Camel and gazed at Tallal. He noticed that the Turk was naked under his bathrobe and Aram's specialty flickered in his mind, bringing a grin to his face. That would "kill" Tallal more effectively than death itself—not being able to fuck! He banished the thought. With two quick flicks of his knife, blood flowed from long and short intersecting slashes on Tallal's forehead. He found no joy in what he had done.

He drove to Boston and Blue Hill Avenue and slept through the night. Early the next morning, he drove to Boston police headquarters on Berkeley Street, walked in and asked to see the chief. The chief wouldn't be in until ten o'clock. All right, he'll wait. He waited until noon and when he asked for the chief again, he was told the chief was too busy to see him. Why not the sergeant at the desk. Mamigon went to the desk sergeant.

"Yes, what can I do for yuh?"

"I cut up a Turk last night."

"Did you kill him?"

"No."

"Why did you cut him up?"

"He killed my wife and children in the old country."

The sergeant nodded. That made sense. "What do you want me . . . us to do?"

"Don't you want to arrest me? Hang me?"

"You didn't kill 'im, did you?"

"No."

"Go on, get out of here. You goddamn foreigners, that's all you do, go around sticking each other. As if we don't have anything better to do than to worry about you dagos."

Mamigon shook his head as he walked out. Well, he tried. These Americans weren't bad at all. They understood the eye for an eye custom. He went back home, changed his clothes, and went to work.

33 ⚭ GOSSIP

"It apparently happened sometime Wednesday night, as far as the coroner can make it. Ghastly."

The city editor of the *Peabody Daily Evening News* was being filled in by his police reporter, Joe Moriarity.

"What makes you say it wasn't meant to be murder?"

"Three things, Vin. The victim had a couple of heavy contusions on his head. The coroner is certain they were knockout blows meant to anesthetize the poor bastard. A cross was cut on his forehead, too.

"Then, the guy who did it—it had to be a guy—cauterized and covered the severed stump of the dead man's penis and balls with that gunk farmers use to stop the bleeding when they geld a horse or steer."

"What's the third thing?"

"That's the real weirdo part: He put the penis in Kosmanli's right palm and sewed the fingers shut over the cock. Can you beat that? Never heard of

such a thing. Everybody on the case believes the killer—the unwitting killer—wanted the guy to come to and find his own prick in his hand—with no
chance of it falling out. Boy, the killer must have been really sore at him
about something."

"And the victim . . . ?"

"Yeah, Kosmanli choked to death. The killer separated the scrotum from
the penis and stuffed it, balls and all, into the man's mouth while he was
knocked out.

"The coroner says the bloody sac slipped down and lodged in the throat,
choking the Turk to death."

"He choked to death on his own balls?"

"That's what the coroner says."

The city editor was shaking his head. "One helluva story but, goddammit,
we can't print those details. Give me a 'graph on it . . . he's a foreigner,
anyway."

The story appeared that afternoon under a one-column headline that
read:

PEABODY MAN, 38, CHOKES TO DEATH

The mutilated body of Tallal Kosmanli, 38,
general manager of a Boston importing company, was found yesterday in his home on Summit
Street, Peabody. His cleaning woman found the
body. He had been dead for three days, according to the Peabody police. The autopsy report
revealed Kosmanli had choked to death on a
piece of raw meat. Police are investigating. The
victim was a native of Turkey and had joined
the Boston firm in 1917. He leaves no known
kin. Police found two horses, almost mad with
thirst, unattended in a barn on the dead man's
property.

34 EUNUCHS

"No foolin', you don't know about Mr. Mamigon?"

"I think I do . . ." From the sound of Piscopo's voice, Emily wasn't too
sure. "What's there to know?"

Piscopo seemed to settle a little deeper into one of the hard chairs he
provided for his customers. For the past Saturdays, Emily had been coming
to his place without Mamigon to eat her meals. The second Saturday she

was there, Piscopo had stood by the table, chatting with her about nothing in particular but hoping she would reveal why the big truck driver wasn't with her. Piscopo had talked briefly to Mamigon each Wednesday when he delivered his meat and produce, but hadn't dare mention anything personal beyond how his injury was faring.

"You really don't know Mr. Mamigon is wanted by the law?" It was the third Saturday and Piscopo had been invited to sit down with her.

"I can't believe that. He's too easy to identify . . ."

"No, no, not by Americans. He is wanted dead or alive by the Turkish police, didn't you know that?"

"No, I didn't," she said defiantly, "and I don't believe you. He would have been extradited—sent back to Turkey if that were true."

"No, lady, Mr. Mamigon wanted for wartime crimes in old country. He big Armenian hero."

"A hero? Why do the Turks want him?"

"He killed hundreds of Turks in the old country."

"Mr. Piscopo, I happen to know that Mah . . . Mr. Mamigon was an officer in the Turkish army during the war. What are you trying to tell me?"

"I am telling you truth. It was during the Exile. Turks move all Armenians out of country—kick them out. They kill hundreds of thousands of them while they doing it. They kill everybody in Mamigon's family. Do terrible things to wife before they kill her. Man name Tallal, Turkish friend of Mamigon in army, kill her . . ."

"Oh . . . I knew that, Mr. Piscopo. But, I . . ."

"Listen, lady. He save hundreds of Armenian women. He take them to seacoast, put them on Greek boat. They escape to Athens where saved girls tell his story. He big hero. Story in Greek papers here maybe five years back."

"When did he kill all those Turks? Why should the police be after him?"

"He stay behind, lady. He do something special to every Turk he kill. Scare everybody in Turkish army while he look for Tallal."

"Something . . . special?"

"Yes. Mr. Mamigon become mad dog at way Turks treat his wife and many Armenian girls, ladies. You know what they do . . ." He rolled his eyes to the ceiling, not looking at Emily.

"What did Mr. Mamigon do? Mr. Piscopo, you tax me with your dramatics."

"Eh? Well, he make *eunouchos* of all men he kill . . . you know."

"You mean . . . eunuchs? He dis . . ."

"Yes, lady. He cut it off and put in right hand of dead man. It was his sign."

She almost spilled the coffee she was drinking, staring at the narrator. "You say he killed hundreds of soldiers and did that to them?"

"Sure, lady. He call them his *Eunouchos* of Hell. He say he join them in hell some day . . ."

"Do you know how he escaped?"

"No, nobody know. Everybody sure he kill Tallal first, then he escape to this country. Lady, he tell me nothing. He no know I know anything about him."

"Does anyone know whether he killed Tallal or not?"

"Everybody sure he never leave Turkey until Tallal dead, that for sure."

"What if he couldn't catch Tallal?"

"Then he never leave . . . or die trying, lady. You no know Mr. Mamigon. He man of steel. He no talk much but he know plenty, think plenty. He man of big honor."

"Yes . . . yes, I guess he is." Emily was sure, now, that calling Mamigon a "dirty Turk" was something he had taken very seriously. And shutting the door in his face was something you didn't do to a man like that. "Do . . . do you know what he's doing now? I haven't seen nor heard from him in three weeks, Mr. Piscopo."

"Oh, that too bad, lady. He good man. Did he say he not see you any more?"

"No, not exactly. I was . . . busy the last time he called on me to come here for supper. I haven't heard from him since."

"Lady, I see him every week. He deliver here. Next time I see him, I tell him you look for him, OK?"

"Oh, no, please don't do that, Mr. Piscopo. I'll get in touch with him."

On the fourth Saturday, Piscopo came right to her table and sat down, like a conspirator, his head leaning forward. "Mr. Mamigon no come, make me delivery to my place Wednesday. He give job to his friend, Carpenito. Carpenito say Mr. Mamigon tell him if he not back on job Thursday, business belong to Carpenito. I no hear from Carpenito or Mr. Mamigon since. You know anything?"

"I haven't heard a thing, either, Mr. Piscopo. I think I'll try and find out," she said, getting up. "I'll be back to let you know . . . and get something to eat. See you later."

She went out to Talbot Avenue, boarded a street car, transferred at Blue Hill Avenue for a Dudley Station car, got off at Grove Hall, and walked to his place. It had taken her over an hour to get there and it was close to eight o'clock but she couldn't see any lights in his flat. My God . . .

She ran up the flight of steps and knocked on his door. She knocked again, her heart hammering, before she heard movement. The door opened without the foyer light going on. Mamigon stood at the door for a second in his work overalls, then nodded without speaking.

"May I come in?"

"Sure." He stepped back, let her enter, and went ahead of her into the kitchen, where he turned on the light. He had been sitting in the dark, apparently.

"Are you all right?"

"Sure, why not?"

"I . . . I had to make sure, that's all."

"Sure, I'm OK. Are you all right?"

"Yes."

"Fine. We are both fine."

"Good . . . I'm sorry . . . I think I disturbed you. Do you want me to go?"

"Whatever you want to do, Miss Hartnett."

"All right, I'll go, but I know something's bothering you. Do you want to talk to me about it?"

"No."

"You are sure?"

"Yes."

"Please talk to me . . ."

"Why?"

"Because . . . because . . . because I care about you."

"I am dirty Turk. Why you care for . . . do you care for him?" He had grinned at the correction.

She took heart at his acceptance of the correction. "Please . . . talk to me." Her voice was low, soft, and pleading.

"Very good, Miss Hartnett, I . . ." He saw the look on her face. ". . . I mean Emily, I will tell you about Tallal but you will be, how do you say—disgusted?"

"You can tell me. I know what you've done."

"You know?"

"Of course I know, Mamigon. You went after Tallal and killed him." She was certain that that business with Carpenito had been part of his preparations in case the Turk killed *him*. "Well, didn't you?"

"Yes, I went after him, but I did not kill him."

"If you didn't kill him, what did you do?"

"I cut the sign of the cross on his forehead."

"That's all? What's to prevent him from coming after you again?"

"He will remember me every time he looks in the mirror to shave. And many women will stay away from him, thinking he is a holy man of some kind."

"I don't see how . . ."

"Emily, he knows now I could have killed, and I did not. He will respect that."

"Mamigon, I should be the last to bring this up, but what about the vow you made to your dead family?"

"Ah, I know."

"You decided not to . . ."

"Emily, I shoveled coal for nearly five years on a steamer. I had much time to think, to repent from some wild thoughts and deeds. I was not about to let Tallal go totally free so I did what I did. But I did something else that a Moslem who lives by the Book of Retaliation will never understand."

Emily was impressed by Mamigon's sudden vocal animation. He hadn't talked so much since his first efforts to extricate himself from her interest in him. "Please, go on."

"I heard Father Vasken preach it many times and had wiped it from my thoughts: The greatest, noblest vengeance is to forgive . . ."

Neither said anything more, the words of Father Vasken sinking deep. Then: "It's all over?"

"I am sure. I cut off his entusiasm . . . (thank you) . . . enthusiasm."

Emily couldn't control herself. She was laughing hard after she corrected him, putting her arms around him. "That's the best euphemism for that thing I've ever heard! I suppose you tagged him for future membership in your band of Eunuchs of Hell?"

Mamigon was thunderstruck, speechless. *How* could she know? Who has she been . . . "How do you know about these things, Miss Har . . . lady . . . Emily?"

She tilted her head upwards, her eyes closed, her lips tight, her eyebrows arched. "I'll never tell . . ."

"I'm not playing, Miss . . . Emily. If you have met someone that knows about me and Tallal in this country, you could be in peril."

"No, Mamigon, it's all right. No one seems to know that Tallal is here. I've only heard about what happened in Turkey, that's all, really, truly."

"You fought me about going after Tallal. I came to your home that Saturday to talk it over, but you . . . closed the door. I went ahead and did what I wanted to do."

"You said you wouldn't have to worry about Tallal because of what you did? Why, then, is there peril . . . danger . . . if I should know someone here who knows about Tallal and you?"

"I talked to Tallal, Emily. He thought Enver had told me where he was. He didn't believe me when I said no."

"He told you that?"

"Yes. He also mentioned a pier where Enver was."

"Well, what do you think? Would Tallal send this man after you again?"

"I think Tallal believes this Enver fellow talked to me. No, Tallal wouldn't trust him."

"I suppose you're going after this man, now." It was more a statement than a question.

"I don't know."

"How do you feel about killing a man, Mamigon?"

He looked at the floor a long time without answering. "It's not difficult when you're defending yourself—it's a natural reflex. It is not too difficult, either, when one is in a passion or rage as I was after everyone in my family was slaughtered, Em. In those days in the mountains and plains of my homeland, my only thought was not to let them kill me too easily. I was determined to get Tallal and take as many as possible with me to the gates of hell." He paused and looked at her. "It is very difficult for me to kill now. The fires are gone. When I finally learned where Tallal was, I was really a prisoner of my own ashes of hate. And I had a vow to my dead young wife. But, I couldn't kill Tallal. I think I killed him in a way he will remember until his dying day . . ."

Neither said anything for a long time. "I'll bet you haven't eaten a thing all day. Would you like to go to Piscopo's for dinner?"

He took her arm, shut the light, and they went to the garage for his car. On the way, she broke the silence. "I haven't seen you in the alley. I waited every day, thinking you might have changed your delivery day."

"I parked the truck outside the alley and used the front door. I . . ."

"I'm sorry, Mamigon. Are we friends again?"

"We never stopped being friends. We were friendly enemies for a while."

They walked into Piscopo's place with arm-waving greetings from the fat one, coupled with a surreptitious headshake from Emily not to give her away.

After they ate dinner, constantly interrupted by the proprietor, they went to his car and drove back to Grove Hall. He suggested she take the car and go home. She swallowed hard and wanted to know why? He hemmed and hawed and finally admitted that he needed a bath. She said she liked the way he smelled—all man—and wouldn't go anywhere except to his place. To stop his mutterings, she heated a pan of water and sponged him down to save the time it would take to heat up the tank. They jumped into bed but something was missing.

"You're remembering the last time we were here, aren't you?"

"Yes."

"We said some hard things to each other. I apologize."

"Yes, we did say some bad things. I did some bad things, too. I beg your pardon, Em."

"No need, darling. I want to tell you something. I was hoping you were angry enough to rape me . . . break my virginity . . ."

"Emily, I have tried and tried to tell you we should wait until we're married. Why won't you let it be?"

"Because I love you very much and want all of you now . . . not sometime in the future that may never be."

"May never be?"

"Mamigon, you might have died last Wednesday and I probably wouldn't have known about it, even today. Tell me, now, would you have wanted to leave me forever, guessing what might have been?"

Mamigon turned over on top of her. They were passionate and never had need to resort to foreplay in the months they had been together, and tonight was no different—with one major exception: After she had climaxed twice with his external ministrations, he positioned himself and pushed in a bit deeper than he had ever gone before. She let out a drawn "ooooooh." He sank his distended member even deeper and could feel her insides giving way. This time, she emitted a long "ohhh." He was as gentle as possible, taking more than two minutes to enter her completely, finally wrenching from her a long, drawn out grunt, ending in a deep moan. After some tentative movements on her part, he began thrusting with purpose, repeatedly pulling out and plunging back in, blood on his organ. Her groans diminished, replaced by an uninterrupted low singsong as her hips began to move.

It was one long orgasm for her, to be repeated innumerable times until her exhaustion was total. Mamigon cradled her and they slept through the noon hour the next day.

35 ❧ TEN GOOD MEN

"Tallal Bey was killed by a *bohglu Ermeni*."

"You know that?"

"I found out how he croaked from one of the drivers at the company."

"How did he die? Who killed him?"

Enver Dash looked slowly around at his audience in the coffeehouse, savoring the hush of expectation. He liked the attention he was getting.

"We cared little for him, but, after all, he was a countryman, a soldier of Islam, and a true believer. He shouldn't have died the way he did . . . and at the hands of an infidel, too."

"Come on, quit milking the goat and tell us. Did he die well? Who killed him? All we know is that he choked to death, eating."

"Eating . . . ? By Allah, you have it wrong!"

"Well, what, then?" Enver could see that his questioners were getting impatient.

"He choked to death on his own balls!"

It was too much for his listeners to grasp. They all stared, waiting.

"That is right. I am not making it up. That's what the newspaper was referring to when it said he choked on a piece of raw meat."

"You're full of *bohg* yourself. You're making it up."

"So be it, you stinking camels, believe me not, but I know what I am talking about. Want to hear the rest?" There was total assent.

"The killer cut off Tallal's donk and balls while he was still alive!" Everyone squirmed a bit, responding with the empathy usually felt by men when violence to the male privates is involved.

"The killer put the sac, balls and all, in Tallal's mouth and told him to eat it. Tallal cried and begged to stop the bleeding first, so the killer did. He wanted Tallal to live without his privates. He put that gunk we use when we geld horses and sheep on his wound. By this time, Tallal passed out. So, I . . . the killer slipped the balls into his mouth and his cock in his right hand. He found a sewing needle and thread and sewed up the hand so the cock wouldn't roll off. He choked on it before the killer left the house. That's where the newspaper got that camel shit about 'raw meat.' "

There was a deathly silence.

"Who told you all this?" It was Gugcel, the old army sergeant.

"I told you, it was . . ."

"No one could know that much detail unless he was there himself."

"I tell you, it . . ."

"Or, you made it all up . . ."

"I swear, I did not make up anything!"

"Then, you were there. Admit it!"

"No, I was not." Enver's voice had achieved that shrill quality.

"All right, then, who is the killer?"

"Were any of you around last December at the other coffeehouse when . . ."

"Never mind that—who is the killer, if you know?"

"I am going to tell you, wait! Remember when the coffeehouse was badly burned? Remember the big man who came in and told me he would be waiting for me outside?" There were murmurs of assent from several listeners. "Well, he's the killer, the man I've been talking about."

"I was not present when the place burned that night. Who is this man supposed to be?" Gugcel asked.

"He's that big *Ermeni* bastard the government chased all over Anatolia after he began mutilating the troops."

"I don't seem to recall. Mutilating the troops?"

"Right. He would kill our men from ambush, leading a small army of brigands, cut off the cocks of all the dead men and place them in their right palms. Ah . . . remember now?" Gugcel's face now had the light of recollection.

"That same cock licker, that same camel fucker, is in Boston right now. He got away from us in the old country after nearly killing Tallal once before."

Gugcel was hard to convince. "You sure you had nothing to do with Tallal's death?" Enver gulped. He knew he had let his mouth run away and he had said more than he should have. It had become the most difficult moment in his life. He had evened the score with that son of a dog and he wanted to crow about it. What a chance it had been. Losing Mamigon in the traffic, getting lost, finally guessing he might be going to Tallal's place, getting there too late but finding his tormenter naked and helpless. He had enjoyed every second of it, especially the screaming. He nodded in the negative to Gugcel. He didn't trust his voice.

"By Allah, Mamigon the Eunuch Maker!"

"Right. He called the men he killed and cut up his Eunuchs of Hell."

"That sonovabitch . . . that boy lover . . . that asshole licker . . ." The epithets came thick and fast as the men reacted to their frustration.

"Wait a minute, Enver. Why haven't the police seized this Mamigon? Isn't murder a crime here, too?"

"The police don't know about Mamigon. Only Tallal and I knew about him. There was one other who knew, too. Remember Ali Souroglu, the wrestler who worked at the company? He knew, and the *Ermeni* killed him only a few months ago. I tell you, men, he's after me right now . . ."

There was an uneasy murmur at this announcement.

"I tell you this, also. This Armenian has vowed to kill as many Turks as possible before he dies. You may be next . . ."

"Camel shit, Enver. Hey, Gugcel, tell us why this Armenian has this big hair across his ass?"

"Enver was in Tallal Bey's police troop. He knows why. The troop killed everybody in the Armenian's village. I heard that Tallal took the Armenian's wife before he killed her . . . killed his kids and his whole family . . . personally."

"No, jest, Enver? Is that true?"

"Yes . . ."

"Not only that, the story goes that Tallal was an army pal of the *Ermeni* and had broken bread and eaten salt in his house . . . got the Badge of Merit from the *Ghazi* himself at Gallipoli. I fought there, myself. A real ball-buster."

"What're you going to do, Enver?"

"I'm going to get him before he gets me, that's for sure."

"How're you going to manage that?"

"The same way I polished off a friend of his—I'm going to gut him."

"What're you talking about?"

Enver stood up and looked around at the score or so around the table. His pride was getting the best of his discretion. Keeping quiet about his triumph in the train station had been eating away at him. "Are we among friends here?" He lowered his voice. "I'm the one who did the killing in the train station six months ago."

"*You?*"

"Yes. He was a close friend of Tallal's killer. He was trying to track Tallal and spent much time in the coffeehouse that burned down . . . remember? A skinny man with a bushy head of hair? Yes, that's right . . . he found out about Tallal right here. I heard some of you talking to him. I followed him and got him before he could tell this Mamigon where Tallal was. Yeah, had to wipe out the trainman, too—caught me doing it. Now, I don't know how the big Armenian found out where Tallal was. The bad thing is, this man knows what I look like. I'm sure I'm next on his list."

"I'd hate to be in your boots with a guy like that after me . . ."

"Better watch out you don't have your own balls for breakfast . . ."

"Keep your legs crossed when you meet him, old horse . . ."

"Wear iron pants and put a lock on it . . ."

"That would give him away. His balls would clang when he walks . . ."

"Leave him alone, boys, he's in enough trouble . . ."

"You fatherless dogs! May the fleas of a thousand camels infest your short hairs!" The tears in Enver's eyes brought the ribbing to a halt. Gugcel spoke up.

"Maybe there's some way we can help you."

"I don't know how. It's my fight."

"It's his fight."

"But that infidel bastard needs to die."

"He's been killing us 'cause we're Turks, not because any of *us* did anything to him."

"That's right. Who the hell does he think he is, anyway, the devil's hand?"

"Why don't we get together on this. Most all of us served in the army back there, didn't we? Any officers here?"

Gugcel said he was a master sergeant in the foot brigades. No one outranked him, the *bash chowoosh*. Everyone now looked to Gugcel whose deportment underwent an instant change as he shifted from tannery worker to master sergeant.

"All right, men. I want ten volunteers—no cooks, bakers, or quartermasters—fighting men, who want to see this thing through."

It was easy to select the men, all suddenly with new light in their eyes, standing a little straighter, listing their former martial proficiencies to the cognizant old sergeant. They were all in their twenties, rugged, tested veterans of the hard-bitten, merciless rigors of service in the Turkish army about four years ago. Time had not made them flabby nor sapped them: the hard, physical work in America had kept them in shape.

Gugcel's new command, with Enver in tow, retired to a corner table to make plans.

36 &LUCK O' THE IRISH?

Emily Hartnett was Irish, through and through. She was going to take direct action and tie up the loose ends Mamigon had left dangling. It was not only his life, anymore. If she was going to give notice and quit her teaching job in the Boston schools, she was going to do it on the sound premise that Mamigon was going to be around in the years to come. She wasn't at all sure that Mamigon's conclusion that Tallal was all through was the correct one. One would think that what Mamigon had done to Tallal would only fan the flames of hate to a degree that even Mamigon's death couldn't quench, she thought. Well, she would find out for herself just how much of a "fixed" pussycat Tallal was now. It wouldn't do any good telling Mamigon what she was going to do; she would do it and get it over with. Her mother had always said it wasn't the "luck of the Irish, it was the pluck of the Irish" in the old country that saw them survive the perfidy of the English, the short potato harvests, the stink of sputtering peat in the hearth, and the vile whiskey distilled and drunk all year 'round to keep warm. She'd find out or her name wasn't Emily Katharine Mary Hartnett.

The Saturday after her reunion with Mamigon, she drove his car to Peabody, found City Hall closed, went to the police station, looked up Tallal Kosmanli's address in the city directory, got directions to Summit Street, and drove out to Tallal's house. It was deserted. A kitchen window was broken. The front and rear doors had small yellow paper signs stuck to the glass warning against trespassers, per order, Peabody Police Department. She wrestled with the thought of talking to the police about Tallal, thought better of it, and went to the newspaper office she had spotted in the square.

She went upstairs to the newsroom, asked to see the back files, and was shown the library—they called it the morgue—where she flipped back to the July Wednesday Mamigon said he had done his deed. She found the news item in the following Saturday edition. She was stunned. Tallal was dead. Mamigon had killed him, undoubtedly . . . no, the story said he had been mutilated . . . but had choked to death . . . ?

Later that day, when she went to Mamigon's flat, she suggested they take a walk to the zoo in Franklin Park. She realized he didn't like the idea of strolling about with a woman, but he agreed.

"I went to find Tallal today."

"I thought you might. Can I . . . May I ask why?"

"I wanted to clear up this business between you two, once and for all."

"And . . ."

"I couldn't talk to him, Mamigon. He's dead."

"Dead? When did he die? I only saw him . . ."

"He died the night you were with him."

He stopped in his tracks. "Emily, I swear to you I didn't kill him."

"I know, Mamigon, I know. He died by accident after you left him that night."

"By accident? How . . . ? What do you mean?"

"I can only guess from the newspaper account that after you left him, he tried to eat something and choked to death."

"Eat something? What are you talking about?"

"Well, the newspaper said he choked to death on raw meat. It must have been steak tartar or something like that."

Mamigon didn't break his stride this time. "Raw meat, huh?"

"That's all it said. I guess you really didn't hurt him too badly, Mamigon, if he had had an appetite afterwards . . ." She gave his arm a squeeze.

Her escort, suddenly busy watching the prancing of three handsome wapiti in their enclosure, muttered something inaudible.

"What was that, dear?"

"Nothing. I guess we don't have to worry about Tallal, anymore."

"No, darling, now we can get married . . . whenever you say."

That brightened his face and cleared the furrows from his forehead. "I suppose you've decided not to worry about this other fellow—Enver—for now."

"Yes, I've decided, Mamigon. Seven, eight years is long enough for a vendetta. It's almost as if you've been in prison. It's time you looked ahead instead of backward."

"You're absolutely right, Em."

They walked all the way to the elephant enclosure and the cages for the big cats before they returned to his flat, not exchanging another word.

The next week, on Friday, Emily was asked by her principal to carry final records to the School Committee offices downtown. It was around two-thirty when she was through with her errand, with nothing more to do for the rest of the day. She was on Beacon Hill, at Somerset and School Streets, when she realized that it was only a fifteen-minute walk to the market district where Mamigon was likely to be. Even if he had left on his deliveries, it was still a place she had been anxious to visit. She went down the hill past King's Chapel across Tremont and School Street to Washington, turned left and walked toward the Old State House past newspaper row where the *Boston Post* and the *Boston Globe* faced each other in two decrepit buildings; dodged traffic as she walked by the round inset in the pavement marking the site of the Boston Massacre; down another block to Faneuil Hall, past the Quincy Market stretching along South Market Street to Commercial Street. His truck should be here somewhere, she thought, if he were still around.

It was close to quitting time—everything shuts down in the market around 3:30—but the sight of her at the few places still open brought work to temporary standstills. Women were a rarity in the market district, and Emily's figure brought long, speculative stares and even a few whistles. The wholesale fruit house of Tekmejian Brothers was ready to close, but old Baron Tekmejian, startled and pleased that such a beauty would address him, told her he expected that Baron Mamigon was probably at the fish piers on Atlantic Avenue, where, he wasn't too sure. Maybe, Trovato & Trovato Company on T Wharf. He told her it was a good three blocks and directed her. Yes, Baron Mamigon had been called there for a late order—which was puzzling because Friday was practically over and most fish deliveries are made on Thursday.

As she walked hurriedly, still hoping to catch him, just to say hello, she knew he would be surprised to see her. She smiled a little at the quiet greeting she would get from him. He didn't go for public demonstration of affection.

Ah, there it was, just backing up to the dock, halfway down the pier, the only truck on T Wharf, about 400 yards away. There were two touring sedans parked farther down the pier that jutted into the waters of the harbor. She decided to stay where she was, at the mouth of the pier, until he was through loading. It wouldn't do to interrupt him in the middle of his work. Plenty of time to say hello when he drove out to stop before turning into Atlantic Avenue. It was remarkable, she thought, at how devoid the area was of people. For blocks and blocks, from where she stood on T Wharf on Atlantic Avenue, there were nothing but piers and warehouses and cold storage buildings. That was Atlantic Avenue—from the vicinity of Foster's Wharf to Lewis Wharf—until it became Commercial Street going toward Charlestown Bridge where the North End began, housing with teeming families of Italian immigrants. Running the entire length of the avenue between Rowe's Wharf and Commercial Wharf was a single railroad track, under the elevated train structure, spinning off spurs to the piers and wharfs. Every avenue, every pier and wharf, was paved in the granite cobblestones typical of Boston's downtown commercial streets.

Once the commercial houses closed for business by three or three-thirty—they opened every morning by three o'clock—the area was almost totally deserted, desolate—absolutely no pedestrians since there wasn't a retail store nor restaurant open within a thirty-minute walk. And there were no residences until the northern end, near the bridge.

Emily wondered how long Mamigon would be loading at the dock.

There were two consistent sounds associated with that section of town, one constant, the other periodic, which she soon realized. The constant sound was the high-pitched calls and screams of the gulls and albatross, wheeling and circling and diving on the water, coming to rest on the roofs of the waterfront buildings. The other was the mind-blanketing roar of the elevated trains—the subway trains—that emerged from their holes in the ground to hurtle across the massive iron trestles straddling many miles of Boston's main avenues, transforming them into shadowy caverns echoing to crescendos of rocketing sound when the train of cars trundled past. She could see the platform high up at the State Street station, without a passenger waiting for or getting off the infrequent trains. She wondered if he would be much longer. Hmmmm. What are all those men doing—piling out of those cars. They're carrying broom handles, it looks like . . . they're coming   this   way . . . no,   they're   heading   for   the truck . . . what . . . what!

Mamigon, who had leaped up to the loading dock and disappeared into the establishment, reappeared, backing up with someone pointing a heavy whaling harpoon at his chest. The man lunged. Mamigon grabbed the weapon and sidestepped his attacker, using the latter's hold on the harpoon to propel him into the back of his truck. Holding the harpoon at the ready, he leaped to the cobblestones of the pier to face the onrushing men from the cars.

Emily began to scream his name, cry his name, racing toward him.

There were ten men, all in nondescript clothing, carrying broom handles, all right, but the handles had long butcher knives strapped to the ends. Former *bash chowoosh* Gugcel had decided on this weaponry for two reasons: the weapons were silent and more of them at a time could be concentrated on the narrow target of one man.

Mamigon backed up the side of his truck to face them. The leader barked a command, and the group split into three, two groups of three "lancers" approaching from the sides; the center group of four approaching head on. The Armenian recognized the maneuver. There would be no escape. He had drilled men in the army in just such hand-to-hand encounters. If only he could say goodbye to Em . . . He could hear her . . . Hope they don't harm her.

"Kill me . . . Don't harm the American *hanum*," Mamigon hollered in Turkish, suddenly relaxing the hostile angle of his harpoon.

Gugcel raised his hand to halt the advance. The afternoon sun glinted on the vicious-looking knives. "We are soldiers of Islam. We do not kill helpless women. Only infidel dogs who . . ."

"Get on with it, you craven bastards." The Armenian spit in front of Gugcel. The old master sergeant didn't move, staring at Mamigon. Some of the Turks began closing in, but Gugcel held his arms out sideways, stopping them.

"Don't I know you . . . ?" Gugcel didn't seem too sure.

Mamigon felt the sudden easing of tension.

"You were at Gallipoli, weren't you . . . ?" Gugcel was still struggling.

"Yes, I'm ashamed to say. I fought for a country that disowned me."

"Now I know you!" Gugcel was grinning from ear to ear. "Stand back, men. This man is the *albay*, Magaros. He saved me and my men when we were trapped fighting the French back in 1914." The intervening years receded from the *bash chowoosh*. He stood at attention, in salute.

Mamigon's jaw slacked. Could this be the sergeant he had found with a handful of survivors in that bullet-ridden forward position? He couldn't remember the face at all. And he had elevated Mamigon's army rank to colonel.

"The *Ghazi* himself decorated this man," Gugcel shouted, still at salute. "Dismiss us, colonel, and begging your pardon, *effendi*."

Mamigon stepped away from the side of his truck, returned the salute, sheepishly, to release the sergeant . . . and grunted loudly as a harpoon slammed into his back.

"Death to the infidel whoremaster!" It was Enver Dash on the loading dock. He had gone back into the store, returned with another harpoon—fish store owners often decorated their walls with such relics—and thrown it into his back.

Mamigon staggered, his cap flying, his hands grappling behind him, trying to reach the haft of the heavy harpoon protruding from his back.

Gugcel took three quick steps forward and held his falling body, lowering Mamigon gently to the ground on his side. Then he carefully pulled the harpoon out. The hook had not penetrated.

Emily arrived almost at the same instant, out of breath, her voice muted as she repeatedly uttered his name.

Two of Gugcel's "troopers" jumped to the dock and grabbed the dancing Enver Dash.

"I . . . I hope you men are happy, now . . . now that you've . . . killed him." The agitated voice, the sobbing words had great effect on the onlookers, who shuffled and edged around, seeking relief from her fierce looks.

"We weren't going . . ."

"He was right. He always said you couldn't trust the Turks!"

"Ssh, *mein Liebling,* it's all right . . ."

"Mamigon!"

"Sssh. Stop that yelling . . ."

"Oh, my dearest, you're alive!" She put her hand under the hem of her dress and yanked on her slip to bring it down. She stepped out of it, folded it into a small square, and pressed it over the wound. "Please, someone, call a doctor, call an ambulance."

One of the men jumped to the dock to use the store phone.

"Where's the sergeant?" Gugcel leaned into Mamigon's line of vision. "Sergeant, no punishment to the man who disobeyed your orders . . . Who was it?" His words rasped at the strain of speaking.

"Yes sir, *albay*. It was Enver Dash, the *araba* driver whose life . . ."

"Good. Now, please go before the police get here. I'll tell them I was attacked by a bandit." The voice was weak, his breathing laboring under the trauma.

The Turk nodded, stepped back, and waved the men to the cars. "You are through, then, with Enver Dash, *albay*?"

"I was never after him, sergeant. He was after me at Tallal Kosmanli's bidding. He's a dumb kid . . . treat him gently."

"Yes, sir. He says you killed the Bey . . ."

"I did. I didn't mean to . . . Sergeant. He broke bread in my house and then killed my wife . . . my *babacks*. You know what the Holy Book says . . . but, I left Tallal alive . . . Allah took him."

Gugcel nodded, squeezed Mamigon's hand and ran to the waiting automobiles.

"What was that all about in Turkish . . . but you shouldn't be talking, dear." She tore her silk stocking on the cobblestones as she brought a thigh under his head for a cushion.

Mamigon closed his eyes, exhausted from his talk. "Did you give notice about quitting?"

"No, darling."

"Why not?"

"I've never been sure you weren't more interested in joining your goddamn Eunuchs in Hell."

"My, such language from the American *hanum,* the teacher of children."

"What's an . . . a . . . *hanum*?"

"Turkish for gracious lady."

"Thank you."

"Are you going to quit teaching?"

"Now I am."

"Why not before?"

"I found out you can't ever trust an Armenian."

Mamigon sighed deeply and resettled his head in her lap. Americans were a cheeky lot . . .

Epilogue
And then they lived . . .

1923

Eksah was in tears, trying to comfort her husband. Tatios was ashen, trying to smile through his tears. Mamigon wasn't showing a trace of emotion, a blank look on his face but his inner torment was evident through the working of his jaw. Emily was to one side, near the front door, her eyes red but dry at the moment.

Mamigon and Emily had returned from a two-week honeymoon trip to Chicago and the falls at Niagara and were now faced with the inevitable. They had driven to Manchester-by-the-Sea to bring little Mesrop home with them. A visit before the wedding and a telephone call on their return was not enough to allay the shock and grief Tatios and Eksah were feeling at the loss of the baby they had grown to consider their own.

It had been a difficult decision. The foster parents had assured Mamigon that they dearly, deeply, sincerely wanted to keep the little boy to grow up with Hagop and Mary. But they were equally sincere in offering back the boy to his rightful father. Emily was torn so much by the situation that she steadfastly refused to help Mamigon make up his mind about taking the boy away from what was an ideal environment for the child: loving "parents," compatible playmates, trees, grass, fresh air, ocean breezes, and, most of all, totally familiar and accepted surroundings. Mamigon and Emily were relative strangers.

Mamigon felt it was his duty to rear the boy and now that he was married, the opportunity was there and the time was not too late. Mesrop was only fourteen months old and would quickly forget his infant years.

Everything was packed and ready for Mamigon and Emily when they arrived the Saturday afternoon of a lovely August day to bring Mesrop to his new home. The children, Mary and Hagop, had been sent to the Sears mansion by arrangement after they said their good-byes, believing Mesrop to be going away only a few days. The baby's things were packed in the back seat, the farewells were said, Eksah hugged Mamigon and Emily and the child once more, and they drove away.

Mesrop began to whimper, then wail mightily as he watched Tatios and Eksah fade from his sight. He kicked and squirmed and cried and howled for almost a half hour before he snuggled up against Emily's breast and fell asleep. He was acclimated within a week, finding new wonders to explore in the apartment and loving the undivided attention he was now getting.

Taking custody of the child had been expected in the Armenian community. Everyone had been waiting for that development although there had been some who were certain the American woman Mamigon had married without warning would "not really care about Mesrop."

"Why should she bother with an Armenian boy?" Mamigon could almost hear the gossip on Sharon Street and West Brookline Street.

"She is a cold-blooded American with few emotions."

"Americans do not have the warm liver we have."

"She must have vamped him during a weak moment, poor, defenseless man."

"He made a mistake wedding a woman so different from us."

"With all those single Armenian women needing husbands he had to marry an alien, humph."

"Have you noticed, he is attracted by foreigners, first to that skinny Turkish girl and now to this old American schoolteacher."

"He could not wait a decent interval, for shame! The mother of his son has been dead only a year."

Mamigon and Emily would provide much pastime.

1934

Mamigon was a changed man. He was still quiet, not given to extravagant expressions nor the dribble of small talk, but he was sociable enough in the company of men and even laughed when the occasion forced him. He took his family on picnics in the woods of the Blue Hills, let the boy swim in Houghton's Pond under his careful eye even though he never went in himself because it was unthinkable for a grown man to be in that state of public undress. He had seen, out of the corner of his eyes, the young women with full breasts cavorting in the water on the beach and had marveled that such nudity was not illegal. But, live and let live, he had come to accept with the quiet grace of a reasonable man who would not dream of forcing his own concepts of propriety on anyone except those in his own family. He certainly wouldn't have allowed his wife to be seen in such nakedness in public and he was certain she wouldn't have wanted to. Emily had made all the difference in the world. They had become a devoted couple, as the world likes to say, in eleven years of marriage, each respecting the other and each seeming to know what the other was thinking even before a word was said.

It was now 1934, Franklin Roosevelt was in the White House trying to save the country with a new deal and Mamigon was trying to pay for another second-hand Autocar cab-over-engine truck he had bought through the unheard of arrangement called "time payments." Emily had advised him that it was better to leave his savings account untouched and use the bank's money to buy the vehicle.

Mesrop, the trauma of leaving Tatios and Eksah long forgotten, was all of twelve now and working on the truck Saturdays and school holidays as well as through the summer. Tatios and Eksah were his loving "uncle" and "aunt." Mary and Hagop were as close to him as ever.

1938

Things were prospering for Mamigon and Emily. He believed in volume to make a profit rather than charging all that the traffic would bear; and his integrity and rigid adherence to business earned for him more customers than he could handle with one truck. He had four now with a small warehouse in South Boston near the rail yards.

Emily had become his business manager. She provided the telephone, bookkeeping, and correspondence services that made his expressing firm efficient, reliable, and profitable. She had her own share of the profits, her own bank account, and had total sway over the once hard-eyed man whose only reason for living had been to kill his enemies without mercy.

It wasn't until his sixteenth year that Mesrop learned of his father's reputation. His "sister" Mary was getting married in an arrangement with a successful young man from Detroit and the clan from all over converged on Boston for the nuptials.

As the wedding day progressed, Mesrop noticed what to him seemed to be an inordinate amount of direct and indirect attention being paid his father. Why did it seem as if every handshake was hard and prolonged? Why did the greeters, almost to a man, tend to be or seem to be conspiratorial in the way they leaned toward the big man and whispered? And, why were there groups of two or more friends and relatives, at various times, holding long conversations with frequent glances or gestures in Mamigon's direction? Invariably, Mamigon would back away from a handshake and always shake his head, making consistent efforts to remain private.

Mesrop finally mentioned his puzzlement to one of his "cousins" from Philadelphia, Sabu, who had changed his name to Val Avery. You can't go on the American stage and become an accepted actor with a name like Sabu Megerditchian, he had announced one day with magnificent disregard for the pride Armenians have in their ancient names. His telling argument was that the name wouldn't fit on most marquees when he, inevitably, became a big star. He was the son of Aunty Ahrussyag, Tatios's older sister, the one who had saved him in the Syrian desert. Mesrop admired him for his verve and bombast, not to mention his wit.

"You really don't know about Baron Mamigon being wanted by the law, do you?"

"Ha, ha, ha. You're full o' bull. Baron Mamigon?"

"Yeah, Baron Mamigon." Sabu's jaw hardened. He wasn't used to being questioned. "Not only is he wanted dead or alive by the Turkish police, but he's also a genuine Armenian hero."

"A hero? Why do the Turks want him?"

"He killed hundreds of Turks in the old country . . . "

"Was he in the army?"

"What army? The Armenians didn't need an army. He did it all by himself. The Turks had killed his wife and kids and he took off after the Turks who did it and killed all he could find. But, here's the best thing . . ." Sabu pushed Mesrop a little to the side to give his next words more emphasis, unwittingly assuming the same air of conspiracy Mesrop had noticed before. "He cut off the cocks of every Turk he killed. Someone heard him say the dead men were his Eunuchs of Hell. What'd yuh think o' that?"

"What's a eunuch?"

"Crissake! You are dumb." Sabu was savoring the entire exchange. "That's a guy with his donk cut off. Hey, Armen," he called out to another cousin, Mesrop's favorite because he read books and didn't concentrate totally on girls and tits. "Mesrop didn't know what a eunuch was, har, har, har . . ."

"He didn't? OK, I give up. What's a eunuch?" The three laughed. Come to find out, Armen had also known about Baron Mamigon. What had been taboo as conversation in Mamigon's family apparently was common knowledge and talk in the Armenian community.

Armen unwittingly contributed the most devastating piece of information. "Yeah, the Turks followed him here and tried to kill him."

"What are you telling me? My father was hunted here?"

"Sure. That's the best part of it, huh, Val?"

"It would make *some* movie . . . fightin' off unknown, unseen attackers . . . beating the crap out of the ones he catches . . ." Val could see himself in all the parts.

"Yeah, and taking off after them when they kill his brother right here in Boston, and they almost nailed your Uncle Tatios. The poor guy was in the hospital with his guts hangin' out for almost a month." Armen had grabbed the story line.

"Geez, nobody told me any of this . . . Sure you ain't makin' it up?"

"Makin' it up? Do you think we would make up such a story about your ma?"

"My . . . ma?

"Yeah, your ma."

"What about my ma . . . ?"

"You know they killed her, too." The second he said it, Armen realized he was breaking brand-new ground and was about to make a killing.

Mesrop laughed out loud. "Yeah, I know all about it. I've known it all along." He had realized immediately this was something else he knew nothing about. Could it be that his real mother was someone he had never even heard of? But he wasn't going to learn about it this way. He changed the subject quickly. "But how come everybody knows about my father? I've never heard him talk about these things, not once."

Armen was sidetracked. "Heck, when he was attacked, he ended up in the hospital at least twice and everybody heard about it."

"What about the eunuch business? That happened in the old country, didn't it?"

"Sure," Sabu said, picking up the lead. "But he was written up in all the newspapers before we were born. He was hot stuff. My mother kept the Armenian papers that printed the stories about him." Sabu held the floor. "I got my ass kicked just this morning by my father because of Baron Mamigon. When all of us got here and were shaking hands, I asked him if he had killed any Turks lately."

"Holy cow, what happened?"

"Nothing much. Before Baron Mamigon could say anything, my father had me by the ear and was dragging me away. Boy, was I mad. My father tells me we ain't supposed to mention things like that in front of Baron Mamigon 'cause it ain't polite. Bullshit! He killed 'em, didn't he? That wasn't very polite as far as all those Turks were concerned, eh? I love the big guy, don't get me wrong. I just wanted to make a joke."

Mesrop realized, upon reflection, that something had been left unsaid, something about his mother that did not have the ring of untruth the way Armen had stated it. Anyway, he had needed this new dimension to help him understand the big, quiet man who seemed to be so distant most of the time. He looked at him with new respect, if that were possible. If only he felt comfortable enough to talk to him about his adventures. Well, maybe, some-day . . .

Mesrop saw a strange sight that day: Emily holding on to Mamigon's arm, closely, with her head resting on his shoulder—in public! She had tears in her eyes during most of the day and Mamigon did much remembering about his little "baby girl" wife he left on the Anatolian plateau, about his darling Guzell, and about Tatios, father of the bride today who was the most important person to Mamigon outside of his immediate family. Come to think of it, Tatios and Eksah were his only "family ties."

Mamigon had definite ideas about how a young man should comport himself in public and in private. There were strict rules about coversation. Mesrop was allowed only four basic answers unless given permission to speak: yes, sir; no, sir; no excuse, sir; I'll try, sir. The boy was also to address every older male as sir. He must never wear a hat in a home or building, never walk with his hand in his pockets, and hold doors open and chairs out for women and older persons. And, women had to be addressed as madam or miss.

The figure of the huge man, still slim and trim in his mid-forties, clad in his American uniform—blue denim overalls and cloth cap—became a famil-iar sight at the high school the boy attended. Mesrop was already nudging six feet and had all the promise of looking like his father, except for his eyes. They were Guzell's and he had become a heartthrob for many of the young, maturing girls.

Mamigon was constantly checking up on Mesrop to make certain the boy did not digress in any way when he claimed he had to stay after school hours. He would stop in when his deliveries brought him anywhere near the school. He would walk into the headmaster's office and ask to see his boy.

The very first time he did that, he had walked in on Mesrop going over galley proofs on the magazine he was helping to edit. Mamigon had been pleased and he said so. (Thank you, sir.)

The next time, the boy had been ordered, without ceremony, to put on his clothes and go out to the waiting truck. Mamigon had found Mesrop run-ning laps in the indoor gym in shorts, training for the track team. Frivolous! You were sent to school to study and learn, not to waste time running in circles and getting tired. (No excuse, sir.) Another time, he found him play-ing chess in a tourney against the team from Boston English. Playing games in school? Shame! (No excuse, sir.) Only the strong intercession of Mr. Alcieri, the chess coach, who spoke to Mamigon in Turkish, saved the boy from being booted out to the truck again. The coach had convinced him that the mental training provided by this acient Persian game would be of tremendous value to the boy. Mesrop came to the conclusion that it was really the Turkish that did it, because Mamigon would ask occasionally, with a touch of fondness in his voice: "And how is Professore Alcieri today?"

1939

But the school activity that made a deep impression on Mamigon was one he never knew anyone would teach or could teach—fencing. Mesrop had been thrilled watching Douglas Fairbanks, Jr., in a swashbuckling movie and joined the fencing club in school, keeping his fingers crossed that his father wouldn't show up and stop him. It was three years, in his senior year, before he was caught. In the meantime, he had become quite expert with the foil, épée and saber even though it bothered him that none of the participants ever looked like Fairbanks or Rathbone when they fenced.

Mesrop was waiting his turn with the épée when Mamigon suddenly appeared in the gymnasium. There was an instant hush because everyone knew what was about to happen. But Mamigon was transfixed by the action and walked over to the fencing master, Mr. Steele, and asked if he could watch, totally ignoring the boy. After about ten minutes, he asked Mr. Steele if his boy was any good at it. He's very good, about the best in all three weapons. Is this training for military action, Mamigon wanted to know. Oh, no, it is for physical fitness and sport, sir. Sport? In the old country I used that (he pointed to a saber) to kill my enemies. Have you had training in these, Steele asked. Mamigon shook his head. Steele looked at him for a moment, waved to Mesrop to come over, and told Mamigon that his boy could easily disarm him, no matter how or what he tried. Mamigon shook his head, but there was a new light in his eyes. Is there a chance I could hurt the boy, Mamigon said, looking over the torso-length padding Mesrop was wearing and the mesh mask he was carrying under his arm. You won't have a chance, I promise you . . .

Everyone stood by as the man of fifty-two and the boy of seventeen squared off in the en garde position, although Mamigon was holding his saber down toward his side, wearing no protection. Mr. Steele signaled to start and Mesrop began with a feint. Mamigon had not watched the fencers for nothing. He knew what the opening gambit was going to be and his saber whistled up and hit the extended blade with such force it snapped in two. Another saber was handed in. They started again but Mesrop held back this time, waiting for his father to attack first. Mamigon realized instantly that he didn't know what to do in a case like this when he wasn't being attacked. He really didn't want to slash at his boy but, the boy's supposed to be good . . . He took a measured swing at Mesrop. Mamigon's weapon went flying. They tried again, Mamigon now not being as gentle. He lost his weapon again on a double riposte. The next time he figured he would really deliver a blow but the act of bringing his weapon back for the swing was all that Mesrop needed. The point of his saber cleanly, lightly touched Mamigon's chest and was withdrawn before the whistling parry came.

Mamigon dropped his weapon and embraced the boy, tears in his eyes. "You could be the scourge of the Turks, my son. I am proud of you." He shook hands heartily with Mr. Steele and did the same with everyone of the twelve boys in the gym. Then he left, waving an arm, firmly convinced that America would be forever because it knew the value of education.

The boy may never have known of the love his aloof father had for him if it had not been for the honors the boy received during high school graduation exercises. The headmaster had called out his name as the "outstanding senior" because of his high marks and many extra school activities. As he made his self-conscious way to the stage to receive his honor, Mesrop was acutely embarrassed and secretly amazed when Mamigon stood up like a swarthy, brown old oak, all alone in a lea of turning faces, waving his cloth cap, shouting in a heavy stentor: "Hoe-ray! Hoe-ray! Hoe-ray!"

Unwittingly, Mamigon stole the limelight as his brief antics caused a low rumble of appreciative murmurs from the parental gathering.

Mesrop was admitted by Harvard College and worked nights at the *Boston Herald* as a copyboy to earn extra money. The regimen was arduous but suited him as it did his father who felt that an active young man needed as many distractions as possible to keep him out of mischief. The major complainant was Emily, who felt very strongly about not seeing Mesrop as often as she would like. In the back of her mind was the war in Europe and the aerial siege of England. She thanked God often that her son would not have to be fighting in it.

1941

At six o'clock in the morning, Mesrop sat with his mother and father at the breakfast table. It was time to say good-bye for a while. He was reporting to the naval receiving station and even though the family had a small gathering the night before, they were up to see him off. Emily was especially quiet. Mesrop noted that she was sitting at the table next to her husband this morning, a place she never had assumed in the past.

"You will write, won't you?"

"Every chance I get, Ma. Don't worry about anything. I'm just going somewhere to be trained to fly an airplane, that's all."

"Isn't flying dangerous? For the life of me, I can't imagine why you chose such a crazy way to serve."

"It isn't dangerous and it isn't crazy, Ma. I've wanted to be in the Navy ever since I can remember and I also wanted to fly. I can do both now. And, anyway, Ma, I look at it this way: If we should get into a war, I would prefer to be a specific target of the enemy instead of being killed by a shell fired off miles away that happens to fall on me. I think it's safer in an airplane, that's all. I think it's time to go, sir."

Everyone got up and Emily embraced the boy and cried. Mesrop had a paper bag with only toilet articles as specified in his orders. They didn't say another word as Mamigon drove his big truck to the fish piers at Boston Harbor where the naval station was situated, a big, old converted office building.

When Mesrop jumped out of the truck, Mamigon got out too, came around to where Mesrop was waiting to say good-bye. The boy was surprised when Mamigon put his arms around him and kissed him on the forehead. He was crying.

"Take care of yourself, my son, fight hard for your country, and don't let them kill you easily." He said it in Turkish, his mouth all twisted, unable to control himself.

Mesrop was embarrassed at the tears and the kiss. He had never seen his father like this . . . he had never kissed him before. He was also amazed that Mamigon had mentioned the possibility of death. The thought had never crossed his mind. We weren't at war, and hell, I'm not going to die. He guessed that, to Mamigon, going into the service meant war and death.

The boy put his arms around Mamigon suddenly, kissed his rough cheek, and ran into the building, crying for the big man who didn't know how to show love easily.

The Navy turned out to be no stranger to Mesrop—a world of discipline, no excuses and hard work, not unlike the world he had just left, the world of Mamigon. It wasn't too long before his inordinate level of innocence about women was quickly smelled out by the rest of the men and, of course, he was immediately referred to as "the passionate Turk."

Mamigon's precepts and concepts of conduct for a young man nearly got Mesrop thrown out of the Navy at one point. He was shooting some practice emergency landings in a horse pasture in Texas when his engine conked out and the plane crashed. He was close to the ground when it happened and his injuries were solely to his head, a wallop solid enough to disorient him for a while. The doctors treated him for a slight concussion and later released him to a Navy psychiatrist, as standard procedure, to see if the bang to the head had any deleterious side effects.

The psychiatrist was a white-haired little man, no more than 2 or 3 inches over 5 feet. Among the casual questions he asked was whether Mesrop was anxious to get back to his girl friend.

"I don't have a girl friend." He said it a bit too proudly because good boys just didn't have girl friends. The doctor must have missed the pride in his voice.

"You know what I mean, girls."

"I'm too busy studying and flying to have time for girls, sir." Boy, was he showing the doctor what a great guy he was, a credit to the Navy. The doctor perked up at this goody.

"You mean, you don't have relations with girls? You don't fuck?" Mesrop was not only surprised by the question but shocked and offended at use of the four-letter word.

"Of course, not . . . sir." He didn't feel like sirring him after he had used such language, lieutenant commander or no.

"Why not?" He was leaning forward when he asked.

"Because you don't go with a girl unless you are engaged to marry her." Mesrop knew he was overdoing it but Mamigon's precepts were to be upheld, dammit.

The poor man almost fell off his chair in, perhaps, delighted surprise and anticipation at what he had discovered lurking in the United States Navy.

"Don't you like girls?" he asked, softly, not looking at Mesrop.

"Of course I do," he said indignantly, "but my father made it quite plain that a good man doesn't fool around until the girl is spoken for and the guy is going to marry her . . . sir.

"Oh, yes, and only after I marry her do I take her to bed . . ."

Mesrop stopped because the doctor had raised his hand in a stop signal, a bit wearily. He shouldn't have laid it on so thick. He should have mentioned Lillian and Gina, the girls he had surreptitiously dated and kissed in high school. The boy was interviewed by a panel of doctors and finally cleared on the basis of Mesrop's description of his father's tenets and dictums.

Mesrop debated whether he should write to his father about these events and finally did, leaving out nothing. The answer he received did more to shed light on his father than anything yet.

Dear Son:

You must have no doubt now that you are in the world of men. This world is different from the world of a boy. As a boy you were not told what this new world would be like because boyhood is a special time. You were not taught anything about the world of women because it was not necessary. That type of learning is reserved for the time you will actually need to know, and it is something that cannot be taught without the teaching itself become vulgar and debasing. It is instinctive, the nature of man. Since you would not need such information until the day you are married and since your bride would also be innocent, then it would become a matter of both of you learning the secrets and joys and marvels of life together, the facts and feelings unfolding for each of you as one. This sort of learning is what binds a man and a woman together for life. It is something that cannot be examined on paper or tried casually in passing. If you do, you destroy the basis of future fidelity.

I will not say to you that the doctors in the Navy were wrong. I will say to you only that they have been persuaded by what they have learned from books and are ignoring their own common sense.

I hesitate to talk to you with such frankness but I think it is about the time: You are not a man simply because you have a penis that cocks at the thought or presence of a woman. You are a man if you cherish the woman with whom an intimate embrace is the end result of deep affection. Nothing more, nothing less.

There is no big secret or special knowledge about these intimate matters between man and woman. They are matters that should be employed and enjoyed privately. It should never be a matter of public conversation, unless a physician is required to correct or adjust what nature might have failed to form properly.

I do not know what else to tell you other than to say I am very much pleased you were able to write to me about something that must have been difficult for you to accept and talk about. I will not address myself to this type of subject again with you.

Your mother sends you her love and affection.

It wasn't signed, as usual. With less than eight hours of instruction he was told to take up his little Aeronca and land her solo. It is a nervous moment in any would-be pilot's life. Mesrop was full of doubts as he eased the throttle forward, wiggled the rudder and ailerons, taxied downwind, turned around, and took off. He made the four turns to the left in a perfect pattern, and let down for an easy tail-first landing, Navy style.

Mesrop wrote to Mamigon with great pride and exultation about his success at flying airplanes. The reply was not what he had expected.

Dear Son:
I am pleased that you are pleased with the way things are going for you in the Navy. I knew, from the day I saw you in the gymnasium and the way you handled a sword that you were going to be a man of excellent reflexes and control. But, do not be so praiseful of your accomplishments at this time. Remember, only a shallow man takes one step and lauds himself for the distance he has traveled.

Your mother is well and sends you her love. Learn your duties well so that you can serve your country well.

It was not signed and was written in Armenian, what Mamigon had learned from Eksah.

1942

He was a brand-new ensign when he cracked up his second Navy airplane. At 600 feet his engine conked out after taking off and the plane slammed into a corn field. He was able to walk away from it. The engine had thrown a piston.

His first baptism of fire was in the Battle of Midway, flying cover for torpedo bombers as the Navy pasted the Japanese fleet in one of the decisive victories of the war. He was landing after his third sortie when he experienced one of the worst things, short of painful death, that can happen to a pilot: His fighter jumped the crash barrier on landing when the arresting wire snapped and his airplane pancaked atop another plane about to take off, killing the pilot, a friend of his. Mesrop wasn't hurt physically, and the squadron leader made him go right up again to prevent him from dwelling on it. Mesrop wrote about it to his father, and eventually received this reply:

Dear Son:
You cannot influence or direct what has already been written as your fate or anyone else's. The Moslems call it *kismet*, which is a far better way of looking at things than our own outlook which we tend to call luck, good or bad. No, your friend was meant to die that way. He could not help being exactly where he was when he died, no more than you could have helped to strengthen the device that should have stopped your airplane. It was meant to be. The secret gnashing of teeth is a sign that you do not understand the verities of life and death. Stand up straight and do not concern yourself with things you cannot control.
You must be inwardly strong. Do not worry about that. You have more important things you should be concerned with now.
Your mother is well and sends her love. We are concerned about your Uncle Tatios who is very worried about Hagop with the Army in Europe. My very best to you, son, and continue to fight hard and well. I am proud of you.

It wasn't signed, as usual.

With each letter from his father, Mesrop began to realize that the man had an intellect that he had rarely worn on his sleeve. The contents of the missives had been a surprise, even though he knew, on reflection, that they shouldn't have been. The man had always seemed to go to the heart of things, whether with words or actions. Perhaps it was words on paper that helped to emphasize the man's true heights of perception and intelligence.

1943

It was in the Marianas that Mesrop lost his fourth airplane during what turned out to be fruitless efforts by the American Navy to soften up the Japanese defenses on Saipan from the sea and air before the Marines were to hit the beach.
On his sixth bombing and strafing run his engine suddenly quit. It may

have been a lucky hit by a soldier below firing at the airplane. While he still had air speed, he glided up as far as the plane's momentum would carry and then turned into a shallow glide to get as far away from the invasion fleet as possible. He brought his airplane upwind, wheels up, canopy open, and bellied into what looked like two-foot swells. Steam and spray arose in a mighty splash when the nacelle bit into the water and the plane slid to a quick stop. It was a good landing. He clambered out quickly onto the starboard wing with his raft, inflated it with a yank of the petcock, lowered his ass into it, and paddled away from the gurgling airplane. It went down in less than three minutes. He was picked up four hours later by an LST and brought back to the carrier fleet.

There was a long delay in the reply to his letter that described the crash landing off Saipan. When it arrived, Mesrop knew why.

> Dear Son:
>
> You lost your "brother" Hagop last week. He died in a hospital in North Africa after suffering some serious wounds in battle with the Germans. Needless to say, your mother and I are desolate for him and for your Uncle Tatios and Aunty Eksah. We all take comfort in the fact that his youth and innocence have given him certain entree to heaven and the company of angels. You are not to feel too sad, my son, other than to shed a tear for the future lack of company and support of a brother. He is beyond the trials of this earth now.
>
> Your own trials in the war convince me that modern warfare requires many different types of skills in order to survive. I was cheered considerably to learn that your unexpected landing on the water left you unhurt and ready for more combat with the enemy.
>
> Your mother is as well as can be expected in these times and sends you her love. If you can manage the time, son, please write to her also with a few comforting words about Hagop. She had come to love him. Her sadness at this time is increased by your absence and what she fears might happen.

1944

He shot down two Japanese fighters in one day during a brief, hot dogfight over Rabaul that lasted all of four minutes. He felt pretty good about it. He felt like a consummate warrior. At least, he kept telling himself that he felt pretty good. He really had a sense of relief that he wasn't the one whose plane had exploded as .50 caliber slugs stitched into it. He envied the guys around him who smoked and cracked jokes. He surely needed something that day and for days afterwards. So, he wrote his father, telling him about the air action and how badly he had felt about killing the Japanese pilots.

The reply was again in Armenian, with no signature.

Dear Son:

   I can understand completely your feelings about killing your
fellow man. It will never become easy or more acceptable with
each death you inflict, if you are a man of conscience.

   You have only one way to spread balm on your suffering
soul. You have to remember why you are doing what you do.
Remember who is your enemy. Your enemy attacked your
country, without warning, and killed thousands of your
countrymen before they were ready to die. That was bad.
They became your mortal enemy by that act and they are still
trying to kill.

   Ask yourself, would they have stopped killing if we had not
fought back? You must see that you have to kill them or be
killed. As an American, you have no choice but to defend
yourself or die.

   I do not pray to God for your safety, my son. The enemy
are also God's children and I cannot ask Him to make a choice
among His children in this terrible thing we call war. There
is no sanctity in it. I know about this all too well.

   Just don't let them kill you easily. I would gladly take your
place in battle but I am too old. The enemy would have no
trouble killing me. I hope I will be able to see your shining
face again before I die.

1945

   He lost his fifth and last Navy airplane in spectacular fashion. It was
shortly after the battle at Leyte Gulf and he was flying patrol with his
wingman, Hamilton. They had ranged into the Sea of Japan and were
ready to return when he spotted a small flotilla of ships through the spotty
cloud cover. It was a Japanese battleship, class unknown, surrounded by
four cruisers and a dozen destroyers. He radioed their position and course
and then the two went down to do a little damage.

   As Mesrop nosed over his airplane he saw Hamilton's bomb hit the
superstructure. Hamilton was pulling up when his airplane disappeared in
a blinding flash.

   Mesrop was boring in now. The split second when he released his bomb
was the instant something hit the starboard wing and the airplane jerked
ever so slightly, but enough to spoil the aim. The bomb exploded alongside
the ship as he pulled up and away, the entire flotilla now throwing everything they had at his airplane. He got away with his airplane peppered and
a small bleeding gash on the top of his head.

   He got back to the fleet, flashed his recognition signal and made his
approach to land on his carrier. He had forgotten about the ragged hole in
the wing. He began to lose altitude too fast and realized he wasn't going to
make the deck. He gunned the engine and inched the stick forward. The
engine coughed once and died. The airplane hit the carrier just below the

flight deck, the impact knocking him out. The guns on the Hellcat began chattering away as it fell backwards into the aft five-inch gun tub, flipped again and plopped into the wake, right side up and floating. He was picked up, more dead than alive.

When Mesrop came to nine days later he was aboard a hospital ship and completely encased in a plaster cast. He was broken up, so to speak—his ankles, knees, back, wrists, and jaw broken; his chest crushed, his nose smashed, and his back teeth gone.

At the San Diego Naval Hospital, his father's letter caught up with him. It had to be read to him by an Armenian WAVE by the name of Katcherian who could read the Indo-European script.

Dear Mesrop: ("How do you pronounce that . . . oh, I'm sorry, I forgot you can't talk with your jaw all wired up.")
    The Navy telegram told us you were alive and hurt badly. Your mother made me go to the Navy office to find out if you were going to die. I waited more than five hours until they found out that you would almost certainly recover. Since you are no longer engaged in combat I was able to go to church and ask God to make you well. Your mother insisted on going with me and she would not leave my side in the church portals. I relented, of course, due to the special circumstances. ("Hey, what kind of a crazy is he? What's he talking about?")
    I feel certain that you gave a good account of yourself before the enemy. I am certain because you did not let them kill you. The force of arms is a stupid way to settle matters of money and land but, once engaged in it, one must follow it to the bitter end, using any and all means to win.
    The Navy says they will not be able to use you any more. That means you will be coming home when you are well enough to walk. You will not feel sad, I hope, at the thought of leaving your comrades-in-arms before the battles are over. You have done your duty and done it well. Tatios Effendi is proud of you, as proud as I am, because you did your best. That is all any man can expect of another. So, do not feel badly about leaving the war to others to finish. I know you would have been glad to have died for your country.

"This guy is crazy, I'm sorry! That's all, sir, and there isn't any signature, nothing . . . who wrote this? I'll have to come back when you can talk. This guy is something!"

1946

Mamigon had certainly mellowed in the nearly four years Mesrop had been away to the wars. He was still driving one of his trucks. And, miracle of miracles, he was going to church services accompanied by Emily and sitting in a pew with her, although he insisted it be the very last pew. Parading down the aisle with Emily was not entirely proper.

It looked as if the war would end soon and Mesrop was making preparations to return to Harvard in another month when the semester began.

Coming back home in 1945 had been a sad time for him, in a way. The President had died in Warm Springs a month before Mesrop was released from active duty and his comrades were going to finish the war without him, by God, just when we had enough ships and airplanes to feel confident we were going to do it.

He was feeling fine, physically. His injuries had healed, on the whole, although he had a tendency to pass out on rare occasions from what the doctors said was caused by a "motor lapse" in his banged-up head. What had surprised the Navy was Mesrop's insistence that he would not accept any type of compensation or pension due to his naval service. He had had the word from Mamigon when the topic had come up in casual conversation.

"What's that word 'compensation' mean?"

"It's what the government is planning to pay me monthly for my war injuries."

"You mean the government pays you because you were hurt as a soldier?"

"Yes."

"Do they pay you if you are killed?"

"Yes. It's called insurance. The family gets $10,000 if the boy is killed or dies while in service."

"Hmmm. And, how much do they pay if you are hurt?"

"Oh, that depends on the disability—how unable you are to live and work properly."

"What does it pay?"

"Well, if you are completely disabled, you get as much as they paid you as a soldier or sailor. If you are half disabled, let's say, you get half your pay. The doctors decide that."

"How much would they pay you?"

"Full compensation, sir. They have me down as 'mentally and physically' disabled."

"My mother's *shawlwar!* You have the honor and privilege of fighting to protect your family, your land, your country from an enemy that wants to kill and then you *bazaar* for money if you are hurt doing what has to be done? I now worry about my adopted land."

"Please, sir, it is the law of the land. Congress has passed these laws to do what it can for its servicemen as a grateful nation."

"Cow dung, my boy. Are you so . . . what you say . . . disabled . . . that you cannot work at anything you want to do? Do you need help from your grateful country or are you simply a suckling at a sow's teat?"

"But, it's my right to collect this money. Everybody else is doing it. I'm also going to get money to pay my way through college from the government."

"You are not my son if you collect money from your government for having served honorably in the service."

Mesrop had thought that dictum over before he answered. "Very well, sir, but I feel I must accept the money they have for me to go to college. The college will not extend the scholarship as long as I have money due me from the government. Is that all right?"

"How much money for the college?"

"I've got about two more years to go and that means about $1,400."

Mamigon had pondered that figure before he nodded his assent. He patted Mesrop on the shoulder to let him know that there were no hard feelings. His hair was still coal black but his mustache was showing a little gray here and there as obeisance to his fifty-eight years. His hawk nose had become a bit more prominent but he was as straight and hard and powerful as he ever was.

Mesrop got his job back as copyboy on the *Herald* with his pay raised to seventeen dollars a week and he started his studies again. He had felt guilty about not being able to give Mamigon any assistance on the trucks. Working on the trucks as a boy and young man had given him a superb physique which the Navy said had saved his life, in the final analysis. Sometimes he longed for the simple work of loading and driving and unloading and then calling it a day without worrying about the job. On rare occasions, Mesrop found the time to drop around to his old haunts at the wholesale market in the shadow of the Custom House and Commercial Street, taking in the smells, the accents, the hustle and bustle.

He was out of one of his courses early on a cold Thursday in March and had three hours to kill before reporting to the *Herald* at five-thirty. A good time to fool around, he thought, and to hell with the research paper he was writing. The market. He would get off the subway at Scollay Square, walk to the market district in back of Faneuil Hall, look around, and then take the long walk to the *Herald* on Avery Street. He might just catch his father there if things were slow.

Mamigon was there, his truck parked in front of the Eknoian brothers' wholesale fruit and produce outlet on Commercial Street.

"What're you doing here, son?"

"Just thought I'd say hello, Boss (he called Mamigon boss from the days he worked on the trucks with him). I'm killin' some time before I have to go to work."

"Nice to see you. Can't put you to work. I'm waiting for last minute calls before I begin the run."

"Well, God be with you. I'll be on my way." Mesrop had made his farewell in Turkish, which he had picked up from Mamigon. He loved using what little he knew of the language.

Mamigon raised his hand. "Son, please don't address me in that tongue. Your mother tongue is English. Your heritage is Armenian and American."

Mesrop was taken aback. "You must hate the Turks very much . . ."

"I do not hate anymore, my son. I only distrust them. I always will."

"Boss, yuh know, I've heard my cousins in Worcester and Philadelphia say terrible things about the Turks, and . . ."

"That's only natural, Mesrop. They hear their elders tell of the horrible things that happened to them and their families in the old country. The children can't help but to assume the same mantle of despair that's translated into hate."

"Why did the Turks do it, Boss?"

"Son, they ruled us as a conquered Christian minority for nearly 900 years. When some of us asked for a political voice in the government, the Turks weren't ready for such democratic nonsense."

"Was that reason to kill us?"

"Son, for reasons too numerous to mention the Turks felt we were no longer to be trusted as loyal subjects because of the demands made on our behalf by the Russians, English, and French."

"So they killed us."

"They tried on a selective basis, at first. Then they decided to kick all of us out of the country in 1915 . . . and they didn't care who or how we died in the process."

"No wonder Armenians hate the Turks."

"It's been thirty years, my son. Hate is a waste of time. The Turk knows what he did. But he won't let his children know. Each country, each nation writes its own history. The massacre of the Armenians will never be a part of Turkish history."

"Does that make a difference?"

"Absolutely, my son. Turkish boys and girls your age will have no information whatsoever about what happened between 1915 and 1921 to the two million Armenians who once lived with their parents. The most they will know is that the great Kemal Pasha, in a fit of compassion, kicked out most of the traitorous Armenians living in Turkey during the Great War rather than killing them, as he had every right to do."

"I can't believe that facts can be twisted so much."

"Son, the Turkish government records will show proclamations and official orders calling for even-handed treatment of all Armenians as they are ordered into exile. These records are what Turkish historians will use in writing the textbooks new generations of Turkish children will read."

"Won't they ever know the truth?"

"What is the truth, Mesrop? You believe what I say to be the truth. You read in your books and hear your schoolteachers tell you what they say is the truth. What is there to disbelieve?"

"There must be many people who are not Armenians or Turks who know the facts."

"There are, my boy, many hundreds if not thousands. But the fact remains that succeeding generations of Turks will not know unless they become world travelers and scholars."

"So . . . ?"

"So, hate is a waste of time. A Turk your age will believe you have lost your senses if you attack him for what his parents did to your parents. Even if he knows all about it and believes it to have happened, it still wouldn't make sense.

"They killed about half the Armenian population in Turkey, son, but I now believe they did us a favor."

"They did us a favor?"

"Yes, m'boy, they did us a favor. We would never have known of the true meaning of the word freedom nor the bounty of America otherwise."

"Wasn't that too high a price to pay, Dad—losing your homeland?"

"Your own countryman said it a long time ago, Mesrop. Someone called Patrick Henry. Emily told me he said, 'Give me liberty, or give me death.' "

"I take it, then, that you have forgiven the Turks for what they did to your family . . . I've known all about it since the day Mary got married."

"I haven't forgiven them, my son. I'm just not passing on any legacy of hate. Do you also know of Enver Dash?"

"Enver Dash? No, sir. Who is he?"

"He's a Turk who was trying to kill me at Tallal's orders. He almost did. He's right here in Boston, son. In fact, he works in the market not four blocks from where we are." Mamigon didn't mention that the Turk was probably the killer of the boy's mother.

"No kiddin'? Does he know you're around? Do you talk to each other?"

"He must know I'm around. You can't miss my trucks with my name on them. He started working at Armour's only a week ago. I saw him last week. He didn't see me. I asked Mr. Smith, the manager, about him."

"Is he still after you?"

"Son, it was twenty-three years ago, back in 1923 when he last tried. I don't think, after all this time, he's going to try again."

"If you say so, Boss. But I'd be careful."

Mamigon grinned. "Do me a favor, son. Before you trot off, check the call boxes for me."

"Sure thing. I'll be right back." Mesrop walked the two blocks to where the boxes, much like mailboxes, were hung for any call cards. A retail merchant who bought anything from the wholesale houses would get calling cards from them, write the name of his retail store on the card, and leave it in such call boxes to let the trucker know there were crates, bags, and barrels or burlaped sides of meat to pick up.

There was one lone card which Mesrop barely looked at and delivered it to Mamigon. "That's it. That's all, Boss. Well, I'll be seeing you."

"Mesrop, would you care to go with me to pick up this stuff?"

"Sure, Boss. Anything special?" Mesrop was puzzled by the look on his father's face.

"I guess you didn't notice the call card. It's Armour & Company . . . where Enver Dash is working."

Mesrop stared at him for a second or two, then grinned to match Mamigon's grin.

"You want to prove to me that you don't hate 'em anymore, right?"

"Something like that, son. Actually, I'm curious myself about that man. You know, way back in 1915 I had him in my gun sights and let him go because he was so young. He must be around forty-five or so now. Let's go."

Mamigon backed up the truck in front of the meat-packing company—there was plenty of room at that hour of the day—and Mesrop went in to present the card to the man at the desk, Mr. Smith.

Mr. Smith looked at the card and spoke into the speaking tube that went into the refrigerator room. "The Alukian order," he called.

In less than a minute the heavy meat locker door swung open and three lamb carcasses dangling from wheeled hooks on the overhead rail came through, pushed by a white-smocked fat man, short and swarthy.

Mesrop had stood aside. He couldn't handle the carcasses because he had to go to work in an office and couldn't afford to get dirty.

Mamigon strode through the front, meat hook in hand, to take the carcasses as they were lifted off the hooks.

The fat man took one look at Mamigon, froze for a split second, then staggered back on shaky legs toward the meat locker. The door had swung shut behind him. He fumbled frantically to unbutton his smock at his belly.

Mamigon looked at him carefully, seemed to recognize the man, and held up his right hand, grinning. The hand was holding the meat hook.

It was Enver Dash, with thirty pounds added to his frame, weighing twelve ounces more because of the short-barreled hand gun he had pulled from inside his smock.

Mamigon saw instantly what was happening and dropped the meat hook. The three shots were almost as one.

Mamigon stood for a long second, disbelief on his face, his head shaking no. Then he crumpled to the floor backward, his blood being sopped up by the sawdust that covered the floor.

Mesrop got to him first, yelling, "Boss, Boss?" He dropped to his knees and put his arm under the big man's head.

"My son, take care of your mother . . . please . . ." It was a whisper.

"I will, sir . . . sir? Father?"

Mamigon opened his eyes.

"Please . . . please don't die now . . ."

He shook his head and smiled, bringing a hand up to the boy's shoulder.

Mesrop's voice caught in his throat as he choked out the words: "How can you say don't hate the Turk? How . . ."

Mamigon's half-closed eyes opened wide, the sweat glistening on his face, soaking his black hair. "Do not HATE. That is the emotion of fools . . . Hatred is blind, my son." His voice had risen above a whisper and the exertion made his hand drop away from the boy.

"All right, Boss, all right. Please hang on, please. We'll get you to a hospital." Mr. Smith had already called the police after disarming and pushing Enver Dash into the meat locker.

"You be a good man . . . take care of your . . . mother . . . I . . ." His face was ashen.

"Is my mother my mother?"

"Emily . . . your mother . . . you . . . your . . . you carried to life by . . . Guzell . . . my Osmanli . . . Turkish wife . . . Guzell . . . Guzell . . ."

His voice faded, his eyes closed.

"Guzell . . . ? Father . . . Who's Guzell?"

Mamigon's eyes opened wide again, a smile spreading on his deathly gray face as he stared at his son. He arched slightly and slumped, never answering, his long bubbling sigh becoming the death rattle.

"My father . . . my father . . ." Mesrop's voice cracked as he slipped into Armenian. "Please, my father . . . I only wanted to find out who I really am . . ." The boy held on to his father's head, then gently, tenderly, closed the staring eyes and kissed them.

"Is he dead?" Mr. Smith had been standing by.

"Yes."

"Do you know why Dash shot him?"

"It's a long story, mister. He took most of it with him."